SIX WEEKS OF SEDUCTION
La Petite Mort Club

Ellis O. Day

I love to hear from readers so email me at
authorellisoday@gmail.com

http://www.EllisODay.com

Facebook
https://www.facebook.com/EllisODayRomanceAuthor/

Closed FB Group (sneak peeks, sample chapters, and other bonuses)
https://www.facebook.com/groups/153238782143373

Twitter
https://twitter.com/ellis_o_day

Pinterest
http://www.pinterest.com/AuthorEllisODay

Other Books By Ellis O. Day:

GO TO MY WEBSITE TO SEE ALL MY BOOKS AND
TO SEE WHAT'S COMING NEXT
HTTP://WWW.ELLISODAY.COM

SIX NIGHTS OF SIN SERIES (BOOKS 1-6)
(AVAILABLE IN PAPERBACK AND EBOOK)

SIX NIGHTS OF SIN SERIES EBOOK ONLY
INTERVIEWING FOR HER LOVER (BOOK 1)**FREE**
TAKING CONTROL (BOOK 2)
SCHOOL FANTASY (BOOK 3)
MASTER – SLAVE FANTASY (BOOK 4)
PUNISHMENT FANTASY (BOOK 5)
THE PROPOSITION (BOOK 6)

The Voyeur Series (Books 1-4)
(AVAILABLE IN PAPERBACK AND EBOOK)

THE VOYEUR SERIES EBOOK ONLY
The Voyeur (Book One) **FREE**
Watching the Voyeur (Book Two)
Touching the Voyeur (Book Three)
Loving the Voyeur (Book Four)

A Merry Masquerade For Christmas

WEEK ONE: THE HUNT

CHAPTER 1: NICK

Nick parked his car and slipped into the back entrance at La Petite Mort Club. He couldn't risk running into anyone who worked there. He'd been without a woman for almost one hundred and twenty-one days and he wasn't going to spend even a minute of his first night with Sarah fighting. God, he missed her. He missed sex but more than that, he missed her— her touch, her taste, her scent. His dick hardened. Fuck, he'd probably come just looking at her.

He exited the elevator and walked to Ethan's office. It was two minutes until midnight. He knocked on the door as he tugged at his pants which had gotten uncomfortably tight.

Terry flung the door open. "I win." He stepped aside so Nick could enter. "Pay up." He held out his hand to Ethan, Patrick and Mattie.

"Really? My own brother?" Nick had signed over his club membership a few months ago to his brother and Mattie had been enjoying himself immensely. As soon as Sarah agreed, he'd talk to Ethan about buying a limited membership for them so they could watch but not participate. It seemed to be working out great for Patrick and Annie. He'd never seen a happier man.

1

"I thought you had enough pride to wait at least until morning." Mattie slapped a wad of bills in Terry's hand.

"The man hasn't had sex in over a hundred days," said Terry. "Pride means nothing to him. His dick's ready to explode at the idea of pussy."

Terry was crass, but accurate.

"Drink?" Ethan stood by the bar.

"Thanks." He'd considered waiting until morning so he wouldn't hear the shit from the guys, but when Sarah arrived with her letter he wanted to be here. He wanted...no needed to see her, to touch her. Shit. He had to stop thinking about her or he was going to come in his pants and he'd never, ever hear the end of that.

"She ain't here yet. So, have a seat." Terry plopped his large frame down on the couch next to Mattie.

Nick walked to the bar and handed his friend the letter, giving Ethan permission to share Nick's contact information with Sarah. "To make it official."

Ethan glanced over the paper. "You're officially pussy whipped."

The others roared with laughter and he chuckled as he picked up his drink. Let them gloat and joke. It'd be worth it when he was with Sarah again.

"What no argument?" asked Mattie. "You aren't even going to defend yourself?"

"He's gone four months without sex all because of one woman." Terry tossed back his drink and walked to the bar to refill it. "There's no defense that'll stand. He's a lost cause. There'll be wedding bells soon."

"Now, hold on." He had to draw the line somewhere. He

wanted Sarah, a lot, but he wasn't ready for marriage. That was a lifetime commitment. "We're just going to date."

"Pleeease," said Terry. "You went without any woman for four months on the hope that this Sarah will want to see you again."

"She will." He had no doubt. She was as hot for him as he was for her.

"Time will tell." Terry looked at his watch. "It's already five minutes after midnight. I guess she's not as eager as you are to rekindle your fucking."

"This is Nick we're talking about. Women love him"— Mattie grinned—"almost as much as they love Ethan."

"They don't all love me." Ethan studied Nick. "I just know which ones to tempt, which ones to chase and which ones to avoid."

"I'm happy for you, Nick." Patrick was leaning against the wall. "Finding the right woman isn't easy, but it's worth it."

"Enough with your love-sick drivel," said Terry. "You're so whipped you can't see straight."

"I know and I love it." Patrick grinned.

Nick was glad for his friend. Patrick and his girlfriend Annie had gone through a rough couple of weeks, but they'd worked it out.

"It's quarter after twelve." He took a sip of his drink. She was late. He was going to wring her hot, little neck. "What time does everyone have for Sarah's letter?" He dropped onto a chair by the couch. "I want in on the action."

"You can't bet—"

"Why Mattie? I've had no contact with her. I have no idea when she'll arrive with her letter." It'd better be soon because

3

for every minute she made him wait to fuck her, he was going to make her wait double to come. Not the first time. Not even the first night or two. It'd been way too long since he'd kissed a woman, tasted her pussy, or heard her moaning his name as her hot, wet cunt clenched around him. He shifted on his seat to ease the pressure in his pants. As soon as he fucked out some of his frustration, Sarah would pay for making him wait, and he'd make sure she loved every minute of it.

Terry walked across the room and pulled a paper off the table by the bar. "Patrick has when the mail arrives."

"You think she'll mail the letter?" That'd take days. He'd kill her. He'd absolutely kill her.

"Yeah. She doesn't like to come out a lot, right? Wasn't it a stipulation in her contract that she could only meet on certain days and times?" asked Patrick.

"It was," said Ethan.

"Shit." He'd forgotten about that. He turned toward Ethan. "Now that you know I'm serious, what's the deal with that?"

"I can't tell you anything and you know it."

"Come on." His friend's bullheadedness over the rules was beyond annoying.

"You know she'll tell him everything once they start dating," said Mattie.

"If they start dating." Ethan glanced away.

"You're kidding, right?" Now, he was getting nervous. Ethan knew things about Sarah that he didn't. "She's not married, is she?"

"No. You know that. It was in the contract."

"I know what was in the fucking contract. I'm asking you to tell me what wasn't." He stood, fear and frustration getting the

4

better of him.

Terry moved between them. "Mattie, on the other hand picked twelve-thirty." He looked at his watch. "You lost."

Nick glanced at his wrist. It was already twenty-to-one. Where in the hell was she?

CHAPTER 2: SARAH

In five minutes it'd be one hundred and twenty-one days since she'd been with Nick. Over two thousand, eight hundred and eighty hours since she'd touched him or been touched by him. She grabbed the bottle of Crown Royal and a glass and went into the living room. She pushed Tank's large, hairy body out of the way and sat on the couch next to him. She ran her fingers through the Belgian Malinois's thick fur as she poured herself a hefty drink. She was going to need it. She missed Nick more than she should, more than was safe.

She picked up the letter from the coffee table. She didn't need to read it. She knew it by heart. It was to Ethan, telling him to give her phone number to Nick. She folded it and put it in its envelope. She took a large sip of her drink and walked into her bedroom. She opened her nightstand and dropped the letter inside. No matter how much she wanted to see him, he wouldn't feel the same. Men like him didn't wait for women;

they just found someone else to warm their beds. He'd probably barely remember her.

Her cell phone rang and she hurried into the living room. A spark of hope flared in her chest—improbable, unlikely, but it could be Nick. She grabbed her phone from the table and the hope sputtered and died. It was her sister, Maisie. She plopped on the couch. "Hey."

"How you doing?" asked Maisie.

A few weeks after her last night with Nick, she'd broken down and told her sister everything. Well...not all the sexual details but everything else.

"Fine." She took a swallow of her drink. It wasn't exactly a lie. She would be fine. Eventually. One day, she'd stop dreaming of him—stop waking in the middle of the night needy and wet for him.

"You sure you don't want me to come over?"

"Yeah." She'd rather be alone. Tank nudged her hand. Correction. She wasn't alone. She had Tank. She kissed his furry head. "I'm just going to watch a movie or read and then go to bed."

"Okay. If you're sure..."

"I'm sure." She knew what was coming. She tossed back the rest of her drink and refilled it.

"Why don't you send the letter?"

"I can't."

"What would it hurt? Best case he sent one too and you can see him again, worse case he didn't and you're right where you are now except you'd have closure."

She'd also have pain—lots and lots of pain. "I can't."

"Sarah, you need to take a chance. What happened with

Adam was sad and it hurt, but not every man is Adam."

"I know." She did. Not every man would choose another woman over her. Not every man would die loving another woman. Not every man would give her a baby. Perhaps, no man ever should. She hadn't wanted that baby. She'd hated Adam so much for choosing Lisa that part of her had hated the child she'd carried, until she'd lost it. "I can't do it again. I can't." She gulped down her drink.

"Sarah…" Maisie sighed.

"Please. Don't. I can't handle a lecture right now." She bit down on her lip to stop from crying. She wanted Nick but he wasn't the kind of guy to be with only one woman.

"Give him a chance."

"To break my heart? No thanks."

"He might not."

She laughed. "You don't know him. He told me he tired of women after a month. He's forgotten about me by now."

"What if he hasn't?"

"Please. He belongs to a high class sex club. There are tons of women there willing to do all sorts of things. I doubt that he even thought twice about me once our contract was up." And that made it hurt so much more.

"You don't know that. He wanted more time with you. You told me he'd said he'd even be celibate for you."

"Maisie, trust me. That's not possible. Nick being celibate is like the sun rising in the west. It's not going to happen."

"He suggested it. You didn't ask him to do it."

"Because he wanted me to agree. He wanted to win. Everything's a game to guys like him. They want everything their way and he was using whatever he thought I wanted to hear to convince me." She paused. "And once I give him what he wants, he'll leave."

"So, you're leaving him first."

"Yes." At least this way she could pretend that he'd thought about her at least a little, pretend she'd meant something more to him than someone to fuck for six nights.

"What if you're wrong? What if he's waiting for you and you don't show up?"

Her heart skipped a beat. She'd hurt him. She didn't want to hurt him. She didn't want him to feel even a little bit of the pain she'd gone through with Adam.

"Think about that, Sarah. By protecting yourself, you may be hurting him."

"Goodbye." She hung up the phone. Her hands trembled as she took another drink. She stood and went into her bedroom and grabbed the envelope from her nightstand. He'd wanted her to bring it to the Club, not mail it. He'd said he'd be waiting for her.

She headed for the door but Tank was sitting on the couch watching her. She couldn't leave him. She grabbed her phone. Maisie would come over and stay with him. He'd be okay for a few hours. She could be with Nick again—touch him, taste him, have him touch her. Her body trembled and then her fingers stilled on the phone. Or, she'd go to the Club and Ethan would take the letter. He'd try to hide it, but there'd be pity in his eyes. She couldn't stand that...that pity. She might even see Nick with another woman. He'd know why she was there. He might even offer her a pity-fuck. The breath hitched in her chest. She wouldn't do that again. She'd never chase after a man who didn't want her. She wasn't that stupid, young girl any longer.

She walked into her bedroom and tossed the envelope back into the drawer. She couldn't, wouldn't give anyone any reason to pity her again. She'd had enough of that for a lifetime.

She went into the living room and dropped onto the couch. Tank curled up by her side. She turned on the television and refilled her glass. She flipped through the stations and drank as her sister's words echoed through her head. Maisie was wrong. Nick wouldn't be waiting for her. She wasn't hurting him; she was saving herself from hurt.

CHAPTER 3: NICK

"Hey, Nick. Why don't you come down into the Club and I'll buy you a drink?" Terry stood, taking his empty glass to the bar. "And anything else you want."

"No." Nick stared at his drink. He'd had too many and not enough. It was two in the morning. Where the hell was she?

"Terry's right." Mattie finished his beer. "Let's go have some fun."

"Fuck off. She's coming."

"Yeah, with some other guy," mumbled Terry.

"You mother..." Nick flew across the room but Patrick and Ethan stepped in his path. "I'm going to beat the shit out of you."

"Man can't take a joke." Terry smirked. "I guess blueballs will do that to a guy."

"Go downstairs, Terry," said Ethan.

"If you change your mind, Nick, come find me." Terry

stopped at the door. "You did your time. You can tell this Sarah, if she shows up, that you were celibate for four months. It'll be the truth."

"Go fuck yourself." He pulled away from Ethan and Patrick and sat on the couch. "She'll show up. She probably mailed the letter."

"That's right." Patrick filled Nick's glass. "If she mailed it today, Ethan won't get it for a couple of days."

Nick tossed back a gulp of his drink and stood. "I'm going home."

"Good idea. I'll drive." Patrick took his keys.

He followed his friend out of the Club. If he didn't leave now, he'd fuck someone. He was hard and ready and he needed a woman but he'd waited too long for Sarah to blow it now. Oh, she was going to pay for these extra days of celibacy.

CHAPTER 4: SARAH

Sarah moaned and rolled over, her hand tangling in Tank's fur. "Lie down."

He nudged her again with his wet nose.

"All right. I'm getting up." The damn dog had an internal timer she could set her clock by. She sat up, head spinning. The half empty bottle of Crown stared accusingly at her. Oh man, she'd tied one on last night.

Tank ran to the back door and whined.

"Okay, okay." She stood, her stomach churning. She needed water, something bland to eat and then more sleep.

Tank whined again.

First, she had to take her dog outside. She stumbled to the back door and opened it. Tank ran outside and stopped, staring back at her. She should work with him more on going out alone, but he got so upset if she were out of his sight. She was pretty sure he feared she'd disappear like Adam. "Okay." She stepped into her backyard, wincing as the sunlight hit her face. "Why did you let me drink so much?"

Tank sniffed around the yard, ignoring her.

"Some friend you are."

He peed and ran back to the door.

"Done?"

He stared at her, wagging his tail.

"Great. Let's go back to bed." She wouldn't get any arguments from him. At eleven years old he was more than happy to sleep most of the day. Although having worked for the military until he'd been wounded in the gunfire that'd killed Adam, he was also used to exercise. She'd bring him back out later, after her nap.

He followed her into the kitchen. She dumped a scoop of dog food in his dish and dropped a piece of toast in the toaster. She drank some water and went into the living room to put away all reminders of her binge last night.

Her eyes fell on the papers scattered over the end table. Flashes of her scribbling and crying flickered through her brain like an old, home movie. She picked them up. They were letters to Nick. There was also the one she'd put in her nightstand. Thank God, she hadn't dropped these in the mail. Talk about pathetic. Even if Nick had sent Ethan a letter, he'd take one look at these and run screaming. No man wanted a desperate woman and she was beyond desperate in these letters—lonely, scared and clingy. Exactly, the kind of woman Nick avoided.

Her phone rang and her traitorous heart once again skipped a beat, hoping it'd be Nick. Ethan and Nick were good friends. Ethan might break his rule and give Nick her contact information without her consent. She found the phone on the floor by the couch. It was her sister again.

"Hey," she answered, trying not to sound as disappointed as she was.

"How you feeling?" asked Maisie.

"Good." She paused. "Like shit. I drank way too much last night."

"Did you—"

"No, and I'm not going to." She grabbed the letters from the table.

"I think you're making a mistake."

"My life. My mistake." The toaster popped and she went into the kitchen. She tossed the letters in the trash as she put her toast on a plate and buttered it lightly.

"I know, but enough about that." Maisie's voice was excited.

"What's going on?" She took a bite of her bread.

"You...well, Peter...well...we—"

"Maisie spit it out. What did you and your husband do now?"

Peter helped Sarah manage her company and he did all the things outside of the house that she hated doing—couldn't do because of Tank. He was a great guy, a great husband and a great employee, except...when he pushed too much. She was pretty sure most of that started with Maisie.

"There was a contest and—"

"Tell me you didn't." She took her toast into the living room and flopped on the couch. "Please, tell me you didn't waste money entering the company in one of those charities—"

"It wasn't a waste because we won." Maisie was almost screaming now and Sarah winced.

15

"Quieter. Speak quieter."

"Sorry." Maisie lowered her voice, but not much. "I'm just so excited! We won."

"What did we win?" She sighed—another hundred dollars and a free hotel stay which she wouldn't accept.

"Five hundred thousand dollars!"

"What?" She stood, hands trembling. Her company did well but an additional half million would be wonderful. She could help so many more animals with that money.

"You heard me. A half million dollars!"

"Oh, my God." She dropped back onto the couch. The ideas of what she could do with that much extra cash making a whirlwind in her head but then reality splashed in the center. "What do I have to do with the money? What are the stipulations? What kind of scam did you get us involved in?"

"Calm down. It's legit. You can do whatever you want with the money as long as it goes to helping animals. The charity is the Norman Jay Animal Rights endowment."

"Oh, they're huge." And reputable. This was fabulous.

"Yeah and you won. They love what you do for animals especially our K9 veterans."

"I can use the money however I want?" She could help service men and women adopt the animals they fell in love with overseas. She could set up subsidized housing for veterans and their pets. There were so many great ways she could expand.

"Yep. You have to give them an itemized expenditure list but as long as it goes for animals they don't care."

"That's wonderful." Her mind stumbled over itself trying to think of the best way to spend this money. "Thank you."

"You're welcome. I hope you'll be more open to us

entering the company in other competitions."

"You know the only reason I don't want you signing us up is because they usually require me to accept the reward. I'm surprised that Norman Jay is okay with Peter going in my place." She sat on the couch. "I'm happy, but surprised."

"Ah…"

Her fist tightened on the phone. "No, don't say it, Maisie. Don't."

"It's a half million dollars."

She flopped onto her back. "I can't. You'll have to refuse."

"We…You are not turning down $500,000. You know how many animals you can help with that. Let alone the publicity."

"I know but…I can't. I can't leave Tank."

"You can. I'll watch him. He'll be fine."

"No. He won't." Her heart was racing. She didn't want to go. She didn't want to accept the award, stand in front of all those people and make a speech. Have them all looking at her. She hated being the center of attention, ever since that party at Adam's parents' house—all the pitying looks and false smiles. She'd only made it through the Viewing because she couldn't see their faces and even if she had, they'd wanted to fuck her, not pity her.

"Calm down." Maisie's voice was firm but gentle. "You can do this. Peter will be there with you and I'll be with Tank."

"I'll have to be gone too long." These events were always out of town.

"Only four hours or so."

"It's here?"

"Yes, in the city. You'll go, eat dinner and accept the award. I'd suggest staying and enjoying the party afterwards, making

17

some contacts but if you can't, Peter will bring you home."

"I...I don't know." She'd still have to make a speech.

"Sarah, I think you need to do this. You're getting worse—"

"It's not me." But it was. Some of her self-imposed isolation was her fear and they both knew it.

"You've barely left the house in four months."

"There's no reason to go out and Tank—"

"Would get used to you leaving if you did it once in a while."

"Stop, Maisie. Just stop." Tank nudged her arm and she rolled over burying her face in his neck.

"Think of all you can do with that money. All the dogs like Tank you can save."

Her heart raced. She didn't want to do this.

"It'll only be a few hours. Three. Three hours for half a million dollars."

She had no choice. She rolled over, staring at the ceiling. "I guess, I can do that."

"I know you can."

"When?"

"In two weeks. I'll come by and we'll look at dresses online." Maisie's voice was filled with excitement. She loved to shop.

CHAPTER 5: NICK

Nick tipped the bottle and chugged. It'd been over a week and still no Sarah. He didn't understand.

"Hey, let's go to the Club," said Mattie.

He ignored his brother. He didn't want to go to the Club and fuck some nameless woman. He wanted to fuck Sarah.

"Sitting here and getting plastered every night isn't doing you any good."

"It sure feels good." He'd get drunk and pass out and then he didn't miss her. Sometimes she visited in his dreams and it was great, until he woke—his dick in his hand and no woman next to him. He took another long drink. Maybe, Mattie was right. Maybe, he should go to the Club.

"Come on. You don't have to fuck anyone. Go and see the guys. Socialize." Mattie tossed him his jacket.

"The last thing I want to do is see the guys. I'll never hear the end of this."

"Nah. Ethan won't tease you. Not about this."

"Terry will."

"Terry's an ass."

"That's true." He grinned.

"Come on." Mattie headed for the door. "I'll drive."

"Why not?" He followed his brother.

When they arrived at the Club, Mattie smiled at one of the young women.

Nick knew her well. She liked to be tied up and spanked. "I'll meet up with you later." He nodded at the girl. "Have fun."

"I plan on it." Mattie walked toward her.

Nick headed to Ethan's office and knocked on the door.

"Come in, Nick."

"You and your bloody cameras." He walked into the room and went to the bar.

"I'm glad to see you."

"Yeah." He didn't have much to say to that.

"It happens to all of us."

"Shut the fuck up." This had never happened to him and he was pretty sure it'd never happened to Ethan.

Ethan laughed. "You'll live. The best thing for a brok—"

"Don't." If his friend said broken heart he was going to punch him.

"For something like this is to jump back into the scene. You'll forget about her. Tiffany and Vicky are here."

"Really?" The twins liked to fuck the same guy. Vicky gave great blow jobs. His dick started to stand at attention.

"Yeah. I'm sure you could persuade them to join you for the evening. They appreciate a man who knows what he's doing."

That might be a problem. He was so horny he wouldn't make it long, but he'd be ready to go again soon. Still, he hesitated.

"Was there something else?" Ethan watched him, his blue eyes seeming to see into Nick's soul.

"Have...have you spoken with her? I mean, she isn't hurt or sick or anything is she?" The flash of pity in his friend's eyes told him all he needed to know.

"She's fine."

He tossed back his drink and poured another. "That bitch." She'd used him and tossed him aside. "Give me something. Her last name. Where she works. Something." No one treated him this way, no one.

"I can't do that." Ethan's calmness sparked his rage.

"You can, but you won't."

Ethan shrugged.

"Fuck you." Nick headed for the door. "I'll find her myself. I don't need you."

"Leave her alone, Nick." There was a warning in Ethan's tone.

"Or what? You'll kick me out of your Club? I'm not even a member anymore, remember?" He left the office, slamming the door behind him as he pulled out his phone and called Patrick.

"Hello." Patrick's voice was raspy from sleep.

"I need you to find Sarah for me."

"Nick?" Patrick was wide awake now.

"She's fine and Ethan won't give me her contact information. The stupid fucking bastard."

"You know I can't do that."

"Why?" His friends were being assholes. "You barely come to the Club anymore. You can find another place that'll let you and Annie watch."

"That's not it." There was a feminine mumble from Patrick's phone and then his muffled voice, like he had his hand over the phone.

Patrick must've moved his hand because his weary sigh was loud and clear. "Okay, I'll ask him but it doesn't matter. I can't give out her information."

The hell he couldn't. "Ask me what?" He was in no mood for twenty questions.

"Annie wants to know why you want to contact Sarah."

"Why the fuck do you think?"

"Gee, Nick." Annie had snatched Patrick's phone from him. "You could want to talk to her, or you could want to scream at her. Which is it?"

"Neither." He liked Annie but she had a habit of sticking her nose where it didn't belong.

"Then why do you—"

"I want to fuck her, Annie. Why do you think? I waited for her. I waited over one hundred and twenty days and she didn't come." He almost bashed his phone against the wall.

"You only want to have sex with her? Get her out of your system?" She didn't sound offended.

"Yes." He took a deep breath. "She thinks she doesn't want me, but she does." It'd been too good between them for her to not want to be with him again.

"So, you want to prove to her that she does desire you."

"Fuck yeah." And then, he'd leave because no one, no one, walked away from him. He'd ended every relationship he'd had

22

and it wasn't about to change now.

"And then what?" Her voice was quiet.

If he told her the truth, she'd never agree to convince Patrick to find Sarah. "Then we see where it goes." It wasn't exactly a lie. That'd been what he'd planned on doing. He'd thought for four long months that she might be the one, but now there was no way. He'd make her want him—make her think about him with every breath, feel him with every step—and then he'd leave. Let her experience an iota of what he was feeling.

There was muffled arguing from Patrick and Annie and then Patrick got back onto the phone. "I'm sorry, Nick. I can't. You knew the rules when you signed—"

"Fuck the rules." His hand clenched the phone so tightly he thought it'd break. "I helped you. If it weren't for me you would've blown it with Annie."

"I know that, but I can't do it." Patrick sighed. "Go to the Club. Lose yourself in some woman. Have fun. You'll find some—"

"Fuck you." He hung up the phone. He didn't want to lose himself in some woman from the Club. He wanted Sarah and he wanted his revenge.

CHAPTER 6: NICK

Nick stared at the computer, unable to think about anything but finding Sarah. He'd done some digging but he wasn't a private investigator. His friends were but they refused to help. Besides Patrick, he'd reached out to Hunter, Patrick's top investigator, but the guy had ignored his calls and texts. His friends sucked.

He clicked through the spreadsheets. He had to focus on business. It'd been almost two weeks since Sarah had dumped him and he had to get over it. He poured himself his third drink. Working from home had its perks. It was two in the afternoon. He was doing better than last week.

The doorbell rang.

He opened the door. "So, you decided to stop ignoring me." He stepped aside so Hunter could enter.

"I wasn't ignoring you. I was working." Hunter strolled across the room and dropped onto the couch.

"Drink?" Nick walked to the kitchen.

"A little early for me."

"It's five o'clock somewhere as they say." He finished his drink and poured another. It was time to get drunk. Someday, when he gave up on finding Sarah he'd go back to the Club but right now he wasn't interested. All he wanted was to find her and fuck her. He didn't even care anymore why she hadn't showed. She obviously didn't want him as much as he wanted her, so all he cared about now was to getting her out of his system.

"Yeah, but I go by our time." Hunter crossed his long legs at the ankle.

"You got my messages?" He sat on the chair near the couch.

"Yeah."

"And?" He hated monosyllabic answers.

"Why do you want to find her?"

"Why does it matter?" Great, here he went again.

"Because it does." Hunter's light brown eyes were sharp in his narrow face.

"Why?" He couldn't pull off the same half-truth that he'd told to Annie on Hunter. The man knew him too well.

"Men have been known to do stupid things when a woman doesn't want them."

"You think I'd hurt her?" He almost stood, filled with pent up passion and anger at Hunter's statement. "Jesus. How long have you known me?"

"A long time and I've never known you to give two shits whether a woman wanted you or not."

"Sarah wants me."

"She just doesn't know it yet." Hunter barked a laugh. "We've all felt like that." He sobered. "And we've all been wrong."

"I've never felt like this," he mumbled into his drink. Sure, there'd been women who'd preferred one of his friends to him, but he hadn't wanted them, not like he wanted Sarah.

"Lucky you."

"Yeah. Lucky me." He was a mess, all because of one woman. "I'd never hurt her." He wouldn't, not physically.

"I don't believe you."

"Go fuck yourself. And get out of my house."

"Hold on." Hunter didn't move. "I didn't mean you'd hit her or hurt her in that way."

"Well, what did you mean?" He was afraid that Hunter understood him a little too well. He did want to hurt Sarah. He wanted her to feel like he did right now—confused, miserable and angry.

"As you said, I know you Nick and you're tenacious but you also lose interest fast. That's why you excel in your profession. By the time you're bored with the small business you're helping, the job's done."

"Yeah?"

"That works for businesses but not women."

"So, you'll only help me if I want to marry her? Is that what you're saying?"

"No." Hunter gave him a disgusted look. "But if all you want to do is fuck her again then...leave her alone. She's—"

"You already found her, didn't you?" There was something about the way Hunter talked about her that reminded him of Ethan. "Tell me where she is, you son-of-a-bitch." He leaned forward, prepared to beat the shit out of the guy if he didn't tell him what he knew.

Hunter leaned forward, eyes locking with Nick's. "Tell me you won't hurt her and I'll tell you what I know."

"I can't tell you that. I have no idea where this will go." He had no plan of letting it go anywhere but the bedroom. Not anymore.

"What's your intention?"

"What are you her father?"

"Fuck you, Nick. You know what I mean." Hunter stood. "Find me when you're ready to answer my questions." He headed for the door.

"Wait." It was now or never. "Yes, I want to fuck her and yes, I'm pissed, but...I can't get her out of my mind." He rested his glass against his head. "I should be at the Club fucking anyone who's willing, but I don't want them. I want her." There it was—the truth, part of it anyway.

"You've had many relationships where you didn't want to see the woman again."

"Yeah, so?"

"What would you have done if they showed up at your door?"

"Kicked Ethan's ass." His mouth dropped open. Fuck. He'd screwed up big time. "I didn't mean that."

"Too late."

"Come on. This is different." Nick hurried over to Hunter.

"The only thing different is that you want more and she doesn't instead of the other way around."

"Fuck you." He turned and went back to the kitchen and grabbed the bottle.

"Let it go, Nick." Hunter walked out the door.

He dropped onto the couch and chugged down some scotch. Hunter was right, the stupid mother fucker.

CHAPTER 7: NICK

Nick hadn't gotten off the couch in days. Hunter's words kept echoing through his head and he couldn't accept them. It'd been different with Sarah. She had to have felt it too, but obviously she hadn't. He'd just been some guy she'd hooked up with like all those faceless women he'd banged. It'd been fun, something to pass the time, but that'd been it.

Damn. This hurt. He pointed the remote at the TV and flipped through the stations. Daytime TV sucked. He grabbed the phone. He'd call the liquor store. Everything was better when he had a buzz. That was a million dollar slogan. Even drunk he was a genius. Now, all he needed was a small liquor business to represent.

His phone rang and he stared at it in his hand, his mind still fuzzy from drinking earlier, or last night, or today. He had no idea what day or time it was. Maybe, the liquor store was calling him. He grinned as he answered the phone, "I'd like six bottles of Glenlivet."

"Nick?" asked Annie.

"Annie?" He sat up, his eyes focusing on her name on his phone. "Everything okay?" He was helping her with her catering/restaurant business, but their next appointment wasn't for weeks.

"No, everything's not okay. What did you say to Hunter?"

"Nothing."

"Really? He's refusing to give you Sarah's contact information because he says you only want to use her."

"That mother-fucker. Why the hell did he say anything to you?"

"Because I asked him to go behind Patrick's back and get Sarah's file."

"You did? Why?"

"Because Patrick is being a stubborn idiot about this, or I thought he was. He's using the same excuses he did to stay away from me—Ethan says. It's Ethan's rules—and that's just stupid. If you're in love with her, Ethan shouldn't stand in your way." She took a deep breath. "And you helped me and Patrick."

"Thank you." He was humbled that she'd stick her neck out for him, because Patrick was going to be pissed.

"Apparently, I'm an idiot and Patrick's right, so thanks a lot. We had a huge fight over this and it was all for nothing because you're a jerk."

"I don't know what Hunter told you but I'd never hurt her." He still had a chance. All he had to do was convince Annie that he cared for Sarah and he'd have her again. Sarah may not want to admit it but she was as hot for him as he was for her. He just had to remind her how good it'd been between them and he could fuck her and move on with his life.

"Really?"

"Really. I don't hurt women. You know me better than that."

"Hmm."

"Please Annie, I'm a mess." That was true. "I need to see her. Talk to her." And fuck her in every position imaginable.

"If she's not interested, what will you do?"

"I'll leave her alone." He ran his fingers across his chest in a cross as if she could see him. "I swear."

"Attend the Norman Jay Animal Rights Dinner this Saturday night."

"She'll be there? Sarah will be there?" His hand shook.

"Don't make me sorry I did this." She hung up the phone.

He wouldn't. Actually, he didn't care. He hadn't asked Annie to help him. That was her decision caused by her woman's heart, filled with love and happily ever after. He didn't want love or a relationship but he did want to fuck Sarah again—over and over until he couldn't see straight and he no longer dreamt of her every night.

CHAPTER 8: SARAH

Sarah's hands fluttered in her lap. She was in no hurry to get to the awards banquet but the car kept moving and that meant they kept getting closer.

"You'll do fine," said Peter.

"Thanks." She wasn't so sure about that, but she smiled. Peter was a great guy. She was glad for her sister. Maisie had the kind of life she'd once wanted—a loving husband and a great kid.

"Don't be nervous."

"I'm trying." They both knew he could say that all night but it wouldn't help. She didn't like crowds. She didn't like parties. She didn't like going or being anywhere but home.

Peter pulled into the hotel parking lot and drove to the front. The valet opened her door. She got out of the car and Peter came around to her side. He handed the valet his keys and a tip and then took Sarah's arm, heading for the building.

"You look terrific. You've gone over your speech a hundred times. You're ready for this."

Her hand squeezed his arm. He was steadfast and strong beside her but it wasn't enough. With each step they got closer and closer to the door. Too soon, they were inside the hotel. The event room loomed ahead. The doors were open. There were hundreds of tables and small platform with a podium and microphone. There were people everywhere. Someone called out Peter's name.

"Give me a minute." It was half-question.

"Sure." She could do this. She could.

Peter walked a few steps away and she wandered closer to the room. She stood to the side of the open double doors. This wasn't like Adam's party. No one would look at her and feel sorry for her...unless she panicked. *That's not helping.* She took a deep breath. She should walk in and go to the bar. No one would stare at her. No one would notice her, but her feet didn't move. She jumped as Peter took her arm. He must've seen her trembling because he turned her toward him and tipped her chin until her eyes met his.

"You can do this. A half of million dollars will help a lot of animals."

He was right. She had to do this. She took a deep breath and smiled, her lips trembling a bit. "I can do this."

"Yes, you can."

"They won't be looking at me with..." She stopped herself from saying with pity but the flash of pain in his eyes told her he knew what she'd almost said. What she'd almost admitted.

"They'll be admiring a smart, sexy, successful woman who runs her own business and is kind and compassionate." He kissed her forehead. "You're stronger than you think, Sarah."

She grabbed the lapels of his tux and leaned against him. "I'm going to be looking at you the entire time."

"That's fine." His hand patted her back in a brotherly caress.

"Thank you." She straightened and took a deep breath. "I think, I need a drink."

"Of course." He grinned as he offered his arm and they stepped through the open doors and into the mass of wealthy, well dressed people. Sarah had never been more terrified in her life.

CHAPTER 9: NICK

A surge of relief followed by lust raced through Nick when his eyes landed on Sarah. She was standing in the doorway, looking better than fantastic. She wore a short, emerald green dress trimmed with black. Fuck, he loved her in green. His eyes trailed down her long legs, stalling at her shoes. Those tiny, wedge heels wouldn't make her unbalanced. It was too bad because he'd love an excuse to steady her and see her eyes darken with desire. He forced his gaze up to her face. It was pinched with fear. Without thinking, he strode toward her. A man walked over to her and she smiled up at him. Nick's feet stopped as if encased in cement. This couldn't be happening, but it was. She'd move on, forgotten about him like he'd meant nothing. She rested her head against the other man's chest and Nick's rage ran icy hot.

She and that man headed for the bar. Nick made his way in the opposite direction, lingering on the outskirts of the room and watching her. While he'd been jacking off and dreaming about her, she'd been fucking some other guy. He needed a drink—a lot of them.

He stopped a waiter, handing the young man a hundred dollar bill and his glass. "Scotch. Glenlivet. Keep them coming."

"Yes, sir." The kid took off, returning a moment later with a full glass.

He gave the kid a twenty and prowled in the shadows of the room. Sarah sipped her drink as she and her boyfriend—the word soured in his mind—moved around the party, chatting and laughing. He finished his scotch and the kid was there a moment later with a refill.

"Thanks." He handed the kid a business card. "Come see me if you're really this ambitious. I'm sure I can find a job for you." He could use an assistant.

"Thank you, sir."

"Drive and dedication should be rewarded." He stared past the kid at Sarah. She didn't understand that but she would. He'd been dedicated to her and she'd move on. That didn't work for him. He wanted her again and he'd have her. Tonight and tomorrow and then she could go back to her limp-dicked boyfriend.

CHAPTER 10: SARAH

Sarah hated crowds. The alcohol was helping a little and everyone had been nice but her nerves hummed with dread. She skin on the back of her neck prickled as if someone were staring at her, but whenever she'd glance around there was no one there—at least no one looking at her. It was probably her fear. The time for her speech was drawing near.

"We should sit down," said Peter. "They're about to start."

The president of the organization was moving to the stage. She nodded, letting Peter lead her to their table. A waiter came by and they placed their orders as the president started speaking.

She stared at the stage, smiling when everyone else smiled, but unable to concentrate on the speech. She couldn't do this. She couldn't get up there in front of everyone. Her hand shook as she finished her drink.

Peter leaned near her ear. "You'll do fine. Just look at me."

She swallowed. Everyone was clapping and looking in her direction. She stood and headed for the stage, taking deep breaths and hoping no one noticed. She needed to calm down or she'd pass out. *They'd notice that.* Before she knew it she was on the stage behind the podium. She stared into the crowd. She opened her mouth but nothing came out.

People were smiling at her, but the longer she stood there, the more those looks started changing—surprise, confusion. If they looked at her with pity she'd die. Her gaze raced to Peter but it didn't help. Panic clawed at her throat. She couldn't do this. She was going to be sick. She glanced at the doors—her escape. If she ran, she could be there in a few minutes. Someone stepped out of the shadows into her line of sight. It was Nick. Her stomach dropped to her toes. She'd never thought she'd see him again. He was so handsome in his tux, the black of the suit matching his hair. He took a drink and his eyes roamed down her body, pausing on her breasts. Warmth pooled in her belly. His eyes locked with hers and he tipped his head.

She found her voice. She could focus on him—look into his eyes. She knew them. She'd seen them filled with lust and passion and desire. The man had seen her at her most vulnerable. He'd tied her up and had made her lose control and she'd loved every second of it. She stared at him as she spoke, her speech pouring from her and then everyone was clapping and the president was handing her a check. It wasn't real. The real money would be electronically deposited into her account.

She thanked him and left the stage. She glanced at the doorway but Nick was gone. She looked around the room as she made her way to her table but he wasn't there.

"You did great." Peter hugged her before holding her chair for her.

"Thanks." She wasn't crazy. Nick had been there. "Did you see the guy at the back?"

"What guy?"

The waiters delivered their meals while another waiter came by and collected their drink orders.

"I...I thought I saw someone I knew."

"Who?"

"No one. No one important." She was going crazy. Next thing she'd be seeing Adam. Maybe, Maisie was right and it was time for her to talk to someone about this.

CHAPTER 11: NICK

Nick leaned against the wall in the hallway his gut tied in an angry knot. He never should've helped her. He should've let her flounder up there. She'd been going to bolt. It'd been as clear in her eyes as her spark of desire when she'd seen him. Did her boyfriend know she still had the hots for her ex-lover? He usually didn't fuck women with boyfriends or husbands but she was his. He'd found her first and the boyfriend could have her back when he was done with her.

The waiter came out and handed him another drink.

"Thanks. What did she say?" He'd sent the kid to spy at her table. He'd expected her to come into the hallway looking for him but he should've realized she'd go back to her little-dicked boyfriend.

"Nothing much. She told her date that she thought she saw someone she knew."

He snorted. She knew she saw him. Her panties were

probably soaking because of it. "What else?"

The kid hesitated.

"Tell me." This wouldn't be good.

"The guy asked her who she thought she saw and she said no one important."

His jaw clenched, grinding his teeth. No one important! She'd had multiple orgasms with him. She'd spilled her guts about her ex and baby but he was no one important.

"Sorry, sir."

"Don't be. I needed to hear it." He'd started, once again, to feel something besides lust for her. She'd been so scared and helpless on stage. He'd had to help her, but that was done. He was going to fuck her twelve ways to Sunday and then leave. "Plus, I always expect the truth,"—he glanced at the kid's name tag—"Tommy. No matter what."

CHAPTER 12: NICK

As soon as dinner was over, Nick was going to have Tommy take a note to Sarah. He was pretty sure all he needed was one moment alone with her and she'd be his for the night. His dick hardened at the thought. He glanced inside the main room. Everyone was still eating. He took a deep breath. He needed to be patient—only another thirty minutes or so.

Sarah stood, excusing herself and Nick had to fight not to grin. It seemed fate was finally on his side. As she walked toward the doors, he moved down the hallway. He had no desire to put on a show for everyone. She stepped into the foyer and headed toward the bathroom. He moved out of the shadows and into her path.

"Nick." She jumped, her hand fluttering to her chest as her eyes roamed over him. "It's really you."

Her words were a soft whisper, almost a caress and his body responded, hardening for her softness. He hated that she had this effect on him—that he was a puppet to the desire coursing through him. He stepped toward her. She licked her lips—a tiny peeking of her tongue—and his control shattered. He grabbed her—one hand on the back of her neck and the other holding her chin. She wouldn't get away, not until he'd tasted her. His lips came down on hers and she squeaked. It was the only opening he needed. He thrust his tongue into her mouth as his body pressed her against the wall. For one second, she remained still and then her arms wrapped around him and she was kissing him back. This was what he'd wanted. What he'd dreamed about for four long months. His hand skimmed up her leg, moving her dress out of his way.

"Nick." She grabbed his wrist, stopping him.

"I need you." It came out like a growl—angry and desperate. He needed to be inside of her now. He moved his hand under her dress, dragging hers with it, and cupped her pussy. "You're so fucking wet. You want this to." He kissed her, hard and demanding. She was soaked for him. For him.

She squirmed and he shoved her underwear aside as his other hand went to his zipper.

"Stop." She pushed at this chest.

He froze. She wasn't wiggling in pleasure. She was fighting him. His arms trembled as he forced himself to let her go. He touched her cheek, his thumb caressing her soft skin. "Sarah." It was a benediction and a plea.

"Let me go." Her green eyes were wide in panic.

"I'm sorry." He backed away. They were in the goddamn hallway.

She pushed past him and hurried to the bathroom. He nodded at a guy who stepped out of the banquet room. The guy nodded back and went the other way. He waited to follow her until the man was in the men's room. It'd been a mistake trying to take her in the hallway, but she wasn't getting away from him. She still wanted him and he didn't give two shits about her boyfriend.

CHAPTER 13: SARAH

Sarah leaned against the bathroom door. Nick was here and he still wanted her. Could she do this? Could she not? Her body wanted him, ached for him. She took a deep breath and went into the stall to pee. She had no idea what she was going to do. She nibbled her lip. She could cut out early and go somewhere with him. Maisie was watching Tank. She'd been planning on staying here for another hour or so, instead she could leave with him. But then what? Then nothing. Tomorrow, she'd be alone again. He wasn't a relationship kind of guy, but tonight...Tonight, she could feel him again. Her body hummed, overriding her mind.

She flushed the toilet and stepped out of the stall. Now, all she had to do was find him. Should she tell him she wanted him? She giggled. That was probably obvious. She'd almost fucked him in the hallway. She turned on the faucet and was washing her hands when the door opened. Her eyes meet Nick's as he closed the door and locked it.

Her heart raced. She knew that look. They were going to fuck. Right here. Right now. Wetness almost ran down her legs. God, she wanted this man. He moved toward her. She turned off the water and dried her hands. He stepped behind her, their eyes still locked in the mirror. He grabbed the hem of her dress and pulled it up, his warm hands rough on the skin of her thighs. Her panties were visible in the mirror, stained from her desire.

"Take off your underwear." His voice was strained as if barely containing himself.

She swallowed but pushed her panties down her hips, brushing against his erection as she bent. He gasped and she gave him an extra wiggle.

"Enough." His fingers dug into her hips as his foot went between her legs and shoved them apart. "Bend forward."

The desperation and need in his voice made her body quiver as she obeyed.

"I'm going to fuck you." He bent and whispered in her ear. "It's going to be hard and fast. I won't last long."

Her arms trembled as she braced herself. She wanted this. She missed it, but she knew it'd hurt a little at first because she hadn't had anyone inside of her in over four months.

He unzipped his pants, his dark eyes almost black. He was like a fallen angel and he was about to fuck her. Her heart raced in anticipation. His dick brushed against her ass.

He licked his fingers and then prodded her asshole. "I should fuck you here."

"No." She shifted away, but he wrapped his arm around her holding her in place.

"Don't tell me no."

"You agreed—"

"That contract is over. Was over four damn months ago."
He was angry now and she had no idea why. "This is different.
This is about what I want." He pushed down on her butthole
with his finger.

"No. You said...we both have to want it." This was
forbidden and God help her, she was getting even more turned
on.

He skimmed around her asshole with his finger, pressing
and caressing. She squirmed at the sensations. If he put his
other hand on her pussy when he did that...

His eyes darkened even more. "You want it. You just won't
admit it."

"I...I don't." She lied, kind of. She didn't want to do this.
Not now. Maybe, not even later but the feelings were
interesting.

"Don't lie to me." He grabbed her hair and pulled her head
back toward him.

"I...I'm not sure."

He let go of her hair. "You will be." He moved the hand
that was on her abdomen lower. "But right now, I'm going to
fuck you here." He dipped his fingers into her folds, stroking.

She moaned and pushed her ass against his erection.

"Tell me you want this." His other hand grabbed his cock,
rubbing it against her opening.

"Condom." Her fingers tightened around his wrist. "We
need a condom."

"Fuck, Sarah." He flicked her clit and she trembled.

"Do that again. Please." She was close to coming. Just
being near him made her almost come.

47

He did and she closed her eyes. He flicked and rubbed her and she moaned, no longer stopping his hand, but pressing it harder against her. Then his dick was there, pushing and her eyes popped open.

"Condom." She blocked her opening. "We have to use a condom."

"Please." He kissed between her shoulder blades. "I'm clean. You're still on birth control, right?"

"Condom." Birth control wasn't one hundred percent effective.

"I don't fucking have one." His fingers grabbed her hips and he started to step back.

"Oh." She shivered as the warmth from his body disappeared. "I do." She grinned as she grabbed her purse. She'd started carrying them during her time with him and she'd never cleaned out this purse. She handed one to him.

"How convenient." He took it but his eyes were shadowed and his face taut with tension. His white teeth flashed as he tore it open and rolled it onto his cock. He pushed her down to the counter, grabbed her hips and pulled her legs apart.

He was angry for some reason but right now she didn't care if he were rough or if it hurt a little. Right now, she needed him inside of her.

"Tell me you want this." He rubbed his dick along her crease, the heat almost burning her sensitive flesh.

"Please, Nick. I want this. I want you." That was all it took and he was inside her. She gasped as his dick stretched her, filling her with his warmth and hardness.

"You're still so fucking tight." He thrust into her, not giving her time to adjust. "You feel so good."

48

"Nick...ouch. Wait." Her fingers dug into the counter. He was moving too fast and too hard.

"Can't." His hand came around and slid against her clit, stroking. "Relax, baby." His hips moved faster and faster.

She squirmed as the pain from his intrusion warred with the pleasure of his fingers and soon the pain was only a tiny spark, lighting her passion. She needed more. She needed him deeper and harder. She rocked against him, clinging to him with her inner muscles, never wanting him to leave.

"That's it." He grabbed her hair, pulling back her head as he kissed her neck, sucking hard as he thrust into her again and again. "I'm close. Come for me, Sarah." He ran his nail gently along her clit and she screamed, her body tightening around him. He thrust into her again, and bucked against her as he came.

He rested his head between her shoulder blades for a moment before pulling out of her. A warmth and lassitude filled her limbs. She wanted to grin and snuggled against him but instead she straightened, letting her dress cover her body. He tossed the condom in the trash and zipped up his pants.

He stared at her, his eyes dark and unfathomable as she pulled on her underwear and then straightened her hair. Her eyes landed on the love bite on her neck. "Damn it, Nick." She touched the sensitive skin.

He grabbed her shoulders, staring at her in the mirror. "I'll mark you wherever I want."

"I can't go back—"

"You're mine." He grabbed her dress and pulled it down, uncovering her breasts. "You're coming home with me, not your little-dick boyfriend."

"What?" She had no idea what he was talking about.

"You heard me." He spun her around and lowered his head toward her breast.

"You can't order me to go home with you." She wanted to do exactly that. She'd planned on doing that, before he'd ordered her to do it. She wasn't his slave or his property. She grabbed his hair to stop him, but his hot, wet mouth came down on her breast and she moaned, pulling him closer instead of pushing him away. God, she'd missed his mouth.

He sucked and licked and his other hand trailed up her legs to her pussy which was ready for him again. She rubbed against him and he moved to her other breast. She was going to come again. Her body tensed, her hips thrusting into him and then he stopped. He took a step back, his breath coming in pants.

"Nick?" She was so close. He couldn't stop. It was cruel. Her breasts jiggled as she drew in great mouthfuls of air, trying to cool her blood.

"You...have...five minutes to make your excuses." His eyes never left her breasts. "I'll be out front in the limo." He took a step toward the door, his gaze slowly moving up to her face. "If you make me come back in here, I'll toss you on the table and take you in front of your boyfriend and everyone else in that room."

"Someone will stop you." She wouldn't want them to, but someone would.

"You're right." He moved closer again, his eyes darting from her face to her tits. "I guess, I'm going to have to prove you're mine another way." His finger ran over the love bite. "These will look great all over your neck and breasts and legs. A nice trail of where I was." He grabbed her and lifted her to the sink.

"No. Don't." She squirmed and he let her slide off the counter. She tucked her breasts back into her bra and dress.

"Five minutes, Sarah." He tipped her chin so her eyes met his. "I'm not kidding."

CHAPTER 14: SARAH

Sarah stared at the door. Nick was an ass and he could sit in his car and rot. She straightened her hair and splashed water on her face. She pulled her makeup from her purse, reapplied her lipstick and used concealer to cover the love bite. She refreshed her perfume and headed toward the banquet hall, feeling each step between her thighs. He'd been rough and she'd loved every second. She would've gladly, no eagerly, gone home with him, if he hadn't been such a jerk. She stopped at the bar and got another drink and then found Peter. Dinner was over and everyone was mingling.

"Hey, you okay?" asked Peter.

"Yeah." She was. She felt more confident and at ease even in the crowd. She would've never guessed that a quickie would do that to her.

"You sure? You were gone awhile." His brown eyes were concerned.

"I'm sure. I ran into an old friend." *And he rammed into me, over and over and over again until we almost crumpled from release.* She took a sip, hiding her smile.

"Let me know when you want to leave."

"I'm good." She wasn't going anywhere until she saw Nick again. He'd be furious with her for disobeying and she couldn't wait. "But if you want to get home to Maisie and Kyle, I understand." Peter doted on his wife and son.

"I can't leave you."

"Really, Peter. I'm good." She touched his arm.

"Is this old friend you ran into a man?" His eyes sparkled with mischief.

"That obvious?" She blushed.

He hugged her. "I'm happy for you, Sarah."

"Don't go planning the wedding. It isn't that kind of relationship. Trust me."

"Then he's a fool."

"No. He's an ass." But tonight he was her confident, controlling, dominant ass.

"Maybe, I should stay."

The look of concern on his face warmed her heart. "No. I'll be fine. He's an ass but I can handle him." She couldn't wait to get her hands on him again, but this time she was calling the shots.

"I'm sure you can." He kissed her cheek. "You're the strongest woman I know."

She blinked back tears. Peter was crazy. She was the weakest woman in the world.

"Do you want me to get a car for you?" asked Peter.

"No. I'll call an Uber when I'm ready to go home." She

glanced away, embarrassed. "I may be late."

He chuckled. "Stay out all night. We'll stay with Tank. I'm sure Kyle is sleeping with him now."

Tank did love her nephew. "I'll be home tonight...or tomorrow morning."

"Have fun." He grinned as he headed toward the door.

She glanced at her watch. It'd been six minutes since she'd left the bathroom. Nick would be fuming by now. She tossed back her drink and went to the bar to wait.

CHAPTER 15: NICK

Nick almost snarled as he looked at his watch for the third time. If she thought he wasn't going to go in there and drag her out, she was crazy. She was his. His! At least for tonight. He pressed a button and the window between him and the driver lowered.

"I'm going inside. I need you to..."

Sarah's ass-wipe of a boyfriend came out of the building and spoke to the valet.

"Never mind." He raised the window as he leaned against the seat. She'd be here soon. His dick pressed against his zipper. He'd take her in the car. There was no way he could wait until they got to his place. He'd already waited too long. That quickie in the bathroom hadn't counted...but damn, she'd felt great. He had no idea why her pussy was special. Before Sarah, he'd believed all women were basically the same, but he'd been wrong. There was something about her that made him crazy

55

with lust and he'd enjoy that until it went away. That meant her boyfriend—his lips curled as he watched the other man get into his car—was out of the picture until he tired of her.

He poured himself a drink. He never fucked women who had boyfriends or husbands, but tonight, he'd make an exception. Nick glanced at his watch. Ten minutes gone. He searched the doorway. She'd probably wanted to make sure her boyfr...Limp-Dick was gone. If he still wanted her after tonight, he'd give her a day to dump the guy. If she didn't, he'd do it for her. She could go back to her dickless-wonder when he was done with her. He smirked against his glass. Not that she'd be able to walk for a few weeks.

He tossed back the rest of his drink. It'd been eight minutes since Captain-Quickie had left. *Where in the hell was she?* He poured himself another drink and waited, his eyes darting between the doorway and his watch. He was going to kill her. He finished his drink and got out of the car.

The driver rolled down his window.

"Mike, wait here. I'll be right back." His heart thudded in his chest at the anticipation of the chase as he strode into the building. She'd better have a good...more than a good reason for not coming to the limo. He'd waited four months and two weeks. He wasn't waiting a second longer.

He opened the double doors into the banquet hall, his eyes searching the crowd. She was standing with a small group of women and men. She was drinking and laughing. She turned toward him as if feeling his stare. She smiled and tipped her glass as if in a toast. *Smartass.* He was going to toss her over his shoulder and drag her out of here caveman style.

He took a step toward her, but stopped as she said

something to the others before strolling in his direction. His gaze went to her hips as they swayed seductively. She looked like a magical fairy in her green, silky dress. Okay, maybe she'd gotten hung up in a conversation. She had just won this award. He'd give her a break, until they got to his house. As soon as he wasn't ready to explode with lust, he'd make her wait to come. He'd bring her to the edge and then back off, again and again until she felt a fraction of what he'd been going through.

"Nick." Her lips twitched and her eyes sparkled up at him.

She was trouble and he didn't care. He grabbed her hand. "Let's go."

"I have something for you." She pulled her hand free and took something from her purse, keeping whatever it was concealed in her fist. She leaned up, sliding her hand into his tuxedo jacket.

He leaned toward her, drawn like a moth to the light. His hands shook at his side. His lips were only a fraction away from heaven but if he kissed her, he wouldn't stop. He'd probably fuck her right here and they'd both end up in jail. Her tongue darted out, wetting her lips.

"Sarah." It was half-groan and half-plea. He needed her right now.

"I know it's been awhile, but I think you've forgotten. I don't take orders from you." She turned and walked away.

He stared after her, his eyes on the way her firm, round ass moved under the dress. He needed to see it shake as he pumped into her, over and over until he came. It took his lust filled brain a moment to realize what she'd said. "Sarah," he called out. It wasn't too loud, only enough to be heard over the music, but there was a warning in his tone.

She kept walking, not even looking back at him.

He was going to torture her for days. Tie her up. Fuck her. Torment her. He'd make her regret teasing him. He hurried across the room, catching up with her at the bar.

"A Glenlivet for my friend and another Crown for me," she said to the bartender.

"Don't bother. We're leaving," he almost growled.

"He may be, but I'm not." She smiled at the bartender and the man filled her drink and put a scotch in front of Nick.

He leaned closer to her. "I will carry you out of here."

She turned, her lips brushing along his jaw as she whispered. "I'll go home with you and we'll do...whatever you want, but not if you make a scene."

Each beat of his heart, echoed in his almost bursting cock. He moved closer until his torso brushed against her side. "Anything?"

Her green eyes sparkled with arousal. "Anything...with a condom. For the first hour."

"Conditions again." He had no idea why he loved bartering with her. It annoyed him that she wouldn't obey but it also turned him on. "I should've expected it."

"You should've."

"But...tonight, you're mistaken." He grabbed her hand and pulled her flush against his chest. "I'm in no mood for games, Sarah. I've waited too long." He was ready to come right now. He was like a bull elephant in musk. "I'm going to fuck you in the next five minutes. It's either going to be in here or in the limo. Your choice."

CHAPTER 16: SARAH

Sarah wasn't sure if she wanted to slap Nick's face or jump him. She both hated and loved his arrogance and bossiness, but there was something wild in his tone that called to her. She wanted to play but there was a time and place for that and by the look in his eyes, it wasn't now. Still, she wasn't going to concede this easily. As soon as they were alone, he'd be in charge. He was too desperate right now to let her lead but it was only with him that she felt this powerful, this in control—and completely out of control. It was crazy.

She stared in his eyes as she picked up her drink and took a sip. She placed the glass on the bar.

"In four minutes I'll move behind you." His voice was whisper soft and it made her shiver. "I'll stand very close." His hand skimmed over her arm, sending desire coursing through her body. "I'll pull up your dress and unzip my pants." He moved a little closer. "Are you a good actor? I hope so because you'll have to pretend that I'm not shoving your underwear out my way and sliding into you." He leaned closer and she could smell the clean scent of his aftershave and the scotch on his breath. "Should I go slow or fast? If I shove into you hard and fast, you'll gasp. That'll draw attention. I don't care but you might." He reached around her and grabbed his drink. She inhaled sharply as his arm glanced across her breast. "Just remember,"—he took a sip of his drink—"it was your choice to stay or leave."

Her pussy throbbed an insistent rhythm for him, but she wasn't quite ready to stop. "You didn't even look at what I put in your pocket."

He reached for it but she grabbed his hand.

"I'm going to walk out of here and get into your limo."

He shifted his hand around so he had a hold of her wrist and he tugged her toward the door.

"Wait."

"Three minutes." His eyes were black with desire.

"I know you won't really fuck me in here." She moved closer to him.

"You have no idea what I'll do." His hand went to her ass and he pulled her against his body—his erection hard and long between them. "I'm past caring about anyone but me."

Heat pooled in her belly. Part of her wanted to tempt him, to see how far he'd go but there was something desperate in his eyes that said he might do what he threatened. She rested her hand on his chest. His heart raced under her fingers. "If you want me to get in that limo you're going to let me walk out of here alone."

"Sarah, don't fuck with me. Not right now."

"I'm not." She reached behind her, causing her breasts to

60

rub against his chest, and grabbed her drink. She tossed it back, letting the warmth fuel her desire to play. "You finish your drink. Give me three minutes." She put the empty glass on the bar. "Your limo is out front, right?"

"Yeah." He squeezed her ass.

"I'm going to get into the limo and wait for you." Her face heated as she pictured how she was going to wait for him. She could strip or get on her back, legs spread, or...the possibilities were endless.

"There's no reason—"

"Please. Do this for me. Play with me."

His jaw tensed but he nodded.

"When I walk out of this room, I want you to finish your drink and then look at what I put in your pocket." She nibbled her lip and he trembled. Oh, this was going to kill him and she couldn't wait. She was so ready for a hard, fast fuck her legs were shaking. "But don't let anyone else see."

"Your time is up."

She tugged on his shirt until he leaned closer to her. "Don't keep me waiting." She slipped from his grasp and strolled to the door. She made sure her hips rolled with each step because his eyes would be on her the entire way but instead of making her nervous, it made her wet.

CHAPTER 17: NICK

It took every ounce of control Nick had not to chase after Sarah. He wasn't in the mood for games but he hadn't been able to refuse her when she'd looked up at him, her eyes sparkling with mischief and arousal.

He tossed back his drink and reached into his pocket. The breath caught in his throat. He knew the feel of lace panties. He didn't need to see them, but he pulled them out, keeping his hand fisted. He opened it a little and his knees almost buckled. She'd been naked under that dress. All the blood in his body surged to his cock as he almost ran out the door.

CHAPTER 18: SARAH

As soon as she was out of his sight, Sarah picked up her pace. Nick wasn't going to wait long. He was too hot for her and that made her nerves hum with anticipation and fear. This had to be a one night thing. She couldn't be with him longer than that. Her heart was too involved already. He'd leave her as soon as he tired of her and he'd tire of her as soon as she needed him.

She headed to the large limo. A tall, handsome driver stepped out of the car.

"Is this Nick…" Damn, she still didn't know his last name. Her face heated at the amused expression on the driver's face.

"Yes, ma'am. This is Nick Macris' limo." He opened the door.

"Thank you." She climbed into the car, her desire dimming.

Obviously, having a strange woman show up and hop in the car wasn't an uncommon occurrence for Nick. His driver hadn't even questioned why she'd wanted to know. If she hadn't been here tonight, it'd be some other woman going home with him. She opened the new bottle of Crown and poured herself a drink, reminding herself that none of that mattered. This was nothing more than a bonus night—one last chance for fabulous sex. She took a large gulp of the liquor and tried to push her irritation aside. He'd made no commitment to her—not that commitments mattered to men like him anyway. She'd been right not to send the letter to Ethan. She shouldn't be going home with him. She definitely shouldn't have had sex with him in the bathroom. God, he made her crazy and she didn't need that. She was crazy enough on her own. This was a mistake. She should go.

The door flung open.

"Mike, take us to my place but go the long way," said Nick as he almost jumped into the car.

Too late. Her hand tightened on the door handle as she squeezed her legs together. Part of her wanted to flee from this man but the other part wanted to submit to him and that's what it would be—at least this time. His face looked carved from stone, his eyes black like a shark's. They narrowed as they landed on her hand grasping the door handle.

He slid across the seat and grabbed her face, cupping it in his large palms. "I would've found you." His lips landed on hers, devouring her mouth as he crushed her to him.

All thoughts of fleeing vanished as her body softened for him. This was what she'd dreamed of every night. This was what had made her ache every morning, empty and alone. She wrapped her arms around him, running her fingers through his thick, soft hair.

"I need you now." He shoved her dress up and unzipped his pants as he pushed her down onto the seat.

"Yes." She spread her legs and reached between them to guide his cock. "Condom."

"I can't wait." He panted in her ear as he shoved her legs farther apart and pressed against her. "Please."

"No." She couldn't risk it. "Condom."

"Where's your fucking purse?" His hands clenched her shoulder, hurting her a little.

"Here." She reached above her head, causing her breasts to rub against his chest. She gasped and he moaned.

"You better hurry." His dick was hot and heavy against her thigh.

She opened her purse, digging through it, items falling out. "Here." She fumbled trying to open the condom.

"Give it to me." He snatched it from her and tore it open with his teeth.

"Let me." She needed to touch him.

"No." The sound echoed through the limo.

She stilled. He'd never, ever yelled at her. She didn't like it. She wasn't going to be with a guy who spoke to her like that.

He took a deep, shaky breath and rested his forehead against hers. "If you touch me, I'll come."

"Oh." She fought a smile. That was okay. She'd pushed this man—this rich, sexy man who could have any woman he wanted—to the edge of his control. Even more wetness pooled between her legs. He may not belong to her forever but he was hers tonight and she was going to use him to her satisfaction.

He exhaled through his teeth as he rolled the condom down his engorged cock. She skimmed her hands across his back, wishing he'd removed his jacket.

"Sarah?" He prodded at her opening.

He may be rough sometimes but he was a good guy. Even now, on the edge he wanted her permission. This would be her last moment of control and she was going to enjoy it. She nibbled her lip.

"Answer me." He grabbed her chin, his grip rough.

She lifted her legs wrapping them around his waist and the tip of him slid into her.

"Sarah..." It was half-groan.

"Yes, Nick. Fuck me." And then he was in charge.

He pushed into her—no finesse, no patience. She gasped at the intrusion. She was still a little sore from earlier and even though she was more than wet enough, this hurt.

"Nick, wait. Please." Her nails dug into his back as he rocked his hips.

"Sarah." He continued to thrust into her, but he slowed his pace and reached between them, caressing her pussy. "You feel so fucking good." He buried his face in her neck.

Pleasure started to build. His fingers coaxing away the pain and igniting sparks of desire. Soon, his thrusting felt good, but she needed more. She rocked with him, following his lead and enjoying the sensation of being surrounded by him again.

"Yes, baby. That's it." He pumped into her harder and faster.

Her legs tightened around his waist, pushing against his ass, helping him go deeper. She needed him deeper. She needed to feel only him.

"Sarah!" He surged forward, filling her over and over.

"Nick..." She was close. He needed to wait but his body

shook and he groaned against her neck as he collapsed onto of her.

She lay trembling under him—her body screaming for release. "Nick." It was a plea. She needed him to help her finish.

"Sorry." He rolled off her.

He thought he was too heavy. "No. Nick. Please. I didn't…"

"You didn't what?" He leaned up, looking at her.

He knew. It was in his eyes which were hard and brittle, not warm and soft like they used to be after they'd had sex.

"I didn't come." She touched his cheek. "Please."

He grabbed her hand, moving it away from his face. "Does your boyfriend always satisfy you?"

"What?"

"What do you do when he doesn't make you scream? Does he eat you out or use his fingers?" His grip tightened on her wrist.

"Stop. You're hurting me." She tugged on her hand and he let go. She started to sit up.

"Answer my question." He leaned over her, ensuring she couldn't move.

For one second she was afraid but that dissipated with her anger. He had no business asking her about her life. "What do you do for the women you don't satisfy?"

"You're the first." His nostrils flared.

Perhaps she should be scared because he was more than pissed, but she wasn't. This was Nick. He'd never physically hurt her. "Lucky me." She shoved at his chest. "Now, get off me."

He moved away, stuffing his dick back into his pants and zipping them up.

She sat up, pulling her dress down and scooting to the

other side of the limo. "You can..." She'd started to tell him to take her home but she didn't want him to know where she lived. She couldn't have him walking in and out of her life until he tired of her.

"I can what? Go fuck myself? No thanks. I've been doing that for months."

"You can take me back to the hotel." She no longer wanted to be around him. She'd go home and shower, wash him away. This memory would go a long way in making their previous pleasurable ones disappear.

"When we're done." He poured himself a drink.

"We are done." Completely and forever.

"Not even close." He took a sip of his drink, watching her over his glass.

"Excuse me?"

"You heard me." His voice was getting softer, more deadly.

Her instincts told her to tread carefully, but her body and brain were a mess of nerves and emotions. "Take me back to the hotel."

"No." He finished his drink.

"You don't seem to understand." She leaned closer to him. "We're done. I'm done. I don't want to do this anymore. I don't want you."

In a flash she was across the limo and half-lying on his lap.

"You made it perfectly clear that you don't want me in your life, but your body wants mine." His mouth came down on hers, hard and demanding.

She tried to keep her lips closed but he squeezed her jaw and she opened for him. She fought it but he was right. She wanted him. Before she knew it, she was kissing him back and then she was completely on his lap, his dick hard again and pressing against her hip.

CHAPTER 19: NICK

Nick grabbed Sarah's leg and shifted her so she was straddling him. He was furious and so fucking hard for her again. He had no idea why this woman turned him on like she did but there was nothing he could do except fuck her until she didn't.

He grabbed her chin. His dick positioned right at her opening. "If you want a condom, you'd better get one."

Rage warred with desire in her expressive face. He held his breath as he rubbed his cock along her opening, hedging his bet. Her eyes drooped with desire and she leaned to the side, grabbed her purse and pulled out another condom. She offered it to him but he shook his head, gritting his teeth. *How many times had she planned on fucking her boyfriend tonight?*

She tore it open, her white teeth flashing. Fuck, she was hot. He could've sworn his dick grew another two inches. She reached between them and he dropped his head back as her hand wrapped around him. She brushed her thumb over the top and he moaned. She gave him a little squeeze as she began rolling it down his length.

"Sarah..." It was a warning growl but she didn't have the sense God gave a gnat because she moved her hand to his balls and gently scraped her fingernail across them.

"Fuck!" He straightened, grabbing her waist and pulling her down as his hips shot up, enveloping himself in her hot wetness.

She gasped and clutched his shoulders.

"Shhh." He was more in control this time. He'd make it good for her. The last time he'd been crazed with desire. "I'll wait. Whenever you're ready." His hands ran up and down her sides as she clenched around him. She was so fucking tight and felt so good he couldn't stop from thrusting upward, just a little.

She whimpered and bit her lip.

He unzipped her dress and pulled it off her shoulders, his nostrils flaring at the sight of her black and green bra. His favorite colors on her, but she hadn't worn this for him. Anger started to seep into his lust and he pushed the bra down, letting her tits pop out.

"These are mine." He bent and ran his tongue over one nipple.

She arched her back, gasping as he shifted inside of her, but it didn't stop her from grabbing his head and holding him to her breast.

"You're so soft." He kissed her breasts, inhaling her perfume and the scent of her. He'd missed this. Missed her...but she hadn't missed him. He'd make sure she did after tonight. He'd ruin her for any other man. He grabbed her hips and lifted her slightly. "Come on, Sarah. Please." He needed to move. He needed to thrust into her—to make her his, but he had to take it slow. He had to make sure she came. He took her breast in his mouth and sucked as he guided her hips. Her movements were slow at first but the more he licked, sucked and nibbled her nipples the wilder she became, lifting and lowering herself onto him faster and faster.

Soon, he was panting at her chest, close to his own release, trying to hold it back as she rose and fell, squeezing him. "That's it baby. You're close."

She tossed back her head, slight whimpers coming from her throat. Damn, she was beautiful. Her eyes closed, her mouth open slightly and her hair cascading around her shoulders as she rode him.

"Oh...god," she moaned.

"Open your eyes." He grabbed her chin, stopping her rhythm.

"Please." She rocked faster.

"Look at me, Sarah." He grabbed her hips, halting her movements.

She opened her eyes. They were bright green and filled with passion.

"Me." He thrust into her hard.

She gasped, her eyes drooping again.

"Open your eyes and look at me." He grabbed her chin again.

Her eyes locked with his.

He pushed upward and her mouth opened on a small groan. He punctuated each hard thrust with a word. "I want...you...to...see...who's...making...you...come." He pulled her down as he thrust up again and again.

Her green eyes stayed locked with his as she came, her

body shaking and her hips rocking in release. Her eyes dropped closed, so he pulled her to him and kissed her as he fucked her harder and harder. He never wanted this to end. She felt amazing and right now she was his—only his—but passion roared down his back straight to his balls and he came, clasping her close.

She collapsed against him, her head resting on his shoulder, her lips on his neck. His hands wandered up and down her back. He could stay there all night but the limo stopped and Mike's voice filled the car.

"We're home, sir."

"Condoms," she whispered against his neck. "That was the last one."

He leaned to the side and pressed a button. "Drive to the nearest gas station." As soon as he let go he said, "Do you always fuck your boyfriend three times when you go out? Or was tonight special because of the award?" He shouldn't ask. It shouldn't matter, but it did. He didn't want her in his life as a girlfriend, not anymore, but he didn't want her fucking anyone else either.

CHAPTER 20: SARAH

"What are you talking about?" Sarah had no idea what was going on. Nick had been switching between wanting her and being pissed at her all evening. She straightened on his lap and inhaled sharply as she felt him shift inside of her. He had been mostly flaccid, but he was growing again. How was that even possible?

"Don't play dumb."

"I'm not. I have no idea what your problem is." She started to crawl off his lap and he groaned, grabbing her hip and stopping her. She raised a brow in challenge.

His eyes flared but he moved his hand, pulled off the condom, and zipped up his pants as she sat on the seat next to him. The limo stopped.

"You're a smart woman. Think about it." He hopped out of the car and stopped at the driver's window for a moment before heading into the gas station.

His clothes were rumpled and his hair was a mess. He looked like he'd just gotten out of bed. God help her, she wanted him again, but she wasn't going to put up with this shit. She zipped up her dress, straightened her hair the best she could and opened the door.

"Um...miss." The limo driver hurried to her side of the car. "Nick will be right back."

"I don't care." She started walking toward the store.

"He wants you to wait here." The driver trailed after her.

"I don't care what he wants." She walked into the store. She had little chance of getting him to tell her anything he didn't want to inside that limo and she had even less than that once she got to his house. No matter how much she wanted answers and how much her mind didn't want to be with him when he was treating her like crap, her body wanted him anyway it could get him. All he had to do was touch her and she was putty in his hands—the last time in the limo proved that.

He was purchasing several boxes of condoms when she strolled up to him.

"My God, how many do you think you'll need?" The words were out before she even thought.

The clerk behind the counter chuckled. He was a young kid and she was pretty sure he wanted to high five Nick.

"What are you doing in here?" Nick wasn't happy to see her.

"I want some answers or I'm going home." She crossed her arms over her chest.

Nick's eyes raked down her body, stopping at the juncture between her thighs. "I still have your present in my pocket."

"I'm well aware of that."

"You're right. We need more." He turned to the clerk. "We'll be right back. I'm going to let my lady pick out the kind she likes best." He grabbed her hand and dragged her to the back of the store.

"Let me go." She tugged, but his grip was tight. "We don't need more."

He stopped by the condoms and pulled her in front of him. "Pick out the ones you want."

His hand trailed up the back of her leg.

"Stop it." She slapped at him. "That's not why I came in here."

He pulled her against him, his dick once again hard.

"Jesus, Nick. Again?"

"Yes," he growled in her ear as his fingers skimmed across her abdomen and down between her legs.

"Oh." She bit her lip. His touch felt so good, but not in here. "No." She burst forward and to the side, taking him off guard. "Not like this. Not in here."

The clerk was craning his neck to watch them, his hand behind the counter, probably stroking himself.

"Then wait for me in the car."

"Don't order me around."

"Don't push me, Sarah."

"What's the matter with you? Why are you so angry?"

He laughed, it was an ugly harsh sound and she almost cried. This wasn't the Nick she knew. She brushed past him. She was leaving.

He grabbed her arm. "You'd better be going to the car."

"I'm going home. I can't be with you when you're like this." She blinked back tears. She didn't deserve to be treated like this.

He pulled her close. "You're mine for the night."

"No."

"You agreed." His hand went to her ass, skimming between her cheeks. "You want this. You want me."

She trembled because she did want him. "Not like this."

"Like anyway I want." His fingers slid between her legs, exploring and caressing. "Remember that." He swatted her ass. "Now, be a good girl and go to the car."

"You're a jackass." Her hand itched to slap him.

He pulled her close again and kissed her, it was soft and coaxing, exactly what she hadn't expected. She was so surprised that she didn't even struggle and before she could stop she was melting against him.

He broke the kiss, his lips still close. "Please go to the car and wait for me."

His eyes were warm now. This was the Nick she remembered.

"Tell me why you're so mad at me." No matter how much her body wanted him, she couldn't go with him if he were going to keep running hot and cold.

His face tensed again and his lips thinned. "You really have no idea?"

She shook her head.

"How can you...Forget it." He ran his hand through his hair. "Please, wait for me in the car."

"I can't go home with you unless you tell—"

"I'll fucking tell you later."

"Promise."

"Yes. You have my word." His jaw clenched. "Now, please

go to the car."

She trusted him and she wanted this night too much to leave without giving him a chance to come clean. She turned and went back to the limo.

When he climbed inside the car a few minutes later he sat on the seat across from her, his dark eyes studying her.

"So?" She'd waited long enough and his gaze was making her skin tingle.

"What?"

"You said you'd tell me what was bothering you." She'd thought about it and was pretty sure he was angry about the boyfriend he thought she had. She could confess that she didn't have one, but it was none of his business. He'd had tons of women since her. It wasn't fair for him to be mad that she'd met someone—even though she hadn't. That was the truly pathetic part. She had no one and there was no way she was going to admit that to him.

"And I will. Later."

"When?" She crossed her arms over her chest and his eyes dropped to her breasts.

"When I'm ready."

"I'm not going home with you until..."

The car stopped.

"Too late." Nick smiled.

CHAPTER 21: NICK

Nick's emotions were in a riot. He was pissed, jealous, hurt and damn it, he still cared for her. He should've been able to fuck her and forget her, but he couldn't. Every time he had her he wanted more. She was a drug to him and that was terrifying. One night wouldn't be enough. He'd have to convince her to let him have more but he wouldn't accomplish that by snapping at her. Unfortunately, he couldn't stop himself. Whenever he thought of her fucking that guy while he'd sat at home dreaming of her and jerking off, his temper exploded. The only time he didn't care was when he was inside her. That settled it. He'd fuck her until he passed out.

He grabbed the bag of condoms and got out of the car. He waited...and waited. "Sarah." He wasn't in the mood for games and yet, she'd been playing them all night.

"I'm not getting out until we talk."

He glanced at Mike and sighed. "I'm only going to tell you

once." He handed Mike a wad of cash and his house keys. "Get the door."

Mike glanced at the limo as if in doubt.

"It's a game." He winked.

Mike was Ethan's driver and was familiar with the games played by consenting adults. Of course, he was also aware that Nick had been celibate for four months waiting for Sarah and that she hadn't been interested.

"I swear. She wants this as much as I do." He grinned to put the guy at ease. "Maybe not quite as much, but she did get into the car on her own—twice."

"Yeah." Mike still hesitated. "But if she changed her mind and wants to go home..."

"She doesn't." There was no way he could carry Sarah and fight Mike. He bent down and peered into the car. She was in the corner fuming, her fingers tapping on her lap. "Sarah, we'll talk in the house."

"No."

He counted to ten. "Yes."

"No. I want to know now."

He took a deep breath. This was risky. "Do you want to go home? And before you answer...think...because Mike is going to take you home if you say that's what you want." His eyes locked with hers and he prayed. He had no idea what he'd do if she said she wanted to leave because that wasn't happening, not tonight.

"I want to talk."

He shot a look over his shoulder at Mike and then faced her again. "Do you want to go home?" Confident now that she wouldn't say yes.

"I might." She lifted her chin. "It depends on what you have to say."

Mike snickered, trying to cover it as a cough.

Nick straightened and took a step away from the car. "Come here, now."

She popped her head out of the limo to glare at him. "I'm not your dog."

That was it. His temper blew. He grabbed her under the arms, dragging her from the car.

"Let me go!" She slapped his chest.

He didn't even bother to respond as he bent and tossed her over his shoulder.

"Damn it, Nick. Put me down." She kicked and her toe landed on his thigh, a little too close to his groin.

"Stop fighting." He wrapped the arm not holding the bag of condoms around her legs, pressing them against his body so she could only give him tiny jabs.

"Help me." She leaned up on his shoulder, appealing to Mike.

The driver shook his head. "I would've if you'd wanted to go home, but you didn't." He moved to the door and unlocked it, holding it open.

"Turn off the alarm." He wouldn't be able to do that with a struggling Sarah in his arms.

"I said maybe! Maybe! Not no."

Mike shrugged as they passed on his way out of the house "You can listen to what he has to say and then leave if you like."

"He's not going to let me leave."

"Of course, I will—" Nick swatted her ass, dragging his hand across the soft curves—"but you won't want to."

Mike grabbed her hand. "Call me if you need a ride home."

"Your card? You're giving me your card while this brute abducts me." Her voice was shrill.

Nick couldn't stop grinning. Boy was she pissed. It was going to be fun redirecting all that passion toward sex. His dick hardened uncomfortably.

"Good night, Mike. We won't need you again tonight."

"I don't even have my phone."

Nick stopped. "Where is it?"

"In my purse in the car." She glanced at Mike who was watching her closely. "Would you get it for me?"

"Absolutely." Mike walked back to the car, retrieved her purse and handed it to her. "If you want to leave, call."

"Thanks." She stuffed the card in her purse as Nick carried her into the house and Mike shut the door behind them.

"Nick, stop this now. You don't want…"

He walked straight into his bedroom, flipped on the light and tossed her onto the bed.

"You have no idea what I want." He dropped the bag, shrugged out of his jacket and pulled off his shirt.

CHAPTER 22: SARAH

Sarah dropped her purse and scooted across the bed, trying to get away from Nick, but when he took off his shirt she stopped, her gaze taking in all that skin and muscle. She shouldn't want him when he was acting like this, but she did. She was embarrassingly wet and she'd die if he found out. Who was she kidding? He was going to find out. They were going to fuck again and her heart raced at the thought. Still, she had to pretend. It made it more fun. She hopped off the king size bed, removing her shoes so she could run.

"Get back on the bed." He walked to his closet.

"Not until you tell me why you're being such an ass." She moved toward the foot of the bed. It was closer to him, but the head was against the wall so she'd have to climb over it to escape.

He turned, his dark eyes roaming over her. "I'll tell you when I'm ready."

"That's not good enough." *The arrogance of that man.* "We're not doing anything...anything, until you talk to me."

He smiled, it was smug and condescending. "You really are adorable." He kicked off his shoes and pulled off his socks. "I let you have control before. It was fun and I wanted you to enjoy yourself." He opened his closet door. "But tonight is about my enjoyment." He turned on the light.

Sarah's mouth dropped open. There were ties and gags and other instruments of...pleasure? Some didn't look too pleasurable.

"Obey and things will go easier for you."

What had she gotten herself into? Her heart shifted into high gear, but her body hummed with anticipation, knowing he wouldn't hurt her. He'd used some of those things that other time, when he'd punished her. She wanted that again. When he'd finally let her come, it'd been so good and the pleasure leading up to her release had been exquisite.

"Take off your dress."

She shook her head. "Not until we talk." Her eyes kept darting between the toys in the closet and his pants. He was hard and ready for her.

"Sarah," his tone was chiding. "I'll give you one more chance to obey." He took a deep breath. "Take off your clothes. All of them and get on the bed."

His tone was calm but a muscle twitched in his cheek. He was on edge. If she obeyed, he'd calm down. That meant he'd torment her before letting her come, but if she pushed him, he'd lose control. Her only chance was getting him to look away.

He pulled out a riding crop and tapped it against his thigh. Her legs trembled. She wasn't ready to be whipped.

"Okay." She reached behind her back and unzipped her dress.

The muscle twitched more in his cheek and his eyes grew darker as he watched the cloth slide down her body.

"What would you like me to do next?" She ran her hand across her breasts, down her stomach and between her legs. She shivered as her fingers skimmed over her sensitive flesh.

"Show me how wet you are." His voice was ragged.

"Nick, please." She didn't like doing this. He'd had his

fingers, his face and his cock buried inside her at one time or another but holding herself open and showing him this private part of her was embarrassing.

"Show me." He stared at the juncture between her thighs.

She moved her leg so her feet were shoulder width apart and opened her lower lips. Her heart pounded against her rib cage. She needed him to look away before she dared run. Wetness gushed at the thought of him catching her. He'd be pissed and desperate just like she was.

"Do you want to go home? Do you want to call Mike?"

She inhaled deeply, the air rattling through her lungs. "No, but I want you to tell me why you were so angry."

"Get on the bed and spread your legs."

She crawled onto the bed and sat, opening her thighs for him.

"Take off your bra and lie down."

She unclasped her bra and tossed it by her dress before leaning back on her elbows.

"I said lie down."

"I want to see you." She needed to see when he turned away.

"Obey me."

"I have."

"I think you want to be punished." He smiled but it was almost a leer.

"I don't." She did. She really, really did.

"Liar." He turned toward the closet. "We'll start with..."

She jumped from the bed, grabbing her dress as she ran. Her bra slid from her grasp but she didn't have time to get it because Nick turned.

"What the hell?"

She darted out the door, slamming it shut behind her.

Now, she had to find somewhere to hide.

CHAPTER 23: NICK

"Sarah, get the fuck back here." Nick raced toward the door flinging it open. *Oh, she was going to pay for this.*

He stepped into his living room but she wasn't there. He glanced at the door. She wouldn't actually leave, would she? No, she wanted this as much as he did. Still he went to the front door and opened it, stepping outside and glancing down the street. He was pretty sure she wouldn't ditch out on her own, but just in case, he closed the door and locked it, entering his security code. "The door is locked Sarah. There's no escape." Now that he'd found her, she wasn't going anywhere until he was done with her.

He moved into the living room. "The alarm is on." He glanced behind the couch—empty. "If you come out now, I won't punish you...much." He strolled through the room, looking behind and under everything that was big enough to hide a petite, one-hundred and twenty pound woman. "You're making my hand itch to swat that bottom of yours." She was also making his dick rock hard. He wouldn't be able to hold out long, not this time, but the next time he would.

He snorted on a laugh. Or not. He was crazy hot for her. Just seeing her wet and glistening, her pink nub already hard and begging for his mouth had made him want to jump her right then. He should've. He wandered into the kitchen and glanced around. Not really anywhere to hide in there.

"I'm not kidding, Sarah. You need to come out now." Okay,

he was getting a little desperate. He liked games but he was on edge and ready to come. He moved to a guest bedroom and went inside. He searched under the bed and in the closet. Nothing.

He went back into the hallway. "This was fun, but I'm done." If she'd actually left, he'd hunt her down and strangle her. Not really, but he would tie her up. Hell, he was going to do that anyway. "I only have a few more rooms to search. I'm going to find you. Be a good girl and come out now. Save yourself some pain."

He searched the bathroom. Empty. Damn her. Where the fuck was she? "If you don't come out now, I'm not going to let you come at all tonight."

Still no movement. She was damn good at this hide-and-seek shit. His hand hesitated at the garage door. He stepped inside and almost exhaled in relief. She was here. He could smell her perfume—faint under the odors of oil and engine. He closed the door, leaning against it. He lowered his voice to just above a whisper, "Come out, come out wherever you are?"

He stalked forward, bending to look under his car. Nope. He moved farther into the garage and she darted from around a cabinet on the other side, racing for the door. He launched himself at her, grabbing her around the waist before she could open the door.

"Nick, let me go." She was laughing and half-heartedly struggling in his arms.

"Never." He shoved her against the door, all playfulness gone. She was warm and soft against him. "No more games, Sarah." His mouth came down on hers hard and demanding.

She opened for him as one of her hands tangled in his hair

while the other one skimmed down his spine. Her legs wrapped around his waist. He needed to be inside her now. He shoved up her dress, his finger dipping into her.

"You're so fucking wet for me." He tugged on her hair. "Open your eyes."

She did.

"For me." He almost beat his chest. "I did this to you." He reached between them and unzipped his pants.

"Condom."

"Fuck." He rested his head against her neck, drawing in deep breaths. "Please."

Her legs dropped.

"Fine." He carried her to the car and put her on the hood. "Stay."

"I'm not your dog."

He shoved her dress up so he could see her pussy, glistening for him. He trailed his fingers along the sides and over her clit, back and forth. "Stay or I'm going to fuck you right now, no condom." He grabbed her hair, pulling back her head so her eyes which were half closed with pleasure met his. "Do you understand? If you don't stay right like this,"—he tugged her legs farther apart—"I will find you again and then we won't use condoms. Ever. Understand?"

She nodded.

"Good." He bent, kissing a trail up her inner thigh. He flicked his tongue over her little nub and then sucked it into his mouth. Her hands grasped his hair, pulling him closer. "Stay. Exactly. Like. This." He punctuated each word with a lick or suck until she was trembling beneath him. "You're so fucking close, aren't you?"

"Yes…please." Her fingers tugged on his hair.

"I'll be right back." He pulled away from her and she moaned. At the door he turned around, "Stay."

"I'm still not your dog." But she didn't move.

He grinned and hurried to the bedroom where he grabbed a condom and then another one and stuffed them into his pocket. He should only need one—one quick fuck to relieve this pressure—but Sarah was addictive and his dick was unpredictable around her. His plan was to fuck her and then take her to the bedroom where he could punish her—for her disobedience tonight, for not writing a letter to Ethan and for finding someone else while he'd jerked off dreaming of her. He almost snarled as he hurried back to the garage. If she'd moved...

He opened the door and she was exactly where he'd left her, except she'd loosened her dress so her breasts were almost exposed. With the hem around her waist, her pussy on display and her nipples almost falling from her dress she was his wet dream come true.

He grabbed a condom, and shoved his pants down, kicking them away as he walked toward her. He tore the condom open and rolled it onto his erection. He grabbed her, pulling her closer to the edge of the car.

"Now, Sarah." It was half-question, half-demand.

"Yes."

She licked her lips and he was inside of her in one hard thrust. She gasped, but her arms and legs wrapped around him, pulling him closer. He needed this and he needed it now. He reached between them and stroked her.

"Please, Sarah." He rocked into her, a little. "I need to fuck you." He kissed her neck. "I can't wait."

"Yes." She tightened her legs.

He held her hips, keeping her in place as he thrust into her over and over. She closed her eyes, moaning as her hands scraped at his back and shoulders.

"Open your eyes." He increased his pace, sliding in and out faster and harder. She was so hot and tight. She was his and he needed her to know that.

Her mouth was open, she was close.

"Open your fucking eyes." He growled in her ear and nipped her.

Her eyes flew open and he leaned up. "Look at me while I fuck you."

She tried, but her eyes kept drooping with her approaching orgasm. He should slow down, make her see him but right now he was too close. He dropped his mouth to hers and kissed her. It was hard and dark and filled with all his pain and desire.

She tightened around him, her hips shaking with her release and he followed, his thrusts getting slower and slower as he came, her thighs milking every last ounce from him.

He dropped on top of her and her fingers caressed his spine. Fuck, he'd missed her. She kissed his neck and nibbled his ear. Did she do that to her little-dick boyfriend?

He shoved off her, yanked her dress over her head, dropping it on the floor before pulling on his pants and picking her up. "Time for your punishment."

CHAPTER 24: SARAH

"What?" Sarah shifted, trying to get free, but Nick's grip was tight.

"You heard me." He carried her into his bedroom and went directly to the closet. "Since, I can't trust you to obey." He pulled out a long cord and walked to the bed. He tossed her in the center and knelt next to her, grabbing her wrists before she could move.

"What are you doing?" She was a little nervous but more excited.

"Tying you up." He said it as if it were the most normal thing in the world.

"What?" She squirmed but he was stronger than her and she didn't actually want to get free. A throbbing had started between her legs again. Only this man made her hot over and over within minutes. "I'll obey. I swear." She lied. That wouldn't be any fun at all.

"Liar." He leaned over her, stretching her arms above her head. He looked down at her, his eyes darkening with desire. "Together or separate? Hmm." He held her hands together and stared at her breasts. He used his other hand to separate her arms, never taking his eyes from her chest. "Separate."

"What? No." She almost flipped over, trying to get free.

He quickly straddled her, his bare chest right over her face. She wanted to run her tongue across all that warm skin. She lifted her head but he sat up. She tugged but her hands were secured to the headboard.

He hopped off the bed and went back to the closet.

"What are you doing?" She leaned up the best she could to watch him.

"You should be more concerned with what I'm going to do." He came back to the bed with more restraints.

He grabbed her ankle.

"Please, Nick. Stop."

He glanced up at her. "Safe word still cat litter?" His lips twitched.

Oh, yes. This was going to be pleasurable torture. "Yes."

He nodded almost imperceptibly and then pulled her leg to the side.

"You don't have to do this. I can't go anywhere." She yanked on her wrist restraints and kicked at him with her other foot. She caught him in the side, causing him to loosen his hold on her ankle. She closed her legs. He grunted and grabbed both her feet, jerking them to the side.

"Behave. You're already in for a long night." He tied one ankle to the end of the bed.

"Nick. Don't. We can talk about this." She bucked but her restraints were secure. Desire pooled in her belly. She was going to be spread open for him, unable to move.

"Talk? That's the last thing I plan on doing." He pulled her other ankle toward the other side of the bed. "Definitely apart for these." His eyes roamed up her leg to her pussy. "Although, maybe later I'll strap them together while I fuck you."

She couldn't stop the shiver that coursed through her. She wanted him and anything he'd do to her, but she had to play. "Please. Not like this."

"Do you remember what I said I'd do if you made me wait longer than five minutes?" He stalked toward the center of the bed.

"You'd toss me on a table and fuck me in front of everyone."

"Not that. We both know that wouldn't have happened." His hand skimmed across her torso, getting close to her breasts on the upward trip and her pussy on the downward, but not touching either. "No matter how much I wanted to, someone would've stopped me." His eyes darkened. "But not at the Club. Maybe, I'll take you to the Club and strap you down like this."

The breath hitched in her throat. Fear seeping into her desire for the first time. She didn't want to be on display. "No. I...I wouldn't like that."

He leaned down until his lips were a breath away. "I don't give a fuck what you like. You blew that."

Panic set in. This wasn't the Nick she knew. This man was furious. "Please. Tell me why you're so mad." Maybe, she should admit to not having a boyfriend, but her sense of fairness struggled to the surface. He had no right to be angry about that. "It can't be my boyfriend. How many women have you been with since me?"

His eyes narrowed. "I said I was going to mark you." His hand skimmed down her stomach.

She shivered as his finger trailed over her mons and downward. He pressed against the side of her pussy and lowered his dark head. She closed her eyes. God, she'd missed this. His lips came down on the juncture where her thigh met her pussy. Her breath stilled in her chest as he kissed her.

"Right here." His hot breath blew over her. "I should have

someone tattoo my name, right here."

"What?" Her eyes flew open and she lifted her head the best she could.

His tongue darted out, licking between her thigh and her pussy. "In big letters, I should have them mark you as mine. *Nick's* would be all it needed to say." He glanced up at her. "Or we could add an arrow, to make sure there's no confusion."

"We're not doing any of that." Her voice was shriller than she would've liked but she wasn't one hundred percent sure he was kidding.

He looked back between her legs. "That may be too close." He kissed her thigh, this one was open mouthed and wet. Her legs trembled as he kissed a little lower. "By the time a guy, your boyfriend, saw that tattoo"—he dragged his tongue up and down between her thigh and her pussy—"he'd be too far gone to care."

He kissed her leg again, adding a little suction, but her thigh didn't need his lips, her pussy did.

"He'd care later, but not enough to stop." He leaned up and stared at her, his eyes hard. "He'd finish fucking what's mine."

He flicked her clit with his finger, causing a jolt of pain and pleasure to zip through her. He waited for her eyes to lock with his. She wanted to beg him to kiss away the pain but this Nick didn't care what she wanted. She dropped her gaze, trying to secretly urge him. His eyes narrowed but he lowered his head. Her breath was coming in pants. If he kissed her right, she'd come. His hot breath caressed where he'd flicked. She didn't need his breath. She needed pressure, touch. He ran his tongue over and around her clit.

"Yes." She flopped back onto the bed, her hands grasping at the restraints.

He sucked her as his fingers came up, playing near her opening.

"Please..." Her hips thrust toward his face.

"Oh, no. Not yet." He blew across her pussy, moving his hand away. "You don't get to come yet." He moved down her body.

"Please, Nick." He was moving away from where she wanted him, needed him.

"I think I'll start here." He kissed her calf.

"There?" That was way too far away. She'd die before he got back where he belonged.

"Yep, right here." He turned her calf and kissed it, sucking hard.

"Ouch."

He caressed the spot with his tongue. "One down, dozens more to go." He moved a few inches up her leg and kissed her again, sucking until there was a sharp pain.

"Damn it, that hurts."

He licked the spot. "Oh, it doesn't hurt that badly." He moved farther up her thigh.

"Yeah, but it doesn't feel good." She was leaning up trying to see but his head was in the way. "What are you doing?"

He kissed her again and then lifted his head. "Marking you as mine." He moved inward on her thigh, his kisses coming faster, harder and closer together.

"Marking me? What do you..." He was giving her hickeys, love bites. She jerked on the restraints but they held firm. "Stop it. Damn it Nick, stop doing that."

He didn't listen, just continued his northern movement. He avoided her pussy, kissing up her hip and down the side of her ass.

"Stop." She was almost in tears. She'd have to wear jeans to hide all of these.

He kissed her belly and moved to under her ribs.

"I don't want you to do this." She wiggled under him, but there was nowhere she could go and nothing she could do, unless she used her safe word, but then it'd all stop and she wasn't ready for that.

"I don't give a fuck," he mumbled against her breast.

Her damn nipple hardened at his nearness. He flicked it with his tongue.

"You're turned on, aren't you?"

"No." She wasn't, not really, but her traitorous body wanted him to keep kissing her. It didn't care how embarrassed she was going to be tomorrow. It only cared about what she was feeling today.

"You shouldn't lie when the truth is right here." His hand dipped between her legs, his fingers exploring her and making her gasp. "You're so wet for me." He shifted up until they were face to face. "Me. You're wet for me."

She swore he would've pounded his chest like a gorilla if his hands weren't busy—one stroking her pussy and the other tangled in her hair, forcing her to look at him.

"You're mine and I want your little-dicked boyfriend to know exactly what you did tonight." His mouth came down on hers.

She pressed her lips together. She didn't want to kiss him. She didn't want to desire this man, but his fingers pressed down on her clit and she gasped giving him the opening he wanted. His tongue darted inside her mouth but she refused to kiss him back. He let go of her jaw, stopping his kiss. She closed her mouth and he ran his fingers gently down her cheek, his tongue skimming along the seam of her lips as his other hand stroked along her pussy.

"Let me in, Sarah." He kissed her eyes. "Look at me, please."

She could refuse angry Nick, but not this man. The place between her legs was molten and aching for him but his fingers were fleeting, caressing and moving on to give butterfly touches all over.

She needed to be closer to him. She opened her mouth and accepted his tongue, sucking on it and causing him to groan before his kiss turned desperate, but this time she was on board. His finger slipped inside her and stroked in and out.

"More." She sucked on his lower lip.

"Fuck." He rubbed his dick against her. "If I didn't have these pants on, I'd be inside you right now."

"Take them off." She did the best she could to touch him but with the restraints she was mostly immobile. "I need you. Please." She was past the point of caring if she begged.

"Does your boyfriend make you cry out in need? Make you beg to be fucked?" He rocked against her again and she whimpered.

"No. Only you."

He stilled, his dark eyes searching hers for a long moment. She knew he saw her desire and desperation but she didn't know if he saw the truth, that it'd been only him. No one else had touched her.

"Time to go back to showing the world you're mine." He buried his face in her neck, kissing as one of his hands skimmed across her abdomen and between her legs.

"Oh, god." She trembled when he hit that spot on her neck—the one that seem to be attached to her pussy. He kissed and suckled until she knew there had to be numerous bruises on her skin but she no longer cared.

He moved down her body, marking her as his, leaving his love bites to prove that he'd been there. He kissed between her breasts and then on them. His mouth moved along her rib cage and across her belly—always open, wet and hot, leaving a sharp sting of pleasure-pain as he branded her.

She was beyond words when he was finally between her legs again. She was nothing but a bundle of raw nerves, her body tense and twitching, waiting for his touch.

"You're so close." He blew across her pussy and she trembled. He bent and licked her, his tongue rough against her sensitized flesh and then he pushed away and sat up.

"Please...please." She thrashed her head back and forth. If only she could touch herself...

He reached behind her, grabbing pillows. His chest was in front of her face. She no longer cared if he got angry. He couldn't punish her more. She was already on the sharp edge of passion. She kissed him, licking and sucking wherever her lips could touch.

"No." His hand went to her head, holding her close for one second before pulling her away. "You don't get to decide." He stuffed a pillow behind her and tugged on her hair. "You made your choice. Tonight is about me." He yanked her hair again. "Understand?"

She glared up at him. She was ready to burst. She was done with this game.

He put another pillow under her and she shifted forward, kissing his nipple. He jumped as if burned.

"Damn it, Sarah. No." He scrambled away from her.

She shouldn't but she couldn't stop from grinning. "You can tie me up but you can't stop me from doing what I want."

"You want to kiss something?" His eyes sparkled.

She swallowed, her eyes dropping to the bulge in his pants. She did. She wanted the control sucking his dick gave her but if she said yes, he may deny her that too. Instead her eyes locked with his and she licked her lips—just a tiny showing of her tongue but it was enough. His control snapped.

She'd never seen anyone move so fast. His pants were gone and he was kneeling in front of her face, his cock straight up.

She could smell his musk, his desire and she gushed between her legs. "You're going to have to untie me." She could lick the side of his dick but there was no way in this position she could get him in her mouth.

"You'd like that wouldn't you?" He leaned forward, grabbing the headboard with his left hand. "I'll feed it to you." He took his cock in his right hand and positioned it at her mouth. "Show me you can obey. Suck my cock."

He ran the head over her lips. It was hot and smooth. Her tongue darted out, tasting the precum on the tip and a deep guttural sound rumbled from his chest. She licked around the head and down the shaft, flicking with her tongue.

"Put me in your mouth."

"Beg me." She continued to lick him. With his one hand

supporting him and the other holding his cock, he couldn't force her head down. Right now, even tied up, she was in control.

"Sarah." The word was a warning growl. "Don't fuck with me." He poked at her with his penis but she shifted so he hit her cheek.

"Say, please. Pretty please and I'll suck you so good you'll see stars."

"Sarah." It was a warning. He was losing it.

Her heart skipped a few beats as his hand on the headboard moved downward, yanking on a pillow.

If he moved the pillows, she'd fall back to the bed and he'd be in control. He wouldn't need to brace himself on the headboard. She couldn't let that happen. She flicked the tip of his cock with her tongue before surrounding it with her mouth and sucking.

"Oh, shit...That feels so fucking good." His hips thrust forward and she gagged as he hit the back of her throat.

She pulled away, licking him again.

"Sarah..." It was a plea and a benediction but she needed the words.

"What do you want, Nick? Tell me." She kissed his dick, letting her tongue trail down it.

"Suck me. Please." His eyes met hers and she opened her mouth wide. His black eyes gleamed with lust as he rocked forward and she took him inside. He started thrusting into her mouth. "Don't...fucking...move."

She popped him out of her mouth and she was pretty sure he whimpered. His hips kept moving and his dick brushed against her cheek.

"Fuck, Sarah."

"Don't talk to me like that. You can't order…"

The next second he had her face in his hands. "Please, Sarah. Suck me. Make me come with this gorgeous mouth of yours." He kissed her.

"Untie me."

He knelt again and untied one of her hands. She grabbed his cock and angled him toward her mouth, taking in only the tip and sucking.

"Jesus…" He hissed as he clasped the headboard with both hands. His hips thrusting and rocking as she alternatively sucked him deep and just played with his tip.

One of his hands tangled in her hair, holding her in place as he rocked into her. "I'm so close." He met her eyes. "Swallow. Please."

She sucked harder and he grunted, his seed spilling into her mouth and down her throat. She swallowed as much as she could until he pulled from her lips. His breathing was heavy as he flopped down next to her. He grabbed her hand and kissed it.

"That was fucking fantastic."

"Nick…" She squeezed his hand. She was still on edge. She needed release.

CHAPTER 25: NICK

Nick entwined his fingers with hers. Everything with Sarah was fantastic. This entire night had been one amazing orgasm after another but tomorrow she'd go back to her boyfriend. Rage shot through him, replacing his satisfaction. She was even more adventurous. She'd obviously been busy playing her games while he'd been jerking off.

"Please, Nick." Her hand trailed across his chest, sending tingles through his body.

"Do you swallow for your boyfriend? Of course you do." He shifted, breaking their contact and untying her other hand. "What do you do when your boyfriend, Captain Quickie, doesn't finish you off?"

"What?"

She stared up at him, her green eyes confused and hurt. He clung to his anger. She deserved this and more. She'd left him hanging—no note, no phone call to Ethan, nothing. She'd left him waiting with his dick in one hand and his heart in the other.

"You heard me." He rolled over, resting his head on his elbow. "I find it hard to believe that your boyfriend satisfies you every time." His eyes roamed up her body. He couldn't squash the triumph that surged through him at the sight of all his love bites marking her porcelain skin. If he were her boyfriend and saw this, it'd end their relationship.

"If you're upset because I have a boyfriend, that's not fair."

"Not fair." He grabbed her wrists, pinning her beneath him.

Not fair was him waiting for her and her not wanting him.

"It's not like you contacted Ethan. Right?" Her eyes searched his face.

There was no way he was admitting what a fool he'd been. "What I did and what you did are two different things." He'd put everything on the line for her, for them and she'd grabbed the first guy she'd met and fucked him.

She struggled under him so he let her go but didn't move.

"Right, because you're a man and I'm a woman. So, I should've waited for you"—she shoved at his chest—"a man who admitted he tired of women after a month."

"I also said it was different with you."

"But it wasn't, was it? How long did you wait before fucking another woman? A week?"

He rolled off her, afraid she'd see the truth in his eyes.

"A day? An hour? Figures." She sat up and started untying her ankles.

"Oh, no." He pushed her back onto the bed. He wasn't done with her yet. His conscience whispered that he'd never be done, but he ignored it.

"Get off me." She shoved at him, but he captured her wrists and held them over her head. "Nick, stop. I want to go home."

"How many times do I have to tell you? Tonight isn't about you." Tonight was his payment for all those nights of celibacy.

He kissed her but she kept her mouth shut. She was so damn stubborn, but he was satiated and enjoyed the challenge. He reached between them, running his other hand over her mound. She hadn't come. She was still wet. Still needy.

"Nick..."

He thrust his tongue into her mouth, stopping her protest. She struggled, trying to buck him off her, but she'd been so close to orgasm that it didn't take much before she was thrusting against his hand, and kissing him back. He moved down her body, kissing and licking. Her hands tangled in his hair as her body tensed. He spread her folds, inhaling her arousal. He'd done this to her. She was dripping wet, her pink little bud begging for his touch. He was done denying her and himself. He was going to feast until she screamed. He lowered his head and licked, long and rough.

"Oh…" Her fingers tightened painfully in his hair.

He blew on her and then took her between his lips and sucked gently at first, but let the pressure build until her hips were thrusting against his face. He stopped, looking up at her.

She was sex personified—her hair tussled, her body flushed with passion and her eyes half lowered and filled with lust.

"Show me what you do when your boyfriend doesn't make you come." He loved saying that. If he said it enough maybe he could imprint in her head that he was the only one who could satisfy her.

"Nick, please."

He grabbed her hand from his head and kissed each finger, sucking gently before putting them between her legs. "Show me."

"Please Nick, make me come. It's better when you…"

He kissed her finger that was on her clit, letting his tongue brush against both. "Show me." He needed to see, to know that her boyfriend couldn't do it for her.

She began to rub along her folds, dancing over and around her clit. It wasn't long before she slid her finger inside herself.

Her hips rocked and the muscles in her thighs tightened. He tore his eyes away and glanced at her face. Her eyes were once again half-closed and a blush rose from her chest through her cheeks.

"You're so fucking beautiful." He buried his head between her legs. He sucked and licked, devouring her as his fingers joined hers. His were longer and the angle was better. He curled them.

"Oh, god...there. Please don't stop." She moved her hand from inside herself and wrapped her fingers in his hair, keeping him in place, but he was done fighting her. He was in heaven and didn't ever want to leave.

He quickened the pace of his fingers, hitting her g-spot, over and over until she was a quivering mass of nerves but it wasn't enough.

"I need to be inside you when you come." He had to feel her clinging to him, wanting him. No one else.

"Yes." Her hands went down his neck and shoulders, scraping her fingernails along his skin as he moved up her body.

He positioned himself and hesitated. "Please, no condom." He needed to feel her. Know she trusted him, wanted him in a way she didn't want her boyfriend.

Her eyes sharpened. "Condom. We have to use a condom."

"Fuck." He reached over to the nightstand and grabbed one, opening it and sheathing his dick before he pushed into her. He pulled almost all the way out and pushed back inside. She was hot and tight as she clasped around him. "You feel so fucking good." She felt better than any woman he'd ever known.

She moaned, wrapping her arms around him. "Untie my legs, please."

"No." He thrust harder and faster, holding her hips in place, making her adapt to his rhythm. His balls tightened and he shifted pushing against her g-spot.

She screamed, her body bucking under him, her muscles tightening and clenching around him, squeezing him. He pulled out and pushed in one more time as he came. He collapsed on top of her. He was never moving again. This was right. This was home and he was going to make her see it too.

CHAPTER 26: NICK

Nick rolled over, his hand searching the bed for Sarah. He was hard and ready to fuck again. Last night had been great. Now, all he had to do was convince her that she was better off with him than Little-Dick. That shouldn't be too hard since no man with any respect would take a woman, even one as great as Sarah, back into his bed when she had love bites from another man all over her body.

His hand came up empty and déjà vu settled in his gut like bad sushi. "Sarah." He rolled out of bed. "I'm gonna kill her."

The bathroom door was open and it was empty. He hurried through his living room and into the garage. Her dress was gone. "Son of a bitch." He ran his hand through his hair. "No. Not again. Not this time." He strode toward his bedroom when there was a knock on the door.

Maybe, she'd gotten locked out, but that didn't make sense. His alarm should've sounded if she'd opened the door. The person knocked again.

"I'm coming." He went to turn off the alarm but it was disabled. He stared at it for several minutes. That couldn't be. He'd set the damn thing. He opened the door.

The waiter from last night stared at Nick, eyes on his crotch. "Ah…I don't need that kind of job."

"What are you doing here?"

"Nothing." The kid backed away.

"Jesus. I like women, okay. Give me a minute." He walked

into his bedroom and came back a moment later with jeans on. The kid still waited outside. "Now, what the fuck are you doing here?"

"You said to come by if I wanted a job."

"Yeah, but I meant a weekday."

"It's Friday."

"Shit. You're right." He turned. "Come in. I need some coffee."

"I can come back later."

"Get in here. You're safe. Like I said, you ain't my type."

The kid followed him into the kitchen. "If this is a bad time, I can come back later or Monday." His eyes darted toward the bedroom.

"It is a bad time, but not for the reason you think." He pulled out his phone as the coffee brewed. "The woman I was with last night left without saying goodbye."

"I take it that isn't a good thing."

He laughed. "Usually, it's a great thing but not with her. She has a tendency to leave before...well, before I want her to."

"Oh."

"Don't oh me. It's not like that. It's just great sex." Fabulous, mind blowing sex and he wasn't done having it.

"Sure. Okay. Whatever you say." The kid smiled. "You're the boss."

"I should record that so Sarah can hear it. Maybe one day it'll sink into her thick skull," he mumbled and the kid laughed. "What's your name again?"

"Tommy."

"I'm Nick." He held out his hand and they shook. "Why don't you pour us both some coffee while I find my wayward house guest." He tapped on his phone bringing up Google and searching for Sarah Daly. He'd caught her name at the event last night. As the winner of the award, it'd been hard to miss.

Tommy slid a cup of coffee in front of him. "Milk? Sugar?"

"A little milk." He grabbed the container from the kid and poured a dab into his mug. "Damn it, there are a ton of Sarah Daly's listed."

"Not her." Tommy took his cup and went and sat on a chair.

"What do you mean not her?"

"They were complaining at the event...actually, before the event. They had to go through the guy that was with her to get in touch with her. It's her business and she won the award but she is seriously unlisted...like they tried and couldn't find her."

"Why did they need to speak to her personally?" So, Limp-Dick worked for her. She sure liked being in control.

"I guess she doesn't go to these events and they wanted a confirmation from her that she'd be there. They aren't in the habit of giving away that much money to an office manager."

"The guy she was with was her office manager?"

"I guess. I just overheard them talking when I was cleaning up the banquet hall after a different party."

"Were they ever able to contact her directly?" He had no plans on going through her boyfriend to get to her. The guy would want to kill him as soon as he saw all the love bites.

"Yeah. The office manager came in and gave them the number on a piece of paper."

"Do you know where that paper went?"

"The office manager took it back after they called."

"You've got to be kidding me. What is she the CIA?" He'd

ask Patrick but that wouldn't go over well. He'd try Annie. She'd already helped him once.

"Not kidding but..." Tommy leaned forward. "Guess whose phone they used?"

"Yours?" He loved this kid.

Tommy's face wrinkled. "No. Not mine. Why would they use my phone?"

Okay. He hated this kid. "Get to the point."

"The manager wouldn't let them use their cell phones for the exact reason you wanted them to have used mine. They used a landline."

"How the hell does that help me?"

"Because they made me go get the phone and then the bigwig made me dial her number."

"Do you still know it?" He was going to pound this kid senseless if he didn't.

Tommy grinned. "Would I tell you all of this if I didn't?" He leaned back in his chair. "I have an excellent memory for numbers."

"What is it?" This is where the kid made the biggest mistake of his life. Tommy would ask for money. He'd pay the kid but he wouldn't hire him and what he could teach the boy was worth a lot more than a one-time payout.

Tommy blurted out the number. Nick just stared at him.

"Do you remember numbers too? Why aren't you calling her?"

"Give it to me again." He added it to his contacts as Tommy rattled it off. "Thanks."

"Aren't you going to call her?"

He stared at his phone. If he called, she might hang up. "Do you have her address?"

"No. Sorry."

He dialed Mike and as soon as the driver picked up he said, "Did…"

"Yes, she called me this morning," said Mike.

"You took her home." All he had to do was convince Mike to tell him where that was.

"No." There was amusement in Mike's voice. "She asked me to come over but also asked for the security code so she didn't have to wake you."

"How'd she know you'd have my code?"

"You had me disarm it last night."

"Shit." He had done that.

"Anyway, when I got to your house she was gone. She'd left a note on the door saying that she'd called an Uber."

"Fuck!"

"Have fun finding her, dumbass. You never should've let her go if you wanted to keep her."

"Shut the fuck up." He hung up the phone and dialed Scott, a friend who worked for Patrick and owed him a favor.

"Hey, I need an address for a number and don't tell Patrick."

"Okay, but then we're even," said Scott.

"Really? You look up one number and that equals me spending hours helping your father?"

"You don't want me to tell Patrick. So yeah, we're even."

"Fine." His friends sucked.

"Give me a minute," said Scott. "I'll call you back."

He grabbed a pen and paper and took a sip of his coffee, his heart pounding as he waited. She wasn't getting away from him that easily. He answered the phone on the first ring. He jotted down the address and turned to Tommy. "You, my boy, need to come back on Monday. Bring your resume."

"I have it—"

"Leave it on the counter and come back Monday." He needed to shower and then hunt down his...What? What was she to him? She wasn't his girlfriend.

"What time?" Tommy walked toward the door. "I don't want to disturb you again."

The kid had the audacity to chuckle and Nick couldn't help laughing. "Eight a.m. will be fine. I'm usually up by five. Today was special." And so was last night and the rest of today was going to be special too because whether she liked it or not, he and Sarah were going to talk and then fuck and then fuck some more. She may not be his girlfriend but she was his. She could ditch her boyfriend or take a break. He didn't care. He ignored the anger churning in his gut at the thought of another man touching her because he refused to get hung up on any woman who'd cheat on her boyfriend.

CHAPTER 27: SARAH

"I'm going to kill him." Sarah stared at herself in the mirror.

Nick had left marks all over her body—down her chest, her breasts, her calves and her inner thighs. She couldn't stop the blush from flooding her cheeks. He'd spent a lot of wonderful time with his face buried between her legs. She was okay with those marks. The pleasure was worth her wearing long pants for a while but the ones on her neck and chest only a scarf would conceal and that was going to cause too many questions.

The front door shut and a car started in her driveway.

"Yes, they're finally gone." She'd been hiding in her room, staying as quiet as possible, for almost an hour waiting for Maisie and her family to leave. She was in no mood for the twenty-questions her sister would barrage her with about last night.

She pulled on her robe and opened her bedroom door, peeking into the living room. Empty. Perfect.

Tank nudged her hand.

"Can I shower first?"

His big, brown eyes looked at the door and he wagged his tail.

"Fine." He'd been waiting to go outside since she woke. Her shower could wait ten more minutes. She opened the door wider and followed Tank out of the room.

"Good morning." Maisie was lying on the couch.

Sarah jumped. "You scared me."

Tank ignored the women and waited by the back door, his tail wagging slowly.

"What are you doing here?" She clutched her robe tighter around her neck and walked to the door. "I mean, why didn't you leave with Peter?"

"It doesn't require both of us to take Kyle to school." Maisie was heading for the kitchen. "I'm going to make some coffee."

Sarah opened the back door and walked outside with Tank. He trotted into the yard and sniffed around, looking for the perfect place to pee. He barely even glanced at her to make sure she was still there. He was getting better and she should be happy about that...No, she was happy about that. "Hurry up, boy," she said softly.

If her sister found out Tank was doing this much better, she'd never hear the end of it. Maisie would prod her to date, to go out and she didn't want to. She was happy with her life. Visions of Nick flashed through her mind—him kissing his way down her body, his eyes dark with hunger, his face hard with passion.

Tank nudged her hand, bringing her out of her fantasies. She shouldn't think about Nick. That was over. She wouldn't see him again. She scratched Tank's ear and opened the door following him inside.

"So?" Maisie sat on a chair at the kitchen counter.

"I'll be right back." It was time to dig out a scarf.

"Wait."

"I need to shower." Sarah walked faster. She had to cover these marks.

"Stop." Maisie hurried across the room, grabbing her arm.

"Oh...my...God!" She pulled the neck of the robe open. "Holy shit!"

"It's nothing." If her face got any hotter they could cook bacon on it.

"Nothing?" Maisie's gaze was part appalled, part amused and part envious. "I have never...ever...seen that many hickeys on one person." She tugged the robe open more. "Did he..."

"Stop it." Sarah fisted her hand in the cloth.

"He did!" Maisie grinned. "Come on. Let me see." She tugged on the robe again.

"I'm not showing you my breasts." She jerked free, thankful that Peter and Kyle weren't here. "I'm going to shower." She turned and headed for her bedroom.

"You naughty girl." Maisie grabbed the back of her robe, stopping her. "Your legs too?" Her gaze was on the skin that was visible beneath the short robe. "I can't wait to tell Peter about this."

"Stop it." She slapped at her sister's hand as Maisie lifted her robe.

"All the way up your thighs. Even on your ass cheeks."

She spun around. "Enough."

"That is so....hot." Maisie was fanning herself. "I may have to go and find Peter right now."

"Please do." She laughed.

"So, who was this Romeo?"

"No one."

"A one night stand? Don't say it. My perfect little sister had a one night stand. Another one."

"The other wasn't one night."

"That's right. It was a six-night stand."

116

"Yes." She glanced at her hands, trying to stop the words but they slipped out. "It was him."

"Nick? You saw him? You were with him last night?"

She nodded, blushing.

"That's wonderful." Maisie hugged her. "I told you that you should've sent the letter."

"No, it isn't wonderful."

"It wasn't?" Maisie raised an eyebrow. "By the trail he left, it sure looks wonderful to me."

"The sex was great, as always."

"What else is there to say?" Maisie grinned.

"You're right. That was it. We bumped into each other—"

"Several times."

She snorted back a laugh. "Yes, several times, but it's over. Done."

"Why? What did you do?"

"Me? Nothing. Last night was a...not exactly a mistake. It was a lovely meeting and now it's over."

"Again, why? Apparently, he's still likes you."

"He still wants to fuck me or he did last night" That was all it was to Nick...and to her. She couldn't let it be anything else.

"Is that all? Are you sure?"

"You don't know him. Yes, I'm sure." She bit her lip. "I mean, he'd probably have sex with me again but he's not the kind of guy to want more than that."

"Did you ask him?"

"No." By Maisie's disappointed look her sister didn't agree. "He told me that he grew bored with women within a month. A month!"

"But you told me he said you were different." Maisie took

117

her hand. "It's okay to be scared but don't let it paralyze you."

She wanted to jerk her hand free. She was so sick of this lecture but getting defensive only made Maisie dig in her heels. "I'm only different because I'm not agreeing to his terms. If I did, he'd tire of me."

"It's possible, but it's also possible that he wouldn't."

"Trust me. That's not going to happen with Nick." She kissed her sister on the cheek. "I'm not scared. I'm practical. Now, make me some breakfast while I shower."

"Cereal?"

"No. Eggs, toast, bacon. The works. I'm starving."

"I bet," Maisie laughed and headed for the kitchen.

CHAPTER 28: NICK

Nick pulled into the driveway at Sarah's house. He couldn't wait to see her face when she saw him at the door. If she thought she could get away from him that easily, she was in for a big surprise. Last night, he'd branded her with his kisses. Today, he wasn't sure if he were going to spank her for sneaking away or fuck her first. He'd been aroused when he woke and the chase had only made him hornier.

He hopped out of the car and headed for the door, his step faltering. That was a damn big dog barking. He'd never considered that Sarah had a dog but he should've. She was running a business that helped dogs. Actually, he was a little surprised that there wasn't more than one bark coming from the house.

Her dickhead boyfriend shouldn't be here. There was no way any man would stay with a woman who came home with love bites all over her body. He smiled as he rang the doorbell. Nope, he'd ended that relationship. Sarah was all his for this weekend, maybe longer. He was going to bury himself so deep in her body that she'd never have sex again without thinking of him.

A woman opened the door.

"Ah, you're not Sarah."

"No. I'm not." She seemed amused.

"I'm sorry." He gave her his most charming smile. She was a cute, little redhead. Her hair was shorter than Sarah's and more on the auburn side but she was definitely a relation. Sister probably. "Is Sarah home?"

"She is. Who are you?" She grinned. "Because you're not Sarah either."

"No, I'm not. I'm Nick." The woman wasn't upset about a guy showing up here so she must not be a fan of Sarah's boyfriend—ex-boyfriend.

"Nick? The Nick?" Her eyebrows shot up her forehead. "Really?"

"Yes." She'd heard of him. That was good. Right?

"Come in." She opened the door wide. "I'm Maisie, Sarah's sister."

He stepped inside, glancing toward a closed door where a dog, a very large dog, was raising a racket.

"That's Tank. Don't worry about him. He's a sweetheart. Do you want some breakfast?" Maisie closed the door and walked toward the kitchen.

"Sure. Thanks." He followed her. "I'm starving."

"So is Sarah. What a coincidence." She smiled at him over her shoulder.

He grinned and shrugged. He had no comment for that. Sarah's sister seemed to like him, but he wasn't going to ruin it by joking about last night. The dog barked louder as he walked past and the door rattled. He couldn't help it, he jumped.

"Oh, don't worry about Tank. He sounds tougher than he is." Maisie's eyes hardened a little. "As long as you don't hurt Sarah."

"Okay. Ah...that's good to know." They were going to have to go to his house. He wasn't going to risk getting torn up when Sarah screamed her release.

"Is it?" She stopped by the stove.

"Yes." He looked her directly in the eyes. "I'd never hurt any female, especially Sarah." *Except in ways she enjoyed*.

"Hmm. Coffee?"

"Please."

She filled a cup and handed it to him.

"Sit. Have some toast. The bacon and eggs are almost done. Cream and sugar are there." She pointed to containers near the butter and toast.

He sat at the counter, adding a little cream to his coffee. The dog continued to bark and growl. "So, where is Sarah?"

"Taking a shower." She began filling three plates.

His dick hardened. Sarah was naked in the other room, her body warm and slippery. He wanted to strip off his clothes and get in the shower with her. She'd be surprised at first, but she'd melt into him. She couldn't deny her body and her body wanted him.

Maisie put a plate in front of him. It was overflowing with food. She put another one that was just as full by the seat next to his and then sat across from him with a plate that looked sparse by comparison.

"Do you want some of this?" He used the fork to point at his food.

"No. I couldn't." She took a bite of her eggs. "Unfortunately, I didn't burn as many calories as you did last night." She sighed. "Having a kid puts a damper on that kind of exercise."

He took a bite of his toast. He was actually blushing. These Daly women could turn him inside out. "How many kids do you have?" That was a safe topic.

"One. We've been trying for another but...no luck yet."

"So, kids don't actually eliminate that kind of exercise." The words slipped past his lips. "I'm sorry."

"No." She laughed. "Don't be." She took a sip of her coffee. "If kids eliminated sex there wouldn't be any more kids."

"That's for sure."

"So Nick, what brings you here?"

"Um, I wanted to see Sarah." It was kind of obvious.

"Did she tell you to stop by?"

The woman's eyes were sharp. This was a test. She damn well knew Sarah hadn't. He was a businessman. When people expected him to lie, he did the opposite. "No. She snuck out of my bed early this morning and took an Uber home."

"She did what?" Maisie dropped her fork. "That stupid...What time?"

"I don't know. I was sleeping." He was usually a light sleeper but she'd worn him out. They'd fucked almost non-stop and his body had collapsed in satiated exhaustion. The side of his mouth curled up in memory. He couldn't wait to do it again.

"I can't believe..." She shook her head and took a sip of her coffee. "She could've called me."

"She could've woken me." Sarah didn't need to call anyone but him for a ride—any kind of ride.

"Yes, she could've done that." Maisie studied him. "Why do you suppose she didn't?"

"I don't know." He said it through gritted teeth because he knew exactly why she hadn't. He wouldn't have let her leave. He would've fucked her until she'd passed out. That'd been his plan for today and the rest of the weekend. It was still his plan. All he had to do was get rid of the sister.

"Hmm." She took a bit of her toast. "Did she tell you where she lived?"

He took a drink of his coffee to give himself some time to think. Maisie knew the answer to that too. "Are you a lawyer?"

"No. I'm worse. I'm a big sister."

He tipped his head. She was protecting Sarah. He appreciated that, but he needed her on his side. Actually right now, he needed her gone. He leaned forward. "You know as well as I do that Sarah didn't tell me where she lived."

"Then how did you find this place? It's unlisted."

"Trust me. I'm aware of that." And the fact that Sarah didn't want to be found by him or anyone.

"So?"

"I know people."

"Hmm." She ate the last of her eggs. "I guess the better question is why did you come here?"

He was pretty sure saying to fuck your sister wasn't the right answer. It was the honest one but not the right one. "I wanted to see Sarah."

"But why?"

"Because I like her." That was the truth or part of it. He liked to fuck her—a lot.

Maisie's eyes narrowed. "Like her? You brand her body because you like her?"

"You saw that." It wasn't a question.

"How could I miss it? You made sure to leave your mark all over her. Why would you do that? Are you that possessive? Do you think she's your property?"

"No. It isn't like that." She was his, but she wanted him too. She did. No one could fake attraction like theirs.

"Sure seems like that to me." She crossed her arms over her chest.

Damn. He'd lost the sister. It didn't matter. Sarah wanted him. *Not enough to leave her number or to contact Ethan.*

"I think you should leave." She stood.

"I'm not going anywhere until I speak to Sarah."

"Said the stalker."

"It's not like that." It wasn't. It really wasn't. "I'd never hurt her."

"Said the stalker. Every damn one of them, right before they do just that." Maisie stood, pulling her phone from her pocket. "Don't make me call the police."

"Don't do that. Please." He stood.

"Then go."

His hands gripped the counter so tightly his knuckles were white. "Not without seeing Sarah. If she wants me to leave, I'll go." Of course, she'll have to say it after he kissed her.

Maisie pressed a button and then another one. "I'm not joking."

The last string to his temper tore. "You know what? Do it. Call the fucking cops." He leaned forward. "I have no record. I'm a respected businessman and they can't do anything worse to me than what your sister has already done."

"What did Sarah do to you?" Her finger froze above the keypad.

"What did she do to me?" He laughed but it was a hard and angry sound. "She stood me up. I waited four fucking months..." No, he wasn't admitting that to anyone. "Forget it." He sat down and took a gulp of his coffee. "Call the cops if you want. I don't give a shit."

Maisie's eyes were wide. "You contacted the Club." She dropped onto her chair. "Oh...You waited for her." She leaned forward. "Did you really go four months without sex?"

"What? No." His eyes darted away from her face. Sarah must've bragged to her sister about the guy she'd strung along.

"Liar." Maisie grabbed his hand. "Have you told her?"

"What? No." He repeated, sounding like an idiot.

"You have to." She jumped up.

"No." He stood, grabbing her arm. "Please."

"Why? She'll be so excited."

"I'm serious. Don't."

"I'm not going to tell her." She pulled her arm free.

"Maisie, who are you talking to? Is Peter here?" called out Sarah.

A huge dog charged into the room and Nick backed against the counter as it stopped in front of him, barking and baring its teeth.

"Nick..." Sarah stood in the kitchen doorway. Her hair was wet and hanging loose. She wore an old T-shirt and sweatpants. Her neck was covered in his love bites and they trailed down under her shirt.

He was hard instantly. He needed the sister and the damn dog gone, now.

CHAPTER 29: SARAH

Sarah's legs almost buckled. Nick was here—in her home. How? Why? Never mind, she knew why. He'd hated her leaving in the middle of the night before and she was sure he hadn't gotten over that pet peeve in the time they'd been apart.

"Can you call off your dog?" His eyes darted from her to Tank.

"Tank. Come." She snapped her fingers.

The dog shot her a confused looked and then stared at Nick again, lips curled.

"Tank. Come." She repeated more sternly.

The dog barked once more before he walked to her side and sat, giving her dirty looks.

"I don't need your attitude today," she mumbled as she scratched Tank's ear. She had enough problems—like the six-foot tall, sexy one in front of her.

"Nick and I were just talking," said Maisie.

Nick shot Maisie an odd look and her sister's lips pursed. She shook her head before saying, "Your breakfast is on the counter. I'm going home."

Nick seemed to let out the breath he was holding. Something was up. She'd have to call Maisie later and find out exactly what'd gone on while she was in the shower.

"Nick, it was nice to meet you." Maisie held out her hand and Nick shook it.

"You too," he said.

"I'll leave you two to talk about..."

Nick's eyes narrowed.

"Things." Maisie smiled sweetly and turned to hug Sarah. "Give him a chance," she whispered.

Sarah stared after her sister's retreating form. She had no idea what to say to him. She could feel his eyes on her, making her ache for his touch.

The front door closed and then a car started and drove down the street.

She turned toward him. "Why..." She knew why he was here. "How..." Asking him how he found her made it sound like she hadn't wanted to be found, which she hadn't but it seemed kind of cruel to say to the man she'd just spent hours fucking.

"How?" His voice rose and his eyes snapped with anger. "How did I find you? Was that what you were going to ask?"

"Ah..."

"Why did I have to look for you, is what I want to know." He took a step toward her but Tank's warning growl froze his feet to the floor. "Lock up your dog."

"No." She rested her hand on Tank's head.

A muscle in Nick's cheek twitched. He was furious but there was nothing he could do. *Thank you, Tank.* She scratched the dog's ear.

Nick took a deep breath. "Please. We need to talk."

"Funny. I wanted to talk last night—"

"And we would've if you'd stayed."

"Pleeease." She moved around the counter—Tank at her side—to put something besides air between them. Whenever he was mad she wanted to sooth his temper with her hands and her mouth. Her eyes dropped to his pants and she nibbled her

127

bottom lip. He was hard for her already.

"Get rid of the dog and I'll show you what you're staring at."

Her face flushed as she raised her gaze to his. She could drown in those dark depths and never come out. He was too dangerous. "I'll pass."

"You sure?" He patted the counter. "This is a perfect height."

An image of her sitting on the counter while he thrust into her flashed in her mind and then one of her bent over while he took her from behind replaced it. She grabbed her plate. "I'm hungry."

"I bet you are." He smirked. "Coffee?" He started to move around the counter and stopped at Tank's growl.

"Orange juice, please."

"I'm just getting us something to drink," he said to Tank. "So chill, buddy."

Tank's growl deepened but Nick moved slowly to the refrigerator. He grabbed the juice and a glass from the counter. "Now, I'm going to come over there by you." He looked at the dog. "And you are not going to bite me." He held the OJ and glass low so Tank could sniff them. The dog moved to Nick's leg.

She giggled at Nick's sharp inhale when Tank's nose pushed into his crotch.

"We're both guys here. Be gentle, boy."

"He's been neutered," she said.

"Oh dude, I'm so sorry." He put the glass down and held his hand out for Tank to sniff.

"Stop it."

"No, really. That's mean."

"It is not." Her face heated. "He can still...do it. He just can't reproduce."

"Oh. That's not so bad then. It's like a doggie vasectomy."

"Exactly." The fact that most dogs didn't want to do it after being neutered didn't count.

Nick moved closer and poured the orange juice into the glass and slid it over to her. His arm brushed her shoulder and she felt the zing to her toes. She wanted this man. Again. Always. She shouldn't. It was going to hurt so badly when he tired of her, but he was here and she didn't have it in her to send him away.

"Why did you sneak out this morning?" His hand skimmed over hers, filling her with warmth.

"I didn't want to wake you."

"That's obvious." His voice rose and Tank growled softly. "Please Sarah, lock him up so we can talk."

"He's fine." She patted Tank's head. "Aren't you, baby."

Nick grabbed the coffee pot from the counter and refilled his mug before going back to his side of the island and taking his seat. "So, why did you sneak out besides not wanting to wake me?" His dark eyes met hers. "Truth, Sarah."

"I'll answer that when you tell me why you were so mad at me last night." She ate some eggs and toast.

His eyes followed her fork to her mouth and her pussy clenched at the desire in his gaze. She'd never thought she'd see him again and here he was—an unexpected gift. She wasn't going to waste it. Life was too short for that.

"I asked first."

"No, I asked several times last night." She took a sip of her orange juice and slowly licked her lips. He shifted on his seat and she barely kept herself from grinning like the Cheshire Cat.

"When we're done talking, we're going to fuck. Right?"

"Truth?" she mimicked.

"Always."

"Absolutely."

He grinned. "I love it when we're honest."

She laughed but a small part of her broke because she was in so much trouble.

"I was pissed last night because I didn't like seeing you with your boyfriend." He leaned back in his seat. "I hate the fact that some guy touched you, kissed you, fucked you." His eyes hardened. "You're mine, Sarah. Only I get to do those things."

Her breath caught in her throat. She wanted to believe him. No, she did believe him but she also knew he wouldn't feel like that forever and she would. "It's not fair for you to be mad at me about that."

"You wanted the truth."

"How many women have you been with since me?"

"That's different." He leaned forward. "Me fucking some women is not the same as you having a boyfriend."

"Why? Don't I get to feel territorial about you?" She did. The idea of him with those women in the Club haunted her dreams.

"Fucking is only physical."

"So, you wouldn't be mad if I'd fucked ten men while we were apart instead of one boyfriend." She knew she was testing his limits and if it weren't for Tank, they'd already be naked and going at it, but she was so sick of his double standards.

"That'd better not have happened." His nostrils flared and the muscle in his cheek was doing the cha-cha.

"But it's okay for you to do that." This would never, ever work. She'd known it before, but stupid hope had blossomed in her heart when she'd seen him in her kitchen. Her mind had lied, convincing her that his being here meant something, but it didn't mean anything except he didn't like to lose.

"Do you really want to know how many women I've been with since you?" He stood, leaning toward her.

She could smell the soap he'd used that morning and his shampoo. The pleasant odor of coffee clung to his breath and she wanted nothing more than to drink it from him.

"Do you, Sarah? Do you really want to know? Because I'll tell you."

"No." She held up her hand. "Please don't." She swallowed. This was going to be hard. This would probably break her, but she had no choice. "I'll give you thirty days, Nick."

"What?"

"You said you usually tired of your women after thirty days. I'm going to give you that. Thirty days. We can fuck when you want." She shrugged. "Mostly. I still have to work and—"

"I don't want thirty days."

Oh God, he was already breaking her heart. "How long then?"

"Jesus, Sarah." He dropped down on his seat. "I don't know."

"Decide on a time. We can go through Ethan—"

"I'm not involving Ethan in this. This is between you and me."

Tank grumbled a low growl.

"Okay. Your call, but I need a time frame." She needed to know when her heart would be destroyed.

For a moment he looked hurt and then his gaze sharpened. "Six weeks. Six weeks of you and me. No one else."

"Okay." She tried to tamp down her excitement but she couldn't. He wouldn't be at the Club. He'd be hers for forty two days.

"No boyfriend."

"I won't sleep with Peter." She could barely stop from laughing. Maisie would be so happy to hear that.

"Or anyone else."

"Nope. You either."

His eyes roamed down her body, stopping on her chest. "Just you. Whenever I want you. However I want you."

"Same rules as before."

He opened his mouth and then shut it, nodding. "Except, not only Saturday nights and one hour during the week."

"Agreed."

"Now." His growl almost sounded like Tank's.

She nodded. "We'll have to go to your place and I'll have to call Maisie—"

"I can't wait." He took her hand.

"Tank." She stood.

"Can stay in the other room."

"He'll get nervous." She couldn't do this here.

"He'll live."

"No." Her heart raced. "He might not. He's old. He'll stress."

The lust faded from Nick's eyes. "Calm down, Sarah. Come here." He let go of her hand and held his arms open.

"We have to stop if he gets upset." She moved around the island. She wanted to be near him, engulfed in his arms. "His heart is bad. He's an ex-military dog. He stresses easily."

Nick took her face in his hands and kissed her. Tank, who'd followed her, growled.

Nick lifted his lips. "Shush. I'm only kissing her. Do you want me to growl when you kiss her?"

She laughed and Tank grumbled.

"Is there anywhere he likes to stay besides at your side?"

"No." Tank was always with her. She bit her lip.

Nick groaned. "Stop that or I'm going to take you right here and let the damn dog bite me."

"I don't think you'd enjoy that." She grinned.

"No, but I will enjoy sinking my dick inside you." He lowered his head and kissed her gently, his tongue tangling with hers.

Tank sighed as he stretched out on the floor.

"See." His lips trailed down her neck. "He's okay." He clasped her hand in his. "Come on." He led her to the living room.

Tank trotted after them.

Nick pulled her close and kissed her. It was gentle again, coaxing. She wrapped her arms around him. His body pressed into hers and she moaned. Tank gave them a dirty look and crawled onto the couch.

"See, he's good." He led her into the bedroom and closed the door in Tank's face. The dog whimpered and scratched at the door.

"Nick..."

"He'll be fine." He kissed her again, pulling her into his arms.

She wanted this but she couldn't risk Tank. She stepped

back. "I think we should go to your house."

"How long will you stay?" He sighed, his lips against her neck, making her shiver.

"I can try and get Maisie to come back over but I know she has things to do today."

"Why does she have to be here?" He moved closer, his hands wandering down her back to her ass.

"I can't leave Tank by himself for too long."

"He's a dog not a kid."

"And he's old and not well." She shoved away from him. Tank was all she had and all she'd have to help her put the pieces back together when these six weeks were done.

"Okay. Fine. Let's just see how he does out there."

She crossed her arms over her chest. "If he keeps crying, this is done. If you don't like it we can cancel—"

He yanked her to him, her breasts pressing against his hard chest. "We're not cancelling. You're mine for six weeks."

Tank barked and scratched at the door.

"This isn't going to work." She wanted to cry.

"Fuck." He backed away, shoving both hands into his pockets.

"I'm sorry. I really am." She was. She wanted him. Yes, it'd only be for a few weeks and her heart would be in tatters when it was over, but she wanted this time with him.

"Let's go." He grabbed her hand.

"Where?"

He opened the door and Tank shoved his nose against her leg.

"My house."

"Give me a minute." She pulled her hand free.

The muscle twitched in his cheek but he only grabbed his phone and walked a few feet away.

She bent and rubbed Tank behind the ears and kissed his forehead. "I'm going to leave for a little bit. It won't be long. I promise." When she stood Nick was staring at her with an odd expression on his face. "Don't."

"Don't what?"

"Don't look at me like that."

"Like what?" He headed for the door.

"Like...like I'm crazy or you feel sorry for me." She hated the pity. She hated it.

"I'm not."

"You were." She knew that look. It haunted her dreams.

He opened the door.

"You go. I'll go out the garage."

"Why?"

"I have to get my car."

"We can ride together."

"Ah...I don't think that's a good idea."

"Why not?" He crossed his arms over his chest.

"There's no reason for you to come all the way back here."

"Don't make this about what's convenient for me." He stepped toward her.

A low rumble rattled through Tank who was standing at her side. She rested her hand on his head. "It's okay."

"Fuck this. You know what?"

She braced herself. It was over before it'd begun. He didn't have the patience for her and her issues.

"Get your car and let's go." He stepped out the door.

"You still want me to come over?" She'd been wrong. He

wasn't ending it.

"Fuck yeah." He was looking at her like she was crazy again.

"Oh. Okay. Good." She grinned and shut the door.

CHAPTER 30: NICK

Nick waited in his driveway for Sarah. What the fuck had he gotten himself into? He'd known she had some issues with her past but not willing to leave the dog...That was crazy. She pulled her car into his driveway and got out. The blood immediately rushed to his groin. It didn't matter how nuts she was. He wanted her.

She walked toward him, her sweats clinging to her hips and those long legs. He couldn't wait to feel them wrapped around him.

He held the door for her. She smiled shyly at him as she stepped inside his home. This time he wasn't carrying her. This time she was completely sober and he had her for six weeks.

He closed the door and locked it. She stood with her back to him, her hands fidgeting at her sides. He loved that she was nervous. It was only fair because his heart still beat an erratic rhythm when he was around her.

She turned—her green eyes bright with excitement. "We don't have long..."

That was all it took to snap him into action. He grabbed her face and kissed her with all the pent up desire from when he'd woke that morning. Her arms wrapped around his neck, pulling him closer.

"I need you now." His hands skimmed along the waistband of her pants, waiting for her consent.

"Yes." She nipped his ear and he growled as he shoved her

pants and underwear down.

She kicked them and her shoes off and he lifted her as he turned, bracing her between the door and his body. She reached between them, her long fingers grasping his dick through his pants.

"Fuck, Sarah." Thank the lord she liked it hard and fast.

"Fuck me, Nick." She unbuttoned his pants and unzipped them, her hand sliding inside and wrapping around his cock.

"I want to taste you." He needed to slow it down—savor the moment.

She stuck her tongue in his ear and he almost roared. Savoring was over. He pulled his wallet out, fumbling with it as he dug for one of the condoms he'd put in there before leaving his house. She stroked him and kissed his neck, her tongue darting out to taste his skin. He grabbed the foil packet, dropped his wallet and tore the package open with his teeth.

He pushed her hand away as he rolled it down his length. "Now."

"Now," she said, grabbing his dick and positioning him at her opening.

He didn't even check to see if she were wet and ready for him. He couldn't wait. He shoved into her in one long push. She gasped and he hissed through his teeth.

"You...feel...so good." He didn't move. He just stayed there wrapped inside her heat.

"Nick," she whispered.

He shoved her shirt up, pushing her bra with it and bent, running his tongue over her nipple. Her hands tangled in his hair, holding him close.

"Please, Nick."

"What do you want?" He flicked her nipple with his tongue as his other hand wrapped in her hair, pulling back her head. "Look at me and tell me what you want."

She opened her heavy lidded eyes. "Fuck me. Please."

"Is that all?" He rocked his hips as his other hand pinched her nipple.

"Yes...oh...no."

"Say it. Say my name. Tell me what you want me to do to you." He needed her to admit she wanted him to do these things, not just someone with a dick.

"Kiss my breasts."

"Who?"

"You." She gave him a confused look.

"Say my name." He yanked on her hair.

"Nick, suck my tits as you fuck me. Please."

He didn't even hesitate. His head dropped and he took her nipple in his mouth, sucking and teasing with his teeth and tongue as he thrust into her, reveling in her whimpers of need as he withdrew and her moans of pleasure as he pushed forward filling her. Her legs tightened around his waist, her feet pushing against his ass.

"Harder, Nick. Please."

"Later, babe." He was enjoying the sensation of being inside her too much to rush it. That'd come later but right now, he moved in and out, over and over, slow and steady.

She was scratching at his back, her feet pushing on him and her pussy clamping down, trying to keep him inside of her.

"Please, Nick. I don't want to wait. I'm so close."

He kissed his way up her neck. "Not yet."

"Now, Nick. Now." She turned her head and stuck her

tongue in his ear again, sending him sailing past pleasure into rut.

"Fuck, Sarah." His fist tightened in her hair and he fucked her faster and harder.

Their bodies slammed against the door, her nails dug into his shoulders and her pussy tightened around his cock like a vise as she shook with her orgasm. He buried his face in her neck as he shoved into her one more time before his body shook with his release.

CHAPTER 31: NICK

Nick inhaled her scent, a slight shiver coursing through him. He could stay like this forever—her wrapped around him, his cock cocooned inside her. She started to lower her legs.

"Where do you think you're going?"

"Nowhere. I just thought I was too heavy." Her hands flitted down his back.

He grabbed her hips, pulling her closer. "Not at all. Hold on." He moved away from the door and she wrapped her arms around his neck as he strode across the living room.

"Where are you taking me, Master?"

"To my bed where you belong." He ran his hand between her butt cheeks. "How much time do we have before you have to leave?" He placed her on the bed, tugging on her legs.

She glanced at her watch. "About an hour." She dropped her legs and sighed as he pulled out of her. "That last one didn't take too long."

"That's your fault." He swatted her ass. She could push him past his control like no one he'd ever met.

"Hey!" She laughed.

He tucked his dick back into his pants and zipped them up. "Don't talk back to your master." He pulled her T-shirt over her head and unclasped her bra. Shit, she was beautiful—long and lean with perfect tits.

"You're overdressed." She reached for his pants.

He slapped her hands away and pulled off his shirt. "There.

Happy?"

"Hardly." Her eyes dropped to his crotch and she licked her lips. "I want to..."

"What do you want, Sarah?" He knew exactly what she wanted and was more than happy to give her every inch...later.

She raised her eyes to his. "I want to suck your cock. I want to feel you grow in my mouth." She got on her knees. "And I want to lick and suck you until you come."

His nostrils flared. "You're going to kill me." Her hands were on his pants again and it took every ounce of will power he had to grab them, stopping her. "Later." He climbed onto the bed and made her lie back on the mattress. He straddled her hips, putting her hands above her head. "First, we're going to talk."

She frowned.

He laughed. "That's all you wanted to do last night and now, you don't want to."

"Last night, you were being an ass."

He shrugged. "I had my reasons."

"Yeah, stupid ones, but—"

"They aren't stupid." She'd fucked another man while he'd jerked off. He was still pissed about that, but she was his for six weeks. Of course, those days were going to be difficult with that damn dog around.

"The double standard you men have—"

"I don't have double standards." He'd expected them both to be celibate. To wait for each other but obviously, he'd been the only one to feel that what they had was worth it.

"Please." She struggled to get up.

He leaned more heavily against her, watching her breasts

jiggle with her efforts. "Damn, you're beautiful." He lowered his head, running his tongue over her nipple and pulling it into his mouth, sucking gently before scraping his teeth across it.

She moaned as her hips pushed upward, searching for his cock which began to harden, answering her call.

"We need to talk about our time together." He blew across her nipple and she trembled.

"Same rules as before." She arched her back, offering her breasts to him.

"No. You agreed that I could fuck you whenever I wanted this time."

"And I can fuck you whenever I want."

"That, my dear,"—he kissed her lips—"goes without saying."

"Then what do we need to talk about." She shifted her hips upward again, trying to rub against him.

"That dog of yours."

"What about Tank?" She stiffened.

"I can hardly fuck you whenever I want with that beast ready to bite me."

"He's a little protective." She struggled in his grasp. "Let me go."

He dropped his hold and rolled off her, sitting on the side of the bed. She sat up and grabbed a pillow, covering herself. That wasn't a good sign.

"How's this going to work, Sarah? How are we going to...play with that dog around?"

She swallowed. "We can meet here for a few hours every day."

"That won't be enough for me."

"It'll have to be enough." She hugged the pillow tighter.

"You suggested the thirty days. You wanted this." He was trying to keep his temper in check but he was losing that battle.

"And we can have your six weeks. I'll come by every day. You pick the time and I'll see if my sister can watch Tank once in a while so I can stay longer."

"No." He stood. "That's not going to work. I want you here—"

"I can't stay here."

"You can bring your dog."

"He doesn't like strange places."

"He's a dog. He'll adapt."

"No. He won't." She climbed off the bed, grabbing her T-shirt and bra.

"Where do you think you're going?"

She hooked the bra and pulled it up, covering her luscious tits. "Home. I'm sorry but this isn't going to work."

"Like hell." In two strides he was around the bed. He grabbed her hand, snatching the T-shirt and tossing it aside.

"Nick, I'm leaving." She tried to pull free from his grasp. "Let me go."

He yanked her to him. "Never." He was hard and ready for her again. "We'll figure this out."

"It isn't going to work. Tank isn't—"

"He must've gotten used to you fucking your boyfriend. He can get used to you fucking me."

"I...he..."

"What? Captain-Quickie didn't make you moan and scream? Maybe, I'll have to gag you." His eyes darkened as he tugged her toward the bed. "Kneel."

144

"What?"

He pushed her against the mattress. "Kneel."

She glared at him over her shoulder but her eyes were gleaming. She was as aroused as he was.

He grabbed her other hand and yanked it behind her back. He walked to his closet, dragging her along with him. He pulled out handcuffs.

"What are you doing?" She struggled but it was a half-hearted attempt.

"You know what I'm doing." He snapped the cuffs around her wrists, making sure they were tight but with the padding they wouldn't hurt. He shoved her back to the bed. "Now, kneel."

She crawled onto the bed. He put his hand in the middle of her back and pushed her forward until her face was resting on the mattress.

"Stay." He strode to the closet, grabbed a riding crop and slowly walked back to the bed, letting her see the crop and giving her mind time to spin with the implications.

"Nick, don't hit me with that."

"That's entirely up to you."

"Me?" Her voice squeaked.

"Yes. Will you cooperate?" He leaned down and kissed the small of her back. "We can figure this out but only if you're willing to compromise." He nipped her ass and her gasp sent the blood rushing to his balls. She was probably soaking the bed with her arousal.

"Please, take off the handcuffs."

"Use your safe word if you really want me to stop."

She nodded and he smirked as he slapped her ass gently

with the crop.

"Ouch. Stop that." She tried to sit up but he placed his hand in the middle of her back again, keeping her immobile.

"You said your dog doesn't like new places." He skimmed the crop up and down her back and over her ass, enjoying the way her muscles tensed and relaxed.

"Yes."

"Why is that?"

"He was in the war. He has PTSD."

He stilled. He should've guessed. That was her business.

"He can't help it. He's sick."

He wanted to punch something. He respected the military men and women...and dogs, but he didn't like them interfering with his sex life. "How did you get him used to your boyfriend?"

"Peter?"

He cracked her ass with the crop, not too hard but not as gently as before either.

"Hey, what was that for?"

He leaned over her, so his dick rested against her hip and his lips were at her ear. "I don't ever want to hear his name when you're in my bed, naked and waiting for me to fuck you." He straightened and ran the crop between her ass cheeks. "Understand?"

"Yes." The word came out almost breathless.

He skimmed his hand over her butt and between her legs to her pussy. "Fuck, you're drenched." He spread her legs and leaned back down, her ass cheeks now cradling his erection through his pants. "You like being punished, don't you." He nipped her ear.

"No."

"Don't lie to me." He brought the whip down, not too hard, on her thigh.

"Oh..." It started as a cry of surprise and turned into a moan.

He was so hard he was going to burst through his pants. "You like being punished, don't you?" He asked again as he caressed her leg with the crop.

"Yes, but not too hard."

His fingers danced between her pussy lips. "Let me be the judge of that." He sucked on her earlobe. "I know your body better than you do." His other hand dipped between her butt cheeks. "You'd like to be fucked here, too."

"Nick..." There was a warning in her tone.

"Later." He kissed her neck and straightened. "What did...Limp-Dick do to get Tank to accept him?"

"Ahh..."

"Answer me." He ran the crop down her back.

"He befriended him. Got Tank used to him."

"Then that's what I'll do." He grabbed her legs and spread them farther apart.

She gasped.

He unzipped his pants and rubbed his cock along her pussy crease. "You're so fucking wet and hot." He skimmed his hand down her stomach until his fingers dipped inside of her. "And so tight."

"Please." Now, she was begging.

He positioned his tip at her entrance. "One day, I'm going to fuck you without a condom."

Her body stiffened and he leaned down surrounding her as his fingers rubbed her hot, slick flesh. "I'm going to come inside you. Fill you with my cum."

"Nick...please."

He stepped away from her and she moaned.

"I should make you beg. I should refuse to fuck you until you agree to no condom."

"I...I can't." She started to get up but he pushed her back down, holding her in place with his hand.

"You can. We will." He snarled. He wanted to make her his in the most elemental way. An image of her large with his child filled his head and for one moment, he wanted that. She'd be his in a way no one else ever had been. A part of him would be living inside of her. His dick throbbed and he couldn't wait any longer. He grabbed a condom and covered his cock. "We'll talk about it later." He positioned his tip at her entrance again and grabbed her hips. He pushed in a little.

She moaned, her ass pushing back against him.

"Hold still." He slid in a little more. He was going to make her scream.

"Please." She rocked back and he slipped inside another inch.

He gritted his teeth. "Hold...still." He slapped her ass and she gasped. He moved forward, her pussy clenching at him, trying to drag him deeper. "Fuck." He shoved inside unable to wait another moment.

She moaned low and long, the sound of pure pleasure making his balls tighten. He wouldn't hold out long. He grabbed her hips and began fucking her hard and fast. She trembled and whimpered as she rocked against him. She was close. He dipped his fingers into her wetness and trailed it up between her ass cheeks. She stiffened as he pressed down on her puckered hole.

"Nick...don't." Her body was clenching around him. She was going to come. She just needed that little push.

"Sarah." He moved his hand away from her butthole and slapped her ass, groaning as he slammed his cock into her.

She screamed and her body tightened for one exquisite moment before undulating in orgasm.

"Fuck!" He shouted as he came, collapsing on top of her.

CHAPTER 32: SARAH

"Nick, my arms," said Sarah. They were getting numb from being restrained behind her back especially, since Nick was still flopped on top of her.

"Hmm. Oh, yeah. Sorry." He kissed the side of her neck and leaned up.

She bit back a moan as he withdrew from inside her. She hated the emptiness when he left. She'd be fine if he stayed inside her always. Of course, that'd make meetings very awkward, even video meetings. She started to giggle but groaned instead as he freed her wrists and the blood poured back into her limbs.

"Here, baby. Let me." He began massaging her shoulders and arms—his strong hands working out all the kinks.

She stretched out on the bed. "That feels so good." This time she couldn't stop the moan.

"You feel good." He kissed the spot where her neck met her shoulder.

"Hmm." She wiggled as a spark of desire warmed her blood again.

His hands moved to her back. "Your skin is so soft." He kissed a trail down her spine. "I'll never tire of touching you."

She stiffened at his lie.

"What?" He massaged her ass.

"Nothing." She tried to relax but the moment was gone.

"It's not nothing. One minute you're as soft and loose as a

noodle and the next your stiff." He sucked on her neck a little. "Like you make me."

His hardening cock rested along the crease of her ass. "Again?"

"You drive me wild." His mouth moved back to the sensitive spot where it met her shoulder. "I've never wanted anyone like I want you."

She bit her lip to stop from asking, for how long.

"What's wrong?" He rolled off her.

"Nothing." She stayed on her stomach, unable to look at him.

"Don't lie to me." He skimmed his hand down her back as if unable to stop touching her.

She took a deep, shaky breath. There was no reason to ruin the little time they had together. "Really. I'm fine." She turned her head and smiled at him.

He was lying on his side, using his elbow to prop himself up and his dark eyes studied her for a long moment.

She feared what he might see in her face. She was crazy for him but that'd send him fleeing faster than anything else and now that she had him, she wasn't ready to lose her time with him. She shifted closer and kissed him. His mouth opened for her and the kiss was gentle without an agenda.

He rolled onto his back, pulling her into his arms.

"I have to leave soon." She rested her head on his chest, his heart beat slow and steady beneath her ear.

"I know." His hand skimmed up and down her back.

"You're not mad?"

His hand stilled. "Why would I be mad?" He sat up.

"Because you're choosing to spend time with your dog instead of me?" He stood, grabbing his pants.

"That's not...You don't understand." She sat up, clutching the blanket around her.

He yanked his pants up. "You're right. I don't." He knelt on the bed and took her face in his hands. "Explain it to me."

"I already did. Tank's old. He doesn't like being alone." She hurried on before he could argue. "Or being in new places."

"He's a dog. He'll get used to it."

She shook her head. "No. He won't and I won't make him." She pulled free from his hold and got out of bed, wrapping the blanket around her body.

"I'm not asking you to get rid of him or anything, just bring him here or stay for more than an hour."

"I can't and you know that." She walked toward the living room. "I've got to go."

He followed her. "You still have fifteen minutes."

She dropped the blanket and pulled on her pants. "Yes, but I don't feel like arguing with you, so I'm leaving."

His eyes darkened while he watched her dress but he didn't say anything. Obviously, he didn't want to argue either.

She pulled on her shirt and grabbed the door handle. "Goodbye, Nick."

"Wait." In one step he had her against the door. He grabbed her jaw holding her in place as he lowered his mouth to hers. This kiss was hot and wet and made her want to wrap her body around his and never let go.

"I'll see you tonight," he said as he broke the kiss.

CHAPTER 33: SARAH

Sarah tried to focus on work but her eyes kept going to the clock on the computer. It was late. Apparently, Nick wasn't coming by. He'd probably never come over again. Even if she'd told him that she hadn't been with Peter or anyone else it wouldn't have made a difference. Nick wanted to fuck and they wouldn't be doing that at her house, not with Tank here. The best she'd get for the next six weeks was an hour of fabulous sex every day. She sighed. Pathetic creature that she was, she'd take it.

She stood and went over by Tank, who was stretched out on the couch. He thumped his tail as she sat down and rested her face on his large, warm side. "I love you. You come first. Always." In the end, when Nick tired of her, she'd still have Tank.

The dog nudged her with his nose.

"I'll never leave you. I swear." She captured his face and kissed his snout. "You and me forever."

CHAPTER 34: NICK

Nick shoved his laptop in his car next to the packages and went back inside his house. He opened his closet, looking over all his toys. He'd bought so many for her, for them. He had at least six weeks and he was going to use every last one of them at least once. Sarah was going to have to learn to be quiet, because there was no way he'd be able to stay at her house with her all day and not fuck her brains out. The damn dog would just have to get used to it. He grabbed the leg and wrist restraints, lube and some other toys and stuffed them in his duffle bag before heading out the door. He got in the car and called Annie.

"Hey, Nick," said Annie. "What's up?"

"First, thanks for...everything. I'm going to Sarah's."

"That's great." She sounded like she was ready to clap her hands.

"Yeah, kind of."

"What's wrong? What did you do?"

"Why are you blaming me?"

"Because I know you."

"Ouch. That hurts." He laughed.

"Tell me what you did?"

"Nothing."

"You called me, Nick." She was growing impatient.

"Well...I told her I'd be over and—"

"You're not there yet? It's almost ten o'clock."

"I know. I had things—"

"Did you call her and tell her you'd be late?"

"No." Shit, he should've done that. "I got busy and—"

"And you what? Forgot about her? What did you have to do that was more important than the woman you lo...are crazy about?"

His breath froze in his chest. Everyone thought he loved Sarah. Did he? No. He didn't. He couldn't. She hadn't even wanted to be with him.

"Nick? What's wrong?"

"I'm starving and I was wondering if maybe I could swing by—"

She sighed. "Go to Patrick's office. It's pizza night tomorrow. Chelsea is still there getting everything ready."

"Great! Thanks. Ahh..."

"What?" She sounded a little pissed.

"I'll need to take one to go. You know with me being late and all."

"I'll call Chelsea and she'll have one ready for you. What do you want on it?"

"Um...I'm not sure. I don't know what she likes."

"You'd better find out if you want to keep her. Good sex only goes so far."

"Yeah, food is very important," yelled Patrick from the background.

"Thanks, Annie." He didn't just mean for the pizza.

"You're welcome but you'd better straighten up. Being late isn't—"

"I know but I got stuck at the pet store."

"The pet store. Oh, Nick. You didn't get her a pet did you?"

155

"No. She has one. A dog that hates my guts."

Annie burst out laughing. "That's why you're late. You were shopping for her dog?"

"Yeah. If I want to have sex, I've got to get that dog to let me touch her."

"You have got to be kidding me." Annie turned away from the phone. "Nick can't have sex because Sarah's dog hates him."

Patrick's laughter grated on his already raw nerves.

Annie spoke into the phone again. "I have got to meet this woman. When can we all go out?"

"I don't know. Maybe, we can have you over one night." He wasn't spending his few hours away from that blasted dog with another couple.

"Patrick, Nick wants to have us over one night."

"When's the wedding," yelled Patrick.

"Shut the fuck up." He started to hang up the phone and hesitated. "Thanks again, Annie."

CHAPTER 35: NICK

The damn dog started barking as soon as Nick pulled into her driveway. He got out of the car, grabbing the pizzas and the other groceries Chelsea had given him. He liked that girl. Annie had called her friend and between the two of them, he now had a very romantic meal complete with two pizzas—one vegetarian and one meat—some chocolate cake, a salad, wine and beer.

The door opened before he moved away from his car. Sarah stood in the doorway, that damn, huge dog by her side still barking.

"Hey," he said.

She looked gorgeous in her jean shorts and T-shirt. His dick hardened as his eyes fell on his marks trailing up her long, thin legs and disappearing beneath her shorts. She could have his piece of cake. He was having her for dessert.

The dog growled as if reading his thoughts.

"Give me a break," he mumbled.

"I-I didn't think you were coming tonight."

"Oh, we'll both come tonight. Several times."

Her cheeks flushed as she stepped aside, snapping her fingers. The dog groaned a little but moved aside.

He paused in the doorway, holding out his hand for the dog to sniff. While Tank was busy checking him out, he leaned in and kissed Sarah. It was soft and sweet, nothing like he wanted, but it'd do until he could get her away from that devil-beast.

"I brought dinner."

"I see." She said against his lips.

"I hope you're hungry."

"I kind of skipped dinner. So yeah, I'm starving."

He followed her into the kitchen and put the pizza and groceries on the counter. "I have some other things. Can I go get them?" He'd never asked if he could stay with her. In the other contracts he'd had with women, they'd both stayed mostly at the hotel, but this was different. This was Sarah and honestly, he had no intentions of stopping when six weeks were up. That was only the amount of time he had to convince her that they should give this a chance long term. He was still hurt that she hadn't sent Ethan a letter, but he could get over that. What he couldn't get over was leaving her.

"Ah...sure. Do you need help?"

His hand trailed down her back to her ass. There was a slight rumble in Tank's throat but he ignored it. "Nah. Make the plates and I'll be right back."

He stepped outside and grabbed his duffel bag and his laptop from the car and went back into the house. He hesitated at the bedroom door. He'd never lived with anyone. This was her house. Maybe, he should ask before putting his stuff in her room. Of course, that'd give her the chance to refuse. He dropped the bag on the floor by the door and put the computer on an end table in the living room.

He went outside again and brought in all the dog toys and other crap he'd bought. Everyone said dogs were like kids and if it were true he was going to buy his way into that damn dog's heart.

Tank's toenails clicked on the kitchen floor as he moved to the doorway. The dog stared at Nick and the bag.

Nick pulled out a large beef bone. The clerk at the store said dogs loved it. "You want this?" He held it out to the beast. Nick could've sworn the damn dog's eyes narrowed before he turned and trotted back into the kitchen.

"What's that?" asked Sarah as she carried the bottle of wine and salad to the dining room table. The plates, glasses and two bottles of salad dressing were already there.

"Nothing." Now he felt foolish. "Just some stuff I picked up for Tank."

She bit her lip and it was like a jolt of electricity straight to his groin, making everything stand at attention. He'd never wanted anyone like this. If it weren't for that dog, he'd have her on the table right now.

"You didn't have to do that." She opened the bottle. "The pizzas are in the oven. Wine?"

"Yeah. Thanks." He walked to the table and Tank huffed and moved closer to Sarah as she sat, pouring the wine.

He grabbed his plate from the other end of the table and took a seat next to her. He didn't come all the way over here to sit a mile away – not that the table was actually that big, but he wanted to be close to her. Hell, he wanted to be inside her. He tugged on the front of his pants to give his growing dick a little room.

"I hope you like Ranch or Italian. It's all I have." She put salad on both of their plates.

"They're both fine but wasn't there some dressing in the bag." He went into the kitchen. "I could've sworn Chelsea said she sent us some of Annie's dressing." He came back with a small container. "It was under the napkins."

"Oh."

He opened it as he sat down. "Try it. Annie is a fabulous cook."

She stuck the tip of her finger into the container and then between her lips. He couldn't take his eyes from her mouth. He wanted to grab her and drag her into the bedroom, or better yet, fuck her right here. Tank growled. That proved it. Not only was her dog a pain in the ass but he was also a mind reader.

"That is fantastic." She poured some on her salad and handed the container to him. "Nick?"

He blinked, dragging his eyes away from her lips and grinning at her blush. "Thanks." He drizzled some on his salad and they both began eating.

"How long have you had Tank?"

Her fork stalled midair and she paled slightly. "Since right after Adam died."

He wanted to bash his head against the table. Talking about her ex-lover and father of her miscarried child wasn't the way he wanted to start their evening. "Oh." He took a big gulp of his wine, wishing it were something stronger.

They ate in silence. The timer went off with a loud ding.

"The pizzas are done." She started to get up.

"I got it." He put his hand on her shoulder. "You rest." He gazed down at her. "You're going to need your energy later."

CHAPTER 36: SARAH

Sarah stared at Nick's ass as he walked into the kitchen. Sexy, hot, dominant, playful Nick was dangerous enough but thoughtful, considerate Nick was turning her heart into mush. Not only had he shown up, but he'd brought dinner and gifts for Tank. She was in serious trouble but right now she didn't care. She'd treat this magical night like a special gift.

He came back into the dining room carrying the two pizzas. "I wasn't sure what you liked, so I had Chelsea guess."

"Anything's fine. Pretty much." This was the second time he'd mentioned Chelsea.

"Try both and I'll let her know which one is your favorite." He slid a slice of each onto her plate and then tossed two of the one covered with meat onto his. He took a bite and groaned. "I have no idea how Patrick isn't as fat as a house."

"Patrick?"

He wiped his mouth with a napkin. "Yeah, he's a friend." He grinned. "Actually, you met him. Kind of."

"Ah...I don't think so."

"During the Viewing. He was the guy who asked you to raise your dress."

"Oh my, God." She wanted to hide. "The two of you are friends?"

"Yeah. He wasn't happy with me for getting you to forego his interview. He swears you would've picked him." He took another bite of his pizza. "Annie is a cooking god." He glanced at her plate. "Try it."

"Okay. Sure." She didn't want to like the food. He liked it enough for both of them and she couldn't help being jealous. She wasn't a particularly good cook. She pushed that thought aside. She wasn't in competition with Annie or Chelsea. Nick would lose interest whether there were other women around or not. She picked up the slice of vegetarian pizza and took a bite. She moaned. It was that delicious.

"See. I told you." He finished his first piece and started on his second.

"This is the best pizza I've ever had." She shoved more in her mouth.

"I'll pass that along to Annie and Chelsea or you can tell Annie yourself."

"You want me to meet her." She almost dropped her food. Good thing she hadn't because she loved her dog but he was not getting any of this pizza. Tank rested his head on her knee and she scratched his ear.

"Yeah. She invited us over for dinner."

"Like a couple?" Her heart beat slowed as if it were trapped in mud.

The muscle in his cheek started throbbing. "Yeah Sarah, like a couple." He tossed back the rest of his wine and refilled it. "We're going to be together for six weeks. We aren't just going to fuck you know."

"We aren't?" That was news to her.

He leaned toward her, his dark eyes snapping. "As much as I'd like to be able to fuck you for twenty four hours straight, even I need to eat and work."

Her heart was suddenly going a mile a minute and her

panties were soaked. This man drove her crazy with lust.

He trailed his finger over her knuckles. "Of course, we aren't going anywhere except my place until Tank is used to me. I'm not giving up my hour of fucking you to have dinner with Annie and Patrick."

"Oh...right." It seemed Annie was with Patrick. No reason to be jealous of her. Not that she was, because she wasn't.

"Eat." He leaned forward and kissed her, it was slow and soft, his tongue playing over her lips but going no farther into her mouth.

She wanted to grab his head and pull him closer but Tank's rumble kept her hands on the table.

He broke the kiss and leaned back, finishing his second slice of pizza.

She took a bite of the meat pizza and put it down on her plate.

"You don't like it?"

"It's good but...too salty. Too much meat."

"Here." He handed her another slice of the vegetarian pie and took the other one from her plate."

She watched as he bit into the pizza right where she'd eaten. They'd done so many things to each other but this was, in a way, more intimate. This was like a couple. She couldn't do this. She couldn't let herself get attached to him except for sex.

"What? Are you one of those women who don't like to share your food?"

"No. It's fine."

"What's wrong?" He dropped the pizza onto his plate. "Because by the look on your face it's not fine. I'm sorry. I shouldn't have taken the pizza from your plate. I should've asked first. I'm used to my family and we always do this kind of stuff."

"No, that's not it. I don't care that you took the pizza."

"Then what is?"

"It's nothing." She couldn't sit here and pretend with him, but the only other option was kicking him out and she didn't want to do that.

"Sarah, tell me." He took her hands in his. "I'm not an expert in relationships. You're going to have to help me here."

"That's the problem." She struggled to keep the panic away as she pulled free from him and stood.

"What? Did I do something else wrong?"

"This isn't a relationship." She nodded at the duffle bag. "All this stuff you brought...Why? What do you expect from me? From this?" She waved her hand between him and her.

"You only want this to be about fucking, is that it?" He stood, grabbing the pizzas. "Fine. I can do that."

Tank growled at his raised voice.

"Shut up and eat." He tossed the dog the slice of pizza he'd taken from her plate as he walked into the kitchen.

The refrigerator door slammed and he came back out and grabbed the other dishes.

"You don't have to clean up."

He shot her a dirty look but didn't say a word.

Tank nudged her hand, his brown eyes dropping to the pizza near his feet.

"You can have it." She grabbed the salad dressing and remaining salad, almost bumping into Nick on his way out of the kitchen.

He mumbled something as he passed her. The front door

opened and shut and her knees almost buckled. She leaned against the kitchen counter and took a deep breath. This was better. It was. She put the salad and dressing away as tears ran down her cheeks. It may be better but it wasn't what she wanted. She wanted him but she wouldn't be enough. The door opened and she quickly wiped her eyes. She walked into the living room.

"Sorry. I forgot this." Nick had his laptop in his hands.

"Stay." The word slipped from her heart and past her lips.

His jaw tensed. "Why? We can't fuck here."

She had to do something to make him stay but there was Tank to consider. The dog sat between them glaring at Nick. "I...I think we can figure something out." She moved forward tentatively and took his hand, Tank at her side. She tugged on his hand, trying to lead him to her bedroom but he refused to move. "I don't think Tank will care if I touch you." She moved closer. "Let's see."

She stood on tiptoe and kissed him. He didn't kiss her back. She ran her tongue across his lip as her other hand trailed down his chest to his cock which was already hard and swollen. His entire body stiffened as she let her fingers caress him while she unbuttoned his pants. She slipped her hand inside, rubbing along his length. He was so hot and smooth. She loved touching him.

"Sarah," he gasped as he wrapped his hand in her hair and thrust his tongue into her mouth.

She melted against him and Tank growled a low warning rumble.

Nick dropped his hands and stepped away. "This isn't going to work." His eyes were dark with desire and his face was flushed.

"It will. I swear." She took his hand again. "Trust me."

"Trust you? Is this what you did with your boyfriend?"

She closed her eyes for a moment. She should tell him the truth but she couldn't. It was too embarrassing that not only had he been the only one in the four plus months but once the six weeks were over, she'd be alone again. "This is about you and me—not your other women and not Pet...anyone else." His jaw was clenched as she took his hand. "Please, let's try this." She let her eyes dropped to his undone pants. "I miss the taste of you."

"Lead the way." His voice was heavy with desire.

She tugged and he followed her into her bedroom. She stopped in front of her bed and grabbed the bottom of his shirt. "This first." As she pushed it up she followed with her lips, kissing and licking from his abdomen to his chest. She relished the feel of his muscles under her hands—all that strength covered by smooth, hot skin.

He raised his arms and she removed his shirt, kissing his lips. This time he opened right away for her and her tongue darted into his mouth for a quick taste. When he tried to meet her tongue with his, she pulled away.

His hands went to capture her face and then dropped at Tank's rumbled warning.

"I think I might like this arrangement." She smiled as she bent, running her tongue over his nipple before sucking it gently.

He moaned, his hands clenching in fists at his side. "Tease."

"Is that what you are when you do this to me?" Her lips moved downward, dipping into his navel.

"That's different."

She nipped his hip as she began unzipping his pants. "No, it's not." She got down on her knees and looked up at him. "This time, I get to tell you when to come."

The heat in his eyes made her gush with need.

"You'll pay for this."

"Not until Tank's okay with you touching me." She removed his shoes and socks. "Sit."

He started to push his pants down and she grabbed his hand.

"Sit."

Tank sat, staring at her. Her eyes darted to the dog and she bit her lip trying not to laugh.

He shrugged and sat. "I'll be panting at your feet too in a moment."

She let the laughter out, surprised he wasn't angry about this. She grabbed his ankle.

"That's not the part of me that needs your hands on it," he grumbled.

"I'm in charge." She began massaging his foot and the tension fled his shoulders.

"That feels so good." He closed his eyes, leaning back on his elbows and moaning a little as she kissed the sole of his foot. He opened one eye. "Not as good as your lips on my cock, but I might have to let you do this while I watch football."

The familiar panic set in. The idea of them sitting and watching TV together was too normal, too much like a real couple.

"I was kidding, Sarah." He was watching her intently now, the tension back in his face and body.

"I know." She smiled.

He grabbed her chin, forcing her to look up at him. Tank growled.

Nick turned toward the dog. "It's okay. I'm not hurting her." His voice was calm and steady. "Tell him, Sarah." He loosened his hold on her chin so she could turn toward the dog.

"It's okay, Tank."

The dog moved a little closer and nudged her with his head, but kept one eye on Nick. She ran a hand through his soft fur. Nick dropped his hold and she kissed Tank's muzzle. "Go lie down, baby. Mommy's okay." She grinned up at Nick. "She's just going to play with her friend's little toy."

Nick laughed. "You mean his great, big, humongous toy."

She kissed the dog again. "Lie down." She used a firmer tone and Tank gave her one beseeching look before trotting over to the dog bed and dropping onto it.

"Now, where were we?" She faced Nick, her hands grasping the waistband of his pants.

"I think you were about to suck my cock." He lifted up so she could remove his pants—his dick standing tall and proud in front of her.

"Yes, I was." She ran her hand along the length. "Oh, it's not wet enough."

"Not wet at all. That's your part."

"Hmm. Yes, it is." She opened her mouth and licked his tip.

He leaned back on his elbows again. "Look at me."

She met his eyes as she wrapped her hand around his cock. It was long and thick and she couldn't wait to torture him like he'd tortured her.

"Wait." He grabbed a few pillows and positioned them

under his back. "Now, I can watch you."

"I think we need something to lubricate you." Her hand wasn't sliding as well as it should.

"There's lube in my duffle bag...but that's in the car." His eyes darkened to almost black. "You'll have to go old school and use your tongue."

"I could go get your bag." She loosened her hold on his dick. "Is the lube flavored?"

"Don't you dare." His hand wrapped around hers but he let go when Tank stood. "Okay. I'm not touching her."

"Lie down, Tank. It's okay," she said.

The dog grumbled and dropped back onto the bed.

She lowered her mouth, licking all around his cock as she stroked him. "Is that better?"

"Much." His eyes had darkened and his cheeks were taut with tension.

"Still. I should've been more careful."

"It's okay." His breathing increased with each passing of her hand.

"Then you don't want me to kiss it and make it better?" She gave him an innocent look.

"No. I mean, you're right." He took a deep breath. "You need to kiss it. Shit, just suck me, Sarah, please"

"Oh, I don't know. You sure made me wait."

"I'm begging you." He said through clenched teeth.

She flicked the head of his penis with her tongue and then licked his precum. "Beg more."

"You're going to pay for this." His hands clenched in the sheets. "Next time. At my place. I'm going to spank you for this."

Her pussy throbbed. She had no idea why that turned her on but it did. "I can't wait." She lowered her lips, dragging her tongue around the head of his cock.

"Fuck, Sarah. Please." He was leaning up staring at her, his face as hard as a statue's.

She locked eyes with his as she opened her mouth wide. His nostril flared as she lowered her lips. She hesitated right above the tip, letting her warm breath tease him.

"For God's sake. Put me in your mouth already."

She shook her head a little and flicked the top of his dick with her tongue. He grabbed her hair and pushed down on her head. Tank growled but Nick was past caring.

"Let go of me, Nick, or I'll stop." She licked all around the tip.

"Don't stop." He dropped his hand to his side.

"What do you want, Nick?" She loved making this man quiver.

"I'm begging you. Suck my dick. Please."

"Good boy." She took him in her mouth and sucked gently. His thighs trembled beneath her fingers. She wrapped one hand around his shaft, moving up and down with the rhythm of her mouth.

"Fuck…" He groaned, his hips thrusting.

She couldn't take him down her throat so she shifted so he hit the side of her cheek and he moaned. She moved her mouth off him and kissed up and down his length and then took him inside again. She sucked as she gently squeezed his balls. His hips moved more frantically and his hand raised and then lowered, brushing across her cheek before grasping the blankets. She took his hand and put it in her hair, keeping her hand over his. Tank was watching but not growling and she didn't care because this wasn't about control now. For Nick, this was about coming and he was close.

"I'm gonna come, baby…"

She sucked harder and squeezed tighter, pushing him over the edge. He burst in her mouth and she swallowed again and again. When he was done, she sat up, wiping her lips.

He was prone on the bed, panting. "Come here." He opened his arm and she crawled up by him, snuggling against his side. "Give me a minute." His hand skimmed up and down her back.

Tank trotted over to the bed, resting his head on the side.

"For what?" She kissed his chest. "Stay, Tank."

"To take care of you."

She wrapped her arm around him. "I'm fine and I don't know if Tank can handle that." She was horny but she was content to let it simmer.

He turned his head and kissed her nose. "We'll be sneaky." He caressed her ass. "I need you naked."

She had no idea how he was going to handle this and that sparked her desire into overdrive. She sat up, pulling off her clothes as quickly as possible. She wanted to feel his naked body against hers. She wanted him inside her but that'd have to wait until Tank was more used to him.

His eyes roamed over her. "Come here and let me see how turned on you got by sucking my dick."

Perhaps she should be embarrassed about that but she wasn't and Nick, certainly, wasn't upset. She stretched out next to him and he rolled to his side, reaching between them.

"You're soaked." His fingers stroked across her pussy.

"Mmm..." His hand felt so good.

"This shouldn't take but a moment," he said as he played with her. "Open for me."

She lifted her leg and put it on his hip, opening herself up to his exploration. Tank didn't move. Nick's fingers teased along her clit and then he dipped one inside of her. She thrust toward him.

"I'd love to bury my face in your pussy." His voice was rough. "You'd like that wouldn't you?"

"Yes," she moaned as he pressed down on her clit.

Tank sat up.

"Your dog wouldn't though."

Right now she didn't care about what Tank wanted. She wanted Nick's tongue on her—in her.

"Take my hand and hold it against your abdomen,"

She did and he pressed inward as he added another finger inside of her.

"Oh..." Her body stiffened as he thrust against her g-spot.

"Like that, do you?"

"Yes. Yes." She moved against him making his fingers hit her harder and harder. He picked up his pace and pressed down more firmly with his other hand. Her muscles clenched and she gasped as she came, rocking against his hand. When she opened her eyes, Nick was staring at her.

"Welcome back." He smiled. It was a pure masculine look of satisfaction.

"Hmm." Her body felt as boneless as Jell-O.

He shifted, Tank coming closer to watch and make sure he wasn't going to hurt her. "I'd pick you up and put you up here, but that dog of yours..."

He crawled under the covers and stretched out on the bed, head on a pillow. He patted the spot next to him. "Come here."

Tank jumped onto the bed, looking from her to him.

"I wasn't talking to you." Nick frowned.

She laughed as she crawled up by her two boys. "He sleeps with me." She got under the covers and wrapped an arm around Nick's waist.

"As long as I get to too, I guess that'll be okay."

She kissed his neck as his arm went around her.

Tank growled.

"I'm not hurting her and I'm not moving. Bite me if you want." Nick's hand trailed down her back to her ass and rested there.

Tank gave him a dirty look but settled on the bed next to her.

CHAPTER 37: SARAH

When Sarah woke the bed was empty. Nick must've left in the middle of the night but where was Tank? She hopped out of bed, pulling on a pair of shorts and T-shirt. Tank never left her side. She prayed he hadn't gotten sick from the stress of Nick being here. She hurried into the living room and stopped. Nick was sitting on the couch sharing his breakfast with Tank. Tank was so busy snacking on bits of bacon that he barely gave her a glance.

"See, I'm not such a bad guy." Nick scratched Tank behind the ears as he fed the dog a bite of toast. "And I'd never hurt your...Mom? Is that how you think of her?" He stared at the dog as if trying to understand Tank's thoughts. "Nah, you know she's not your mom. She's not hairy enough and I'm the only one gets to lick her ass."

She laughed and Nick turned, a smile taking over his face. He looked like a boy with his rumpled hair and morning stubble. Okay, maybe not a boy, but still adorable.

"Good morning." He nodded toward the kitchen. "I made breakfast."

"I see." She smiled even though fear clawed at her throat. This was too good. It wouldn't last. *But enjoy it while it does.* She hurried to the kitchen. "Did you save me any or did you use my portion to bribe my dog." She tried to make her voice sound normal but must not have succeeded.

"Is everything okay?" He followed her, Tank trotting after

174

him.

"Yeah." She tossed a piece of bread in the toaster. "Why?" She had to calm down.

"You seem upset." He glanced behind him. "It's okay that I fed him human food, right?"

"What? Yeah." It was great. He was great and that was the problem.

He moved closer to her but Tank stepped between them. The dog wasn't growling anymore but he wasn't ready to surrender either.

"I'm not going to hurt her. Ever." Nick patted Tank's head as he took Sarah's hand. "I wish you'd both believe that."

"Nick....I know you won't hurt me."

"Do you?"

"Yes, of course. I let you tie me up, more than once." Her toast popped and she pulled free from his grasp and focused on buttering the bread.

"That's not what I meant."

"I trust you. I do." She took a bite of toast as he watched her.

"Hmm." He began cleaning up the dishes.

"I can get it."

"I made the mess." He leaned toward her and kissed her lightly. "My mother raised me right. She'd tan my ass if she found out I'd left the cleaning of the kitchen for you because you're a woman."

"I think, I'd like your mother."

He closed the dishwasher and started it. "You will and she's going to love you."

Her heart started racing again. "Going to? As in..."

"I go there every third Sunday for brunch. The whole family gets together." He took her hands. "I'd like you to go with me tomorrow."

"Me?" Her voice squeaked like a scared mouse. "Tomorrow?"

"Yeah." He kissed her fingers.

"Why? I mean, this will be over in a little over a month. Do you take all your contracts to see your mother?" She knew the answer to that.

"Okay." He dropped her hands. "I'll go alone." He strode into the living room.

She'd done it again. She couldn't stop pushing him away and for some reason it was hurting him. He shouldn't care. This was temporary. She waited to hear the front door close, but it never happened. She walked into the living room and he was sitting at the table working at his computer.

He wasn't leaving. Her heart melted a little. "I'm going to shower." She walked past him, trailing her hand across his wide shoulders. "Want to join me?"

CHAPTER 38: NICK

Nick stared at his computer, the text on the screen nothing but a blur. He wasn't an idiot. Sarah was trying to manipulate him with sex. Every time he tried to make what they had about more than fucking, she stopped him cold and then offered sex. He was done playing that game. He was going to stay here and keep working. The sound of running water drifted into the living room. She was probably naked—the hot water running down her soft skin. He closed his laptop. They could talk later. Right now, he needed to fuck her. The blow job last night had been great but he wanted to be inside her, feel her tighten around him as she came.

He went out to his car and brought his duffel bag back inside, leaving it on her bed next to Tank. The dog sniffed it and then stretched out and closed his eyes. He patted Tank on the head.

"You may hear some noises, buddy. Just ignore them please. Or better yet, listen to this." He grabbed his phone from his pocket, found a radio station and turned it up all the way. Tank sighed. "That's a boy." He tossed his shirt and pants on the floor, grabbed a condom from his duffel bag and walked into the bathroom, closing the door behind him.

The shower door was translucent enabling him to see everything. She had her eyes shut, the water streaming down her face and body. He could stare at her all day. She was grace personified—long and lean with supple breasts and a perfect ass and her legs...They just went on and on. His dick grew even more as he imagined them wrapped around him, pushing on his ass as he thrust into her.

He stroked his cock a couple of times as he moved toward the shower. She turned, half-startled and then smiled, her eyes dropping to his dick before coming back to meet his. He opened the door.

"I thought you weren't coming," she said.

"Oh, we'll both be coming." He moved in front of her, so close they were almost skin to skin. "But you're going to have to be quiet."

"Is that what the radio is for?"

It was a low noise in the background. "Help distract Tank, for when you moan."

"Pretty cocky aren't you?" Her hand skimmed down his chest toward his dick.

"Very cocky, as you can see."

She wrapped her hand around him and he pulled her close, capturing her mouth with his. She opened immediately and he deepened the kiss. Her other hand tangled in his wet hair. He broke the kiss and moved to her neck as she stroked him. He'd have to stop her soon, but not yet. He nipped her neck and she moaned.

He moved to her ear. "Quiet, baby."

"Sorry." She tightened her grasp on him and he moaned. "Shhh."

"Tank doesn't care if I moan." He swatted her ass.

She kissed his neck and his hands pulled her closer to him, so his erection and her hand pressed against her pussy. He moved her wrist off him and rubbed against her, making sure the hard length of him stroked against her clit. She gasped.

He grabbed her hair and pulled back her head. "Quiet, because I'm going to fuck you even if that dog tears down the door."

"Sorry." Her green eyes darkened with heat.

He backed her against the wall as he kissed her. The foreplay would have to wait because she was making too much noise and he wasn't going to lose this chance. He grabbed the condom from the soap dish where he'd dropped it when he'd entered the shower and tore it open. He slid it down his length and lifted her legs. She immediately wrapped them around him. He positioned himself at her entrance, letting only the tip slide in and then he kissed her. It was quick and she followed his lips wanting more. His hands cupped her breasts, as he watched her face and pushed in a little more.

"Please," she whispered.

He lowered his head and took a nipple in his mouth, sucking and teasing it with his teeth and tongue. Her feet pressed into his back, pulling him closer. He should make her wait but he couldn't. He shoved inside all the way and she groaned long and low.

"Quiet." He could swear he heard Tank get off the damn bed. There was no way he was stopping. Even if he wanted to, he couldn't. He pulled almost all the way out, lowering his head to capture her lips so her whine of protest slid into his mouth and so did her gasp of pleasure as he pushed back into her. She clamped around him, so tight and wet. His balls tightened as he thrust into her. He'd devour her if he could. Stay like this forever, fucking her into eternity.

"Nick..." Her hands clasped at his shoulders as her thighs

tightened and then she shook, her lips trembling against his as she came, clutching him tighter as he pulled out and shoved back in again and again.

"Sarah" He buried his head in her neck, grasping her hips and holding her in place as he came.

They stayed like that for several minutes, both almost panting.

"So, shower sex it is for a while." He swatted her ass.

"Except when we go to your place." She kissed his ear.

"For an hour." He wasn't happy about that. He wasn't happy about a lot of this but he'd put up with almost anything for her. Now, all he had to do was convince her that he was the guy for her instead of her limp-dicked ex-boyfriend.

"I was thinking." She untangled her legs from around him and picked up the soap. She rubbed it on a rag and began running it over his chest.

"Yeah." Damn, he was going to be hard again in a few minutes is she continued to bathe him.

"I...It hasn't been easy. I haven't been easy."

He ran his thumb over her nipple. "I just had my way with you and you didn't put up an ounce of resistance. I'd say you've been pretty easy."

"That's not what I meant." She slapped his chest.

He kissed her because he could. Her eyes were sparkling with amusement and she was hot and naked and with him. There was no way his lips could stay away.

"Anyhow, I know it isn't easy being here with me and Tank. I thought that maybe...I could talk to Maisie and see if she can stay with Tank for a few hours next weekend."

"Yeah?" Hours of having her however he wanted her and

making her scream was a wet dream of his.

"Yeah." She glanced down. "And I...I thought we could go to a hotel."

"Why not my place?" He had some toys he needed to introduce her to.

"Ah..." She flushed and it was so adorable that he kissed her again but this one was a little darker a little deeper. She moaned softly when he stopped. She re-soaped the rag and moved it around to his back, her breasts brushing against his chest as she cleaned him.

"Is there a reason you don't want to go to my place?"

"Well, I kind of need to set some things up. There's...something I'd like to try."

That was it. Tank may not be listening but his dick was certainly standing at attention. "The professor and student again." Please, please be that because he wanted to experience that fantasy again.

"No, but we can do that later."

He lifted her chin and kissed her nose. "What do you have planned?"

She nibbled on her lip and he almost took her right then. "I've made you mad a couple of times already and...I think you may have to punish me."

"You're right. I do." He moved closer but she didn't back away, so he grabbed her hips and pulled her into him. "You've been a bad girl."

"I have." Her hand with the rag trailed between his ass cheeks.

"I have plenty of toys for exactly that purpose at my house." He rubbed his cock against her clit and her eyes almost crossed.

"But I have to set it up." She pulled away a little, but it was too late for that. She was his now.

"You can set up whatever you want at my place." He yanked her back to him. "Now, put your hands against the wall. I'm going to fuck you again and it's going to be hard and fast." He started to turn her around.

"Wait."

"I can use the same condom. I haven't taken it off yet."

"That's not it but is that safe?"

"Yeah." He had no idea and didn't care. There was no way she hadn't used one with Peter so she was clean and the birth control she'd had implanted when she'd signed up at the Club was good for years. "Now, turn around."

"No. Wait." She struggled and he almost ground his teeth to powder but he let her go. "I need to be there without you. I want it to be a surprise."

"I'll give you a key."

"You're okay with giving me your key?" Her mouth was open a little in shock.

"Not my key. Your key to my place and yeah." Maybe this would convince her that he wanted more than six weeks.

"Really?"

"Really." They could talk about it later, right now he needed to be inside her. He grabbed her shoulders. "Now, put your hands on the wall before I have to punish you."

Her eyes sparkled. "You can't with Tank here."

"Don't try me."

She grinned and spun around putting her hands flat against the wall. He took in the sight for a moment—all her succulent bare skin, her body leaning forward, her tits brushing against the cold tile. He ran his hands down her sides and over her hips and then up the back of her thighs, letting his fingers trail between the cheeks of her ass.

He moved closer so his mouth was at her ear. "One day, you're going to let me fuck you here." He skimmed his finger around her asshole. "Aren't you?"

"M...maybe."

"You liked it when I touched you here before, didn't you?"

"Ah..."

He moved his hand to her pussy. She was slick with her own desire. He trailed his fingers from her pussy to her ass, making her wet there. "Don't lie to me." He pressed against her little puckered hole.

"It was okay."

He kissed her neck. "One day you'll let me and you'll love it." He grabbed her hips. "Open for me."

She widened her legs and he moved closer, positioning his dick at her opening and thrusting inside. She bent forward, but he grabbed her waist pulling her upright. In this position she'd have no ability to thrust back at him; he was in control.

"Wrap your arms around me." He moved inside her as she lifted her arms up and around his neck. He kept one hand on her hip as the other moved to her front caressing her mound.

"Oh, yes. Right there." She tried to thrust into his hand, but he kept her still as he teased her with long, slow strokes. "Please Nick."

"Patience, baby." He was going to keep the pace slow and steady—enjoy the feel of her tight, wet cunt clasping onto him, all around him.

"You said hard and fast."

He chuckled in her ear. His baby liked to come. "I changed my mind. You feel too good to go fast. I never want to leave."

She stiffened in his arms. She was pulling away from him again. Not her body but her mind and damn it, he wanted all of her. He gently pinched her clit and her body responded, pushing aside her worries. He kissed her neck, letting his tongue dip into her ear as he continued thrusting into her while toying with her clit, around and around—interspersing light, teasing strokes with short burst of pressure.

Soon, her body was tightening but not in worry, in ecstasy. He moved his hand so he was cupping her pussy, every thrust making his palm brush against her sensitive little nub. His pace increased. No matter how much he wanted to fuck her all day, he couldn't delay any longer. His balls were hard and tight—ready to explode. He found the spot between her shoulder and neck that drove her wild and bit down as he shoved into her hard. She screamed as she writhed against him, her pussy clasping onto his cock and pushing him over the edge.

WEEK TWO: COWBOY FANTASY
CHAPTER 39: NICK

Nick was running late. He'd dragged Tommy to a meeting with a new client and when it was over, the kid had pestered him with a hundred questions. He was proud of how well Tommy was doing, but tonight was not the night to be late. It was Friday and Maisie was coming over to watch Tank, which meant he got to see what kinky fantasy Sarah had in store for him. Both of his heads couldn't wait. He texted Sarah.

NICK: On my way. Be ready.
SARAH: I'll see you at your place. Change into your costume.

His dick rose. A costume? Interesting.

NICK: I can pick you up.
SARAH: No. I'm waiting on Maisie. I'll see you there.
NICK: I'll come home and wait with you.
SARAH: No. That's OK.

Nick clenched his teeth. She was pushing him away again and he was done with it.

NICK: I'll be there in a few. No reason for us both to drive.
SARAH: Please don't. I'll meet you there.

NICK: No. I'll pick you up.
SARAH: It's out of your way.

She had no idea where his meeting had been. She hadn't asked. She never asked where he was going or how long he'd be gone. She didn't ask him to pick anything up and wouldn't go shopping with him. She preferred to have her groceries delivered. He wanted to do couple-things but obviously what he wanted didn't matter.

NICK: It isn't out of my way.
SARAH: Please. Don't do this.
NICK: Why don't you want me to pick you up?

He knew the answer but he wanted her to admit it. It took several minutes but she finally replied.

SARAH: I like having my car.

He almost threw his phone out the window. She'd let Peter drive her to the awards banquet but she didn't trust him to get her home to her damn dog. He wanted to tell her to forget it. All of it. Him. Her. Them—even though to her there was no them. But he couldn't. He was crazy about her. No, he was more than that. He was in love with her. It was a scary feeling but not nearly as scary as losing her.

NICK: Fine. See you there.

He felt like an idiot but he wasn't giving up. She was crazy about him too. He only had to prove to her that she could trust him. That he wasn't Adam, the dick. He wouldn't knock her up and abandon her. He wouldn't tell her he loved her and then change his mind.

He'd tell her he loved her now if he thought it'd make a difference but those words didn't mean anything without trust. Unfortunately, he had no idea what else to do to prove to her that he was serious about them. He stayed at her place, slept in bed next to her, had sex with her and only her, cooked meals, helped clean the house and helped take care of her dog and yet, any time he tried to move the relationship a little further along, she pushed him away.

She'd refused to go with him to his mother's house for brunch. His sister's birthday was in a few weeks and when he'd asked her to go to the party with him, she'd, of course, said no. Sex was great. Better than great, even though he still couldn't fuck her around the damn dog unless she was on top, but every time he tried to get her to do something couple-like she'd panic.

Of course—he shifted on his seat, tugging on his pants to give his swelling cock a little room—that led to some fantastic sex, always in the bathroom except once in the back seat of her car inside the garage.

He turned down the road toward his house instead of Sarah's. He could go get her. Push the issue. Make her trust him enough to ride with him instead of driving herself. She had to learn that she could depend on him. He'd get her home to her dog on time, but that'd start things off on the wrong foot. He was pretty sure he was going to get to punish her tonight but he didn't want to really fight, not tonight. They could argue tomorrow.

He pulled into his driveway and drove his car into the garage. He went inside the house and his feet froze as he turned on the light. He swayed, all the blood rushing to his cock. Sarah had better get here soon or he'd have to jerk off because tonight was going to be hot.

CHAPTER 40: SARAH

Sarah shoved her phone in her purse as she walked out of her bedroom.

"Everything okay?" asked Maisie.

"Yeah." If Nick being pissed at her again was okay.

Maisie just stared at her.

"It's fine." Her sister had a way of reading her like no one else. "Nick was going to come by and pick me up."

"And you refused?"

"Yeah. It was out of his way." She looked down at Tank. She wasn't good at lying to her sister. She had no idea where Nick had gone so she had no idea if it were out of his way.

"Mom, you coming? We're going to turn on the movie," yelled Kyle from the living room.

"I'll be there in a minute. You two can start." Maisie lowered her voice. "I have some info to dig out of my sister."

"It's no big deal."

Maisie grabbed her arm and led her to the front door.

Sarah rested her hand on Tank's head. He nudged her thigh. "Go on. Go get some popcorn." The dog was a popcorn beast. He nudged her once more and trotted into the living room to join Kyle and Peter.

"He seems to be doing a lot better," said Maisie. "I think having Nick around is good for him." She turned to her sister. "And you. So, don't screw it up."

"Hey!"

"Why wouldn't you let him pick you up? So what if it was out of the way. Men like to be in charge. They like to believe they're taking care of us."

"I had to be sure I could get back here on time for Tank." She couldn't tell her sister that she couldn't let Nick meet Peter.

"Stop blaming everything on that dog."

"I'm not." She almost took a step back at the anger in her sister's voice.

"You are and you have been. Ever since Adam died you've been hiding. Somehow,"—she raised her hand in the air—"you found a guy who's crazy about you and willing—"

"He's not."

"He is. He's practically moved in and I doubt you made that easy on him. Lord knows, Tank didn't. Yet, it's been a week and he's still here."

"Yeah. One week. Only one week." Not a month. He hasn't had time to get tired of her yet.

"He tracked you down."

"Like a stalker." Nick wasn't a stalker but she hated losing arguments.

"Like a guy who's crazy about a girl he can't find." Maisie smiled. "He's only a stalker if you aren't interested. Otherwise, it's romantic."

"Please."

"It's the truth and I know you're interested." Maisie's eyes gleamed. "That outfit proves you're interested. Exactly, what are you and Nick doing tonight because I know you aren't going line dancing."

She was not going to explain her sexual fantasy to her sister. "I've got to go before he gets more upset. He hates when

190

I'm late." *Especially, since he's going to be in costume staring at the suspension bar.*

Maisie grabbed her and hugged her. "Give him a chance, Sarah. He really cares for you."

"I am."

Maisie frowned.

"He's living here, right?"

"Yeah, but let him live here." Maisie placed her hand over Sarah's heart.

"I'm scared." Her breath hitched.

"I know." Maisie hugged her again. "It's always scary to open yourself up, but"—she glanced into the living room—"it's worth it."

"I'm trying." It was just so hard to trust anyone, especially a guy like Nick.

CHAPTER 41: SARAH

Sarah pulled into Nick's driveway. She turned off the car, her hand hesitating on the door handle. She'd made him angry several times this week and earlier tonight. Did she really want to go inside his house and let him tie her up and do whatever he wanted to her? An insistent throb pulsed between her legs. Yes, she did. She absolutely did. She trusted him not to hurt her physically. Everything he'd do to her tonight would bring her pleasure.

She got out of the car and walked up to the house. She stared at the key in her hand. There was no way he gave one to every woman he slept with, but that didn't make her special. She had to remember that. She was already too attached to him and it'd only been a week.

She stepped inside and he was sitting by the bar on a stool she'd brought. He was drinking his scotch, his dark eyes burning her with his perusal. Damn, he looked sexy in a blue denim shirt, worn blue jeans, cowboy boots and hat. He was ready to play and she was already wet for him. She glanced at the suspension rack unable to quite believe she wanted to do this, but she did. She wanted him to string her up. She'd be completely helpless and at his mercy.

CHAPTER 42: NICK

"Ma'am," Nick said, using a drawl as his eyes raked over her body.

She was dressed as a peasant girl with a long, tan skirt and white, scooped-neck blouse. His palms itched to skim up and under that skirt. Would she be wearing conventional underwear or would that too be part of the costume? Exactly what kind of underwear did farm girls wear? He couldn't wait to find out.

"Mister." She fought a smile as she placed her purse down on the table and locked the door behind her. She tugged her shirt up, covering her breasts.

"You're old man Johnson's daughter aren't you?" He took another sip of his drink. He loved that shirt. It was too big for her and kept slipping down, giving him a peek at the top of her breasts.

"Y-yes, sir."

"And what brings you to see me?" He shifted toward the bar, more to hide his erection than to play the part. "I'd think I'd be the last man you'd be searching out." He had no idea if this were how old time cowboys talked, but he was always willing to try his best for a fantasy.

"It's about my brother, sir."

"The brother who tried to steal my horses?" He finished his drink and poured another. He turned to face her again.

"H-he didn't mean it, sir. He's only a boy."

"Thirteen is not a boy."

"He's a good boy, sir." She took a step closer, trembling slightly.

She should've been an actress. She looked innocent and scared. His eyes darted to the suspension rack and his dick swelled more. He'd had to jerk off before she got here, otherwise he would've grabbed her and fucked her the minute she'd walked in the door. He took a swallow of his drink and tried to focus on the game at hand, not her naked and strung up for him to touch and kiss and fuck in any way he wanted. "He's a horse thief."

"Please sir, he can't be whooped. He'll never live through it. He's frail and sickly. Always has been."

"He should've thought about that before he tried to steal my horses." He shrugged. "The law's the law."

There was a slight frown between her brows. She'd probably thought he'd suggest that she sacrifice herself for her brother but he needed to be sure she was ready for this and so did she.

"Please, mister."

"And what would you have me do?" He spun around on the bar stool so he was facing her. He almost grinned as her eyes dropped to his crotch and then back to his. Her face was flushed but he was pretty sure it wasn't from embarrassment. She wanted his dick as much as he wanted to give it to her.

"Tell the sheriff that it was a mistake. That you ain't pressing charges."

"Why would I do that?" He sipped his drink, letting his eyes linger on her breasts. "What's in it for me?"

"It's...it's the Christian thing to do and I swear he won't do it again."

"Don't much care for doing the Christian thing." He let his eyes go to the rack and then back to her. She was staring at the suspension hook now and her face was a little pale. She may be having second thoughts. Good, it'd be a better fantasy if she were a little nervous. "And you can't promise he'll never do it again." He turned in his seat, putting his back to her. "Go home, little girl."

"I'm not a little girl." She stepped forward until she was standing directly behind him. "Please, mister." She took a big, shaky breath. "I'll do anything."

He turned, his legs brushing against her skirt. "Those are some big words for such a little girl." He bent taking the hem of her skirt in his hand and rubbing it between his fingers as he pulled it upward until her knees were revealed. "You should go home before you get hurt."

"I'm not a little girl." She reached around him and poured some of the Crown Royal that was sitting next to his bottle of Glenlivet into a glass and tossed it back. She slammed the glass down on the bar.

He raised his brow. "I'm impressed. You can down a shot, but that doesn't make you a big girl."

She stepped closer until she was between his legs. "Mister, I'm prepared to do whatever I have to in order to free my brother. Even take his place."

He wanted to bury his face in her chest, lick his way across those tempting mounds of flesh and hear her moan, long and loud. Fuck, he missed hearing the noises she made when she came, but it was too early in the game for that. He turned slightly, pouring more Crown in her glass and handing it to her. "Your brother is set to be whipped."

195

She swallowed and he watched her throat muscles work. He clenched his teeth to keep from grabbing her shoulders and pushing her down to her knees so she could put that long, lovely throat to better use.

"I know, sir, but he's frail and sickly. I'm strong."

"Hmm." He wasn't into hurting women even when they wanted it. He usually avoided those parts of the Club. Sarah had left him a note with the basic premise of this fantasy but he didn't know if she really wanted to be hit with a lash. She hadn't left one here with the other props so probably not, unless she thought he had one. He didn't. "You sure?"

She nodded. "Yes, sir."

"What's your name?"

"Sarah."

"We'll need to take off your blouse."

Her face heated and she cast her eyes downward. "Can't you whoop me with it on?"

"No. The material in the shirt will get stuck in the cuts."

Her head snapped up and her eyes met his. He kept his face stoic but relief surged through him. She didn't actually want him to hurt her. He ran his fingers across her cheek. Her skin was warm and soft. He'd never tire of touching her. "Cat litter still your safe word, right?"

Most of the apprehension left her eyes and she nodded.

Time to get back into character. "Are you sure you want to do this for your brother? He might not learn his lesson if you take his punishment."

She jutted out her chin. "I'm sure and he's learned."

He poured them each a hefty drink. He handed her the whiskey. "You may need this."

She nodded and chugged the alcohol, coughing a bit. She handed it back to him.

"Let's get started then." His hands went to the top button of her blouse.

She grabbed his wrists. "You swear you'll tell the sheriff to let him go?"

"I'll even write it down." He moved away from her and grabbed pen and paper from his desk. He wrote a note saying that her brother was to be freed because he wasn't pressing charges. It'd been a misunderstanding. He carried it to her. "Can you read?"

"Of course, I can read." She reached for it and he let her take it. She read it. "Thank you." She slipped it into the pocket of her skirt.

He sat down on the bar stool. She'd moved away a few feet. "Now, come here." He took her hand and pulled her closer so she stood between his legs again.

"I can unbutton my own shirt."

"I'm sure you can, but I'm in charge and I want to do it." His hands moved to her first button, his finger caressing the soft skin below. "May I?"

"Yeah...I guess."

He took his time, moving down her chest and exposing more and more of her warm skin. He let his fingers brush against her, causing her breathing to increase with each touch and then he froze. "What's this?"

"A camisole. All women wear them."

"Hmm." He ran his finger across the cloth. "It's soft."

"It's supposed to be."

He slipped a finger underneath, caressing her skin. "But

this is softer."

She stiffened. "Is this part of the whipping, sir?"

He bit the inside of his mouth to keep from laughing. So, she wanted to be persuaded to fuck him. "We could do other things. Instead of the whipping."

"I'm a good girl."

"Shame." He moved on to the next button and the next. When they were all undone he pushed the blouse off her shoulders and let it fall to the floor. His mouth watered. She wore no bra, only the camisole—her pert breasts accentuated by the satin. Her nipples were already hard and pointing at him, begging him to taste them. If he lowered his head a little, he could take her in his mouth. The satin would get wet and the friction would drive her wild. He ran his thumb over her nipple.

"Sir, please." Her voice was a bit breathy.

"Your brother was supposed to get forty lashes." He couldn't take his eyes from her breasts. He needed to taste them, make her moan. It'd been too long since he'd heard her deep throated sounds of pleasure.

"Y-yes, sir." She grabbed his wrist stopping him from his steady caress. "I can handle it."

"I'm sure you can." She may have stopped his hand from moving but his thumb still rested on her nipple. "But how about we agree to only thirty-five lashes on your back?"

"That's kind of you, sir, but why?"

He forced his eyes up to her face. "I'll give the other five to your front."

Her eyes widened and she started to shake her head.

"With my tongue."

She froze, her eyes dropping to his mouth. "I...I don't

know."

He moved his thumb again, her hand no real deterrent. "I promise. You'll like it."

"I...I'm not sure."

"Let me show you. Just one kiss." He absolutely had to taste her through that camisole. He was pretty sure his life depended on it. "Please."

"O-kay but only one kiss."

He couldn't help the half smile. "One kiss only takes away one lash."

"Okay."

He lowered his head, blowing across her breast. She was frozen before him, not even breathing. She would soon. No, soon she'd gasp.

"Ready?" His lips brushed against her nipple as he spoke.

"Ye-yes."

He opened his mouth, running his tongue over her little nub and then around, again and again. Her hands went to his shoulders. She was trying so hard not to push closer to his mouth, but he'd win. She'd surrender. He closed his lips around her breast and sucked as he grabbed her ass pulling her closer.

"Oh..." She moaned—one long purr as her back arched, offering her tits for him to worship.

He sucked and licked—the satin hot and sticky in his mouth. He wanted to move to the other breast but he forced himself to stop. "Do you want to trade in all five lashes?

"Yes." Her voice was more a plea than a word.

"Are you sure?" He couldn't help teasing her.

"Yes, mister." Her hands tangled in his hair, pulling his head toward her chest.

He chuckled against her other breast before taking it into his mouth. He moved one hand from her ass and rubbed the wet satin across her nipple while he suckled and teased her other breast. She was holding him close now, not wanting him to move as she gasped and moaned. He moved his other hand off her ass and began pulling up her skirt. He needed to be inside of her.

She broke out of her sensual fog as his hand brushed against her bare thigh. "Mister, stop."

He froze, resting his head between her breasts. "Sarah, I need you now. We can finish this later."

She pulled away from him. "I'm a good girl, mister." Her hands were trembling and she was unsteady on her feet.

He took a deep breath and counted to ten. Obviously, his Sarah wasn't ready to quit. He loved her fantasies but sometimes her dedication to them was frustrating. He took another deep breath. He'd give it one more shot. "You can trade in all your lashes for one night with me."

"I'm a good girl, mister."

"You liked what we just did." When she opened her mouth to argue, he quickly continued. "Don't deny it. You held me to your breasts. You moaned in pleasure." He grabbed her hand, pulling her close again. "You're wet and achy between your legs, aren't you?"

"No, sir." She flushed, looking down at the floor.

"Liar." His hands rested on her waist. "It's okay that you are. It's natural. It's good. We'd be good together."

She raised her head, meeting his gaze. "I think you should whip me now, sir."

"As you wish." He grabbed the bottom of her camisole and

pulled it upward.

"Sir." She crossed her arms over her chest, stopping him from taking it off.

"Can't have the cloth getting in the cuts." He tugged on her wrist but she refused to uncover her breasts. "Move your arms, Sarah."

"Leave it. I'll take my chances with the cuts."

"Your brother would've been shirtless."

This time it was her jaw that clenched, but she raised her arms and he removed the camisole, letting his head get dangerously close to her breasts.

"Are you sure you don't want to trade in some more lashes?" He said so close to her nipple that she had to feel his hot breath.

"I can handle thirty five."

"Then let's get this done." His chest brushed against hers as he stood, causing her to gasp. He smirked as he strode to the suspension bar and picked up the cuffs.

"I thought you used rope." She walked stiff legged over to him.

"That'd hurt your wrists." He took her hands and clamped the cuffs around them, making sure they weren't too tight. He raised her hands, which were both cuffed together, over her head and attached them to the hook. It was low enough that her feet touched the ground but she had to stand on tiptoe.

He stepped back, his dick screaming for him to let it out. He could do anything he wanted to her now. She was helpless and knowing her, she was wet and ready for him. "Are you sure about this, Sarah?" The question was for both the fictional and real Sarah. "I promise you'll enjoy a night with me much more than thirty-five lashes."

"Just give me my punishment, sir." Her lips trembled. She was actually a little afraid.

"I don't have a whip. The sheriff was supposed to bring that, and I'm not accustomed to whipping young girls." His eyes met hers, letting her know that he meant that. He wasn't into hurting woman.

"Then I guess you'll have to use your hands."

"I could or"—he unbuckled the belt that had come with the costume—"I could use this."

Her eyes widened. Good. He'd surprised her. He'd bet a fortune that she'd checked out his closet of toys and had thought she could persuade him to use his hands. She could and would, but right now it was time to show her that she'd just put him in charge of her fantasy. He pulled off the belt and let it hang in front of her, long and ready to inflict pain. He stepped closer. "Anytime you want to trade in some whippings, let me know."

He put the two ends of the belt together and snapped it. She jumped, her breasts jiggling as her nipples hardened even more. She'd been turned on when he'd threatened to spank her. He'd push her to the edge of desire—swat her a few times and she'd cave. Then he'd get to fuck her while she hung suspended—completely dependent on him. Damn, he loved her fantasies.

CHAPTER 43: SARAH

Sarah hung, arms extended over her head and breasts bare. She was completely vulnerable. Nick could do anything he wanted. She should be scared and she was a little, but she was more excited. Part of her wanted to tell him to fuck her right now. He'd be in complete control. She'd be at the mercy of his thrusts, his pace. She squeezed her legs together. She was so ready for him, but she wanted this fantasy. She'd imagined it for some time

The snap made her jump. She hadn't considered the belt. It'd just been part of the costume. It wasn't supposed to be part of the game. She didn't want him to really hurt her, not too much. A little pain before pleasure was good. Great actually. He'd taught her that, but not too much.

He walked around her and snapped the belt again. She jumped—her pulse racing and thrumming between her legs. He moved closer. She could feel the heat from his body against the bare skin of her back.

"So pretty." He ran the cold, hard belt buckle down her spine.

She couldn't stop the tremble that shimmered through her. He wouldn't hit her with that. Would he?

"I don't want to mar this skin." He kissed her shoulder, moving her hair to get access to her neck.

Her knees shook in anticipation and then his mouth was on that spot between her neck and shoulder that seemed to be linked to her pussy. Her knees gave out, causing her to hang from her arms. "This ain't part of the deal, mister." She struggled to speak when all that wanted to come out was a moan.

He stopped kissing her but didn't move, his hot breath cooling her wet skin. "That's the problem, little Sarah." He nibbled her ear. "You didn't think this through. I can do whatever I want to you." His voice was deep and dark and more wetness pooled between her legs.

"You promised, sir."

"You want your brother not to be punished and he won't be. You're taking his place but I don't whip women. Not hard."

Even though she trusted him, relief washed through her. "But we agreed I'd get thirty-five lashes."

"Do you want me to whip you with the belt?" His mouth was at her ear, his words almost a thought in her head.

"No."

"Good." He stepped aside. "You'll be punished, but not with this." He moved in front of her and tossed the belt aside.

"With what then?" She couldn't help it. Her eyes dropped to his crotch where his dick was straining at his pants.

"Oh, you'll get that but it won't be a punishment."

"I don't want to have sex with you."

He took one long step and he was only inches from her. He grabbed her hair in his hand, pulling back her head. "I could fuck you right now." He grasped her pussy through her skirt and she bit back a moan. "Here or here." He reached around her and grabbed her ass, letting his fingers shove the cloth of her skirt between her butt cheeks. "And there is nothing you can do about it."

She moaned. She couldn't help it. She was at his mercy and she loved every second of it.

"But, I won't." His eyes were dark and hot. "Until you beg."

"I'll never beg."

"We'll see about that." He grinned and walked away.

Sarah hung there, trying to see over her shoulder to figure out where he went and when he was coming back. She couldn't see anything but she could hear. She closed her eyes and listened. He was in his bedroom. Her heart pounded in her ears. His closet full of toys was in his bedroom.

"Tired?"

She squeaked as her eyes flew open. He stood in front of her again. "Mister, you're as quiet as a cat."

He'd taken off his shoes and his shirt. All that smooth, hot skin was only inches away. She knew how good that broad chest felt and the way his muscles moved as he thrust into her. She wanted to run her fingers around his nipples and down that chest but she couldn't. She squeezed her legs together instead and he grinned.

"Ready to beg?"

"I'll never beg." She might pant and weep and plead, but not beg. She nibbled on her lip. Okay. She'd eventually beg, but she was going to hold out as long as she could.

He raised the riding crop that he'd kept hidden behind his back and traced her lips. "I won't damage these. They're going to be sucking my cock soon."

She inhaled, trying to imagine how that was possible if she were up here, and he slid the crop into her mouth.

"Show me. Suck it."

She turned her head. "You're disgusting, mister."

"And you're going to love every dirty, naughty thing we do." He moved closer, letting the crop trail between her breasts. He bent and inhaled. "I can smell your desire." He grabbed her skirt and started pulling it up. "Your pussy is already dripping for me, isn't it?"

It was, but she had to stick with the part. "Stop it. Hit me with the crop but leave my skirt alone."

His eyes hardened and he tapped her breast, not too gently, with the crop. She whimpered.

"You don't get to tell me what I can and can't do." He skimmed the crop over her other breast and she tensed. "Count. That was one."

"One." She wasn't sure she could take thirty-five. That'd stung.

He moved around to her back, dragging the crop along her skin. He quickly swatted her back twice. She gasped.

"Count."

"Two. Three."

His hot mouth came down where he'd hit her and his tongue scraped along her skin, soothing the sting. His hand went to the back of her skirt.

"Wh-what are you doing?"

"Making sure you know I'm in charge." He unzipped her skirt and let it slide down her legs. "A slip. Nice. I think we'll leave that on...for now."

"Thank you."

He moved to stand in front of her, his hands trailing up her thighs pushing her slip upward.

"Y-you said you were leaving it."

"I am, but not your panties." He grasped the waistband and

pulled them down, letting his fingers skim across her skin as his face lowered with her underwear.

She tried so hard to concentrate on her character and how upset the girl would be but all she felt was desire. She knew the pleasure that mouth and those fingers could give and her body craved it.

He picked up her skirt and tossed it aside and then he stood with her panties in his hand. He turned them inside out and rubbed his finger over the crotch. "These are soaked." His eyes met hers. "Surrender now. All I want is a please."

She clamped her mouth shut to stop from agreeing. The bulge in his pants was huge and looked painful. She should do this for him. Take away his hurt, but even her lust filled brain knew that was an excuse. She was so turned on she could barely see straight but she wasn't ready to let him win. "Never."

His lips thinned before he shrugged. "Suit yourself." He tossed her panties aside, walked to the bar and looked inside a box that he must've brought from his bedroom. He grabbed something and walked over to her. He was holding two toys that were about two inches tall and cylindrical. Her pussy clenched in anticipation. They didn't look like any dildo or vibrator she'd ever seen but he was the expert.

"We're going to make these"—he flicked her nipple—"extra sensitive." He placed the device over her nipple and turned the top.

"What are you doing? What is that?" She gasped. The pressure was intense.

He turned it again and again.

Her head dropped back and she moaned. He gave it one more twist, flirting with pain and then started on her other breast. She tried but she couldn't hold back another moan.

"That should work nicely." He grabbed her face, making her look at him. "How does it feel?"

She was almost panting. It felt tight and hot. "Four and five."

His brow wrinkled in confusion before he smirked. "Only thirty exquisite tortures to go." He dropped his hold and moved behind her.

She tensed, not sure what was coming next. She'd never make it through thirty more...things.

He pulled up her slip, the satin tickling her thighs.

"I thought you were leaving it." She trembled, wanting his hands on her.

"I am." He leaned in by her ear. "I'm pulling it up, not down." He tucked the hem into the waistband leaving her ass bare.

"Beautiful." He skimmed the riding crop over her butt cheeks, the leather hard and thin.

She jerked forward as he brought it down on her ass. "Ouch." She couldn't help it. That'd hurt.

He hit her again.

"Hey. Ouch." She was pretty sure that had left a mark.

"What did you think was going to happen? You chose not to fuck me. You wanted this." His hand came down, slapping her ass. "Count."

"Six. Seven. And eight."

"Good girl." He touched her butt cheeks, massaging. There was something slippery—oil perhaps—on his hands. It was soothing the sting. "I don't want to leave any marks on this pretty, pink ass."

His fingers drifted between her cheeks as he kissed the underside of her butt. She was pretty sure from the angle that he was kneeling behind her, his hands cupping her ass and his lips and tongue playing along her cheeks and legs. He continued caressing her, his fingers sliding between her thighs but not touching her, coming close but never straying to her pussy. She needed his touch there. She needed him to stop teasing. She tried to push back but being perched on her toes didn't give her enough control.

He kissed her back where her butt met her spine and stood, his hands wandering around her stomach and toward her breasts. "I think it's time to remove these." He flicked the suction cups on one of her breasts and she moaned. "Yep."

He walked away and came back with two glasses. He took a drink of his and put it on the table. He held the other glass to her mouth. "Have some."

She drank, the whiskey sending a warm path down her throat.

"How are your arms?"

This must be a break from the game. "Okay. A little sore."

"I'll be right back." He left and when he returned he had a harness of some sort. He took her arms down from the hook and her legs almost buckled as the blood rushed back into her limbs. He pulled her close as he unhooked her hands. "Sorry. I should've done this first but I thought you'd beg sooner."

"I'll never beg you, mister." She wasn't ready to stop the game.

"Yes, you will." He hooked her into the harness and refastened her hands in the restraint before attaching her to the hook again. "Better?"

"Yes." Her arms still hurt but most of the weight was on her back and shoulders now.

"Good." He grasped one of the cups on her breast and untwisted the top, before pulling it off. "Beautiful."

His eyes almost sparked with desire. She looked down as he unhooked the other device. Her nipples were huge, engorged. He ran his thumb over one of them, pinching it slightly and she gasped. It was like he'd jolted her with electricity.

"See how sensitive you are now." He skimmed the riding crop across her breasts, around and around her nipple.

"Please." If he slapped her there now, it was really going to hurt.

"Please yes? Or please no?"

"No."

"Are you sure?" He tapped it gently across her nipple and her knees did buckle. "I think you want it."

She did and she didn't. The slight tap had been exquisite, the pain shooting to her pussy and making it clench.

"Count."

"Nine."

He tapped the crop against one nipple and then the other, fast and hard like a sting.

"Oh…oh…Nick…" She was going to come. All he had to do was touch her. "Please."

"Are you begging?"

"No." She said through clenched teeth and he smacked her nipple again.

"Count."

"Ten, eleven, twelve." He hit her again. "Thirteen." And

again. She rolled her head back, her body arching toward him, offering her breasts to him. "Fourteen. Oh. Please." And then his mouth was there—hot and wet, sucking on her and pushing her to orgasm. She screamed, her body twitching and her legs giving out beneath her.

He continued to suckle her engorged nipples and she moaned a long keening sound.

"Fuck, baby. I love the sounds you make." He grabbed her face and kissed her. It was hard and desperate, his tongue taking over her mouth. "Say it, Sarah. Beg me to fuck you. Tell me you want my dick so far up inside you that you scream."

She shook in his arms. "I'll never beg you."

His eyes met hers. His were angry or maybe desperate. "Fuck." He took a step away from her. He grabbed his drink and finished it. "Okay." His breathing was ragged. "You still want to play. Fine. You came. Now, it's my turn."

He moved to the stand and turned a crank, lowering the pulley. "Get on your knees."

She hadn't even realized that the height was adjustable. She should've since it wasn't custom made for her.

"Get on your knees."

She wanted to suck him, make him beg, but she had to keep to the part. "Why, sir?" She knelt in front of him.

"You'll see. Actually, you won't." He grabbed a cloth from the box and went behind her. He tied it around her eyes.

"No. Don't." She shook her head and he slapped her ass. She jumped. It was tender from the blows from the riding crop. "Fifteen."

CHAPTER 44: NICK

Nick was so hard he was going to come in his pants if he didn't do something fast. Sarah was so fucking hot, with her nipples engorged and still glistening from his mouth and her ass bare, and tinted red from his slaps. He couldn't believe she'd come just from him sucking her tits. That'd been his mistake. He should've paid more attention to her body but the sounds she'd been making—the little mews and moans—had driven him mad.

He'd been sure she would've begged him to touch her pussy, but she was so damn stubborn. So now, little Sarah was going to suck his cock and give him his release. He moved in front of her. Her nostrils flared and her head shifted. Being unable to see added to the intensity. "Open your mouth."

"Why?"

"Don't make me use the belt." He'd never do that. A belt was hard to control and he didn't want to actually hurt her.

She opened her mouth and he ran the crop over her lips. She jerked a little in surprise. He couldn't stop the smirk. She'd expected his cock. "What did you think I was going to put there?" He kept stroking her lips with the leather tip.

"I...I don't know but please don't hit my face." Her voice trembled.

Damn it. He should've left the blindfold off so he could see her eyes. She didn't really think he'd hit her face, did she? It didn't matter because he wasn't going to. "You still have twenty more lashes to go."

"Not my face, please mister."

"What are you willing to do to save your face?"

"I'm not begging you to have sex with me." Her jaw jutted out stubbornly.

"That's good because I don't want you to beg me because you're afraid."

"Why else would I beg?"

He bent so his lips were close to hers. "So you can come again."

"Come?" Her cheeks heated. He was pretty sure it was desire because his Sarah wasn't embarrassed about her orgasms but it did play well in the game.

"That's what it's called. That thing your body did while I was sucking your beautiful, little titties." He grabbed one, squeezing gently and she moaned. "I want you to make that sound when my dick is in your mouth."

"What?"

He straightened and unzipped his pants. He grabbed his cock and stroked it. He was already close. Just the thought of her lush lips wrapped around him was almost enough. He rubbed his dick across her cheek. "How does that feel?"

"O-okay."

"Describe it." He ran it along the other side of her face.

"It's hot and hard, but smooth."

"Taste it." He skimmed it across her lips and she stuck out her tongue. It was fleeting and too soft but he couldn't stop his moan.

"Salty..a little."

"Again." He held still in front of her mouth and she licked

him, lapping at his tip like a kitten with milk. He grabbed ahold of the suspension rack to steady himself.

"Sixteen." She twirled her tongue around his head and up and down his shaft. "Seventeen."

"Yes, that's it. Take me in your mouth and suck."

"That'll be eighteen, nineteen and twenty."

"Fine." Right now, he would've agreed to anything. "Open your mouth."

She opened wide and he almost came right then. With her arms bound above her head, blindfolded, kneeling and mouth open, she was every guy's erotic fantasy come to life. He slid his cock into her mouth and she sucked, her cheeks hollowing with the effort. She bobbed on his dick, sucking and licking as he thrust into her mouth. She was so hot and wet and the friction was killing him. His balls tightened.

"Fuck, Sarah. I want to come on your breasts. Is that okay?" She did her best to nod or he was pretty sure it was a nod. It might not have been because she sucked even more as he pulled out of her mouth. He stroked himself once twice until he came, spurting all over her chest. He rested his head against his arm, panting. As soon as he caught his breath, he knelt next to her. His hands caressing her breast and capturing some of his cum. "Was that okay?"

"Yeah."

"Open." He ran his finger across her mouth, painting her with his semen.

She licked her lips and he moaned. She opened her mouth. He scraped another blob of his cum and put his finger in her mouth. She sucked, causing his balls to tighten and his dick to perk. He pulled his finger away and kissed her.

"You are so fucking hot." He said against her lips.

"Only fifteen more to go," she said.

"Fuck me." He grabbed her chin and devoured her mouth. She drove him absolutely wild. He pulled away and stood. "Stand up." He grabbed her around the waist to help her as he cranked the handle raising her arms high above her head.

He took a step back and stared at her. She was even hotter with his cum sprinkled along her chest. She was his. He'd marked her and he was never letting her go.

CHAPTER 45: SARAH

Sarah strained, listening for Nick. She had no idea what he was going to do next. She should've made him exchange more whippings for the blow job. With as hard and ready as he'd been, he probably would've agreed to let it count for the rest of them, but then the game would've been over.

He moved closer. She could smell his cologne and the scent of aroused male. The heat from his body made her nipples peak. She was horny again. Sucking his cock always made her hot. She'd thought she'd gotten off on the control—having that hot, sexy man, moaning and groaning, needing her to continue—but this time, with her arms bound he'd been in control and she'd still gotten wet—soaked actually.

"Drink." A glass pressed against her lips.

It was water this time. "Thank you."

"I thought you might be thirsty."

"Your salty cum does that to me."

He laughed. "Ah, I see the real Sarah is here now."

"Sorry." She should've stayed in character.

"Are we done?" he whispered in her ear. "I'd like to fuck you now."

"I'm not begging."

He ran his hand over her cheek. "We both know you will, so why fight it?"

"I won't." She tipped her head away from him. He was right. She would beg, especially now that he'd found his release.

If she'd really wanted to win this game she would've ended it when he was too horny to think straight.

"So stubborn." He kissed her nose and then ran the crop over her face.

She flinched. He wouldn't hit her in the face. He wouldn't— she was almost positive.

It trailed down her neck and she swallowed. He let it ride the wave of her throat and then ran it down her chest.

"Where should twenty one fall?" He rubbed it across her nipples and then slapped it against her abdomen.

"Oh!" That'd stung. "Twenty one."

Slap. Against her hip.

"Twenty-two." Her other hip. "Twenty three." Her eyes were starting to tear up. Those little snaps hurt.

Then his mouth was on her skin, kissing and soothing the burn with his tongue. He moved to her other hip and kissed across her abdomen. She leaned toward him, following that mouth. She wanted him between her thighs. He smiled against her stomach before his face was gone and...slap. The crop came down right above her pussy.

"Shit," she gasped. He wouldn't actually hit her down there, would he?

"Count." His voice was tense.

"Twenty four."

He trailed the crop along her thighs and then hit her twice, once on each leg.

"Twenty five. Twenty six."

A second later, like before, his mouth was soothing her but this time through her slip. His open mouth made the satin silky and hot against her skin and then he was gone, leaving the cloth sticky and cold.

The crop skimmed over her pussy and she tensed. "Please, don't."

It slipped between her legs, rubbing her swollen lips. It was hard and long. Not thick enough or mobile like his fingers but it was pressure and she needed pressure...right there. She moaned, her hips thrusting against the crop, all thought of the pain it could cause slipping from her mind.

"You're dying for it." He whispered in her ear as he rubbed the crop along her slit. "Beg me so we can both get what we want."

Her mouth opened on a silent scream as he rubbed her clit. She took a deep, shaky breath. "I'll...never...beg."

He tapped her mound with the crop. It was fast and hard and she screamed—part from the pain but mostly the pleasure. He did it again and then he was on his knees. He grabbed her hips and kissed her through the slip. His tongue pushed the satin against her pussy. She tried to lean forward, to get closer, but he tightened his hold on her, keeping her still.

"Count."

"Twenty-seven. Twenty-eight."

"God, you taste sweet." He yanked her slip down and his lips were on her flesh. She trembled, her body racked with passion as he sucked and licked and nibbled. He grabbed her legs, lifting them and wrapping them over his shoulders. He reached up, yanking her blind fold off. "Look at yourself."

At some point while she'd been blindfolded he'd moved a mirror in front of her. She was naked, suspended by her arms with her legs dangling over his shoulders. His chest was bare, his lean muscles on display as he knelt before her. His hands were on her upper thighs, holding her open for him. He was staring at her pussy and then he buried his face between her thighs. She gasped as his tongue thrust into her, exploring. She trembled as he shifted her position, the muscles in his broad shoulders bunching. He kissed her deeper, curling his tongue.

"Oh!" Words were beyond her now. She opened her mouth, trying to breath and her breasts jiggled in the mirror. Her body trembled, shaking with release, clutching him closer as she came.

"That's it, baby." He kept licking and sucking, shoving two fingers into her as his mouth moved to her clit. "Get ready again."

"I can't." Her head hung forward. Her body, drained.

"You will." He grabbed her hips and buried his face in her pussy again.

She couldn't. He was wrong. She was worn out. Exhausted. That orgasm had wrung her dry, but he kept sucking and kissing and then his fingers hit that spot and the sparks flew like a fire barely out, roaring to life again. One of his hands crept between her ass cheeks and he pressed on her opening. She shivered, no longer afraid. It felt too good. "Oh god, Nick." She was going to come again.

He pulled his head away, untangling her legs from around him. "Not so fast, baby.

Her knees buckled as her feet hit the floor. He couldn't stop. Not now. It might kill her.

He stood, walked to the bar, grabbed a condom and moved to stand behind her. He removed his pants, kicking them aside before he pulled her legs back—kind of like they were playing wheelbarrow except her top half was hanging from the restraint. Her entire body tensed, waiting for him. This was what she wanted. Needed. This was better than his tongue and fingers. He moved closer, widening her legs and sliding into her slowly.

"Faster." She was helpless. She couldn't push backward. She could only hang there waiting for him, taking what he gave her.

He grabbed her hair, wrapping it in his fist. "Slower."

"No," she whimpered. Her body was so sensitized it tingled.

"Yes." He hissed in her ear. "You're mine, Sarah. Mine to do with as I want." He pushed in a little more. "Fuck, you feel so good." He nipped her ear and she shook.

"Please, Nick, please." She was almost crying. She needed him to push her over the edge, make her come.

"Shhh." He kissed her ear and slid in a little more. "Trust me."

"I-I do."

"You don't." He pulled out and an actual sob broke from her lips. "Trust me." He said again as he pushed into her, going a little farther than before.

"Yes."

He tugged on her hair, pulling her head to his shoulder as he shoved in all the way. She gasped and he kissed her neck, licking and sucking as he thrust into her. Her top half swung forward and back with each motion of his hips, but Nick held her close, impaling her. He was the only thing grounding her and she tightened her legs around his waist as much as she could.

"Hold me."

"I got you." He moved his hand from her hair but she kept her head in place for his lips. His fingers found her breast and began plucking at her nipple all the while he kept a steady thrust in and out, in and out. Her body tightened and she moaned long and low as she came. Nick stopped moving and held her close, his breath hot and heavy in her ear. He was still hard inside of her as he pulled out.

"Nick?" she whispered.

"I got you." He kept one hand on her waist as he walked to her front. "Wrap your legs around me." His face was taut with tension but his eyes were warm.

"No...I can't." She couldn't do it again.

"Shhh. You can, baby." He kissed her. "For me."

She'd do anything for him. She tightened her legs as he put them around his waist and slid inside of her.

"Look at me, Sarah." He grasped her chin.

She opened her eyes and stared into his.

"Trust me." He kissed her and started moving his hips.

His eyes were bright with passion but warm with something she couldn't name. It made her want to hold him close. "I want to touch you."

"Not yet." He shifted, bending his knees a bit and thrusting upward.

"Oh, yes, right...there." Pleasure sparked inside of her again and her eyes drifted shut.

"Look at me. Watch me while I fuck you." He grabbed her chin again. "Open your eyes."

They fluttered open.

"Trust me, baby. I'm here." He hit that spot again and she gasped. "It's me, making you feel this way. Me. No one else.

Me."

She almost sobbed. She should tell him that there'd been no one since him, but he increased his pace and kept hitting that spot, making pleasure shoot though her. Her body coiled and her legs tightened around his waist.

"That's it. Come for me, baby. Come for me." He started pushing into her faster and harder and she broke, crying out as her body quivered. His hand moved to her hips and he pulled her into him as he thrust forward, groaning his release.

They stayed like that—his head buried in her neck, his hands on her waist and her legs wrapped around him. At some point, it could've been minutes or hours later, he lifted her up and removed her from the hook.

"Put your arms around my neck," he whispered.

She groaned as the blood flowed back into her arms and she dropped them over his head.

"I got you. I've always got you." He carried her into the bedroom and placed her gently on the bed.

He removed the harness and the cuffs, tossing them to the floor. He turned to leave.

"Where are you going?" She was exhausted but she wanted to sleep in his arms, not alone.

"I'll be right back." He bent and kissed her. It was soft and warm. "You couldn't force me to leave." His warm eyes sparked a little. "Even if you try."

She stared after him as he disappeared into the living room. For a second, she thought he was talking about more than right now, more than tonight, but this wouldn't work. It couldn't. He'd never be happy with her. No man would anymore. She was broken, damaged. Her heart raced. He'd

222

leave as soon as he realized how fucked in the head she really was.

He came back into the bedroom with a bottle of water. "What's the matter?" He hurried to her side, putting the bottle on the nightstand. "Are you hurting?" His hands skimmed over her arms, shoulders and chest where the harness had been.

"No. I'm fine." She touched his face. She was in so much trouble but she had to take a chance. She couldn't keep pushing him away. She had to at least try to keep him. She took a deep steadying breath. "I'm just exhausted."

"Oh." He smiled shyly. "Yeah, it was intense." He grabbed the water and helped her sit. "Drink."

She took a sip and then began almost chugging it. She was dying of thirst. When it was almost gone, she handed it back to him.

"Good sex can make you thirsty." He put the bottle on the nightstand and stood.

"Now, where are you going?" She was getting a bit annoyed. She wanted to curl up and sleep and he kept leaving.

"I'll be right back, I swear." He chuckled as he went into his bathroom. He came back with a wash cloth and another bottle of something. He sat on the bed and ran the wet cloth over her chest, removing his semen. When he was done, he poured whatever was in the bottle into his hands. He rubbed them together. "Need to warm it up."

"What is it?"

"Oil." He began massaging her arms and shoulders.

She moaned again. It was warm and soothing and his hands were strong, working out all the stress of being suspended from her muscles.

223

"You'll be a little sore tomorrow, but this will help." He dragged his hands down her chest and over her breasts.

"If you start this again, I'll kill you." She was in no mood for another round.

"Sorry. I can't help it." He leaned forward, kissing her nose. "You're too hot for your own good." He massaged her arms a little more.

"Please, just hold me." The words slipped out. She closed her eyes, wanting to pull them back because they were vulnerable words.

She heard the bottle being placed on the nightstand and then he slid into bed with her, pulling her into his arms. He covered them both with the blankets and kissed the side of her head. She tried to relax but she couldn't. She should've never said it. He'd be different now.

"Sarah?"

"Hmm." She was a coward. She'd pretend to be almost asleep.

"Look at me." He tipped her face toward him. "Please." She opened her eyes.

"Are you okay? Really okay?"

She nodded. *No, I'm completely fucked up and I was fine with it until I met you.*

He stared at her for a long time before he leaned down and kissed her. It was warm and filled with caring not passion. "I'll hold you anytime you want me to." He kissed her again. "All you have to do is ask."

"Really?" Again the word slipped from her mouth. This exhaustion was making her tongue loose.

"Yes." He kissed her again, this one a little warmer. "I'll

even hold you when you're pushing me away." His sexy lips turned up at the corners. "I'm a stubborn guy."

She couldn't stop the small smile. "Thank you."

"Thank you." He kissed her again and then leaned back. "If we don't stop this, I'm going to be fucking you again and I'm not sure you can handle it right now."

She groaned. "No. No way. Keep your hands and dick to yourself."

He tightened his arm, pulling her against his side. "What about my mouth?"

"That too." She rested her hand over his heart. It beat strong and steady in his chest.

"Okay." He sounded disappointed. "Only for a bit, though."

They'd fooled around and fucked for hours, but he wanted more. "Do...Did the others go longer?" Again with the loose lips. "I'm sorry. I shouldn't have asked. It's none of my business."

"Damn it, Sarah."

"I said I was sorry. Don't answer." She rolled over, trying not to cry but her emotions were jumbled.

"I'm not mad you asked and I'll answer. Yes, some of the women at the Club went longer. Some of them can go...too long for one man."

"Please, I don't want to hear this."

"Too bad. I'm going to tell you." He leaned closer. "This...What we did was perfect. It was the best."

"Don't lie to me."

He leaned over her, his hand on her shoulder. "I'm not lying. Yes, I've been with other women. I've done a lot of things but nothing...nothing...has ever made me feel like I do when I'm with you." He turned and flopped onto the bed.

"Really?" She said it soft, almost hoping he wouldn't hear.

"Really, Sarah." His tone was disgusted.

"I'm sorry."

"Don't be fucking sorry. Just stop treating me like I'm some one night stand." He got out of bed.

"Nick..."

"What?" He ran his hand through his hair.

"I...I don't want to fight."

"Too bad. Let's get this out in the open. Ask me whatever you want. I'll tell you the truth."

She shook her head. She wasn't ready for this.

"Come on." He leaned down, hands on either side of her head. "You want to know something. Ask."

"Fine. Okay." She took a deep breath. She had to remember that she was only one of hundreds to him. "How many times have you done this before...with other women?"

His nostrils flared and his eyes narrowed. "I've done similar things at the Club with...about eight women."

It was like he punched her in the chest. About eight women. He couldn't even remember the exact number.

He grabbed her chin. "But I have never done it here with anyone. I've never brought any of them here. I've never moved in with any of them and I never, ever fucking invited any of them to meet my family." He let go and crawled into the bed, rolling on his side away from her. "Now, unless you have more questions, I'm going to sleep."

She couldn't process this. He'd done so much with so many other women but he was telling her that she was special. She wanted to believe him. No, she did believe him but how long before she became nothing more than number nine?

CHAPTER 46: NICK

Nick couldn't say how long he lay there listening to Sarah pretending to sleep. He had no idea how to prove to her that he was serious about this, about them.

Right now, he hated his past and yet, if he hadn't been a member of La Petite Mort Club he never would've met her. He rolled onto his back. She was on her side, facing him. She had her eyes closed.

"I know you're not sleeping."

It took a moment but she opened her eyes.

"I swear to you, that as long as we're together there won't be any other women." He shifted onto his side and scooted down so he was looking into her eyes. "I don't want anyone else."

"Why do you have all this stuff if you never bring anyone here?"

"For you." He grinned. He'd enjoyed every minute researching and shopping for all these things.

"But...you had it that first night."

"I did." He ran his thumb over her cheek. He'd never tire of touching her.

"But..."

His smile slipped. It looked like confession time was here. Suddenly, he didn't care if he looked like a fool. "I bought it waiting for you. I was sure you'd want to see me again." His eyes dropped. Admitting his flaws didn't come easily for him, but he'd do it for her. "I tend to be a bit arrogant at times."

"You...you contacted Ethan." Her fingers were a whisper on his chin.

He raised his eyes. "Yes." He didn't have to say anything about his celibacy. He wasn't ready to admit to that since she'd immediately gone out and started dating her business partner.

"I'm...sorry."

He shrugged. It still hurt but he had her now and wasn't letting her go.

"I-I wanted to...contact Ethan but I figured you'd moved on."

"I didn't." He kissed her, his tongue slipping into her mouth and playing softly with hers. "I haven't." He leaned closer, deepening the kiss. "I won't."

She pulled away, putting her hand on his chest to stop him from lowering himself on top of her. "I can't, Nick. I'm exhausted."

"Sorry." He rolled to his back and pulled her to his side. "Later."

"Definitely." She kissed his chest.

His hand skimmed down her back and rested on her ass, his fingers moving back and forth in a soft caress.

"I'll go to your sister's party with you, if Maisie can watch Tank and if you still want me to go."

"Really?" His hand stilled.

She laughed. "Yes. Really."

"You don't know how happy that makes me." He kissed her and this time it was filled with heat and passion. "Get some sleep so I can show you exactly how happy I am."

CHAPTER 47: SARAH

Sarah hurried into her house. She had to get her sister and family out of there before Nick came home. She paused, her hand hovering above Tank's head as he nudged her. Home. This wasn't Nick's home. No matter what he'd said last night, he'd never stay with her. She was too messed up for anyone. She had to remember that this was only temporary—wonderful, but temporary. Tank nudged her again and she scratched his ear.

"Hey, you're home early." Maisie yawned as she came out of the guest bedroom and went into the kitchen. "Where's Nick?" She started making coffee.

Sarah followed her sister. "Still sleeping at his place." She put a couple of slices of toast in the toaster. "Doesn't Kyle have baseball practice?"

"No, he has a game this afternoon."

Shit. She had to at least get rid of Peter. A car drove by and she glanced at the door. The toast popped and she jumped. "You guys have plans for the day besides Kyle's game?"

Maisie poured two cups of coffee. "Do you need us to stay?"

"No!" She almost clamped her hand over her mouth.

Maisie turned and handed her a cup. "What's going on?"

"Nothing." She put some cream and sugar in her coffee and buttered the toast.

"You're acting like you did when we were kids and we'd done something wrong." Maisie took a piece of toast and sat on

229

one of the chairs by the counter. "Spill it."

She sighed. It was time to come clean. "I...um..." She sat. "Nick kind of thinks that Peter is my ex-boyfriend."

"What?" Maisie almost spit out her coffee.

She shrugged.

"What the hell, Sarah? Why did you tell him that?"

"I didn't. Not in words." She tore off a piece of her toast and slid it back and forth on the counter. "He saw us at the awards banquet and assumed."

"And you didn't correct him?"

She shrugged again. "I didn't want to admit that I hadn't been with anyone since him. It was only supposed to be for that night and then he showed up here and...well, things kind of got out of control."

"Out of control? He's living here. How long do you think I can hide my husband from him, especially since we watch your dog when you two run off to have kinky sex?"

"It's not..." She blushed. It was very kinky. "Tank doesn't like..." This was even more embarrassing.

"What? What doesn't Tank like?" Maisie leaned closer. "Does Nick tie you up? Spank you?"

"Stop it." Her face was on fire now. If her sister only knew.

Maisie frowned but a gleam came into her eyes and the hair on Sarah's neck stood on end. That look was never good.

"First, you need to tell Nick the truth."

"Why? It'll be over in a month or so." Her mood dropped through the floor. She didn't want to go back to being alone.

"I don't think so. Not unless you make it end." Maisie grabbed her hand and squeezed. "Give him a chance, honey. He's crazy about you."

"Yeah, until he learns that I'm actually crazy." She wiped a tear off her cheek.

"You are not crazy."

"What do you call a hermit then? A person who can't stand crowds? Who doesn't like to go out?"

"Sarah, this is good." Maisie hugged her. "You need to talk to someone. Get help."

"I know." She sobbed against her sister's shoulder. She should've done it years ago when it was only a little thing—a little flutter of fear not the full-blown panic when others looked at her, believing they felt sorry for her because something horrible was going to happen. If something bad happened again, she wouldn't survive.

Maisie squeezed her tighter. "Oh honey, you don't know how long I've waited to hear you say those words." She kissed her sister on the top of the head. "You're going to be fine. You're strong. You can get through this." She kissed her again. "But you need to tell Nick."

She shook her head. "I can't. He won't understand."

"Then he isn't good enough for you." Maisie leaned back, taking Sarah's hands in hers. "But I think he will understand. No guy would put up with all this if he weren't mad about you."

"You have a point." She bit her lip.

"You'll tell him then?"

"Yeah." She would. As soon as she was better or mostly better.

"Good." Maisie stood.

"Where are you going?"

"To wake my husband and son so we can get out of here." Maisie turned toward her. "But you owe me for this."

"What exactly do you think I owe you?" Her sister was loving and sweet but Maisie could also be a little nuts.

"Does it matter?" Maisie looked at the kitchen clock. "Tick-tock. Nick could get here any minute."

"Fine. Go. I owe you."

Maisie grinned and hurried into the other room. She came back a few minutes later and poured another cup of coffee and threw in two more pieces of toast. "We'll be out of here in five."

Sarah glanced at the door. Hopefully, that'd be soon enough.

Maisie sat next to her again. "I want you to watch Kyle for us this weekend coming up."

"That's all you want?" That was nothing. She watched her nephew a lot.

"You'll have to take him to his game."

"Okay." She could drop him off and come back later or stay in her car.

"And, I want to know where to go or where to get...things."

"Things? What kind of things?"

"You know." Maisie's face turned red. "Kinky things. I want to try some with my husband."

"Oh." Now her face was red. "I-I don't know. I guess you could get them on online or something."

"You've never bought any handcuffs or restraints or anything? I mean, I don't want to get crappy ones that might break or cause a rash."

"No." She'd never tell her sister that she'd bought the suspension rack. "Nick supplied...supplies that stuff."

"Ask him."

"I couldn't." She'd die of embarrassment.

"You owe me."

"Maisie, I can't ask him that."

Peter came into the kitchen. "Ask who what?"

"Nothing," they both said.

"Okaaay." He grabbed a cup of coffee and the toast off Maisie's plate.

"Where's Kyle? We need to go," said Maisie.

"What's the hurry?"

"I'll explain later." Maisie looked at Sarah and smirked.

This was going to be embarrassing.

Peter sat down, sipping his coffee.

Kyle stumbled into the room, rubbing his eyes. "What's for breakfast?"

"Toast." Maisie took the two slices from the toaster and buttered them, handing them to Kyle.

"Hey, what about me," said Peter after he shoved the last bite of his bread into his mouth.

"You can have mine." Sarah handed him her slice, giving Tank, who was begging at her side, the little piece she'd torn off.

"Come on," Maisie tugged on Peter's arm. "We need to go."

"I haven't finished my coffee," grumbled Peter.

"Take it with you." Sarah wanted to shove them out the door.

"Kyle, get your shoes," said Maisie.

The kid stumbled into the living room.

"Come on, Pete, before Sarah changes her mind." Maisie winked at her sister from behind her husband. "She's agreed to watch Kyle next weekend. Friday through Sunday afternoon."

"Why?" Peter's eyes darted between the two women.

"Remember those things we wanted to try?" Maisie gave her husband a speaking look. "But can't with Kyle around."

Peter frowned and then grinned. "This weekend?"

Masie blushed. "Yep."

"Kyle, let's go. We'll stop at Denny's for breakfast." Peter hurried to the door.

"Find out where I can get some of those...things." Maisie hugged her. "And talk to Nick about...everything." She turned and then stopped. "And tell him the truth about Peter." She playfully slapped her sister's shoulder. "I don't like him thinking you two...You know."

"Okay. I will." Later. Much, much later.

CHAPTER 48: NICK

Nick sat up in bed. God damn it. He was alone again. He was sick of this shit. He grabbed his phone and then threw it back onto the nightstand. Fuck her. He got out of bed and pulled on a pair of shorts.

He went into the kitchen and started the coffee. He searched his refrigerator. The cleaning lady who came once a week had thrown out all the perishables, like he'd told her. He shut the fridge and grabbed the cereal, tipping the box up to his mouth.

He went into the living room and opened his old laptop. He sat at the counter eating cereal and waiting for it to boot up. He had no idea what else he could do to make her trust him. He'd thought they'd made some inroads last night, but obviously he'd been wrong.

His phone rang. It'd better be Sarah apologizing. He wandered back into the bedroom and grabbed his phone. It was Patrick.

"Hey," he said when he answered.

"Hey. Annie wanted me to call and see if you and Sarah can come by for dinner next Saturday."

"I don't know. I'll have to ask her." He was pretty sure she'd say no. She never wanted to go anywhere or meet his friends. He'd only met her sister on accident. She was keeping him at arm's length emotionally and it was time it stopped. "Actually, why don't the two of you come by my...our...Sarah's house?"

"That's okay with her?"

"I don't know. I'll tell her later." They were going to fight anyway. He may as well make it a big one.

"Um...remember when you helped me realize what a dick I was being to Annie?"

"Yeah." He knew what was coming. His friends were assholes.

"Let me return the favor. You can't just invite people to her house without talking to her."

"I'm living there too." Let the shit fall where it may.

There was a long pause and then, "Really?"

"Yeah." He couldn't help the grin that spread across his face. He loved living with her—sleeping with her, waking with her in his arms—except today when she'd snuck out again.

"That's great." Patrick moved his face away from the phone. "They're living together, Annie."

"I have to meet this woman," yelled Annie from some other room.

"Tell her she will. Next Saturday," he said.

"Nick...You should still talk to her."

"I will. Later. It's my house too and I can invite friends over." Sarah may not have accepted the fact yet, but he was there to stay.

"Um, yeah. I guess, but..."

"Don't worry. Come over at eight." He started to hang up and then said, "Hold on. Annie's still cooking right? Or do I need to pick up something?"

"We're going to their place instead," yelled Patrick to Annie. "Are you still cooking or do you want Nick to get takeout?"

"I'll bring dinner," yelled Annie.

"Great. I'll see you guys next week." He gave Patrick directions and then packed more things to take to Sarah's.

CHAPTER 49: NICK

When Nick got to Sarah's the door was locked. Tank was already barking but he knocked anyway, as he tried to keep his temper in check. He was glad she was being safe but he needed a key. She opened the door, wearing a pair of exercise pants and an old T-shirt. With her hair pulled back in a ponytail and no makeup on she looked sixteen. Images of last night tumbled through his head—her hanging naked, his face buried in her pussy, making her scream.

"Hey," she said and stepped aside, bringing him out of his fantasy and back to the reality of the fight that was to come.

"I need a key." He walked past her into the living room.

"What? Oh, yeah. I guess." She closed the door.

"I'm living here, right?" He tossed another full duffel bag onto the couch.

"Ah...yeah, I guess."

"You guess?" His voice rose and Tank moved closer to her but didn't growl. That was progress.

"I don't want to fight. I'll get you a key."

"Good but we're going to fight. We need to get some things straightened out."

"What, Nick? What needs to be straightened out?"

Her face was starting to flush. She was getting pissed and he was glad because his anger was simmering right under his skin. It had been since she'd refused to let him pick her up last night.

"This." He pointed to her and then himself. "Us."

"What about us?" She stressed the last word and it made him want to punch the wall.

"There are some things we need to get settled."

"Like what?" She sat on the couch, her face a calm mask but her hands were clenched.

"Like you sneaking out in the morning."

"I had to get home. You were still asleep."

"I woke up at seven and you were already gone. It's not like I slept all fucking day."

"I thought you needed your rest." She smiled slightly at him. "But you seem rested now." She bit her lip.

He wanted to groan. No, he wanted to grab her and fuck her, but that was her game. "It's not going to work this time, Sarah."

"What isn't going to work?" She opened her legs slightly.

He didn't think she did that on purpose but she might've. "You distracting me with sex."

"What?" Her eyes widened. "I don't do that?"

"Yes, you do. Every time you push me away."

"I don't push you away." She glanced down and his stomach clenched. She was doing it on purpose.

He sat on the couch next to her. Tank's lips curled up slightly but there was no growl.

He gave the dog a slight nod. Point taken. He lowered his voice. "Why do you do it? I would've taken you home this morning. I would've picked you up last night."

"I know, but..."

"But what?"

"It's just happening so fast." She touched his hand and he

captured hers bringing it to his mouth for a kiss.

"We've known each other almost six months," he said.

"And more than four of those we weren't together or even speaking." She pulled her hand away from him. "I can't jump into this knowing that you'll..."

"That I'll what?" He knew what was coming and there was no way he'd keep his anger checked. He stood and walked to the other side of the room because he was in no mood to get bit. "What do you think I'll do?"

She shook her head. "Please, Nick. Let's just drop this."

"You think I'm going to cheat on you? Like that asshole Adam. Well, I won't."

She took a deep breath as if trying for patience. "It's not that."

"Bullshit. Tell me the truth, Sarah? Why don't you want to meet my family? Why won't you meet my friends? What do I have to do to prove that I'm not Adam?"

"I agreed to go to your sister's party with you and...I know you're not Adam..."

"But..." This was going to hurt.

She looked down at her hands that were still clenched in her lap. "But how can I trust that this"—she waved her hands between both of them—"is real. That what you feel is real and not some game or conquest when you told me that you tire of women after thirty days."

"You set the time limit between us this time, not me." He couldn't stop from moving closer to her. He wanted to shake some sense into her. Kiss her until she believed what he said. Believed in him. Tank growled, stopping Nick's feet. Smart dog because if Tank wasn't here, he'd be touching her, kissing her and fucking her by now. It was the only time he felt that she was truly his. "And I told you that it's different with us. With you."

"It's only different because I'm not clinging to you. Because I won't submit to everything you want." Her voice was soft and sad. "As soon as I do, it's over."

"That's not true." But a whisper of doubt crept into his head. "You know what? I can't argue with you about this anymore." He had to get out of there. He had to figure out if she were right. He strode to the door and left.

CHAPTER 50: NICK

Nick sat in Ethan's office, sipping his third drink.

"I told you to leave her alone." Ethan was sitting at his desk planning the seasonal parties.

"I couldn't. I can't."

"Nick, she's been hurt enough."

"I know." He ran his hand through his hair. "Why do you think I'm here and not with her right now?"

"Because you had a fight."

"No, shit. I told you that." He grabbed the bottle and filled his drink. "Usually, we fight and then fuck. Even with that stupid-ass dog of hers." He smiled. "He's actually a great dog. He protects her and..." He shrugged. He liked dogs, always had. "If only he'd let me touch her, he'd be perfect."

Ethan burst out laughing. "You can't touch her and yet you're living there, sleeping with her and not fucking." He laughed harder. "Oh, I can't wait to tell Terry about this."

"Ha, ha, very funny." It was official. His friends were dicks.

"It's a great story. Nick, the man who can't go a day without fucking, went four months waiting for the elusive, magical pussy. He'd tasted it once and couldn't get hard without it."

"Shut up."

"Then,"—Ethan continued—"he found it again and now he can't touch it, tap it or taste it."

"Shut the fuck up. I'm warning you. Sarah is more than a

pussy."

"They all are." Ethan sobered. "I just didn't think you knew that."

"Of course...." He paused. He had thought of the women as conquests. He was good to them. Made sure they enjoyed themselves but he never cared about any of them. Never thought about them except as someone he could fuck.

"Unbelievable. I think you're finally growing up." Ethan clapped his hands slowly a couple of times. "It's about time."

He deserved this. He'd hunted, dated and fucked his way through a lot of women. Many were here for only that reason and they understood what he'd been offering but others had liked him, a lot, and he'd hurt them.

"So, what are you going to do now?"

"I don't know." He took a large gulp of his drink. "She said something that bothered me. She said that as soon as she gave me what I wanted, I'd move on."

"She's a smart woman."

"I...The way I feel about her..."

"That's your MO, Nick. It always has been even in business."

It was true. That's why what he did suited him. All the work was temporary. He moved in, helped a floundering company and then he was done. He continued to collect royalties but he didn't do any more of the work. He moved on to another company, another challenge. "I don't want it to be like that with her."

Ethan sighed. "I don't know what to tell you. You're going to have to figure this out on your own, but don't hurt her any more than you already have."

"I haven't hurt her." He'd die first.

"If you end it today, you think it won't hurt her? She told you what'd happened to her."

"That's the problem. She keeps sticking her past in our way. I'm not that cock-sucker, Adam. I wouldn't dump her at a party—pregnant and alone."

"From what I understand, Adam didn't know she was pregnant and she wasn't pregnant until after that party."

"Whatever." Okay, so he had his facts a little jumbled. The truth was he was worse than that asshole. Adam had moved on because he'd fallen in love with someone else, whereas he moved on because he was bored.

"Do you want my opinion?"

"Yeah." He wasn't sure he did.

"I've seen you chase women before. I've even seen some get away. You never, ever went to these lengths." Ethan's eyes sparkled. "Are you really living there and not having sex?"

"We have sex. It's just...quiet sex in the shower and very quiet sex in bed."

"Oh, this keeps getting better and better." Ethan roared with laughter again. "By quiet sex, you mean—simple, boring, non-kinky, quiet sex."

"It's never boring." Even quiet sex with Sarah was better than the best sex he'd had with someone else. "And it won't be forever. The dog's getting used to me."

"Right." Ethan didn't sound like he believed a word of that. "The point is...Is there any other woman you'd do this for?"

"No." It was like a vice was removed from his chest. He did care for her.

"I think that answers your question."

"Good. Now, the next one is how can I get her to trust me?" He couldn't live his life with her pushing him away. He'd grow tired of it eventually, but he wasn't going to give up without a fight. "She keeps me at arm's length."

"Apparently, you have the dog to thank for that." Ethan chuckled.

"Emotionally. Not physically." He'd said it before and he'd say it again. His friends were assholes.

Ethan sobered. "Give her time, Nick."

"I have. I mean what else do I have to do? I moved in. Uninvited, by the way. I'm putting up with vanilla sex and not as often as I'd like. She refused to meet my family." If he mentioned that she'd finally agreed to go to his sister's party, Ethan would tell him again, to give her time and he didn't want to hear it. "She also refuses to meet my friends. Shit." He grabbed his phone. He'd forgotten to tell her about next weekend.

"Everything okay?"

"Yeah." He texted her that Patrick and Annie were coming by Saturday for dinner and that Annie was bringing the food. He put his phone down. She'd be pissed but she should be somewhat over it by the time he got home.

"What you need to do is be there. Every day. Always. Give her more time. It's only been a week."

"Yeah. I guess." It felt longer because he'd been in a relationship with her for his four months of celibacy. Those same four months she'd been fucking that ass-wipe Peter.

"I'm going to tell you something I've never told anyone." Ethan took a big breath. "When I go into a store—grocery, department, any kind of store—especially one I've never been in, my blood pounds. I break out in a sweat. I look for exits and possible places of ambush. I've been out of the military for years and I still go through this. I know that the odds of someone shooting at me are slim to none. I know that the chances of stepping on an IED are basically nonexistent, but my body doesn't listen. It reverts back to survival mode."

"And you're saying it's the same for Sarah?"

"Same? No. Similar? Yeah, I think so."

He stared at his drink. Ethan might be right. She'd freaked out that one time he'd tried not to use a condom and when he'd given her the facial. She could need to talk to someone professionally, but he couldn't broach that subject if she didn't trust him.

There was a knock on the office door.

"Yeah," yelled Ethan.

Mattie opened the door. "I heard you were here." He strode inside, nodding at Ethan.

"So, Ethan ratted me out."

"You looked like you needed a drinking buddy and I can't be him today." Ethan tapped the laptop in front of him. "I have parties of debauchery to plan."

"Come on, I'll buy you a drink," said Mattie.

"I think I got most of everything figured out." He tossed back his scotch. "Thanks, Ethan."

Ethan nodded, but his eyes were already locked on the computer. "Still gotta figure out what to do about that dog." He looked at Mattie, his lips twitching with amusement. "Your brother has been forced to have quiet sex in the shower and sometimes in the bed, in order to not get torn apart by his girlfriend's dog."

246

"You have a big fucking mouth." He'd never live this down. Never.

Mattie's jaw dropped open for one second before he laughed. "Oh brother of mine, you need help. You've turned into as much of a pussy as Patrick."

"I should've gone over there."

"You should've," grumbled Ethan. "Actually, go now." He waved his hand. "I have work to do."

CHAPTER 51: SARAH

Sarah sat on the couch, trying not to cry but as soon as Nick's car pulled out of the driveway, she let the tears fall. She didn't just cry, she sobbed. Tank crawled up by her, nudging her with his hard head and licking the tears off her cheeks.

"I love you, baby." She hugged him, burying her face in his soft fur.

She'd known Nick would be mad about her not being there when he woke but she hadn't expected him to leave. Not yet. Not this soon. She sat up and wiped her eyes. It was probably better that he left now. She was falling in love with him more and more every day.

She went to her desk and tried to work but her mind kept drifting. Every time a car drove by her eyes would dart to the door, hoping it was Nick, but it wasn't.

She started to do housework. It wouldn't take her mind off him but at least she'd get something done. She opened her dresser to put away her laundry and Nick's clothes were in there. He'd made a small space for his shirts next to hers. The same was true for his underwear and socks.

It was no wonder he'd left. She'd been horrible to him. She hadn't even tried to make him feel welcome. She could've made some room in her closet and dresser but instead she'd kept pushing him away and now he was gone. She'd ruined this not him.

Her phone beeped and she grabbed it. It was a text from

Nick. She dropped onto the bed, biting her lip to keep from laughing. She looked at Tank who was sitting next to her, head tipped to the side. "He's coming back." She hugged her dog. "He's coming back. He invited people over without talking to me, and I should be furious with him but...he didn't leave me. It isn't over."

She hurried to the dresser and began cleaning out her clothes, making room for Nick in the drawers and her life.

When she'd put away all his clothes that were in the laundry she stared at his duffle bag. That was his personal space. She shouldn't go through it, but if they were a couple...Her heart raced and her breath was coming in short gasps. She inhaled deeply, fighting off the panic. No one could promise forever but she could at least give this relationship a chance. Try. Really try. She grabbed her phone and dialed her friend that worked with the PTSD dogs.

"Shelly." Sweat was trickling down her back and her hands were shaking.

"Hey Sarah, what's up? How's Tank?"

"Good. Really good. I...I'm calling about me."

There was a long pause and then Shelly said, "What do you need?"

"The name and number of that doctor." She took a deep breath, wanting to vomit. "I threw it away the last time you gave it to me."

"I'm not surprised. You weren't ready." Shelly's voice was calm. "This is a good thing, Sarah. I'm glad you called. Give me a moment to find it."

The time seemed like forever as thoughts tangled in her head. What if the doctor couldn't help her? What if nothing could? She'd be alone. She sat on the bed and wrapped her arms around Tank. She loved him but he wasn't enough, not any more.

"Here it is. Dr. Jemma Smileworth. I'll text you her info."

"Thanks." Sarah's phone beeped and she had the information.

"Sarah, this isn't going to be easy but...it's good and I know you can do it. Give it time. Work the process and it'll get better. I promise."

"Thank you." She hung up and stared at the text for a long time before dialing the doctor and setting up an appointment.

CHAPTER 52: NICK

Nick and Mattie sat at the bar watching a football game. It was the second one they'd watch. Nick tossed back his shot and followed it with a gulp of his beer. He was drunk but it wasn't helping him forget about Sarah.

The cute bartender came by and rested her hand on his, "Another round?"

She had dark hair and dark eyes and she'd been giving him hints all day that she was more than interested but he wasn't.

"Sure," said Mattie, before he could answer.

She smiled at Mattie and poured the rest of the pitcher into Mattie's mug before going to fill it up.

"I should go." At this point he was going to have to call an Uber because neither of them were in any condition to drive.

"Nah, come on. You wanted a drinking buddy and I took the day off just for you."

"Thanks, but it's getting late."

"It's five o'clock."

"I've been gone a while."

"Jesus, you might as well be married."

"Not quite." Although the idea of being married to Sarah wasn't as unappealing as it should be. She'd be his and no one else's. She'd actually have to go to court to get rid of him. He grinned as he finished his beer.

"She's probably still pissed at you anyway." Mattie tapped the shot glasses when the bartender brought the full pitcher back. "Two more." He handed her some money and she left again.

"Yeah, and getting more pissed the longer I'm gone."

The bartender filled their shot glasses and gave Mattie his change. His brother tipped her a ten and let his eyes linger on her cleavage.

She smiled at him. "I get off in an hour. You gonna buy me a drink?"

"Absolutely," said Mattie.

"Great." She turned and walked away to pour another drink.

"I'll stick around for an hour but then I'm gone." He'd be his brother's wingman, not that Mattie needed it, especially with the bartender. She was set on getting laid by one of them.

"Right, you get to go home to your quiet sex." Mattie laughed. "Oh right, she's mad at you. You don't even have that to look forward to."

"I'll have you know that Sarah gets as turned on as I do when we fight." He almost sighed. "Pissed off sex is great." All sex with Sarah was great.

"Oh, angry sex is the best but you"—Mattie slapped his shoulder—"don't get to have that. Not with her dog around."

"Fuck." His brother was right. For a minute, he'd forgotten about Tank.

"You should get him a friend. The poor guy is probably lonely. There you are, fucking his master and all he gets to do is stare at you."

"He's neutered. He's not jealous."

"Even neutered guys need love."

"You're an idiot but..." He tossed back his shot. "You know

what? That's a great idea." He texted Ethan and chugged his beer.

"I don't like how you said that."

His phone beeped and he read the text. "Mike will be here in fifteen minutes to pick us up." He refilled his glass and topped off his brother's. "Drink up."

"Why are you calling Ethan's driver instead of an Uber?" Mattie downed his beer.

"Because Uber drivers don't let dogs in their cars."

"What dog? What are you going to do?" Mattie refilled his beer.

Nick downed his drink. "I'm going to take care of the Tank situation."

CHAPTER 53: NICK

The pound was ready to close when Nick and Mattie showed up. Luckily, Bob, the guy who worked there, was a regular customer at Mattie's garage so he let them into the building.

Nick wandered up and down the lines of cages. This was the saddest place he'd ever been.

"You need to hurry," said Bob.

"What about this one?" asked Mattie. "He looks so sad."

Nick walked over to the cage where Mattie was crouched trying to coax a brown and white, long haired dog over.

"That's Diamond," said Bob.

"What's the matter with her?" asked Mattie.

"Heart-broken," said Bob. "Her owners surrendered her and another dog. The other dog got adopted and Diamond has been like this ever since."

"Why would they only take one?" asked Mattie.

"Happens a lot," said Bob.

"You shouldn't let them separate the dogs," said Nick. It was wrong to break up a pair.

"Then they'd both be dying tomorrow."

"Tomorrow?" said Nick and Mattie.

"Yep." Bob pointed to the sign on the cage. "Due out date is today. Today was her last chance to get a home."

"Shit." Nick didn't need another fucked-up dog. He bent and called to her. She turned her head to stare at the wall.

"You have to take her," said Mattie. "We can't let them kill her because she's sad."

He stood. He was a sucker. "Fine. We'll take this one." Now, he'd never have sex again. Diamond and Tank would team up against him and get too upset any time he looked at Sarah.

"You sure?" asked Bob.

Mattie had wandered over to a lone puppy. "This one is due out today too."

Now, this was more like the kind of dog he needed. It was a young, all black puppy. That would keep Tank busy. "Okay. I'll take this one instead."

"What other ones are going to be killed tomorrow," asked Mattie.

Nick wanted to beat the shit out of his brother. He didn't need to deal with this. "We don't have time—"

"This one." Bob pointed to an old, black dog with a gray muzzle. "And this one." It was a brindle pit-bull type dog. "He's scared of everything, poor guy. Found him running the streets. Had some cuts that weren't accidents." He moved down the line. "And this one." He pointed at a hound dog, with floppy ears and a bouncy attitude. He moved to the next cage. "This one has tomorrow before he has to go." It was a Rottweiler. "People are afraid of him because of how he looks, but he's just a big baby." He opened the cage. "Aren't you, fella?" The rottie almost knocked him over as he clamored for attention.

"I need a drink," mumbled Nick.

"Sorry, can't help you with that." Bob pushed the rottie back into the cage and closed the door.

"The limo," said Mattie.

Bob's eyes brightened. "I wouldn't say no to a drink while

you decide."

"Let's go," said Mattie.

The three of them left the kennels and headed to the limo. It was probably the worst mistake he'd made in a day full of mistakes.

CHAPTER 54: NICK

"Are you sure this is a good idea," whispered Mattie.

"Yeah. Of course." Nick tugged on the two leashes, pulling the hound and the old dog behind him. The older one was lagging as if he were already tired and the younger one was busy sniffing the hallway at the Club. The black puppy in his arms licked his cheek. "It's okay, sweetheart. You get to come home with me."

He didn't bother knocking on Ethan's office door. He just barged inside. "Ethan," he yelled.

"Back here," answered Ethan.

"Come on," he said to Mattie.

"I don't think this is a good idea," whispered Mattie, none too quietly.

He shoved into the back room. Ethan and Terry were sitting at the table playing poker.

"What the hell?" Ethan dropped his cards.

"Jesus, Nick," said Terry. "Are you planning on taking your girlfriend's dog out in a dog fight or do you never want to have sex again?"

"Had to tell him, didn't you?" His friends gossiped worse than women.

"Of course, but what the fuck are you doing with...five dogs?" Ethan's eyes darted between Nick and Mattie. "In my Club?"

Nick closed the door, dropping the leashes and putting the

little dog in his arms down. "This was your fault." He went to the bar and poured himself and Mattie a drink—not that either of them needed another.

"My fault? I wasn't even with you," said Ethan.

Mattie turned the two dogs he held loose. Diamond moved to the far side of the room and leaned against the wall, looking sad. The pit-mix slunk across the room and hid under Ethan's desk.

"You called my brother." He pointed at Mattie. "This was his idea."

"Hey, wait a minute." Mattie grabbed his drink. "I said you should get a dog—one—to keep Tank busy while you and Sarah fucked." He took a sip. "Poor guy is probably lonely."

Ethan scratched his head. "That might work but why five?" The hound ran over to him to be petted.

The oldest dog already had his head resting on Terry's thigh.

Nick flopped down on the couch. "They were going to kill them. All of them." He picked up the puppy and she licked his face, her tail wagging so hard and fast she was wiggling all over his lap. "Even this little sweetie."

"Sarah's not going to be happy about having another five dogs," said Ethan.

"If you were married, I'd offer to represent you." Terry had been one of the best divorce lawyers in town, but he left that kind of work to his employees now and mainly handled business law.

"I'm not keeping all of them."

"What are you going to do with them then?" Ethan's voice was tense. "You aren't leaving them here."

"I think you should have an office dog. It'll be great for the place." He nudged Mattie who'd sat next to him.

"Yeah. Women love dogs," said Mattie.

"I don't need a tool to pick up women," growled Ethan. "And none of these dogs are staying here."

"I'll take this one." Terry patted the old dog.

Nick's mouth dropped open. He hadn't expected that, not from Terry.

"What? I can't like dogs?" Terry actually looked offended.

"No. It's just..." He had no idea what to say. Terry wasn't the warmest guy but he was a pure dom and he supposed dogs were natural submissives.

"I hate going home to an empty house and"—Terry shrugged—"we all know how Nick can be. We either help him or he'll whine at us for eternity."

"I don't whine. I persuade."

"Whatever. I figured I'd take the oldest. It won't be around as long." Terry scratched the dog's ears and it closed its eyes in ecstasy.

"You work all the time and when you're not working, you're here," said Ethan.

"I sleep at home. I'll hire a dog walker."

"That one doesn't like to walk much," muttered Mattie.

"Perfect," said Ethan.

"Mattie?" yelled a guy from the other room.

"Back here, Jake" answered Mattie.

"You invited my sou chef here?" Ethan gave Mattie a disgusted look.

Jake walked into the room. The hound and the puppy raced over to him. He bent and petted them, laughing as they pushed

259

against him knocking him to the floor. "What's going on?"

"Your shift is over, right?" asked Ethan.

"Yeah." Jake continued petting the dogs.

"Get a drink," said Ethan. "You'll need one."

"Thanks." Jake stood and made himself a drink, topping off the others' glasses with their beverage of choice.

"Nick needs homes for four of these dogs," said Ethan.

"Three," corrected Nick. "I'm taking one."

"Which one?" asked Ethan.

"The puppy."

Ethan pulled out his phone.

"Who are you texting?" he asked.

"Annie. She loves dogs."

"Great idea." He should've thought of that.

"Patrick is going to be pissed," said Terry. "Annie's been pestering him about getting a dog and he doesn't want one, not yet."

"I know." Ethan grinned. "Serves him right for fucking Annie when I told him to watch out for her."

"What's his problem?" Jake nodded at Diamond who was lying on the floor next to the wall with her head on her feet. "He sick or something?"

"No." Nick tried not to snarl. People were so cruel. "She was surrendered with a friend. The friend got adopted and she didn't. She's been sad ever since."

"That ain't right." Jake walked over to the large, fuzzy dog.

"They tried to get them adopted together but the people didn't want her," added Mattie.

"What kind of fuck-head does something like that?" Jake knelt and let the dog sniff his hand before petting her. "Who wouldn't want her?" He lowered his voice and spoke to the dog. "You're a pretty girl and sweet." She licked his hand.

"Looks like you found a home for another one," said Ethan.

"What? No. I can't." The dog nudged Jake's hand and wagged her tail. He looked at her. "I would but I can't. I work too much. You'd be lonely."

The dog turned her head away from him and sighed. It was the sound of sadness and defeat.

"Ah, shit. Fine. You win." Jake bent and kissed her head. "You come home with me."

"Only two to go," said Ethan.

CHAPTER 55: SARAH

Sarah lay in bed, staring into the darkness. Tank was curled up on Nick's side. Yeah, the jerk already had a side. A side that was filled with her dog and not him. It was after midnight and he still wasn't home. Damn, there she went again, moving him in and giving him more access to hurt her.

She rolled over. Maybe, he wasn't coming back. No, he'd made plans for next weekend. He was coming back but it'd be after he'd fucked every woman at that stupid Club. She'd rather be alone than with a man who cheated on her and it was cheating. They'd agreed to monogamy for six weeks. It didn't matter that they'd had a fight. She expected...demanded fidelity, something he couldn't provide. It was over. She would not—would not—put up with a cheater.

A car pulled into the driveway and Tank sat up barking. She wasn't ready for this confrontation. She wasn't ready for this to end, but life never cared what she wanted.

There was a knock on the door.

"I'm coming." She took a deep breath and crawled out of bed. She had on a T-shirt and sweats. She should put on a bra but it was only Nick and she wasn't letting him in anyway. She walked to the door. "Go away."

"Sarah, it's Ethan."

"I...I'mm...snot go...ing away." That was Nick and he sounded drunk—very drunk by the slurred words. "Why do yous want me...ta go away?" Now, he sounded hurt.

"Sarah, please open the door," said Ethan.

"No. He's not coming in this house after spending all day at your Club fu…." She decided to leave it at that. She didn't even want to imagine all the things he'd done.

"Saarahhh…pleeease. I neeeed you." Nick again.

"He wasn't there for that. He was only there to annoy me." Ethan paused. "Please, Sarah. I swear he didn't go into the business part of the Club."

She hesitated. Ethan had no reason to lie, plus she wanted to believe him. She unlocked the door and opened it.

"Saarahh." Nick grinned and lurched toward her.

Tank growled softly.

Ethan staggered forward, keeping his arm wrapped around Nick's waist, holding him up and veering away from the dog.

"Oh, good lord." She stepped aside. Nick was plastered. "Tank, down." The dog sat by her legs, a low rumble in his chest.

"Where to? He ain't light." Ethan eyed the large canine.

"Sorry. This way."

"Saarahh, I misssed you." Nick mumbled as Ethan followed her into the bedroom, half-dragging Nick.

"Stay." She shut the door in Tank's face. She didn't need him biting Ethan.

Ethan dropped Nick onto the bed, repeating her command. "Stay."

Tank growled and scratched at the door.

Nick sat up, grabbing her hand and kissing it. "Come here, baby."

"I'll be right back." She blushed as she pulled her hand away from him. "I have to show Ethan out."

"Hes can find his owwn way out." Nick reached for her

263

again but she easily dodged his hand. He frowned, staring at her. "Don't be mad at me, baby. I'm sorry."

"I'm not." She leaned down and kissed him softly, but he grabbed her, his hand going to her ass and pulling her onto the bed.

"Ah...Sarah...I...ah, there's something of Nick's in the car that I have to give you." Ethan fidgeted at the door, obviously not wanting to exit and face the growling dog.

She shoved away from Nick, breathless. Even drunk that man could kiss. They hadn't had drunk sex yet. Apparently, tonight was the night because as much as she should be mad at him, she wasn't. She was too happy that he was back.

"Baby, pleeease. I neeed you." Nick started unbuttoning his pants—a large bulge already pressing against his zipper.

She had to get out of there before Nick exposed himself. She opened the door, grabbing Ethan's arm. "Tank. Down." She led Ethan out of the bedroom.

Ethan pulled free and bent. "So, this is Tank." The dog sniffed his outstretched hand. "I heard a lot about him."

"I bet you have and none of it favorable." She laughed.

"Nah." Ethan was scratching behind Tank's ear. "Nick loves dogs."

"Tank sure likes you." She'd never seen her dog take to anyone like this. Tank already had his head pressed against Ethan's chest as his tail wagged slowly.

"We veterans recognize each other."

"How did you..." She wanted to slap herself in the head. "Of course, you know." Ethan had run an extensive background check on her before she'd signed up at the Club. He probably knew what she usually ate for breakfast.

"I'm sorry about Nick." Ethan stood.

She glanced at the door and as if sensing her, Nick hollered, "Saraahhh, hurry up. I need to be inside you."

Her face had to be redder than blood right now.

"I'm really sorry about Nick," mumbled Ethan.

"He's drunk." She looked Ethan right in the eyes. "You swear he wasn't with anyone else?" She and Ethan weren't close but she didn't think he'd lie to her about this.

"No. Not while he was at the Club. He and Mattie went out drinking. I don't think he was with any women then either."

But he wasn't sure. He couldn't be.

"But that's not why I was apologizing."

"Oh."

"He wasn't supposed to find you. It was against the rules."

"Oh. That." She bit her lip and then continued, "Actually, I'm glad he did."

"Saarahh, get in here now. I need you to suck my dick," yelled Nick.

"Really? You're glad." Ethan's eyes sparkled.

She was going to kill Nick. "Yes, but he won't be getting that for a long time."

Ethan laughed and then sobered. "Still. He shouldn't have gone after you. I would've kicked him out of the Club but he'd already signed over his membership."

"He did what?"

"He didn't tell you?" Ethan's eyebrows rose.

"No." Apparently, Nick had some secrets too.

"He signed over his membership to his brother."

"When?"

"About two months after you last saw each other."

265

She almost lost her breath. He hadn't used the Club for more than two months before he found her. He could've been with someone outside of the Club but..."Why?"

"I think it's obvious but you'll have to ask him." Ethan headed for the door.

She didn't want to ask Nick. "Please Ethan, why would he do that?"

"I shouldn't have said anything. I wouldn't have if I'd known he hadn't told you. I figured that would've been one of the first things he'd mentioned." He shook his head. "The man is a genius at business but he's sure fucking this up."

"Damn it, Sarah," yelled Nick. "Come to bed."

Ethan hesitated at the door. "Give him a chance. He's a good guy and he's trying." He grinned. "Maybe, too hard."

"What do you mean by that?" By the humor in Ethan's eyes, this wasn't good.

"Step outside with me for a minute." He opened the door. "And leave Tank inside."

"He gets upset—"

"It'll only be a minute. I swear."

She stepped outside, leaving Tank whining at the door. Great. Now, she had two males whining in her house.

Ethan walked to his car and opened the door, crawling half inside. "Come on. It's okay." He straightened and a skinny, brindled Pitbull followed him out of the car.

"Oh, you got a dog." She moved toward them and bent, extending her hand for the dog to sniff. The dog came forward, head down and tail tucked between his legs, but wagging frantically. "You're a good boy." She petted him and glanced up at Ethan who was watching her with a smirk on his handsome face. "He's a sweetheart."

"Glad you like him because he's yours."

"What?" Her voice was a little shriller than it should've been and the dog jumped away.

"You heard me."

"I have a dog."

"Okay. It's Nick's then."

"No." She glanced at the house as if she could see him.

"Yes." Ethan handed her the leash. "He thought Tank needed a friend."

"I'm not taking this dog." She kept her fist closed.

"Then he goes back to the pound and his time was up." The dog stood between them, cowering as his tailed continued to wag. "Apparently, this guy had a hard life. He was found on the streets and he'd been abused. Pits have a hard time finding homes as it is, but when they're nervous like him, people stay away."

"You keep him."

"That's not going to happen."

"You need a dog. I don't."

"If Nick couldn't persuade me to take any of the other four, you're not going to talk me into taking this one."

"Four?"

"Yeah." His lips twitched. "There were five whose, shall we say, time was up and another one who would've been killed the next day. Mattie took the other one and Nick found homes for the four. That left this guy." He patted the dog's head and the dog leaned against his leg.

"Nick took them all."

"Yep." Ethan took her hand and placed the leash in it. "He

saved six dogs because of you." He turned and got into his car and drove off down the street.

She looked down at the dog who was staring up at her. "What am I going to do with you?"

By the time Sarah got the dogs settled, she was ready to kill Nick. She couldn't just put the two dogs together which meant she'd had to take the new dog around back and leave him in the yard. Then, she'd gone into the house, letting Tank sniff her as she shoved him into her bedroom where Nick was snoring peacefully. She'd been so pissed she'd wanted to shake him awake but then she'd have to deal with him. Instead, she'd coaxed Tank to jump onto the bed. The dog was not a gentle jumper and he'd half landed on Nick which had unfortunately caused nothing more than a grunt.

She'd left the room and let the new dog into the house while she'd prepared the guest bedroom for him—putting down food, water and one of Tank's dog beds. Finally, she'd sat on the couch, letting Tank sniff her but he was more interested in the scents coming from the guest room. He sniffed under the door, whimpering a little. The new dog didn't make a sound and that was a good sign. He didn't appear to be aggressive with dogs.

"Come on." She called Tank and locked him in the bedroom with her and Nick. Nick was stretched out on his stomach sound asleep, with the covers tossed over his hips. He was naked, or at least his upper body was and since he'd been horny before he'd gone to sleep she was pretty sure his lower body was just as bare. She stared at all that glorious skin and muscle. She ran her hand down his back and over his ass. Wetness pooled between her legs. Even angry with him, she wanted him. She pulled off her clothes and cuddled up next to him, soaking in his warmth.

CHAPTER 56: NICK

Nick rolled over and groaned. His mouth felt like he'd eaten a towel and his head pounded. He was home, in bed, but he had no idea how he'd gotten here. Last night was a bit of a blur. He got up and went into the bathroom. He turned on the shower and stepped in, letting the cold water snap him awake. He rested one hand against the wall and opened his mouth, drinking the water until it turned warm. He shut his eyes and let it soak into his skin, cleaning out the poisons of the alcohol. He should know better than to go out drinking with Mattie.

Things always got out of hand with his brother. The kid was an expert at finding trouble and convincing him to do the stupidest things. His mind tumbled over images and his heart began to race. Mattie belonged to the Club now but he hadn't gone there, except to talk to Ethan. They'd gone to a bar and had watched football. There'd been the cute bartender, but he hadn't touched her. He hadn't touched any woman. His heart beat normal again. He didn't know what he would've done if he'd fucked up his chance with Sarah.

He turned off the water and got out of the shower, drying off. He brushed his teeth and went into the bedroom. He needed to get something to eat and go back to bed for a few hours. A nice round of sex would help clean his blood too. He opened his duffle bag. It was empty. All his clothes were gone. They were going to have a chat about this. He grabbed a towel from the bathroom, wrapping it around his waist before storming out of the bedroom. She was sitting at her desk working.

"We need to talk." He was done with her pushing him away.

"Yes, we do." She glanced at him. "Get dressed first."

"I would if I knew what you did with my clothes. You can be pissed at me if you want but throwing them out won't make me leave. I can go to my place and get more."

Her eyes widened, but she remained silent. "Are you done?"

"We aren't even close to done with this conversation."

"I put your clothes away." She turned back to her computer.

Away? What did she mean by that? He walked slowly back into the bedroom and to the dresser. He opened the drawers, almost reverently. His clothes were piled next to hers in neat stacks.

"We...we can get another dresser if we need to."

He spun around. She was standing in the doorway, looking nervous.

"Thank you." His heart almost exploded as he moved toward her.

She nodded, her gaze sliding down his body, making his dick even harder, and then back up to meet his.

"Where's Tank?" He closed the bedroom door. Breakfast could wait.

"Stationed outside the guest bedroom." Her breathing picked up a notch. She was as turned on as he was.

"He okay?" He stopped in front of her, waiting to touch her, making her want it as much as he did.

She nodded, her tongue darting out to wet her lips. His eyes stayed on those lips. They'd be soft and warm and she'd open for him without any coaxing.

"I missed you." He ran his hand over her cheek and then around to the back of her neck.

"I wasn't sure you were coming back." Her hands were on his chest now, just resting there.

"Always." He lowered his mouth to hers, unable to wait another moment to taste her.

Her arms went around his neck, pulling him closer as she opened for him. His tongue played with hers, as his hands pushed up her shirt, taking her exercise bra with it. He cupped her breasts, tweaking her nipples and she moaned into his mouth. There was no movement outside the door—no Tank whining or barking—but he'd have to make this quick. He lowered his mouth to her nipple sucking gently, teasing it with his teeth and tongue. She pressed his head closer and moaned low and loud.

He shoved her shorts down as he continued to torment her with his mouth, half-listening for the damn dog. He was pretty sure he heard toenails on the floor but then they stopped. She kicked off her shorts and underwear and his hand stroked between her legs. She was hot and wet, ready for him.

He kissed his way up her neck as he slipped one finger inside of her. "I want to drop to my knees and bury my face in your pussy but you won't be quiet, will you?"

"I...I can't." She was thrusting against his hand now. Apparently, she'd missed him too.

"I need to hear you cry out when I fuck you and we only have so much time before Tank comes whining." He shoved two fingers inside of her, his dick hardening even more at the way she clung to him. He skimmed his thumb over her clit.

"Please..." Her hands were clawing at his back. She was more than ready.

He grabbed her leg, lifting it to his hip. With his other hand, he grabbed his cock and positioned it at her entrance.

"Condom," she whispered in his ear.

He gritted his teeth. It'd only take one second and he could be inside her with nothing between them. "Please, Sarah. Not this time." He kissed her hard on the lips and rubbed the tip of his dick against her clit. "Just this one time."

"We...can't." Her body was still pulling him close, her leg tightening around his hip.

"It'll be okay. I swear." He kissed her ear and pushed forward, letting the tip of him enter her. She felt fantastic—hot and wet and tight.

"No." She stiffened, dropping her leg. "Stop it."

"Fuck." His body trembled as he took a step away from her. "Why? Fucking, why? We're living together. You're going to give me a key. Why can't we fuck like a couple?" He'd been so close to perfection.

"Why?" She shoved him away. "I've told you a hundred times. I could get pregnant. You can't swear that won't happen." Her face was flushed and her eyes sparked green fire.

"And if you did, would it be that bad?" The idea of her belly swollen with his child didn't frighten him as it should but apparently it appalled her.

"Oh, not for you, but for me and the baby...that's another story." She pulled down her bra and shirt and grabbed her clothes from the floor.

"What kind of ass do you think I am?" It hurt that she didn't know him better than that.

"I know exactly the kind of ass you are. You're the kind that pays for a woman to have an abortion or just sends her and his kid money so he can feel good about himself."

"I'd never do that." He grabbed the towel from the floor, wrapping it around his hips. "If you wanted an abortion"—that thought killed him—"we could discuss it and if that's what we decided of course I'd pay, but if you had our baby I'd insist on being a part of his or her life."

"Don't you dare start changing your story now. You made it very clear how you felt and what you'd do."

"What are you talking about?"

"During the Interview." She stepped into her underwear and shorts, her anger shifting to disbelief. "You don't remember do you?"

"I..." His mind scrambled, trying to recall the conversation. He'd been so hot for her that day.

"You had all the answers for a possible pregnancy."

Through this entire fight, he'd still had a raging hard on, but that...that memory killed it.

"I see you finally remember. That's why we need to use condoms." She turned and left the room, slamming the door behind her.

He dropped onto the bed. He'd been an arrogant ass. Ethan was right. He'd been like a child. He ran his hand through his hair.

"Don't forget you have a dog to take care of," she yelled from the other room.

A dog? Tank was her...Oh shit. More memories from last

274

night flipped through his head. Not only was he an arrogant ass but he was also an idiot.

CHAPTER 57: NICK

Nick stepped out of the bedroom, not sure how to talk to Sarah about this. She was in the middle of the living room putting up a dog cage.

"Need help," he asked.

"No. I got it." She hooked the last piece into place. "I'll take Tank into the bedroom while you take Sweetie out back."

"Sweetie? You named the Pitbull, Sweetie?" He grinned but she didn't crack a smile. It was going to be a long day.

"Yeah, unless you want to call him something else. I had to call him something when I brought him in, alone, last night and took care of him this morning while you slept."

"I'm sorry about that." He was going to have to work hard to get back on her good side and—his eyes roamed over her slender body—back in her pants.

"I'm going to take a bath. That'll give you time to let him explore the yard and the house before Tank and I come out of the bedroom."

"Okay. Sure." Obviously, he wasn't invited to the bath, even with a condom. "Is there anything you need me to do?" *Like join you? Fuck you? Eat you out until you scream?*

"Just take care of your dog." She closed the bedroom door behind her and Tank.

"Got it." It was time to kiss some serious ass and not in the way he enjoyed.

His best bet was to do what she said...for now. He went to

the guest room and grabbed the leash from the door handle. He opened the door. Sweetie was lying in the corner. He had a dog bed but he wasn't using it. Instead he was as far away from the door as possible. Sweetie wagged his tail but didn't move.

He squatted and called to the dog. "Come here."

Sweetie stood, keeping his head down as he crept toward him. The poor dog jumped when he put his hand on his head to pet him. He bit back a curse. He'd like to find the bastard who'd abused this dog and kick the crap out of him.

"It's okay." He gently ran his hands down the dog's sides, letting Sweetie get used to him. "You want to go outside?"

Sweetie continued to wag his tail with his head down. Nick hooked the leash onto the collar. "We'll get you a new collar. This one is garbage." It was the flimsy one that'd come from the shelter. He stood and led the dog out of the bedroom and toward the backyard. "We'll get you a really nice collar. We'll get your name on it and a tag with my phone number so if you ever get lost, you can find your way back." He patted the dog's head as he opened the back door. "You have a microchip but this would be just in case that didn't work. Technology doesn't always you know."

He stepped into the yard. Sweetie seemed okay as Nick walked him around, checking the fence to ensure the dog couldn't escape. He let him off the leash. Sweetie stayed right by his side. He grabbed a ball that must belong to Tank.

"Here, boy." He tossed it.

The dog stared up at him, wagging his tail.

"Go get it," he prodded.

The dog didn't move.

"Damn it." He was in enough trouble. He didn't need Sarah

pissed because Tank's ball was in the middle of the yard. "You're supposed to be doing this," he grumbled as he went to retrieve the toy.

Sweetie glanced at the door and at Nick's retreating form. "Come on." Nick bent and grabbed the ball. The damn dog stared at him and then went and stood with his nose to the door. Apparently, Sweetie was done with the outside.

When they went back inside it was the same thing all over again. Sweetie didn't even bother to sniff or explore the house. Instead, he ran to the guest room and waited at the door. As soon as Nick opened it, the dog hurried to his corner and curled up.

Nick sighed. "I don't think you're going to be much help to Tank."

Sweetie wagged his tail, his head lying on his paws.

Nick grabbed the dog bed and moved it to the corner. Sweetie stood and then got onto the bed, circling a few times before lying down.

"You'll probably make Tank worse." It was all Annie's fault. She'd fallen in love with the puppy. He'd tried to get her to take Sweetie too but she'd wanted a playmate for the puppy and had settled on the hound. That'd left him with the neurotic Pitbull. He grabbed the bowl of food and water and moved them closer to the dog. "If I can't even have quiet sex anymore, you're a dead dog." He bent and petted Sweetie. "Just kidding, buddy. We'll figure it out."

He went into the kitchen and started making something to eat. It was almost lunch. This might be his chance. He moved to the bedroom door only hesitating a moment before walking inside. He patted Tank who was stretched out on the bed and

278

tried to sound casual as he walked into the bathroom. "I'm making something to eat. Are you hungry?"

His dick went from flaccid to painfully hard in less than a second. Sarah was in the tub, her hair piled on top of her head, tendrils falling around her face. There were a few bubbles but he could see almost every detail of her long, lithe limbs. Her face was flushed from the heat of the water. "Sarah..." It was a benediction. He worshiped her, wanted to worship her with his body.

"No. I already ate." She stared at him.

He wasn't giving up yet. "Do you want me to wash your back or your hair?"

She swallowed and her green eyes darkened. He took a step closer. There was hope.

"No." She took a deep breath. "Not this time. Please, close the bedroom door when you leave."

His stomach knotted and his dick protested. All he had to do was touch her and she'd cave, but the hurt in her eyes stopped him. He nodded and left. Shit, he had some apologizing to do.

CHAPTER 58: SARAH

It'd been so hard to tell Nick no, but Sarah had to stay strong at least for an hour or so. The problem was she wanted him as much as he wanted her. She'd missed him last night but they needed to talk. Sex didn't solve everything, although it did put a soft glow around their problems. She got out of the tub and dried off.

She dressed in a pair of shorts—ones that flattered her long, thin legs—and put on a push-up bra and tight T-shirt. Oh yeah, she and Nick would have sex, but he'd pay first. Now that she knew him better, she didn't think he'd actually meant what he'd said about a baby, but if he did feel that way there was no future for them. She dabbed on some perfume and dried her hair. She was in this for the long haul—either until he left or they decided they wanted different things. She had to give him a chance to explain.

When she went into the living room, Nick was sitting on the couch watching football. Tank trotted straight to the guest room.

"You could've put Sweetie in the cage." That was why she'd put it up.

"He wanted back in the bedroom. He's still scared." He turned toward her and his eyes darkened.

Her nipples hardened and she started getting wet—just by a look.

"Sarah—"

She walked toward her desk. "He can't hide in the bedroom the rest of his life." She stopped mid-stride. That'd hit a little too close to home. "I'm going to take Tank outside. Put Sweetie in the cage. He needs to get used to us. Used to new things."

"Shouldn't we give him tonight? This is all new."

"No." She swallowed. "He had last night and all of today. If you give him too much time, he'll get comfortable being alone and won't want to change."

Nick's eyes sharpened and that familiar panic started to claw its way up her throat. She couldn't have him looking at her like that. Not with pity. "Tank, come." She hurried to the door before she lost it.

Once outside, she took a deep breath. She hated that look, especially on Nick's face. Logically, she knew it didn't mean he was leaving her—going off with the woman he loved and then dying—but her mind wouldn't believe it. She needed to see Dr. Smileworth. She needed to get better, not only because of Nick but for her. She followed Tank around the yard, taking deep breaths and by the time they were back at the door she was breathing normally again. When she stepped inside Sweetie was curled up on the blanket inside the cage. Nick was still on the couch but he was sitting as close to the dog as possible.

"Look how he's looking at me," said Nick. "It's like I betrayed him by making him come out here."

Tank hurried over to the cage, his tail wagging as he sniffed around the enclosure. Sweetie didn't move, just continued to stare at Nick with disappointment.

"He'll get over it. He'll like being out here soon." She hesitated again. "It's for his own good." And so were her sessions with the therapist.

"If you say so." Nick glanced at the dog. "She made me do it."

She laughed and Nick smiled at her, making her heart melt.

"Sarah—"

"You need to call your friend and cancel." She interrupted him again. She wasn't ready to let him touch her and that's where his tone was leading. Her body was already responding. She moved across the room to her desk. It was safer.

"What friend and cancel what?"

"Next weekend. You should've spoken with me before you made plans." Her eyes went to the dog. "Among other things."

"I know. I'm sorry. I should've talked to you before getting the dog but..."

"Nick, if we're going to try being a couple—"

"We aren't going to try. We are a couple," he snapped.

"If we're a couple we need to discuss big things...like getting a dog."

"I just said that."

"What made you think getting another dog was a good idea?"

"Do you have to talk to me from across the room?" He was really getting pissed now.

"It's safer this way."

"Safer? I'd never hurt—"

"I'm not afraid of you." Her face heated. "I missed you too and...if we're close, I don't think we'll finish our conversation."

"Oh." He grinned and patted the couch. "Then I insist that you sit right here so we can talk."

"Too bad." She laughed.

"What did you say? I can't hear you from over there." He patted the couch again.

"Seriously, Nick."

"I am serious."

"I'll sit by you as soon as we're done talking."

He sobered. "Okay. I'm sorry about Sweetie, but once I got to the pound and realized that he was going to be put down...I couldn't leave him." He looked at the dog. "He'd already had a rough life. We can give him a better one." He looked at her. "It may not be perfect, but what is? I'm not perfect, but I'll love him and keep him forever."

She was pretty sure her heart stopped. She didn't think he was just talking about the dog. "What about the other ones?" Now, she was only half-talking about the dogs.

"Other ones? Who told you that I—"

"Ethan said you adopted five dogs."

"Ethan has a big mouth," he mumbled.

She bit her lip to keep from smiling. He didn't realize it but Ethan's loose lips had wedged Nick further into her heart.

"Actually, between Mattie and me we adopted six. Mattie is getting a Rottweiler that was due to be killed today. He had to wait for him to be neutered before taking him home. We took the other five to the Club."

Her face must have twitched or something because he started speaking faster.

"I didn't go into the business part of the Club. Only the office area to talk to Ethan. I swear."

"I know."

"How do you know?"

"Ethan."

"Oh."

"And before you complain about his big mouth, I wasn't going to let you in last night. I won't tolerate cheating."

"I understand and I agree." His eyes had sharpened.

"Good." Like she had anyone to cheat with.

"Are we done talking?" He patted the couch. "I think I'm all talked out and could use a break." He glanced at the dogs. Tank was lying by the cage. "Tank seems preoccupied."

"We still have more to discuss."

"I was afraid you'd say that."

She tried not to laugh, but he was so damn cute. "You haven't called your friend yet."

"Why do we have to cancel? You'll like Patrick and Annie and you'll love Annie's food. It was her pizza recipe—"

"I already made plans for us"—she held up her hand—"and before you tell me that I shouldn't have made plans without talking to you, I did it for you. I had to agree to watch Kyle next weekend if you want me to go to your sister's party or if you ever want to spend another weekend at your place."

"If *I* want to? Like you don't want to do that too." He captured her eyes with his. "Admit it, Sarah. You can't lie to me. I was there."

Her face heated and it was going to heat more. "Yes, I like going where we...can do whatever we want as much as you do."

"Then why don't you come over here and we'll see just how into Sweetie Tank is."

"Call your friends."

"And then you'll sit by me?" He pulled out his phone. "In the bedroom."

"What about on the couch?"

284

"No reason to test Tank too quickly."

"True." She was more than ready to give in to his demands.

He hit a button on his phone, waited a moment and said, "Hey Patrick, we have to cancel next weekend." He paused. "We're babysitting Sarah's nephew." He rolled his eyes. "Stop laughing. I don't know." He walked over to her, holding out his phone.

"What? I don't want—"

"Annie wants to talk to you." He raised his voice. "Since Annie is a pushy brat, it's best to just hear her out."

"Hey," yelled a female voice from the phone.

Nick, put the phone in Sarah's hand. "Talk to her. You'll like her," he whispered.

"Hello?"

"Sarah, I can't wait to meet you. I've heard so much about you. Nick is...Stop that, Patrick." Annie's voice came back to the phone. "Sorry. Apparently, I'm not allowed to tell you how much Nick pined for you...Hey, stop it." There were muffled sounds of arguing and then Annie came back and sighed. "I like kids and if you don't mind we could still come over."

"Um...I don't know." She glanced at Sweetie who was sniffing in Tank's direction.

"I understand. That's okay. I just want to meet another couple. All my friends are single. So, Patrick and I don't do too much with them."

"If you don't mind hanging out with a ten year old then I'd"—she glanced up at Nick—"we'd love to have you come over."

"Really? Great."

"Do you want me to make...buy anything?"

"The booze," yelled Patrick.

"Just supply the drinks," said Annie.

"Are you sure?"

"I love to cook so yeah, I'm sure." She almost squealed. "This will be so much fun. I can't wait to chat and...Oh, sorry. I have to go."

"Okay. Bye." She hung up the phone and gave it back to Nick.

He caught her hand, his fingers caressing her skin. "Thank you."

She nodded as he bent, kissing her softly. He straightened and tugged on her hand.

"We still have some things to talk about." Not that she actually wanted to talk right now, but she liked making him work for it.

"We can talk in the bedroom. We'll undress as we talk. Kind of a tribute to our first night together." He tugged again and she stood.

She was already wet and ready for him, this would only make it that much more exquisite. Unlike that first time, she wasn't nervous only eager. She followed him into the bedroom, glancing at Tank. The dog was watching her but he didn't move even as she shut the door.

Nick was right in front of her, his chest brushing against hers. "Getting that dog was a good idea. Admit it."

"It was an excellent idea."

"I love when you admit you were wrong." He grinned.

"I never said we shouldn't get a dog. I said you should've talked to me first."

He kissed her nose. "Same thing. It would've taken time

and we wouldn't be in here...alone...right now. Admit I was right."

"Fine."

"Good. Now give me your shorts."

"Oh, is that how this is going to work?"

"Yep."

"If I remember correctly, you remove them."

His smile spread across his face. "That's right. I do."

"So, you were wrong and that means I get your shirt."

"Ladies first." He lifted his arms.

She took her time and not just to tease him. If he'd let her, she'd spend hours touching his body, but it always led to sex. Not that she minded that. Not at all. She trailed her hand up from his waist, enjoying the smooth warmth of his skin under her fingers. He was so hot and hard—everywhere.

"You're a tease," he muttered.

"It's my turn. Deal with it." She pushed the shirt upward so it trapped his arms.

"Payback, baby," he growled around the shirt that was resting right under his chin.

"I'll deal with that when it happens." She squeezed her legs together in anticipation as she raked her nails down his chest, and then back up to circle his nipples.

He let out a low guttural groan and pulled his shirt over his head.

"Hey, I'm not done yet."

"You'd better hurry. This game is ending fast." His hand rested on the back of her head and the other one came to her hip. "I missed you last night. And this morning. And this afternoon."

She glanced up at him and licked her lips, enjoying how his eyes darkened. She lowered her head and kissed his nipple, pulling it into her mouth and teasing it with her teeth and tongue.

His head dropped back. "God, Sarah." One hand held her to his chest as his other one pulled her hips against his. He was hard and throbbing.

She couldn't stop her hand from going farther southward and stroking him through his pants. "You have too many clothes on." They both did. She was done with this game. She unbuttoned his pants but he stopped her before she could unzip them.

"My turn." He backed her against the door and knelt.

Her body melted at the thought of the pleasure to come. He leaned forward, trailing hot, open mouth kisses across her abdomen. "I love these shorts." His hands skimmed up and down her legs, in a whisper-like touch. "But they have to go. Rules are rules." He grabbed her shorts with his teeth and tugged them downward, but only one side lowered. "Oops. Have to take care of this." He kissed his way across her body again, but this time he was lower—his mouth dancing over the top of her pussy.

She shivered from the heat and promise. He grabbed the other side of her shorts with his teeth and lowered them. He pushed her legs apart so that the shorts didn't drop. "Gotta fix this." He kissed his way to the other side. His mouth still not low enough.

He tugged on her shorts and she brought her legs together, so they could fall to the floor. He rested his mouth on the top of her mound, breathing against her hot, needy flesh. She buried her hands in his thick, silky hair, pulling him closer, but the most he'd do was give her teasing little licks through her panties. She could fix this. She grabbed the waistband of her underwear, but he stopped her from pushing them out of her way.

"Question, Sarah. That's the game."

His hot breath teased her and she shivered. "Did you really sign over your membership to your brother?"

He froze like a naughty statue kneeling before her.

"It's okay if you didn't. I didn't expect you to. I was surprised." Happy was a better word. "I mean, I didn't really believe it when Ethan told me." But she'd wanted to believe him. "Two months without going to the Club would've been a very long time." She stopped herself from saying for a guy like you. He hated it when she said that and she was in no mood to fight. She wanted sex.

"You have no idea," he grumbled, his mouth still pressed against her pussy—so close and yet so far from where it needed to be.

Now, she stilled. Her hands were back in his hair. She didn't remember moving them there, but she must've. She let the silky, soft strands slip through her fingers. "You actually gave up your membership? For me?"

He looked up at her, his eyes searching hers for something. "Yes."

"Oh, Nick." Her heart wanted to explode and melt at the same time. She cupped his face and started to lower herself toward him.

"Oh, no." He grabbed her waist. "I answered your question. I get my prize." He yanked her panties down so fast she gasped, but that gasp turned into a moan as he lifted her leg over his shoulder and kissed her. He didn't play this time. He went right for the promised land—his tongue claiming her as he held her open, his fingers playing with her clit.

She collapsed against the door, her body shaking. She was going to come fast this time. His lips moved to her clit and he sucked as his fingers dipped inside her, searching and then pressing against her g-spot.

"Oh, oh, Nick." Her hands dug into his scalp as she came, her body trembling and clenching as he continued to finger her and suck her clit, sending her crashing over the edge.

She hadn't even stopped shaking when he hopped to his feet. The sound of his zipper made her blink and then he was sheathing himself in a condom.

"Tank's whining," he said against her mouth.

He was right. The dog was right outside the door, whining softly. She wrapped her arms around him. "You'd better fuck me fast then."

"You got it."

His mouth came down on hers, swallowing her moan as he shoved into her in one long thrust. He kept kissing her as he pulled almost all the way out and pushed back in to the hilt. She couldn't stop her moan of pleasure. He always filled her just right. He was long and hard and he thrust into her again and again. She clung to him, wrapping her legs around his thighs. He lifted her higher, his hands on her ass as he slammed into her. She bumped against the door and Tank whimpered louder.

"Hurry." She broke the kiss and shoved her tongue into his ear. That always made him lose control.

"Fuck, Sarah." His pace became faster, more desperate—all rhythm gone but her body tightened in response.

He grabbed her hair, pulling back her head for his kiss as he rocked into her. He bent his knees a bit, shifting his angle and she screamed as he hit a spot so deep and so sensitive that it sent her flying into her release. Her body clutched at him, not wanting him to leave and then he was back, hitting that spot again, but this time he stayed there, his body shaking and he groaned in her ear as he came.

He was still inside her when he carried her to the bed. He slid out as he placed her under the covers. He kissed her and walked to the door, opening it for Tank.

The dog raced into the room and hopped on the bed. She patted the side, not Nick's side, and the dog nudged her before stretching out next to her. Nick crawled into the other side, pulling her close.

"Tank's getting better," he said. "He didn't try to bite me."

She laughed. "No, he didn't."

"Sweetie is going to work great. I know it." His hand skimmed down her body and slapped her thigh gently. "Soon, I'll be able to turn you over my knee and give you the spanking you deserve for torturing me all the time."

"Torturing you?" She leaned up. "Oh, I forgot to tell you something." She bit her lip. "Tell. Ask. Whatever."

"What?" His hand skimmed over her skin, sending little sparks of desire through her satiated limbs.

"Ah…"

"Don't be shy. Haven't you learned that after sex, a man will give you anything you want?"

She smiled. "No, I haven't learned that, but thanks for the tip." She kissed him. "I don't have all that much experience with relationships, as you know."

"Well, there was Peter."

"Um. That wasn't...Let's not talk about him." She was going to have to tell him sooner or later, but later sounded good to her.

"Good idea."

"You know that we're watching Kyle next weekend."

"Yep. You made plans for us without talking to me, but you didn't get into any trouble for it." He smiled. "See why you need that spanking?"

"I told you why I did that." She kissed him again, but this time his lips captured hers for a sweet moment before she leaned away, slightly breathless. "Maisie wants to...wanted me to ask you..."

"Yeah?"

"She wants to try some kinky stuff and she has no idea where to get the things or what to get." She lowered her face to his chest. "This is so embarrassing."

"Embarrassing? Why? I had you strung up and hanging—"

"Trust me, I remember." Those memories started a heat in her belly. "But, that was us, not my sister."

"Sisters." He laughed. "I just went through this with Patrick."

"You need to explain that because I'm imagining all kinds of things that I hope aren't true."

"Annie is the sister of one of Patrick's best friends. Let's just say he had a hard time coming to grips with his desire to fuck her in every way imaginable."

"Oh." She laughed. "That's much better than what I'd imagined. I was thinking that Patrick strung up his sister like you did me."

"What? No." He sounded appalled.

"Will you help Maisie? Will you tell her what to buy?"

"I'll do better than that." He crawled out of bed and came back a minute later with his phone. He got back in bed and punched a contact. "Ethan. Yeah, I need a favor." He paused. "No, I didn't adopt any more dogs. Shut the fuck up." He mouthed asshole to her. "No. Sarah's sister and her husband." He held the phone to his chest. "She wants to do this with her husband, right?"

"Yes." She slapped his arm. "Of course."

He turned back to the phone. "Sarah's sister, Maisie, and her husband want a tour of the Club."

Sarah's mouth dropped open. Her sister was in for a big surprise.

"Yeah, they want to start experimenting. I don't know. Probably just together but you'll have to ask them. Yeah, give them a room and put it on my tab. Next weekend." He looked at her. "What days?"

"Friday through Sunday afternoon."

"All weekend, starting Friday," he said into the phone. "Thanks." He hung up and tossed the phone on the nightstand. "There. Done. You can tell Masie she owes us the weekend after." His hand trailed down her back and rested on her ass. "And you owe me too. It's my turn to pick the fantasy."

"I thought we were going to your sister's party?" Hopefully, he'd changed his mind.

"We are, but we won't stay long." His hand began exploring her backside. "After that, we'll go to my place. You. Me. Toys."

"What fantasy did you have in mind?" Suddenly, she was

looking forward to next weekend.

"I'd like to go back to teaching school."

WEEK THREE: THE APOLOGY
CHAPTER 59: SARAH

The bed moved and warm, strong arms wrapped around Sarah, pulling her close.

"Hmm." She wiggled against Nick. She no longer dreamt of Adam, only Nick. "Is Kyle asleep?"

He kissed her neck. "Yep."

"What time is it?"

"One." His hand slipped under her shirt and rested on her belly.

"One? Kyle has to go to baseball practice tomorrow morning."

"I know. We kind of got carried away." He'd bought the latest video game system and games and the two of them had been playing since Maisie had dropped Kyle off after school. "He promised he'd get up with no problem."

"He's a kid. They always say that." Kyle was going to be a crab tomorrow. "You're going to have to make him take a nap. Not me." Kyle felt he was too old to nap.

"A nap." Nick sounded offended and then he kissed her neck again. "Actually, a nap could be nice." His hand caressed her stomach. "It'd give us a little private time before Patrick and Annie come over."

She couldn't help the slight tension at the mention of his friends. She wasn't sure she was ready to meet them. They might hate her or what if they noticed she was different?

"You'll love them." He pulled her closer. "Don't worry."

"I'm not good with new people."

"It'll be fine." He kissed the back of her head. "I promise."

She entwined her fingers with his against her stomach. "Okay." She was trying to believe him, to trust him.

He kissed her head again. "I'm sorry about what I said."

"What are you talking about?" She rolled onto her back.

"When we first met." He leaned on his elbow, staring down at her. "I'm not going to lie to you. I meant what I said at that time or I think I did. I mean, if you'd gotten pregnant and had wanted to abort, I don't think I would've thought twice besides paying. But if you'd kept it...I think...I hope, I would've been a part of that child's life." He brushed some hair from her face. "I was an ass. I know that now." He raised her hand to his lips and kissed it. "Because of you. Ethan told me that I'd grown up a lot since I met you. I didn't agree until I realized what a dick I'd been."

She stared at his handsome face, so earnest. She didn't know what to do with this information. He wasn't denying that he'd said and meant those horrible things but people changed. Adam had changed. He'd stopped loving her. Now, Nick had changed but he still wanted her.

"I...hope you can forgive me. Trust me. One day." He kissed her hand again and stretched out on his back.

She was glad he wasn't staring at her, expecting her to forgive him—to forget—right now, because she couldn't. Tank nudged her, probably sensing the tension. She stroked the dog's fur. She needed to say something. He deserved that much. "I'll try. That's all I can promise."

He rolled over again so they were face to face. "Thank

296

you."

"It…it isn't easy for me to trust, especially that."

"I know." He took her hand again. "I promise. I won't ask about the condoms again. You decide when you're ready."

"If I'm never ready?" She wasn't sure she'd ever be willing to risk that unless she was married and ready for kids.

His eyes dimmed a bit. "I'll live with it, but…"

"But what?" Here it came. He'd try and persuade her. Try to convince her to see things his way.

"One day…you'll have to do it without condoms if you want kids." He swallowed, his eyes searching hers.

"I know." She wasn't ready to think about him and her that far down the line. *Liar.* It was the entire point of them living together. They were in a relationship and relationships moved forward to marriage and kids, at least for her they should.

His eyes dimmed a little more when she remained silent. "Okay." He rolled onto his back, but his arm went around her, pulling her to his side.

She rested her head under his arm and her hand on his chest, feeling the beat of his heart. Did it belong to her? If it did, for how long?

CHAPTER 60: SARAH

Sarah and Annie sat on the porch sipping wine and talking. She really liked Annie. The other woman was outgoing and friendly and it was nice to have another woman to talk to. For years, her only friend had been her sister.

"I can't get over that he's mine." Annie stared through the sliding glass door where Patrick and Nick sat on the couch playing video games with Kyle.

"Yeah." She felt the same about Nick, although she couldn't help worrying that her possession was on borrowed time. As soon as he figured out how fucked up she was he'd bail. Who wouldn't? She'd been afraid tonight would give him clues but Annie had been so friendly and open and the doctor's suggestions had helped. She'd focused on breathing and keeping contact with the things that made her most comfortable. Her hand had stayed either on Tank or Nick for the first part of the evening, but she was relaxed now.

"Your nephew is great," said Annie.

"He is." And so was Nick.

He was Kyle's new hero. Besides the video games which were the key to any young boy's heart, he'd even taken Kyle to baseball practice today. Nick hadn't said anything, probably because of Kyle's presence, but he'd been upset that she'd stayed home. She'd wanted to go and sit with Nick on the bleachers in the sun while Kyle practiced. She'd wanted that more than anything but she wouldn't have been able to do it.

She couldn't handle the openness of the field and even the small crowd of parents and players made her nauseous. She would've had to stay in the car. Nick wasn't stupid. He'd see there was something seriously wrong with her and she couldn't let that happen. Not yet. Not until she was better. She didn't have to wait until she was cured...only better. Good enough that he wouldn't run away from her screaming.

"And Sweetie seems to have settled in." Annie glanced at her. "Hopefully, he's just what Tank needs."

She stiffened a moment. Was that a jab at her? That Nick was what she needed?

Annie flushed. "Nick was pretty drunk when he got the dogs so don't be mad at him."

"I'm not." But she might be, depending on what he'd said.

"It's not a big deal. I mean...I...Patrick and I like to experiment too."

"What are you talking about?"

"That Nick got the dog so that you and he didn't have to always have quiet sex."

"I'm going to kill him." She covered her face with her hands.

Annie laughed. "No, it's sweet. I mean, he must really care for you to go to the trouble and the fact that he adopted all those dogs." She sighed. "Now, that's the kind of guy who's a keeper." She grinned. "You should've seen Patrick with Sophie—the puppy. You'd think the dog was made of glass the way he'd handled her and cuddled her." She took a sip of her wine and fanned her face. "I mean, my uterus was clenching. He's going to make such a good daddy."

"Are you?" Her eyes dropped to Annie's stomach.

299

"No. Oh, my God, no. Not yet." Annie looked back at Patrick who must've felt her gaze because he turned and smiled at her. It was sweet and loving with the hint of heat, making Sarah melt at the thought of having that with Nick.

"But, hopefully someday not too far in the future. I want to give my business a few years of focus and then, yeah, we'll try and get pregnant."

"I'm glad for you. You'll both make wonderful parents."

"How about you and Nick?" Annie looked at him. "He's great with Kyle and the whole dog thing." She waved her hands. "If he cares this much for Tank and Sweetie, he'll care even more for his kid."

"Yeah. I think you're right." And she wasn't just saying that. Nick would make a great dad. It didn't matter what he'd said that night during the Interview. He'd be a terrific father and she needed to tell him that.

CHAPTER 61: NICK

"Is he asleep?" Nick closed his computer. Tonight had gone well. Sarah and Annie had gotten along and Kyle was great. However, it'd caused a whole lot of thinking on his part.

"Yeah." Sarah sat on the couch next to him, curling against his side.

His cock began to stiffen, but he put his arm around her, content to just hold her for a while.

"Sweetie and Tank are in there with him." Her hand skimmed up and down his thigh.

"Are they?" Apparently, she wasn't in the mood to just be held and that worked for him too.

"Yep." Her hand trailed over his cock, whisper soft and fleeting.

"Will Tank stay there all night?" He captured her hand, pressing her fingers against his hardening dick.

"Don't know. I closed the door most of the way and both dogs are in bed with him." She pulled her hand out from under his and stood. "I think as long as Sweetie stays in there, Tank will too."

"Did you want to watch TV or something?" He kept a straight face at her look of surprise but it wasn't easy.

"Or something."

"What did you have in mind?"

She leaned down, giving him an eyeful of her cleavage as her lips brushed against his ear. "I want to suck your cock until you come in my mouth."

He was hard before but now he'd have a problem walking. "If your nephew wasn't in the other room, I'd have you on your knees right now."

"If Kyle wasn't in the other room, I'd have your dick in my mouth." She turned and walked into the bedroom, her hips swaying with promise.

He hurried after her, closing and locking the door behind him. "Take off your clothes. I want you naked while I fuck your mouth."

She pulled off her shirt, dropping it to the floor. She shimmied out of her pants. "You sure you don't want me to keep this on?" She touched her breast through the white lace bra.

He could see her nipples, the little pink nubs poking through the lace. The blow job was going to wait. He had to taste her. He moved forward, grabbing her around the waist and holding her in place while he took a nipple in his mouth, sucking her through the cloth and rubbing the wet lace across the sensitive nub.

Her fingers tangled in his hair, holding him close. His other hand trailed down to her pussy.

She grabbed his wrist, stopping him. "I started my period today."

"So." He moved to her other breast, teasing the nipple with his teeth and then stopped. "Sorry." He took a step back. "If you don't want to...I get it. Are you cramping?"

"No. I mean, I was but I took some Tylenol. I'm fine."

"Good." He grabbed her and tossed her on the bed.

She laughed and started to sit up as he pounced on her,

settling between her legs.

"Now, where were we? Oh, that's right." He lowered his mouth to her breasts again and her hands went to his hair, but instead of pulling him to her, she tugged keeping him away from his luscious prize. "You can suck my dick later. Actually, I'll insist, but right now, I need to worship these." He unhooked her bra and yanked it off, freeing her soft mounds.

"You still want to...you know?"

He raised his head. "What? Fuck?"

She nodded.

"Of course. Shit. Sorry. I'm really trying not to be so...pushy. Don't you want to? I mean, it's okay if you're not in the mood. We can just sleep." He rolled off her. He couldn't believe he was going to say this. "You don't even have to give me a blow job. I can go without sex for a week." He didn't want to. It'd been hard enough without her around but sleeping by her every night and being with her most of the day and not fucking her would make him a blithering mess of a man but he'd survive somehow.

"Not in the mood? Of course, I'm in the mood." She sat up. "But you don't mind the mess?"

"Sarah, I'll fuck you any way you'll let me—hard, fast, slow, messy, clean, kinky, or straight." He sat up, his hand caressing her cheek. "I don't care about your period, but don't do this because you think I have to have sex. I love making love to you but we can wait if you're not in the mood when you're ragging."

"Really?"

Fuck, it was going to be a hell of a week. "Yes." He kissed her. It was gentle without heat, only caring.

"Thank God."

Damn, she didn't need to be so happy about abstaining.

"I'm always so horny when I'm on my period. Crazy horny." She hopped out of bed. "These are old sheets, but let me grab a towel." She hurried into the bathroom.

Crazy horny? Did that mean extra horny? She was the horniest woman he'd ever met. He was right. It was going to be a long week—a gloriously long week of fucking. She came back carrying an old navy towel. He shoved the covers out of the way and helped her stretch it out on the bed.

She crawled up by him. "Now, let's get these off." Her hands went to his pants.

He lifted letting her tug his pants down. She straddled his legs, and leaned forward, kissing his chest and working her way down his body.

Her tits swayed as she moved and then she blew across the tip of his dick. His body tightened as she grasped him, stroking his length. "Needs some wetness."

He needed that mouth on him. His balls tightened as her tongue came out, licking all around the top and then up and down his shaft. "Put me in your mouth." His hands tangled in her hair.

She breathed on his dick and kissed it but kept her lips together. He tried not to, but he couldn't stop from pushing her head down.

"What do you want, Nick?"

"Suck me. Open that gorgeous mouth of yours and let me fuck your face."

"You get points for being specific." She grinned.

He groaned as she took him in her mouth, sucking and flicking his dick with her tongue. His hips thrust upward as she bobbed down, her breasts swaying and her nipples hard with her excitement.

"Fuck. That feels good." He pushed her down more as she sucked, her one hand stroking him as her other cupped his balls. He was close, his body tensing. He tugged on her hair. "Enough." He groaned as she sucked harder. She was going to make him come in her mouth. He didn't want that. Tonight, he wanted to be buried deep in her body. He grabbed her face and pulled away. She let him slide from her lips.

He rolled over, pinning her beneath him as he yanked off her panties. "Tampon?"

"Yes." She reached between her legs, but he stopped her hand.

Her eyes widened as he pulled gently on the cord that hung from her pussy.

"Nick..." Her voice was unsure.

"There's nothing we shouldn't know about each other. Nothing bad about anything between us. Nothing dirty or taboo." He tugged and slowly pulled the tampon out of her.

He tossed it in the trash by the side of the bed and reached for a condom from the nightstand, but there was nothing there. "Where'd they go?"

"In the drawer." Her hands were busy stroking his side and hip. "I didn't want Kyle to come in and see them."

He bent, opened the drawer and grabbed a condom, rolling it down his length. He shifted so he was over her again and took her hand, wrapping it around his cock as he lowered himself to her. "Put me inside you."

He braced himself on his elbows, letting her guide him to her opening. She rocked her hips, rubbing his dick against her clit and moaning.

"I love the sounds you make. It makes me so fucking hot for you." He kissed her hard, his tongue tangling with hers but more of him needed to be inside her—deep inside her. "I need you."

She gasped, her body clenching around him, holding him tight.

"You feel so good." He rocked into her in long, slow strokes. In and out. Over and over. "Every time, you feel better...and better." His pace increased. One day, he was going to spend hours fucking her, but not tonight. Tonight he needed to feel her clenching around him, needed to know that she was his. That this life was his—him and her together.

"Oh, Nick. Faster." She rocked against him, clasping onto him as he withdrew. She wrapped her legs around him using her heels to help him fuck her harder.

She was close. He could feel her body tensing and her breath was coming in short pants. He reached between them and flicked her clit as he captured her mouth, stifling her scream. Her muscles squeezed his cock. He wouldn't last long. He pulled out and held her hips, keeping her still, as he shoved back into to her. She was even tighter than before, spasming in release. His back straightened and his body thrust over and over, lost to his climax. He dropped onto her, unable to move.

Her hands ran up and down his spine. After several moments he rolled off her pulling her to his side.

"Nick?"

"Hmm." He was beyond words.

"I...Tonight was fun."

"Yeah." He kissed the top of her head. "Kyle's a great kid."

"Yeah. He is. Thank you for taking him to baseball practice."

"You're welcome. How did your appointment go?"

"Fine." She rolled away from him and got out of bed.

"Where are you going?"

"To get a tampon. I don't want to bleed all over the bed." Her cheeks flushed as she hurried into the bathroom.

He started to roll up the towel, but decided against it. They'd have sex at least one more time before morning. He stretched out. He'd been pissed and disappointed that she hadn't wanted to go to baseball practice with them. It was a family-like thing to do and he'd wanted her with him. He needed to show her that he'd be a great partner, not only in bed, but in her life.

She'd made some lame excuse about having an appointment. It was possible. Her business wasn't a normal nine-to-five organization but she'd been having a lot of appointments lately. She never talked to him about them or anything else. He'd brought up his work and offered to help her with hers on several occasions, but she'd always refused or sidetracked him with sex. It ate at him that her ex was her business partner which meant she may be seeing him at these appointments. He forced the stab of jealousy aside. He trusted her. He had to. He only wished she'd trust him.

She came back into the room and crawled in bed. "I've been thinking about what you said...in the Interview and last night."

"Yeah." He pulled her closer afraid she was going to try and escape, run away from him.

"Have you ever..."

He waited but she remained silent. "Had a kid?"

She nodded, her cheek rubbing against his chest.

"No."

"Abortions?"

"No. I've never gotten any woman pregnant." Not that he was aware of anyway.

"Did you mean it when you said that you'd want to be a part of your child's life?"

"Yes." *God, yes.*

"What about what you said in the Interview?"

"Shit, Sarah." He'd thought he'd explained this but obviously he hadn't. "I was an ass. I already admitted that. I probably meant what I said at the time. I know I would've supported them, and I hope, if that had ever happened I would've wanted to be part of the kid's life but...I don't know if I would've then."

"But now, a few months later, you're different?" By her tone, she didn't believe him.

"Yeah. If you get pregnant, there is nothing, not even you, that will keep me away from our kid." His hand moved to her stomach and for one second he imagined her belly round with his child.

"What if I wanted an abortion?" She leaned up, watching him.

His eyes snapped to her face. "No. I mean, we'd need to talk about it, but I'd do everything I could to talk you into carrying our child." He glanced away from her. "If you didn't want to be a part of our lives, I guess I couldn't force you." Although, he'd try.

She touched his cheek. "I'd never not be a part of my

child's life."

He didn't like how she'd said my child and not our child.

"I think you'll make a good dad one day." She leaned forward and kissed him.

This was dangerous ground for her and that meant for him too. "You really think so?"

"Yeah." Her hand rubbed circles on his chest.

"Thanks. You'll be an excellent mother." Hopefully, his kid's mother.

CHAPTER 62: SARAH

Sarah sat in Dr. Smileworth's office, actually eager for this session to begin.

"How did the dinner with Nick's friends go?" asked the doctor. For a woman with the last name of Smileworth, she didn't smile much, but she was kind, motherly and an excellent doctor.

"Good." Sarah, however, couldn't stop smiling. "Actually, it was great. Annie is wonderful and Patrick is a very nice guy." She played with her purse strap for a moment, not sure if she should continue.

"And there was no problem with the fact that Patrick had been one of the men who'd been on your list and had seen you at"—the doctor looked down at her notes—"the Viewing?"

"No. I mean, I was nervous at first. It was more than a little embarrassing that he'd seen me in my underwear, but he'd acted like a gentleman. Of course, I'd been worried that it'd be this uncomfortable secret that everyone but Annie would know." She wrung her hands in her lap. "I didn't like that. I know what it's like to not know something when everyone else at the party does."

"Did you tell Annie? How did you handle this secret, Sarah?"

"I didn't have to say anything." She looked up at the doctor. "Annie already knew. Patrick had told her. She laughed as she brought it up. It was out in the open and...over. It was no big deal."

"How did that make you feel?"

She hated those six words but she needed to dissect these feelings in order to get better and she had to get better. "Good. I worried for nothing."

"And?" prodded the doctor.

"I was glad that Patrick had told her. Glad for her and him. They seem good together. I was also happy that I didn't have to tell her and ruin her relationship with Patrick or have her not believe me." She hesitated.

The doctor's blue eyes were warm and patient. Too patient. The doctor would wait all hour for the hard answers and if they didn't come out today, Smileworth would bring them up again. So, there was no sense in delaying.

"I was also a little sad. I wish Adam had told me about Lisa before he'd come home. I know he didn't do it to hurt me. We were young and foolish and he wasn't expecting to see me, but he still could've told me. He could've called or written. Something." She blinked back tears.

"Why do you think that still hurts you so much? It was a long time ago. Like you said there was no malice and you were both young."

"I...I don't know."

"This only works if you're honest with yourself."

"Okay." She wiped the tears off her cheeks. "I guess, I wish I'd meant something to Adam." She shook her head. "No. I did mean something to him...just not enough."

The doctor handed her the box of tissue and Sarah wiped her eyes.

"I also...Annie is very open." Her face heated. "She'd been

the maid that'd walked in on me and Nick…" There were some things she was very uncomfortable discussing with the motherly doctor. "When I first realized, I almost froze in fear. I-I could feel the panic clawing at my throat. I-I thought that…" She'd thought they'd all see her fear and realize how fucked up she was.

"What happened, Sarah?"

She blinked, the memory, the panic fading away. "Nothing. Annie brought it up. Talked about how embarrassed she was and how mad Nick was when I'd fled. We all laughed." Her face had to be scarlet by now. Talking to the doctor about her hangs up and past was hard enough but about her sex life was a little too embarrassing.

"Don't be afraid to tell me anything." The doctor actually smiled. "I may be an old woman now, but I was young once."

"Okay." She couldn't help smiling back.

"So, you're glad that they came over?"

"Yeah." She took a big, deep breath. "It's a relief. This is actually working."

"Yes, talking through these things does work, but it takes time."

"I know." She didn't have time. "I agreed to go to Nick's sister's birthday party with him."

"Is this an intimate gathering like the dinner with Patrick and Annie?"

"No. Nick's entire family will be there. It's a large family." She was breaking out in a cold sweat just thinking about it.

"We should discuss this further."

"Okay." She wasn't backing down on this. She couldn't.

"With Nick here too."

That wasn't going to happen. "He's very busy right now. He

has several new clients."

"Sarah, going to a party, a large family party isn't a good idea. Not yet."

"I went to the award banquet and gave a speech." She'd almost bolted for the door too, but the doctor didn't need to know that.

"That was a huge accomplishment, but it was also different. You were there with your brother-in-law who you've known and trusted for years."

Okay, maybe the doctor did need to hear about this. "Yes, but it was seeing Nick in the crowd that got me through the speech, not Peter."

"You didn't mention that there were problems."

"There wasn't. Not really. I froze on stage but only for a moment and then I saw Nick and everything was fine."

"Hmm."

"Nick will be with me at the party. I won't be alone." She could do this. She had to do this.

"I still think it's a little early for something so similar to the situation with Adam."

"This isn't the same. Nick's with me not another woman."

"I know but triggers happen." The doctor leaned forward and took her hands. "Recovery takes time. If Nick truly cares for you, he'll understand that."

"You don't think I should go." It was like the air was let out of her body.

"Not this time. Next time, maybe." The doctor squeezed her hand. "You're doing great but you need to take smaller steps. If you jump in, you may lose the ground you've already gained."

"I understand." Between now and the party she was going to have to take a lot of small steps because there was no way she was backing out on Nick.

"Good. Let's go back to your dinner party. How did talking about the Viewing and the Interview with Annie, Patrick and Nick, make you feel?"

"Like I said embarrassed at first, but good. Once it was out, there was nothing to be scared about." She wanted to roll her eyes. "And yes, I see where you're going with that."

"Smart patients are always a blessing."

"Nick and I talked about some other things too, after Annie and Patrick left."

The doctor waited patiently for her to continue.

"He was great with Kyle. I swear Kyle idolizes both him and Patrick, but especially Uncle Nick as he started calling him." She stared down at her hands in her lap.

"And that's a problem."

"No. Yes. I don't know. I mean when...if Nick leaves Kyle will be crushed."

"I'm sure he'll get over it. Kids are resilient and Kyle still has his parents and you."

"Yeah." They both knew it wasn't actually Kyle she was worried about. "When I first met Nick, he'd said some things about kids." She paused, feeling a little disloyal talking about this. "I was worried about getting pregnant and he...he didn't want to use protection."

"I see."

"I insisted and he said that he'd pay if anything happened."

"For an abortion?"

"That was up to me. He didn't care." That was the worst

314

part. "I could get an abortion or he'd pay child support."

"And that bothered you?"

"Of course, it bothered me. A child needs his parents not a paycheck."

"Like your baby would've needed both you and Adam?"

"Yes." Her hands were shaking now. "Even if Adam didn't love me, he would've been in his child's life."

"And Nick won't."

"That's just it. We talked. He apologized. He was very honest about it. He...he doesn't feel that way anymore and I believe him."

"But?"

"I think he'd make an excellent father."

"He sounds like he would."

"You really think so?" She needed an outside opinion. She wasn't sure she was thinking with her head.

"It doesn't matter what I think."

She hated when the doctor did this. "Yes, I think Nick would make a great dad."

"If he were around."

That was the problem. "I don't think he'd abandon his kid even if he left me."

"Do you think he's going to leave you?"

"Yes. No. I don't know." She didn't want to talk about this.

"And that frightens you."

"Yes, but it shouldn't. I mean, no one can promise forever. Even marriage isn't always forever."

"How do you feel about Nick now?"

Her deep breath was shaky. "I'm crazy about him, and it scares me to death."

"Strong emotions are always frightening."

"When Adam left...died and so did my...our baby, it almost broke me. It might have if I hadn't had Tank." Sweat was trickling down her back. She took deep breaths to ease the panic away. "If Nick leaves me, I might not survive. My life isn't perfect but it's a good life. I have work I love and family."

"But it's not enough, is it?"

"No and that's Nick's fault."

"Is it?"

"Yes. I was fine...happy before I met him."

"Then why did you go to the Club?"

Damn. The doctor had her there.

"Sarah, our time is almost up and I want you to think about this." The doctor leaned forward. "You cannot control what other people do. You could not control Adam falling out of love with you and in love with Lisa. You could not control Adam dying. You can't control what Nick will or won't do in the future." The doctor took her hands. "All you can control is how you react. What you do."

"Thank you." Sarah stood and the doctor let go of her hands and walked her to the door.

"Bring Nick with you next time. I'd like to talk to both of you."

Panic flared to life. "Ah, he's so busy with work right now."

"We can meet at a different time. I have evening appointments on Tuesdays and Thursdays. Talk to him and call me."

"One of us still needs to be there for Tank." That was a lie and she was pretty sure the doctor wasn't buying it.

"Then send him alone. I'd like to get his input on some of

these things."

She swallowed. "I'll tell him."

"Sarah, if Nick can't take an hour out of his day for something this important to you...maybe, you should think long and hard about this relationship."

CHAPTER 63: SARAH

Sarah sat in her car at a stop light. She had to do something. Dr. Smileworth was getting more and more adamant about meeting Nick and that wasn't going to happen. She had no intention of telling Nick anything about her problems.

Her stomach grumbled. It was almost lunch. There was a Chili's up ahead. Her hands shook but she forced herself to turn into the parking lot. She stopped the car and stared at the building. She had to do this. She had to get better faster. The doctor was pushing and Nick was getting suspicious. He hadn't said anything yet, but he'd asked her to go out with him on several occasions. He'd tried the movies, dinner, dancing, a concert and a play and she'd found some reason to refuse each time. Usually, she sidetracked him with sex but more and more, she'd see the doubt in his dark eyes and for days afterwards she'd catch him watching her closely as if trying to puzzle her out. She couldn't afford for him to realize that she was nuts. She had to get better.

"You can do this. It's just lunch." She got out of the car and walked to the restaurant—her stomach doing flips. She opened the door and went inside, wiping her sweaty palms on her pants.

"Hi, how many," asked the young hostess.

"One." Her voice squeaked but the hostess didn't seem to notice.

"This way."

She followed the woman to the table, the noises of dishes and chatter making her head spin. A man glanced up at her. She looked away. She could not pass out. She would not pass out. This had been a mistake. She needed someone here—Nick, Maisie, Tank, Peter—someone she could hold on to, someone to make her feel that everyone wasn't staring at her and that her world wouldn't collapse around her.

"Your server will be right with you." The hostess waited for her to sit and put a menu on the table.

"Th-thank you." She stared at the menu, ignoring all the people around her. *They aren't watching you. They aren't.*

"Can I get you something to drink?" The waiter was a cute, young guy.

"Margarita. Double."

"Frozen?"

"No. Straight with salt."

"Coming right up." He smiled again, his eyes roaming over her, but not with pity, with interest, sexual interest.

That she could handle. She smiled back. "Thanks." As soon as he left, she stared at the menu again, pretending she couldn't decide what to order. She shouldn't have come here. She should go.

The waiter delivered her drink and she ordered a turkey club with fries. He took her menu. She pulled out her phone. She had to have something to look at, but this wasn't helping. She took a big gulp of her drink and gasped slightly. It was definitely a double. Her hand shook as she put the phone on the table. She leaned back, and forced herself to look around. No one was looking at her—not with pity, not with interest, not at

319

all. It was great. She sipped her drink, a feeling of relief and pride slipping through her. She could do this. She was doing this. A woman looked up at her. She gave the lady a slight smile before looking away. She was the one staring and she had to stop. She grabbed her phone and started checking emails.

The waiter came back with her food and she ordered another drink. She was in a restaurant. Alone. It was liberating.

When she finished her lunch and her third margarita she left. Lunch had been awesome. She was making progress. She truly was. She couldn't wait to get home to Nick. She wished she could share this with him, but then she'd have to explain why going to a restaurant was such a big deal. Still, she could jump his bones. Warmth spread through her belly and lower. She pulled her keys from her purse and dropped them on the ground. Oops. Maybe, driving wasn't such a good idea. She'd had thee margaritas—all doubles. She wanted more margaritas and Nick.

There was a Walmart was across the street. She could go shopping. Panic tickled her spine but the tequila flicked it away like a pesky bug. She'd gone to lunch alone and no one had cared. She could do Walmart.

She texted Nick.

SARAH: I'm going to Walmart. We're having tacos tonight and margaritas. Be ready.

She walked across the street. She was really doing this. Her phone beeped.

NICK: Okay. Do you need me to do anything?

SARAH: Yeah. Me. I need you naked in bed.

She giggled as she waited for his reply.

NICK: I take it your meeting went well.
SARAH: Fabulous and now I need liquor and sex. I need
your hard cock so deep inside me that I can't speak.
NICK: Sounds like you've already had the liquor.
SARAH: Only three margaritas. They were great.
NICK: Where are you?
SARAH: Walmart.
NICK: Which one? I'll pick you up.
SARAH: The one by Chili's. Stop at your house and get your
handcuffs first.
NICK: Don't drive. I'll be there in about forty minutes.

Sarah slid the phone in her pocket and stared at the door
as people walked past her. A few glanced at her but it didn't
matter because it wasn't pity on their faces; it was irritation.
She was blocking their path. She giggled again. Irritation she
could handle.

She walked inside and grabbed a cart. It'd been years since
she'd been in a Walmart. Nothing much had changed. The
layout was different but the place was still packed with people
who were busy—babies crying, people pushing carts and filling
them, and no one paying any attention to her. It was perfect.
She was surrounded by people and yet more alone than in her
house.

CHAPTER 64: NICK

When Nick found Sarah at Walmart she had a cart full of stuff. "Hey, what you got there?" He was trying hard not to laugh. She was adorable when drunk and happy and today she was both.

"Isn't this place great?" She grinned at him. "They have everything." She dug in her cart and pulled out some oil. "This heats up with friction." She leaned close to him. "I think we can get some friction going, don't you." Her eyes dropped to his pants.

He snatched the lotion as a few people glanced at them. "Yes, I think we can." He grabbed the cart. She was so damn cute. Her hair was rumpled and she had a silly grin on her face. He wanted nothing more than to kiss her but that'd get him in trouble because one kiss with Sarah was never enough. "Come on. Let's go home and try out your oil."

"I'd like that." She trailed after him. "Did you get the handcuffs?"

"Shhh." He laughed as a few women glanced at them.

"Oh. Right. Sorry." She took his hand, intertwining her fingers with his. "I'm glad you're here."

"Me too." This was the first time she'd made him feel like she wanted him for more than sex. Before her, he never would've thought being wanted only for sex would've bothered him, but he wanted more with her. He could hold her hand for hours, just being near her made him feel—full, content and happy.

They got in line and he pulled out his wallet.

"I'll pay for my stuff." She dug in her purse.

"I got it."

"No. I went shopping. I picked it all out. I'm paying."

That wasn't happening but she was stubborn and he wasn't in the mood to fight. If they did that here, they'd only fight. If they did it at home, they'd fight and fuck.

She pushed in front of him to get to the cashier.

"Did you remember limes?" He'd seen them in the cart. "We need them for the margaritas."

"Oh, I don't know. I think so."

"Check the bags. We don't want to forget them."

She started searching the bags and he paid the cashier.

"Here they are?" She grinned at him, holding up the bag with the limes.

"Great. Let's go make some margaritas." He led her outside to his car.

He loaded the groceries and got into the car. She was flopped against the seat, staring out the window. He prayed she didn't pass out before they got home because she was so cute and all the talk about handcuffs and oil had him rearing to go.

"I want to give you a blow job while you drive."

"Oh, no." He stepped on the gas. They needed to get home soon.

"Oh, yeah." She leaned toward him.

He put his hand on her forehead, keeping her from lowering herself to his lap. "As soon as we get home." Her hand skimmed over his thigh and across his cock. "We don't even have to get out of the car. We can do it in the garage."

She slid her hand inside his pants. The breath hissed between his teeth.

"Sarah, stop. I'm driving." Her hand wrapped around his growing cock. "It....fuck. That feels good."

"Let go of my head and it'll feel better."

"If I let go of your head, we'll get in an accident."

She ran her thumb over the tip of his penis. "Stop the car."

"I can't stop the car. We're in the middle of the street."

She laughed. "Pull into a parking lot."

"We'll get arrested." Shit, when had he become some old eunuch? No, this was crazy. He wasn't going to let her suck him off in some parking lot. "Sarah, we can't." He stopped at a light and grabbed her hand, shoving her back to her side of the car. "Stop it."

She frowned, her lip jutting out in a pout. "Fine."

"As soon as we get home—"

"No. I don't want to do it now."

His jaw clenched as he followed the other cars. "This isn't a good side to you."

She shrugged. "It's your fault. I was having a great day." She smiled. "A wonderful day. The best day I had in years and now you ruined it. All I wanted to do was suck your dick, but no, you're too scared."

"All you wanted to do was get us killed or arrested. Jesus, are you sure you only had three margaritas?"

"Yeah, but they were doubles. Oh,"—she bit her lip and a jolt of heat went straight to his crotch—"I had a shot too. No two shots of tequila."

"Fuck." He drove faster. She was going to pass out before he got her home and then he'd have to take a cold shower or jerk off. Neither was appealing. "So, what happened that made this such a great day?" Changing the subject should keep her awake and away from his dick.

"I went to Walmart and Chili's."

"Okay." He glanced at her. "What happened there that was so wonderful?"

Her mouth opened and then snapped shut. "It's not important. It was just a good day." She turned and stared out the window.

"Tell me. Please." He was getting really tired of her keeping secrets and pushing him away.

"You wouldn't understand."

But Peter would. He didn't say it but he wanted to. "Who did you meet with today?"

She paused. "No one."

"You said you had a meeting."

"I did."

"Then who did you meet with."

"It was personal."

Personal. Fuck. She wasn't cheating on him. She wasn't. She'd called him because she was horny. Women who were fooling around with their old boyfriends didn't do that. "You said it was a business meeting."

"It was. It was a personal, business meeting."

He pulled the car into the garage and got out, grabbing the groceries. She grabbed the bag of limes and stumbled into the house.

"Do you want a margarita?" She called out from the kitchen.

"I think you've had enough." Now, he sounded like his

parents. What the fuck was she doing to him?

Sweetie ran up to him as he walked into the kitchen and dropped the bags on the counter. Tank was sitting at Sarah's feet.

"You're right. I don't feel like making margaritas." She tossed the lime that she'd cut into a bowl. She added the salt shaker, grabbing the bowl and the bottle of tequila. She strolled toward him, her hips swaying seductively.

He leaned against the table, his anger disappearing as all his blood flowed to his cock. He could fight with her later.

She put the limes and salt on the table and opened the bottle of tequila. "Body shot." She grabbed his shirt and pushed it up, letting her tongue trail up his chest as she removed his clothes. She grabbed the salt and sprinkled it on his wet skin. She licked him again before taking a swig of tequila. She snatched a lime from the bowl and bit into it.

His eyes never left that pink, perfect mouth. He wanted it wrapped around his dick like she'd promised. "My turn." He grabbed her shirt but she slapped his hands away.

"No. Tonight, I'm in charge."

His spine stiffened. He wasn't in the mood for her games, but he'd play for a little bit. "May I have a drink?"

"Not yet." She pulled out a chair and sat. "Take off your clothes."

That was a command he could get behind. He unbuttoned his pants and unzipped them slowly, watching her eyes follow the descent. As he pushed his pants down she licked her lips and his knees almost buckled. He kicked off his shoes, pulled off his socks and removed his pants. She was staring at his cock and it liked the attention, growing under her perusal like a tree

326

grows from the sun. He moved forward. Sitting in that chair, she was at the perfect height to suck his dick.

"Stop," she said when he was only inches away from being close enough for her to touch him. "Get into the bed."

He nodded and turned walking into the bedroom. He swore he could feel the heat from her eyes on his ass. She followed behind him—close but not too close. He crawled onto the bed and leaned against the headboard. She put the tequila, salt and limes on the night stand.

"Can I have a drink now?" All he needed was to touch her and this game would be over.

"Where are the handcuffs?"

Yes. Thank you, God. He'd have her tied up and be inside her in a moment. "I tossed them in the bag with the oil." He started to get out of bed.

"Stay. Where did you put the bag?"

"On the kitchen counter."

"Wait here." She called the dogs who'd followed them into the bedroom. She returned a moment later, closing the door behind her to keep the dogs out. She tossed the bag on a chair and threw the handcuffs at him. "Put these on."

"What?" He caught them. "No. Fuck no." There was no way he was wearing them. He wasn't in the mood to be tortured, even with pleasure.

"I've worn them. Now, it's your turn."

"I don't want to."

She frowned. "Please. For me."

He groaned. "Sarah…"

"Don't you trust me?"

"Of course I do, but…" This wasn't about trust it was about

327

control and he liked to be in control but so did she…sometimes.

"The last time, I told you not to touch me you cheated."

His mind scrambled to the past. "I was steadying you. You almost fell."

She laughed. "It may have started that way but you kept touching." She started unbuttoning her shirt. His eyes followed her fingers. "Please, Nick. I want to be in charge."

"Fine." He slid the chain around one of the headboard rails and put his hands in the cuffs. "Happy." She didn't know it but there was an emergency release. He wasn't restrained any more than he wanted to be.

She removed her shirt, keeping her green lace bra on.

"I love that color on you."

"I know." She removed her shoes and pants. "Why do you think so many of my undergarments are this color?"

She crawled onto the bed, straddling him. He could feel the warmth from her pussy. He shifted upward a little but she leaned over, her breasts brushing against the side of his chest as she grabbed the tequila, two limes and the salt.

"Lick." She tipped her head, offering her neck.

"That's not what I want to lick," he mumbled before running his tongue across her skin.

She shivered and sprinkled some salt where he'd kissed her. "Again."

He did, taking in the salt mixed with the taste of her.

She tipped the bottle to his lips and he took a gulp. She leaned forward with the lime in her mouth. He bit and then spit it out, capturing her lips. Her tongue tangled with his as she rubbed against his erection.

"Touch me," he whispered against her mouth. He needed

328

her hands on him. "Stroke me."

"Not yet." She sat up, keeping her pussy a few inches above his cock. "I'm thirsty, but you need to lie down."

He rocked his hips upward, pressing against her hot cunt and she moaned. He slid down the bed, the restraints coming with him. He shifted until he was flat on his back, his arms above his head.

"That's a good boy. You deserve a present." Her eyes locked with his as she kissed and licked her way down his body.

She kissed his hips and across his abdomen, skipping around his erection. She lifted her head, her eyes now on his cock. He tensed waiting for her to put those lips and that tongue on his dick. She blew across him, her breath hot and fleeting.

"Please, Sarah." He needed her. He was ready to burst.

She licked around his head and flicked him with her tongue.

"Suck me, baby. Please."

She stroked his cock as she took him in her mouth, sucking and bobbing.

He moaned. Her mouth felt fantastic, hot and wet and it was making the best suction. She hummed against him and the vibrations made his hips buck. "Fuck. Do that again."

Instead she lifted her head, letting his cock slip from between her lips. "Not yet. I get to come first."

"Sure. Okay. Ladies first. Unhook me."

"No." She sat up, removing her panties and then her bra. She straddled him again, moving up his body until her pussy was right above his face. "Ready?"

"Yeah. Come here." He couldn't wait to sink his tongue

inside her. She was hot and gleaming right above him—just out of reach.

CHAPTER 65: SARAH

Sarah couldn't believe she was holding herself over Nick's face, making him eat her out. He didn't seem to mind, his eyes were black with desire. She grasped the headboard and lowered herself. He was staring right at her pussy and then his tongue was there, licking her in one, long, smooth stroke. Her fingers tightened on the headboard and her arms trembled as he lapped at her.

"Lower, baby." His words vibrated through her.

She moved downward and he buried his tongue inside her, his nose bumping into her, so close to her clit. She gasped. "Nick..."

He pulled his tongue from her and licked up the side, teasing her clit—one side and then the other. Her thighs trembled. She wanted to collapse onto him but she didn't want to smother him.

His tongue darted inside of her and then he repeated the process. "Let my hands go so I can stroke you with my finger," he said between licks.

She wanted to but if she did that he'd take over. She shook her head. "Keep licking and suck me, please."

He moved his face so his lips were on her clit and he sucked, sending flashes of pleasure shooting through her body. He stopped and flicked her with his tongue. Then his lips were back on her nub and he sucked her into his mouth, gently scraping her with his teeth. It was too much. It hurt and felt fabulous all at the same time. She buried her face against her arm to muffle her scream as she came. Her grip tightened on the headboard as her hips bucked against his face. He continued, licking and sucking, making her orgasm go on and on.

As her body slowed, his kisses slowed. After a few minutes she caught her breath and lifted off him. She wiped his face with the blanket and then kissed him, tasting herself on his tongue. She reached between them, wrapping her hand around his cock. It was slick with his precum. He was close to losing it.

"Sarah, please. I need you."

He did. He was rock hard and the head of his dick was purple. She grabbed a condom from the nightstand, opened it and slid it down his cock. She grabbed him, stroking him slowly as she lowered herself. She stopped when only his tip was inside her.

"More." He thrust upward and slid in a little deeper, but she stayed above him.

"Wait." She was still in charge. He loved to torture her by keeping her dancing on the edge of release. It was time to pay him back.

"I can't. Please." He thrust upward again but this time she lifted off him.

"Hold still or I leave."

"Son of a bitch." Now his jaw was tense with anger and frustrated passion.

"Will you behave?" She was probably pushing her luck. He'd make her pay for this later and that thought made wetness surge from her.

"Yes," he almost hissed.

She lowered herself, letting the tip of him slide inside again. His nostrils flared but he didn't move or say a word. She lifted and lowered herself again, taking another inch or so inside of her. "That's it. You feel so good, Nick." She raised and lowered again, riding him slowly, taking more and more of him with each descent.

Sweat trickled down the side of his face but besides for the muscle in his cheek, he didn't move. He was her toy, to play with and ride. She set the rhythm. She set the pace. She kept moving up and down, slowly and finally, she took him all inside. He was huge and hard, filling her and making her moan. She placed her hands on his chest, angling his dick so that he rubbed against her g-spot with each rock of her hips. Sparks flew through her blood. Everything disappeared except him and her—the motion, the pleasure. She rocked faster and faster. His hips started moving too but she didn't care. It was better this way. He hit that spot harder and harder. Her body tightened, clinging to him as she lifted—not wanting to let him leave. His hips moved faster and faster causing his cock to slam against that bundle of nerves and giving her body no respite from the pleasure. Her hands clasped his shoulders as her body tightened and shook from her release.

"Keep moving baby, please." He was still thrusting into her. He was close, but not there.

She wanted to stop, to sleep but she didn't. She was in control but she had to make this good for him too.

"Harder, baby."

She pushed against him and soon her body was tingling again with the friction. His hands were on her ass, pulling her tighter against him. He shifted her upward, his mouth latching onto her breast and he tugged on her nipple with his teeth before sucking hard. The pleasure went straight from her breast to her groin. She was going to come again. Her body was tightening, her motions becoming frantic. His fingers dug into her hips as he thrust into her and then he froze. His body stiffened as he came. His dick pressed against her g-spot, making her come again, riding his waves of orgasm with her own.

Her arms were like wet noodles and she collapsed on top of him. His hands skimmed up and down her back.

"You cheated again," she said against his neck.

"I lasted longer than I'd thought." He slapped her ass. "Be grateful."

She lifted up so she could see his face. "I am grateful. " She kissed him gently before climbing off him and curling up by his side. She'd done great today. She was definitely getting better.

WEEK FOUR: THE PARTY

CHAPTER 66: SARAH

"You look great. Relax." Nick's hand rested on the small of Sarah's back as he led her to the huge, expensive house.

"Thanks." She'd spent hours deciding what to wear and how to style her hair. Not only did she want to make a good first impression on Nick's family but looking good gave her confidence and she needed as much of that as she could get. She wore a green pastel sundress that hugged her curves. The color flattered her pale skin and her hair, which was gathered in an elegant chignon. The only flaw in the outfit was the flat sandals. "Even the shoes?" High heels would've looked better but she would've been worried about falling all night.

He stopped, turning her toward him. "Those shoes are sexy as hell." His warm, brown eyes searched her face.

"But they're flats."

He pulled her close until her chest brushed lightly against his suit coat. "They're on you. They're sexy. You look great." He kissed her.

It was only a quick brushing of his lips but she felt it to her toes. Her hands went to his waist. She wanted to bury her face in his chest and hide.

"My family will love you." He kissed her forehead. "Ready?"

"Yeah." Not at all, but the time had come. She took a deep

breath as he rang the doorbell. She could do this. She'd been able to give the speech at the banquet and that had to be worse than meeting his family.

A good looking older man opened the door. "Nick." He pulled Nick into his arms for a quick hug.

"Dad." Nick hugged his father and stepped back. "I want you to meet Sarah."

She smiled. Nick looked a lot like his father except leaner and younger. "Nice to meet you." She extended her hand, praying the man wouldn't hug her. She wasn't ready for that.

"Believe me, the pleasure is mine." He shook her hand and stepped aside as he hollered, "Bella, Nick's here and he's brought his girlfriend."

She preceded Nick into the house and with his father's proclamation, the chattering died down and everyone in the room turned toward them. The blood rushed from her face and she swayed. They were all staring at her. It was happening again.

"You okay?" Nick's pressed up behind her, his words a whisper in her ear. His hands were on her waist, comforting, supporting.

Her chest eased and she breathed, relaxing a little against him. She wasn't alone. This wasn't the past. Nothing bad was going to happen.

"Sarah, are you okay?" He moved to her side, his arm around her, his hand still on her waist.

"Yeah." She smiled at him. "Just got dizzy for a moment." It wasn't a lie.

"Do you need something to eat? Drink?"

"No. I'm fine." She kissed his cheek. "Thank you."

"Nick." An older lady wrapped her arms around him, a huge smile on her face.

It had to be Nick's mother. She was dark and lean, just like him. Most of the others had started talking with each other again.

His mother kissed his cheek before turning toward her. "You must be Sarah. We've heard so much about you." She clasped Sarah's hand in both of hers. "Between us ladies, I've been waiting years for him to bring a girl home."

"Mom." Nick sounded both irritated and amused.

"I was starting to wonder if he were one of those gays." Bella winked at her as she dropped Sarah's hands.

Sarah laughed. Nick was the most heterosexual man she'd ever met.

"Hardly, Mother. I was only waiting to find the perfect woman." He kissed his mom's cheek, but his fingers intertwined with hers. "Only the best for my mom."

"Oh Nicky, you are the charmer." Bella took Sarah's other hand. "Come, let me introduce you."

She tried not to but her grip tightened on Nick's hand. She needed him with her. There were too many people here.

"We'll both come." He kissed her fingers, seeming to understand.

Her heart slowed and she smiled softly at him as they followed his mother around the house.

The next several hours passed like minutes. She'd been introduced to too many people to remember. Most were family and extended family but there were also friends and business associates of Nick's sister and her husband. They were both doctors and highly successful ones by the look of the house and yard.

Nick led her outside, handing her a glass of Crown.

She took a deep breath and then a sip of the drink. It was her second of the night. The warmth of the alcohol helped to steady her nerves. He pulled her into his arms and kissed her; it was warm and dark with banked passion.

"How about we go upstairs?" His hand wandered down her back to her butt.

"We can't." She felt heat rush to her belly as she leaned into his erection, unable to stop herself.

He kissed her neck. "Your mouth says no but your body says yes." He squeezed her ass.

She turned her face so her lips were against his ear. She breathed softly and could feel the muscles in his arms clench. "Listen to my mouth." She kept her lips there, dying to put her tongue in his ear. It always sent him straight over the edge.

"Do it and I'll haul you upstairs so fast everyone"—he turned so his lips were almost touching hers—"will know exactly what we're going to do."

She swallowed. Nope, that wasn't going to happen. "We can't."

"We can." He leaned away from her, but kept his hands on her hips. "No one will notice. We'll sneak upstairs. We can be done in a few minutes. No one will even realize we're gone."

"That fast, huh? Is that supposed to entice me?" She skimmed her fingers over his chest, wishing she could remove his shirt. He looked great in the black suit with white shirt, but he looked better naked.

"You like it fast and hard." He leaned forward again, so his lips caressed her ear. "I can take you against the door. I'll shove

338

your dress up. I won't even take off my pants."

"We can't." She closed her eyes, desire swirling like a tornado inside her. She wanted to do it, but...Who was she kidding? She was going to do it. They both knew it.

"Hey, there you are." Nick's youngest sister Maria came outside.

"We'll finish this discussion later," he whispered before turning toward his sister, keeping his arm around Sarah's waist. "What do you want?"

"I need to steal Sarah for a minute." Maria nodded toward the door.

"Why?" asked Nick.

Sarah didn't mean to but she shifted closer to him.

"Aunt Roe is thinking about adopting a dog. I thought Sarah could talk to her."

"Sure. Lead the way." He took Sarah's hand, following his sister into the house.

Several older ladies were sitting around the kitchen table and other women and men filtered in making plates of food, chatting and eating. A few people looked their way as they entered, nodding or greeting them but quickly went back to their conversations.

Maria led them to the table and introduced the women.

"What kind of dog are you thinking of adopting?" Sarah asked.

"Oh, I don't know. Not a puppy."

"There are plenty of older dogs that need homes." She started talking in earnest with the older woman. Her fear fleeing as she warmed up to her favorite topic.

Nick whispered in her ear, "I'm going to go talk to my

cousin, Mitch. I'll be right back."

She stiffened. He was leaving her. She took a deep breath. She was fine. Everyone was friendly. This wasn't the past. This was now. This was Nick, not Adam. "Okay."

"You sure?" His hand was still on her waist. "I can stay until you're done talking."

"I'll be fine."

He kissed her cheek, using the opportunity to whisper, "Upstairs. Later."

She flushed as she turned to the women and merged back into the conversation. They discussed getting dogs from rescues and from the shelter. She was pretty sure Aunt Roe, as the woman had insisted she call her, was going to go and look at the shelters tomorrow.

"So, you rescue dogs for a living?" asked another elderly woman. "How nice."

"Yes, I do and it's a great job. Sad sometimes, but great."

"Sad? How? You rescue them," asked the lady next to Aunt Roe.

"Yeah, but sometimes they can't be saved. I mainly work with dogs that have issues."

"What kind of issues?" asked Aunt Roe.

"Sometimes physical but most often psychological."

One of the younger cousins laughed. "How do dogs get psychological issues?"

She hated this closed minded attitude but the girl was young. "Usually, from abuse. Imagine living your entire life with someone who beats you, starves you and on the best days ignores you. You never go anywhere. You never see anyone but your abuser. Or, you may see others walking by on the street but no one helps you." Her heart picked up its pace. She should change the topic. She glanced around for Nick.

"That's horrible," said Aunt Roe.

Nick was talking to a woman, an attractive woman with blonde hair. She wasn't a relative. She had her hand on his arm, leaning in to whisper in his ear. Sarah took a deep breath. It meant nothing. Nick wasn't Adam. She forced her eyes back to the table. "They can also get damaged from work."

"Work? What kind of work?" The young girl laughed again. "My dog just stays on the couch all day."

"Many dogs have jobs. I have a former military dog. He was injured during duty. His handler died." Her voice broke. Not his handler—Adam. Adam had died. She didn't want to talk about this—not here, not ever. She looked for Nick but he wasn't there. Her heart started racing.

"Oh, that's terrible," said the young girl.

She couldn't freak out. She had to calm down. She took a deep breath. "Yes, it was. Tank hasn't been the same since." She needed to get out of there. She needed Nick. Her eyes landed on the shadow of a man going upstairs. It was Nick. He'd just turned the corner at the top when the woman he'd been talking to made her way to the stairs, glancing around before following him.

Sarah's heart stuttered and then raced. This wasn't happening. He wouldn't do that, but he was. No, it hadn't been him. A lot of these guys were family and looked like him, but if it wasn't him, then where was he? Her eyes scanned the other room.

"Are you okay?" asked Aunt Roe.

Her head snapped back to the table. She tried to say yes,

she was fine, but when she opened her mouth no sound came out—only her breath. It was coming in pants. She couldn't get enough air.

"I don't think she's okay," said a petite, auburn-haired young woman who worked for Mattie, one of Nick's brothers.

"Lena, get Nick," said Aunt Roe.

The auburn-haired girl darted from the room.

Aunt Roe took Sarah's arm. "It's okay, honey. Sit down."

She shook her head. She couldn't sit. She couldn't stay, not when they were all looking at her like that...with pity in their eyes. She clutched her stomach. Nick was with that other woman. She was alone. Something bad was going to happen. Someone was going to die. She couldn't breathe. She couldn't think. She stumbled backward as blackness stole her vision, first the people on the outside of her sight disappearing and then everyone else.

"Nick," someone yelled.

Her knees buckled and blackness swept over her.

CHAPTER 67: NICK

Nick came out of the bathroom and Lena, a friend of Mattie's, grabbed his arm.

"Something's wrong with Sarah."

He shoved past Lena and raced into the kitchen. Sarah was on the floor, women surrounding her. "What happened?" He pushed through to her side. She was so pale. "Call 911."

"Already did," said his sister.

He lowered his face to Sarah's. She was still breathing. He felt for her pulse. It beat slow and steady. "What the hell happened?"

"I…I don't know," said Aunt Roe. "One minute we were having a nice conversation and the next she was pale and gasping for air."

"Then she fell," said Maria.

He cradled her in his arms. "Sarah, baby. Wake up." He brushed the hair from her face.

The soft sounds of a siren drifted closer.

"Someone go outside and wave them in. They don't need to waste time searching for the house," he yelled.

Maria and Lena hurried out of the room.

Sarah's eyelids fluttered. He touched her cheek.

"Nick?" Her green eyes were confused.

"Yeah, baby. I'm here." He ran his thumb over her cheek again. "You okay?"

"Get out of the way," yelled Maria, making room for the

paramedics.

"The baby?" Sarah grabbed his hand.

Nick felt the blood drain from his face. Sarah was pregnant. Before he could say anything, the paramedics pushed him aside, asking her questions and taking her vitals.

"I'm fine," she said but the paramedics continued their job.

"You need to go to the hospital," said Mom who'd pushed through the crowd and was holding Sarah's hand. "Let them check you out, honey." Mom kissed her hand. "Do that for me?"

Sarah nodded, her eyes going to Nick. He tried to move to her side, but the paramedics had her on a stretcher between them, escorting her out of the house.

"I'm coming with you." He trailed after them.

"We're taking her to Mercy General," said one of the paramedics. "You can meet us there."

He watched as they loaded her into the ambulance and drove away. Her eyes looked haunted as she stared at him.

"Go, honey," said his mom. "Call us and tell us how she is." Mom hugged him, handing him Sarah's purse.

CHAPTER 68: NICK

At the hospital Nick paced, wanting to pull his hair out. Sarah was pregnant. How was that even possible? She was on birth control and they always, ALWAYS used condoms. Even that first time in the bathroom at the award…That was only a few weeks ago. It wasn't his. He dropped on a chair, putting his head in his hands. She was pregnant with someone else's kid—Peter's kid.

"How is she? What happened?" Maisie hurried over to him with an older lady.

"I…I don't know." He'd used Sarah's phone to call Maisie on the way here. "She passed out. I don't know why." It was over. She'd go back to Peter. She'd want to give their relationship a try, for the baby.

"Hi, I'm Sarah's mother, Betty." The older woman extended her hand.

He stood and shook it. "Nick."

"Thank you for helping my daughter."

"Mom," said Maisie, that one word both a chastisement and a warning.

"Excuse me," said a young, male doctor. "Are you the family of Sarah—"

"Yes," he said.

"Are you her husband?"

"No," said Maisie.

He should've never called her. He would've lied. "I'm her

boyfriend." It was a weak title—temporary, fleeting, inconsequential. She'd had dozens of boyfriends over the years and he was only one of them and soon, he'd be an ex-boyfriend.

"I'm her mother."

"I'm her sister."

They were claiming her. They had rights to her and he had none. He was nothing to her. What'd remained of his heart was ripped to shreds.

The doctor and the two women stepped aside.

"Thank God," said Maisie.

Sarah's mother followed the doctor and Maisie walked over to him. "She's going to be fine. They're running a few more tests but it looks like she just passed out."

He sighed in relief. "I want to see her."

"I know. Give my mom a minute."

He didn't want to. He wanted to run in there and see her, touch her, make sure she was okay but he nodded.

"I'll go say hi now so you can be alone with her." Maisie pulled out her phone as she walked away. "Honey, she's fine. Passed out."

He waited for what seemed an eternity but was actually only about ten minutes before Sarah's mom and Maisie came back into the waiting room.

"She's all yours," said Maisie.

He stood, more nervous than he'd ever been in his life.

"I'm going to take Mom home. Are you guys going to your place or hers tonight?"

"Are they going to release her?"

"Yeah, in a few hours," said Maisie.

"I think we'll go home." At her look he added. "Her house.

You guys can still stay if you want."

"No. We'll go home." She took his hand. "You've been wonderful to her."

"Maisie," said her mother with the same warning in her tone, but with a hint of humor. "Why is it okay for you to say it but not me?" asked Betty as they walked down the hallway.

He hurried to her room but hesitated at the door. She was lying in the bed in a hospital gown. She looked so small and helpless. He wanted to wrap her in his arms, cocoon her away so no one could ever hurt her again.

"Nick." Her eyes searched his face.

He moved toward her without even thinking. He took her hand and kissed it. "How do you feel?"

"Embarrassed."

"Don't be. You...What happened?"

She stared at their hands. "I passed out. I hadn't eaten much and...it must've gotten to me."

He ran his thumb over the soft skin of her hand. He didn't want to ask but he had to. "Is...is the baby okay?"

"Baby?" Her eyes shot to his.

"It's okay." He wasn't mad. He was crushed but it wasn't her fault. "You said something right after you came to." He was going to lose her. He wanted to bury his face in her neck and beg her to pick him. He'd love the baby no matter what. It didn't have to be his. The father could see his kid, of course, but Sarah was his.

"Oh, Nick. I'm so sorry."

He felt tears build at the back of his eyes. He looked anywhere but at her.

She touched his face. "Nick, I'm not pregnant."

His heart thrilled, seeming to come to life again and then guilt danced at the edges of his joy. "You lost it?" She'd be devastated.

"No." She pulled her hand from his and cupped the other side of his face. "I wasn't pregnant. I just had my period, remember?"

"I completely forgot." Relief washed through him, but stuttered over one tiny fact. "Then...why did you say that?" He hadn't misheard her.

"I...I don't know. I was confused, I guess." She hesitated. "I'd been talking about Tank and Adam right before I passed out and..." Her eyes locked with his. "Who was that woman you were with?"

"What woman?"

"The cute, little blonde. I saw you go upstairs with her."

"I don't know what you're talking about. I never went upstairs."

"Don't lie to me. You were talking to her and then you went upstairs. She followed a few minutes later."

"Wait." His dark eyes sparkled. "You saw Tina." He laughed but stopped short at her death glare. "Steven's wife. My brother, Steven." He leaned down and tried to kiss her but she moved her face. "I think you saw them sneaking upstairs not me."

She stared at him, searching his eyes.

"I didn't cheat on you." He leaned closer and this time she didn't move when he kissed her. "I wasn't going to cheat on you." He kissed her again. Her lips were so damn sweet and she was still his. He'd be the one to get her pregnant. "I'm never going to cheat on you." This time, he let his lips linger and her hands drifted to play in his hair.

"Promise," she said against his mouth.

"Absolutely."

"Ahem."

He pulled away as a nurse walked into the room. "A few more tests and then the two of you can leave." The older woman smiled. "And finish what you were doing."

"That we will." He laughed. He liked this nurse.

CHAPTER 69: NICK

Nick sat in the waiting room, paging through old magazines and playing on his phone.

"Nick Macris?"

"Yes." He looked up. An older woman was walking toward him a frown on her face. "And you are?" Someone who didn't care for him that was obvious.

"Dr. Smileworth." She raised her brow as if that meant something to him.

"Are you Sarah's doctor?" She wasn't the guy from before but perhaps they'd called in someone else.

"Yes."

"Is she all right? Did something come up in the tests?" This couldn't be happening.

"I'm sure everything is fine but—"

"You're sure everything is fine? You're her doctor you should know if her tests are okay or not."

"And you should've come to see me before taking her to a party. A party." She huffed the last part as if he'd taken Sarah on a jaunt to North Korea.

"Look, I have no idea what you're talking about."

"I'm Dr. Smileworth."

"You said that." He glanced around. Perhaps she'd escaped from the mental ward of this hospital.

"You have no idea who I am, do you?"

"You're Dr. Smileworth." He watched television. He knew

how to placate crazies.

"I should've expected this." The doctor sighed and sat next to him. "I'm sorry."

"For what?"

"For thinking you're an ass and treating you as such."

His mouth dropped open. This doctor, who looked like an olden-time grandmother that baked cookies and blushed at an innocent kiss, had just called him an ass.

"I've known Sarah for years and I have a fondness for her that perhaps I shouldn't, seeing as she's now my patient." The doctor sighed again. "But I'm only human and I thought I could help. Actually, I believe I am helping."

"What exactly are you talking about?" He felt like he'd passed out and woken in another world.

"I told Sarah I wanted to speak with you. She said she told you but you were too busy."

"Who are you again?" He held up his hand to stop her. "And don't say Dr. Smileworth. I got that part."

"Sarah gave me permission to speak with you but my office would be a better location."

"I'm not leaving."

"Of course not, but you could come by on..." She grabbed her phone from her purse and started paging through her calendar. "I have an opening on Wednesday."

"Now. Now is better." He wasn't waiting until Wednesday to find out what was going on.

"Of course." She smiled. "I think you may be good for Sarah after all."

"Of course, I'm good for her."

"Sarah began seeing me a little while ago."

"For what?" Panic flicked his heart again. She couldn't be seriously sick. Life wouldn't be that cruel.

"For PTSD."

"Sarah wasn't in the military."

"It doesn't only affect people in the military or first responders. I don't know what you know about her past but Sarah went through some trauma."

"I know about Adam and the baby."

"Good. I wouldn't have discussed that with you without clearing it with Sarah first."

This explained a lot. "You've been seeing her for an hour a couple of times a week, haven't you?" It wasn't business and it wasn't her ex.

"Yes. I've wanted to help her for years but she never contacted me no matter how much we tried."

"We?"

"Her family, her business partner, the vet who treats her dogs, others at her work." She paused. "Everyone who loves her."

He clenched his jaw to keep from snapping at the older woman. Her business partner—her ex-lover—was not allowed to still love her.

"I was surprised—happy, but surprised—when she called me. We were making progress but that wasn't enough for her. She wanted to get better faster as if she had a deadline."

He was that deadline. He didn't need the doctor to say it.

"That's when I asked to speak with you. I'd hoped you could help me make her understand that these things happen over years, not weeks."

"She never told me." She'd never told him anything.

"I understand that now." The doctor patted his hand. "I was furious when Maisie called me and told me what'd happened. Sarah should've never gone to a party. She wasn't ready."

"I didn't know. I would've never taken her if I'd known." He'd never have left her either.

"Now you do." She pulled out her phone again. "I think we should all talk."

"I'll be available whenever you need me but Sarah has to ask. She has to be the one to tell me about...this...her issues."

"I'd think this incident would cover that."

"She's saying she passed out because she didn't eat." She was lying to him—not avoiding the truth but actually lying. "She doesn't trust me." That hurt more than he liked.

"Sarah has a hard time trusting." The doctor patted his arm. "She needs patience and understanding."

Great. Patience wasn't his strong suit.

CHAPTER 70: SARAH

As soon as Sarah got home the tension fled as she wrapped her arms around Tank. He was safe. She was safe. Sweetie nudged her and she made it a group hug. "You did good, baby." She kissed Tank's head. "You stayed alone. Just the two of you." She'd thought she'd been doing well too.

"Maisie was with him most of the night." It was the first time Nick had engaged her in conversation since they'd left the hospital.

"I know. She asked me to text her when we were leaving." She straightened, giving the dogs one last pat each.

"Why? Didn't she want to see you?"

"Ah...She thought I'd want to rest. She'll come by tomorrow." She needed to tell him about Peter but now was not the time. Something was going on. He was too quiet and he kept giving her funny looks but Maisie had sworn she hadn't said a word to him about anything.

"Do you want something to eat? Or drink?" He walked toward the kitchen.

"No. Thanks."

"You said you passed out from not eating."

"Yeah. You're right. I probably should eat something, but I just want to soak in the tub and go to bed."

"Go. I'll make you something and bring it to you."

She went into the bathroom and stripped as the hot water filled the tub. She sank into its warmth, relishing the heat as it flooded her body. She'd messed up, pushed too hard. She was pretty sure Nick had believed the story about her passing out from hunger but he wasn't stupid. He already sensed something was wrong because she never wanted to go anywhere. Maybe she needed to see the doctor another few times a week. Dr. Smileworth had suggested that she go to a facility for a month or two but she couldn't. She'd never be able to hide that from Nick, plus she had to be here for Tank.

Nick came into the bathroom with a plate of cheese, crackers, fruit and a bottle of water. He also carried a folding table. He set it up and put the food down. "Let me know if you need anything else."

He looked fabulous. He'd looked immaculate when they'd left in his white, button-down shirt, with a black tie, black jacket and black slacks but now, with his tie and jacket gone and his shirt rumpled, he looked more real, more touchable and she wanted to touch him. She wanted him to make her forget everything but him and her.

"I'm sorry about not being able to play school tonight, but you could join me in the tub." She sat up, causing her breasts to peek from the water.

"You should eat." His eyes raked over them, making her nipples harden.

"I can eat with you behind me." She stared into his eyes. "Even inside me. You could feed me while you fucked me."

He took a deep breath, his dark eyes still fastened to her breasts. "I-I don't think that's a good idea. Not tonight. You need to rest." He turned and fled the room.

Damn it, now he thought she was frail. She'd have to convince him that what she needed more than anything was him inside of her. Only then did she know without a doubt that he was hers.

WEEK FIVE: BACK TO SCHOOL

CHAPTER 71: NICK

Today, Nick was going to convince Sarah to confide in him. It'd been a little over a week since the hospital and she was still claiming that she'd passed out from not eating. He was done with the lies. She'd gone to see the doctor this morning. When she'd gotten home, he'd asked some casual questions about her "meeting" but she'd either ignored him or deflected. He would've pushed the issue but he'd had an appointment that he couldn't miss. However, that was over and the time had come. She needed to trust him or this wasn't going to work.

He pulled into the driveway and went into the house. The dogs greeted him at the door. "Sarah?" There was no answer. She hadn't left. That wasn't her thing, unless she'd gone out alone to test herself. The doctor had said that she was trying to hurry this along which was stupid. He headed through the living room toward the bedroom. She'd better be here or he'd track her down and...The blood rushed from his head to his dick. His cardigan was draped over a desk that'd been moved from their home office into the living room. There was a note on the desk.

Nick,

Sorry your visit from Mary, Lucy and Ms. Applewood was delayed, but they're here now. Get dressed and lock the dogs in the guest room. There's a new bone in there for each of them.

Turn on the radio, just in case we make too much noise. Let me know when you're ready.

Sarah (alias: Mary, Lucy and Ms. Applewood).

He'd never in his life gotten undressed and dressed so quickly. Not only was there a cardigan but also an ugly button-down shirt. Perfect for the sleazy professor.

He sat down, his dick already pressing against his trousers, and called out, "I'm ready. The professor is at his desk."

The minutes ticked by. He fidgeted in his seat, tugging at his pants. She'd better hurry or round one of this fantasy was going to be quick. He couldn't tear his eyes from the bedroom door, not sure who was going to come out first.

There was a knock.

"Yes." He forced himself to look at the computer screen.

"Do you have time for a meeting, professor?" asked Sarah as she stepped into the living room, her white Catholic school-girl shirt tied at her waist. Her skirt shorter than it should be, showing long, long legs.

Lucy. Thank God, it was Lucy. He could fuck Lucy. He would fuck Lucy. "How can I help you, Lucy?" He leaned against the back of his chair, as if at ease when in reality he was ready to pounce.

Sarah strolled forward, her hips rolling as she walked. His dick hardened even more, tenting the loose slacks. She had her hair in pigtails again and her lips were painted a luscious red.

"I need you…"

Oh, she was going to get him. Every fucking inch of him.

"To help me with science." She leaned forward on the desk, letting him get a glimpse of her white lace bra.

358

"Science?" He slowly raised his gaze to her eyes. "I'm an English professor." Or at least that was what he'd been the last time.

"I know, but you're such a good teacher." She sauntered toward him, pushing between him and the desk before moving his computer out of the way and sitting down. She kicked off her shoes and rested her foot on the chair between his thighs.

"Thank you, Lucy. I try. Hard. To please." His eyes were locked with hers. He wanted to grab her foot and put it on his cock, but he waited, letting her be the aggressor this time. "How can I be of assistance?"

"We're studying the laws of attraction and"—she ran her foot over the bulge in his pants—"you know all about that."

"So do you." Her foot was magic on his cock but he forced himself to remain still, to act unmoved.

"Yes, but I need practice with…friction." Now, her foot was pressing more firmly against him, teasing the line between pleasure and pain.

"I'll help but only if you do exactly what I say." Time for him to take control.

"Of course, professor." She smiled.

"Friction works best when everything is ready. Wet and ready."

"Really?" Her eyes widened as if surprised. She was a great actor.

"Yes. Are you wet and ready, Lucy?"

She put her hand on her breast and ran it slowly down her body to between her legs, her mouth opening slightly with the pleasure she gave herself.

"Move your skirt. I need to see if you're doing it right."

She leaned back on one elbow as her other hand slowly pulled the cloth out of his way. Her hand trailed back between her thighs, stroking herself through her underwear.

"Spread your legs."

She did, her foot sliding off his cock to his thigh. Her white lace panties were wet and getting wetter with her ministrations.

"I think you're wet enough."

"You may want to check and make sure." She kept stroking herself, as if unable to stop.

"No."

Her eyes, half closed, snapped open.

"You need to make sure everything is wet." He unbuttoned and unzipped his pants. "I'm not nearly wet enough for good friction."

"What do you want me to do, professor?" She licked her lips as he pulled his pants down, freeing himself.

"Wet my cock, Lucy."

"How?"

"However you want." He wanted those lush lips around him, sucking him until he came.

She closed her legs, pulling off her underwear and tossing them to the floor. Okay, her pussy juices lubing him up worked too.

"Spread your legs. I need to see you."

She did. She was ripe and glistening.

"You're right. Maybe, I should check. You don't seem quite wet enough." He needed to taste her. He leaned forward but she put her hand on his shoulder, stopping him.

"You said I needed to make you wet."

"I did." He stared at her pussy. It was only inches away. He could smell her heat, her arousal and he was going a little crazy. If she didn't let him taste her soon, this game would be over.

"Then sit back in your chair and let me make you wet."

"You have no idea what you're asking." His breath shuddered in his chest as he leaned back.

She stood, hiding that sweet treat between her thighs. It was worse than not tasting her, but then she was straddling him, her small hand wrapped around his cock. She rubbed along his length. He grabbed her hips, lifting her up above him.

"You're not wet enough," she gasped, as she continued stroking him.

He grabbed a condom from the desk drawer and slid it over his length. "Take me inside and make me wet, Sar...Lucy."

She moved his hands to her breasts and then wrapped her fingers around his dick again. She held him as she rubbed her pussy along his length, teasing him with her heat.

"I need to be inside you." He moved his hands back to her hips, taking control.

"I'm not done making you wet, professor." She grabbed his wrists, putting his palms back on her tits.

"Fuck." He'd play but he'd play dirty. He tore her shirt open and she gasped, her downward stroke falling to the side and his dick poked at her thigh. He unhooked her bra and pushed it down as his lips landed on her breast, teasing and sucking her nipple.

She moaned as her head dropped onto her shoulders and her back arched, pushing her breast against his face. Her hand was still wrapped around his cock, squeezing. He put his fingers around hers as he continued to torture her nipple with his tongue and teeth. She lifted up, her eyes closed, and as she

361

came back down, he adjusted his angle and she sank onto him.

"Oh," she moaned, sinking farther down.

He kissed his way to her other breast as he moved his hands to her hips and pushed her downward until he was fully sheathed inside of her.

"Now, for the friction." He lifted her and brought her down as he thrust upward.

She grasped his shoulders, resting her head against his neck, and began moving on him, matching his rhythm. She felt so good, so right. She was his. The only one he wanted. The only one he needed.

"Ride me faster." He pumped into her.

She stuck her tongue in his ear and he lost it. All games were done. He grabbed her hips and fucked her hard and fast. She whimpered in pleasure as she let him take control. He latched onto her nipple with his mouth, sucking hard. Everything was rushing to his balls. He wouldn't last another minute. He ran his finger through her wetness, playing with her clit until her body tightened around him and trembled with her release. Her back arched and she clung to him, her pussy muscles clasping onto him in the sweetest torture. He shoved into her and held still as he came. He wrapped his arms around her, never wanting to let her go, but she kissed his cheek and stood.

"Thanks for the lesson, professor. I think I understand friction now." She turned and headed for the door, holding her shirt together. "Mary may need some help though. She's also having trouble. I told her to talk to you."

Man, he loved this fantasy. "Thank you, Lucy." He was more than ready. Well, it'd take some time to get hard again, but that was perfect because Mary would need some persuading.

CHAPTER 72: SARAH

Sarah hurried into the bedroom and tore off her clothes—not that there was much left to remove. Damn Nick, had ruined her shirt. She grinned as she ran some warm water on a washcloth and cleaned herself. She loved making him lose control and the best way to do that was to take control from him until he couldn't stand it anymore.

She sighed. She would've loved to have stayed in his arms and napped—great sex did that to her—but it was time for Mary to make an appearance. She pulled her hair back into a ponytail, changed the red lipstick for a pink gloss and wiped off her makeup.

She dressed in her plain, white panties and bra, put on a clean shirt, tucking it into another skirt that looked exactly like Lucy's, only longer. She took a deep breath and tapped on the door.

Nick's firm—"Yes, come in."—made her shiver with anticipation.

This man drove her crazy with lust. She stepped into the room. "Professor?"

He looked up from his computer, his eyes narrowing on her. "Yes, Mary."

He didn't look pleased to see her but she could fix that. She stepped into the room. "Um...I was wondering...that is Lucy said you might be able to help me with some science."

"Why would I do that, Mary?" He leaned back in his chair,

crossing his arms over his chest.

"Um…" She hadn't expected that. She loved playing these games with him. He took the part to heart and seldom did what she anticipated.

"The last time I helped you, you rushed out of the room"— his eyes were hard—"before we finished your lesson."

That was unfair. He'd been ready to take Mary's virginity. Her only recourse had been to run, but Mary wouldn't argue. "I'm sorry, professor. I was scared."

He relaxed a little. "There was no reason to be frightened."

"You…you promised that I'd still be a virgin and you were going to…going to…" She couldn't help the slight challenge that flashed in her eyes.

A spark of amusement flared in his. "Nonsense. I was going to honor my word. You would've left here the same as you came in."

She struggled to keep from laughing. He wasn't lying. Mary didn't actually have a virginity to lose.

"Now, run along Mary. I don't have time to tutor students who don't trust me."

That one hit too close to home and by the look in his eyes he wasn't just talking to Mary. "I do trust you, professor." She took another small step into the room. "I swear. If you promise that we won't…you know…"

"We won't what? You need to tell me exactly what you don't want to do." His eyes were getting dark and dangerous now and it was drawing Sarah closer.

"I…I don't want to have sex with you." At the tightening of his lips she added, "Or anyone. I'm not ready."

He stared at her for a long time.

Too long. She couldn't take the silence, the inaction, inattention. She was wet again and she needed to keep playing—feel his fingers, his mouth. "Will you help me professor? Please."

"I suppose." He motioned to the chair in front of his desk. "Have a seat and we'll talk."

She smiled and closed the door behind her, moving over to the desk and sitting primly, keeping her legs pressed together.

"Now Mary, with what do you need help?"

"Um...science. We're studying friction and I just don't understand."

"Hmm." He leaned back in his chair. "In order for me to help you with that, I'll need to know that you won't run."

"You promise we won't...you know, do it?"

"I promise."

"Then I promise, I won't run."

"I'm not sure I believe you." He watched her closely.

"I swear, professor."

"I believe that you believe you won't run but...I think you'll get frightened and instead of talking to me"—he tapped his chest—"and letting me help you, you'll run."

Again, he wasn't just talking to Mary. She swallowed. "I swear, professor. I'll do whatever you say and I won't run."

"I need to be sure." He stood and took off his tie.

Her eyes widened. He was going to restrain her. He was going to tie up little, virgin Mary. Damn, she hadn't expected this and it was so hot.

He stood before her. His crotch was at eye level and it was an eyeful. He was already hard and ready. Little Mary might get fucked today.

"Put your hands behind your back."

"Why?" She didn't move. "What are you going to do?"

"You promised to do what I said."

"But..."

"Do it or go. I don't have time for games."

"O-okay." Oh, he had time for games. He was an expert at games and she couldn't wait. She leaned forward, putting her arms behind her back.

"No. Behind the chair."

She did as he said and he walked behind her, tying her hands together. She shifted, testing the knot.

"Is it too tight?"

"No." It was just tight enough to let her know that she was his—helpless, at his mercy. She tried to act nervous, to stay in character, but a throbbing was beating an insistent rhythm between her thighs.

"Good." He walked to his chair and sat down.

What the hell was he doing that far away? She needed him in front of her, touching her, kissing her.

"Mary, friction is good. Try and get loose, move your hands a bit. Your arms."

She did as he said and his eyes dropped to her chest. She wiggled more, making her breasts shift and bounce. She may be tied up but she wasn't helpless in this game. She could still drive him crazy.

"See Mary, that's friction. Do you feel it in your hands and arms?"

"Yes."

"Do you like it?"

"No. Not really. It kind of hurts." But she did like it—not

367

the bite of the cloth around her wrists but the anticipation of his friction.

"Small hurts can feel good."

"I don't understand." Before she met him, she hadn't understood that, but now she did and he was so right.

"You will." His eyes were almost black now, like a shark's ready to strike.

She shivered, squeezing her legs together and he smirked.

"Let me demonstrate." He stood, picked up his chair and carried it around the desk, placing it close enough so that their knees brushed when he sat. "You're new to this, so we'll start slow."

She wasn't sure she could handle slow. The spicy scent of his cologne and the heat of his body were making her ache. Too bad she couldn't be Lucy right now.

He put his hands on her knees. They were warm and strong. He squeezed gently. "There. A little friction."

Not exactly, but she kept her mouth shut.

He ran his hands up and down her thighs, his long fingers on the outside and his thumbs coming closer and closer to where she needed him to touch. She squeezed her legs tighter together. She wanted to let them fall apart, give him an opening, but Mary wouldn't do that.

"Do you like this friction?" His thumb skimmed along the seam of her thighs.

"I...I don't know."

"Relax." He leaned forward and kissed her gently, his lips barely grazing against hers. "You liked my kisses, didn't you?"

"Yes," she whispered.

He kissed her again, this time with a little more pressure.

He ran his tongue along her lips. "Open for me."

His thumbs pressed more firmly between her thighs and his mouth was on hers. She wasn't sure if he meant her lips or legs so she opened both and his tongue darted into her mouth, gently exploring as his hands pulled her legs farther apart. His fingers danced along the soft skin of her inner thighs. She squirmed, wanting to touch him, to bury her hands in his hair but she couldn't.

He pulled back from the kiss, breathing heavily. "Mary, you are a sweet little thing."

"I want to touch you, professor." This game was going to end fast. She didn't have it in her to deny him. "Please, untie me."

"Not yet." His hands now rested at the juncture of her thighs, his thumbs almost touching her pussy. "Do you want more friction?" He pressed in a little, making her gasp.

"I...I don't know." It took everything she had to stay in character. "You promised that we wouldn't..."

"And we won't. I won't fuck you."

He kissed her again but this time his tongue took control of her mouth as one hand held her head still for his invasion and the other rested so close to where she needed him. Too soon, he broke the kiss, his nostrils flaring as if unable to get enough of her scent. She wanted to scream, beg him to touch her, but she remained silent. Being a virgin was starting to get on her nerves.

"But I am going to teach you all about friction—all except that one lesson." He pulled her legs farther apart as he kissed his way to her ear. "Friction works best when both parties are wet, especially if one item is tight and the other large." His thumb caressed her through her panties and she gasped. "You like that don't you?"

"Yes." She pushed her hips toward him. Mary was a virgin but she could feel pleasure and his fingers brought that in truckloads.

"You'll like this even more." He rubbed along her pussy, stroking her and glancing over her clit.

"Please..." She trembled.

"Little Mary is enjoying this lesson but I think you've learned enough."

"What?" she almost screamed. She hadn't learned near enough.

There was a soft woof from the guest bedroom.

Nick put his finger on her lips. "Shhh."

Damn, she'd forgotten about Tank.

"I'll be right back. Don't move." He grinned at her over his shoulder as he walked into the kitchen and grabbed a couple of dog cookies. He disappeared down the hallway and was back a moment later.

"Now, where were we?" He sat back down, his eyes raking over her.

"You were teaching me about friction." She held his gaze as she widened her legs. Okay, maybe Mary was being a little too eager but Sarah no longer cared.

"That's right. We were done with the lesson."

"No." The word slipped from her lips without thought.

"No?" He smirked, all male confidence. "Okay. I guess we can continue."

Thank God.

"There are all kinds of friction, Mary." His fingers went to

370

her blouse, slowly unbuttoning her shirt and kissing his way down her chest.

"Please, untie me." She knew the pleasure that was coming and she needed to touch him, hold him to her.

"No," he said against her belly before running his tongue around her navel.

She ached to end this game, to shove his head between her legs but the damn restraints were secure.

He sat up. "You're a very beautiful girl, Mary."

"Th-thank you." Okay. What was he up to?

"You have nice breasts. I'm going to taste them now. Show you how friction feels here." He cupped her breast and flicked her nipple. She whimpered. "You like that don't you?"

"I-I don't know."

"Let me help you decide." He reached behind her and unhooked her bra, pushing it out of his way. His hands captured her breasts, squeezing as his thumbs caressed her nipples. "Have you decided? Do you like this?"

"Yes." *Yes, yes and yes.* She arched her back, pushing her breasts into his hands.

"You should think about sex, Mary. You'd like that even more."

"I-I'm not ready."

"Fair enough." He lowered his mouth and kissed all around her nipple—first one and then the other—but never taking her into his mouth.

"Please, Ni...professor, please."

"Please what, Mary?"

"I-I don't know but I need...something." She was squirming on the seat. She knew exactly what she needed but Mary didn't.

He moved his face to her ear, his breath a harsh whisper, "If I give you what you need you have to promise to do something for me."

"N-not sex."

"Fine. Not sex." He almost snapped.

"Then okay."

"Promise you'll do whatever I say."

Now, she was nervous. He wouldn't try and fuck Mary in the ass would he? She wasn't doing that.

"You need to trust me...Mary." His eyes searched hers, letting her know that he wasn't talking to Mary. "You have to know that I won't do anything you don't like or don't want to do." His tone was kind of hurt as he pinched her nipple.

She moaned, leaning into his touch "Okay. Yes. Whatever you want."

He kissed her neck and then nipped her. She shivered. She'd just made a deal with the devil—the handsome, sexy, going to make her scream in delight devil.

"Good girl." He kissed his way down her neck and across her chest. It seemed like forever before his mouth finally latched onto her nipple. He sucked, sending heat all the way to her pussy which wept for him.

"Please. I need to touch you." She moaned, her arms yanking against the restraints.

He ignored her, leaving hot, wet kisses as he made a path to the next breast.

"Please, untie me."

His only answer was to move downward, kissing his way across her abdomen and belly. He dropped to his knees, his hands holding her legs apart as he licked and sucked his way up her thigh.

She trembled, trying to remember how nervous she'd been the first time she'd been eaten out. "Wh-what are you doing?" *Don't stop. If there's a God in heaven, don't stop.*

"Friction, Mary. Remember, it's better when wet." He lifted her, pulling off her underwear. His long finger caressed her folds and she groaned. "You're wet, Mary, but you could be wetter." He slipped his finger inside of her.

"Oh...professor." Her head dropped back as he stroked her, relieving some of the tension while building more.

"You feel so good, Mary." His hot breath tickled her pussy as he thrust his finger in and out of her. "Look at me."

She opened her eyes. His face was tight with desire, his eyes black and gleaming.

"I'm going to make you wetter, Mary, and then I'm going to make you come."

"Ah..." She bit back a scream as his mouth lowered, feasting on her juices, lapping and licking and flicking while his finger thrust into her. He added another finger, stretching her as he worked her clit with his lips and tongue. Her hips jerked, rocking with his rhythm. She was so close already. All she needed was a little more—pressure, speed, something. He put another finger inside of her and she moaned long and low, trembling on the edge of orgasm. His other hand drifted across her lips, as he sucked her clit. She screamed as she came, but his hand covered her mouth, muffling most of the sound.

He gave her one more, long lap with his rough tongue and then sat back on his heels, wiping his face. He glanced down the hallway. "All's quiet. Your turn." He stood. His pants tented in front of her. He unzipped them.

She knew what he wanted but now that she'd come it was easier to stay in character. "You said we wouldn't—"

"I'm not going to fuck you, Mary. You're going to suck my dick until I come in your mouth."

"Um...I don't know, professor." She was more than eager. She loved sucking his cock, making him beg, but Mary would be nervous.

"You promised."

"O-okay."

He pulled his dick from his pants. It was big and hard, the tip purple with need. "Open your mouth, Mary."

He held it to her face. She opened her mouth. He rubbed his cock along her lips. "Lick it. Kiss it."

She ran her tongue across the head and he groaned. It was a raw guttural sound that went straight between her legs. She was doing this to him. She was making him feel like she'd felt— desperate, on fire. She licked along the top and up and down his length.

"That's it, Mary." His hand tangled in her ponytail. "That's a good girl."

She pulled away. "I want to touch you."

"Take me in your mouth." He increased the pressure on her head.

She opened and he slid between her lips. He leaned forward, his dick going farther down her throat. She gagged.

"Suck, Mary." He braced one hand on the back of the chair as the other pulled the tie, removing the restraint.

Her hands wrapped around his cock. He was thick and hot. She sucked harder as she stroked him, bobbing her head, finding her rhythm.

"That's it." He tugged on her hair. "That feels so fucking good."

She sat up, letting his dick slide out of her mouth with a pop.

"Don't stop." He pushed her back toward his cock.

"Someone's knocking." She jumped up.

"What?" His eyes were glazed with desire and confusion.

"I've got to go. It's Ms. Applewood."

"No. Fuck no." He reached for her as she hurried to the door and slipped into the bedroom.

"Damn it, Sarah! No. Fuck that, Sarah," he yelled.

CHAPTER 73: NICK

Nick was going to kill Sarah or Mary or...fuck. He should've known better than to untie her, but he'd wanted to feel her hands on him as she sucked him off. He almost cried as he stuffed his dick back into his pants. Someone pounded on the door.

"What?" He was done with this fucking game.

"Professor," Sarah walked back into the room.

He wanted to grab her, shove her against the door and fuck her until she couldn't stand but she...she looked unapproachable. She had her hair up in a bun and she wore a suit with a white shirt buttoned all the way to the top, not leaving even a peek at her luscious skin let alone her tits.

"Ms. Applewood?" Round three had begun and he was rock hard and ready.

She nodded.

"What do I owe this pleasure?" Because pleasure was how it was going to end, one way or another.

"I've heard rumors that there are things happening in here that are unprofessional at best and illegal at worst." Her voice was ice cold and her lips were pinched but her eyes still gleamed with heat and desire.

Apparently, the good professor had been caught with his pants down—almost. "There's nothing going on in here except a professor helping...teaching his students." That wasn't a lie. He was teaching them all sorts of things.

Her eyes landed on Mary's white panties. "Teaching what exactly?"

He wasn't sure how this part was going to play out but he was eager to discover if Ms. Applewood was as prudish as she appeared. "All kinds of lessons that young girls"—his eyes roamed over her—"and women require." He leaned against his desk, his pants still tenting from his erection.

Her eyes narrowed and then a blush heated her cheeks as her gaze landed on his crotch. She quickly looked away. "I can assure you that no young girl or woman needs the kind of lessons you're teaching."

"We both know you're lying." He moved toward her, slowly.

She took a step back. "I'm not and I'm going to report this to the principal."

He was on her in a minute, his large body trapping her against the door, his hands on either side of her head. "Please, don't do that." He was close enough that his breath feathered across her lips as he spoke.

"I...I...Let me go."

"I'm not touching you." He wasn't although his dick was almost pressing against her. It really, really wanted to touch her but he kept his hips away.

"Y-you're keeping the door closed."

"Only so we can talk...privately."

"I don't think there's anything we need to discuss." She straightened. "I'm not stupid. I know what's going on in here."

"Do you?" He was going to give this prude exactly what she needed and wanted. He let his hand caress her cheek. "You're an attractive woman, Ms. Applewood, why do you hide?"

"Stop." She shivered under his touch.

"I don't think you want me to, not really."

"I...Nonsense."

"What's your first name?" He whispered against her ear and she trembled.

"Sarah."

Fuck, yes. He almost groaned. "Sarah, I'd like to kiss you."

"No." She pushed on his chest and he grabbed her hands, keeping them against his body.

"It's only a kiss, Sarah. How long has it been since you've been kissed?"

"That's none of your business." She stiffened but it only increased his desire to make her melt under him, around him.

"It's not but I asked just the same."

"Well, I'm not telling you and I'm not kissing you. You can't charm me out of reporting what you've been doing."

"I'm not trying to." He kissed her ear and she gasped. "I'm just a man near an attractive woman."

"I-I'm not attractive."

Okay, she'd given him the clue. He should've picked up on it from her appearance but all his blood was in his damn cock. "Of course, you are." He reached behind her head and unhooked her hair, pulling it out of the bun and letting it cascade down her shoulders. "Your hair is beautiful." He wasn't lying. It was soft and fragrant and he wanted to feel it against his skin. "You should wear it hanging loose like this all the time. It highlights your cheekbones." His fingers trailed along her face and down to her lips. "And these..." She took his breath away. "So, red and lush." He leaned closer. "So, ready for my kiss."

She didn't move, her hands still resting against his chest, as he lightly brushed his lips over hers

"And your body"—he inhaled, growing even harder at the scent of her perfume and arousal—"is a wet dream waiting to be explored."

"Stop talking like that." She tried to sound outraged but there was a hint of breathlessness in her voice.

"Waiting for me to explore." He kissed her again as he started unbuttoning her blouse.

"You can't." Her hands tangled with his, stopping him.

"I can." He kissed her neck and she tipped her head. "You want me to."

"I don't." She stiffened in his arms, trying to push him away from her.

"You do." He kissed her ear. "Listen to your body." He ran his thumb over her nipple. It was pebbled and hard, begging for his lips. "How long has it been since you listened to your body?"

She didn't answer but she pushed her breast into his touch.

"It can be our secret. Yours and mine." He shoved her bra down, leaving it hooked so the cloth pushed her breasts up like an offering. He kissed her nipple, letting his tongue drag across it, slow and rough.

Her hands grabbed his head.

"No one needs to know. In here with me, you can be a woman with a woman's wants"—he shoved her skirt up around her waist—"and a woman's desires." He stepped closer so his cock rested against the juncture between her thighs. "Tell me you want this, Sarah."

"Yes, professor. Please." Her breath was coming in needy pants and her eyes were bright with desire.

That was all he needed. He tore off her underwear and

unzipped his pants. His dick bounced, causing him to gasp. He was so hard and ready for her. He grabbed a condom from his pants pocket, tore it open and rolled it down his cock. He grabbed her thighs lifting her and she wrapped them around his waist. He'd die if he didn't sink into her right now. He positioned himself and pushed into her in one long, hard thrust. She gasped and trembled in his arms but the feel of her so hot and wet, clenching at him was all he really noticed. He was past foreplay, past technique. He was in rut. In and out he thrust, fast and hard. Her legs tightened around his waist as her back bumped against the door.

"You...okay?" If she said no he'd go mad. He'd curl into a ball on the floor and weep.

"Yes." She whispered, nipping his ear. "Fuck me harder, Nick. I need it."

Hallelujah. He increased his pace. She was so hot and wet, so tight. She was perfect. His fingers dug into her hips as she clung to him—her arms, her legs, her pussy all wrapped around him—but it wasn't enough. He ground his mouth against hers, pushing his tongue inside her. She whimpered, the sound reverberating through him making his balls tighten and lightning shoot down his spine. He wouldn't last much longer, but she had to come first. He nipped her bottom lip and then sucked it. She broke apart, trembling and clasping onto his cock, milking him. He came apart, only coming together again inside her, with her.

It was minutes later before his heart slowed and he could speak. He held her a little longer, unwilling to break this connection, this closeness. At this moment, there was nothing but him and her. She unclasped her legs from around his waist, apparently ready to separate.

"Fuck, I love this fantasy." He kissed her neck. He loved her but she wasn't ready to hear that and he wasn't going to say it until she trusted him.

She laughed. "For a minute there, when Mary left, I thought you hated it.

"I did. At that time." He kissed her lips, unable to stop himself. "But I really like Sarah Applewood."

"Good. She likes you too and I think she's going to be a regular visitor."

"I can't wait."

"She has a bit of a dominatrix side."

"Fuck me." He dropped his head on her shoulder. "You're trying to kill me."

WEEK SIX: THE FIGHT

CHAPTER 74: SARAH

"Damn it." Sarah wanted to toss her computer across the room.

"What's up?" Nick sat on the couch working on his laptop.

"The deal fell through. They won't agree to the price. Not on paper."

"What deal? The apartments for the vets with pets?"

"No. That fell through weeks ago. We'd decided to build a shelter instead." She wanted to cry. The new shelter would've been perfect. They could've saved and rehabilitated at least one hundred more dogs.

"Oh. You never mentioned the other wasn't going to work out." He closed his computer. "Let me take a look."

"No. Thanks though." She had to talk to Peter.

"Sarah, let me help. It's what I do." He walked toward her.

"Thank you, but I can take care of this." She closed her computer and the hurt on his face almost made her cringe.

He squatted by her and took her hands. "I can help you. It's what I do and I'm damn good at it." He kissed her knuckles. "Please, let me take a look. They may not be able to back out at this juncture without fines."

"I know that. I'm not an idiot. I've been running this business for years."

"I didn't say you were an idiot." The muscle in his cheek

began to twitch. "But sometimes fresh eyes can help."

Her phone rang. It was Peter. "Thanks for the offer." She leaned down and kissed him. She'd love to take him up on it but first she had to tell him about Peter because her brother-in-law's name was all over the documents and Nick would realize that her supposed ex-boyfriend shared a last name with her sister. "We can talk later, but I have to take this."

CHAPTER 75: NICK

Nick was calling it a day. It was early but he didn't care.
Today had been a disaster. First, there'd been that almost-fight
with Sarah. He was losing patience with her. It'd been two
weeks since his sister's party and she still hadn't told him the
real reason she'd passed out or about her doctor appointments.
He'd tried on numerous occasions to get her to let him tag
along with her on her "errands" or "meetings" as she called the
appointments, but she'd always refused, using one excuse or
another. To say their relationship had been tense was an
understatement. He kept trying to get her to trust him enough
to tell him she had a problem and she kept trying to sidetrack
him with sex. To be honest, it worked. Tank had gotten used to
them fucking and nothing was being held back. They did lock
the dogs out of the bedroom when they were going to get
rough or use restraints.

Sometimes, when she screamed Tank would trot over to
the bedroom, his toenails clicking on the tile and then he'd sniff
along the bottom of the door for a few minutes before leaving.
Her damn dog trusted him more than she did.

He would've had it out with her this morning, but she'd still
been on the phone when he'd left. His day had gone downhill
from there. He'd had to cancel one of his contracts with a
customer and even though it was unpleasant, he always did that
in person. The guy had argued and then pleaded, but the man
refused to follow his advice and even though it'd cost him a

small fortune to back out at this stage, he refused to have his name associated with a failing business. Then, he'd met with two different business owners Tommy had found. He'd have to talk to that kid. Tommy was smart and ambitious but the kid promised more than they could deliver. Both businesses had expected miracles without any work. Basically, it'd been an expensive, wasted day. All he wanted was to go home to Sarah and lose himself in her softness.

He turned down her street. The neighbor's car was in the driveway and that was odd because Maisie was the only person who had visited Sarah while he'd been staying there. He parked the car and walked inside the house. He'd been wrong. It wasn't the neighbor's car. He'd only assumed that it'd belonged to a neighbor because he'd seen it on their road several times over the past few weeks. Obviously, the old adage about assuming was excruciatingly accurate because he'd certainly been played for an ass.

Sarah sat at the table with her ex-boyfriend. Tank and Sweetie trotted to the door, tails wagging.

"Nick, you're early." Her eyes were wide and her face had paled. It was clear she hadn't expected him home.

He patted the dogs and walked toward the kitchen. He was surprised his legs were working because his body was numb which was good for her little-dick boyfriend because otherwise he'd kill the guy.

"Hi, we haven't officially met." The ex stood and held out his hand. "I'm Peter."

Nick was going to punch the man in the face. He'd wanted her to fire him but that was a lawsuit waiting to happen so he hadn't even suggested it. He stared at the ex's hand for several long minutes. He should shake it. Act like nothing was the matter—be sophisticated—but he felt anything but cool and calm about Sarah. She was his.

"May I speak with you for a minute?" She touched his arm.

He wanted to slap her hand away, but nodded instead.

"I'll be right back." She smiled at her ex.

Nick wanted to shove the guy through the door and then shake her or tie her up. She belonged with him.

"Ah...that's okay. I should go. I have to get Kyle anyway. We can finish this tomorrow," said Peter.

"Are you sure?" She asked. "This will only take a moment."

"He said he had to go." Nick's words were short, static bursts of anger. "And, just so you know, I'll be here tomorrow. All day." He wasn't giving them another moment alone.

"Okay. Great." Peter glanced at Sarah confused.

She closed her eyes as if she were barely keeping her temper. Nick almost snarled at her. He was the injured party, not her.

"Tank, Sweetie, come." He headed for the backdoor, the dogs following. As soon as Limp-Dick left, they were going to fight. The dogs didn't need to hear it. He let them out and returned to the living room. Peter was gone and Sarah was standing near the table, her hands fidgeting at her sides.

She looked like a little girl, lost and scared. Some of his anger dissipated. "How long have you been seeing him behind my back?" He poured himself a hefty drink, not bothering to fix her one. She could get her own. He tossed back half of it.

"I haven't."

"Don't lie to me. He's been here before. I've seen his car on the street." The fact that she'd been sneaking around, even if it were only for business tore him up. She could've seen the asshole when he was home.

"Yes, but—"

"I get that you may have to see him from time to time, but you didn't need to wait until I was gone." He didn't want to ask. Shouldn't ask. But he had to. "Did you sleep with him?" He could swear his heart froze, waiting for her answer.

"What? No. How can you even ask that?"

His heart started beating again. He could work with this. This he could salvage. He finished his drink and poured another. "I can ask because you didn't tell me he was coming over among other things. How many times has he been here in our house when I was gone?" He strode toward her.

"It doesn't—"

"Answer me." He was close enough to smell her now and his cock hardened. Fuck, he wanted this woman. Even if she'd cheated on him, he'd want her and that scared the hell out of him.

"I don't know. I haven't counted." She crossed her arms over her chest. "But if—"

"That many." His head almost exploded. "You've been lying to me this entire time." About everything. Her lover. Her health. Every fucking thing.

"I haven't lied to you."

"You did." He stepped closer wanting her to see how much danger she was in, how close to losing control he was. "You invited him over when you knew I'd be gone. Why? So you could flirt? Fuck?"

"I get why you're mad."

"Oh great. That makes everything all right. You validate my

anger. Fabulous." He strode back to the bar afraid that if he stayed near her a moment longer he'd either hit her or fuck her and he never, ever hit women.

"That's not what I meant."

"Do you want to be with him? Are you counting the days until this is over between us?" He poured another drink. He'd thought they'd been doing well. Sure there were some issues but nothing they couldn't work out.

"No. Damn it Nick, let me fin—"

"I don't want him here. I don't want him in this house unless I'm here."

"Peter is not my boyfriend." Her voice was whisper soft. "He's Maisie's husband."

"You were sleeping with your sister's husband?"

"No. God, no." She walked over to him and held her hand out, slowly placing it on his cheek as if he were a wild animal and right now he felt that way. "Peter was never my boyfriend."

"But...you said." He couldn't stop from resting his face in her hand.

"I know and...I'm sorry."

"Why?"

She dropped her arm and poured herself a drink, tossing back half of it. "I didn't want you to know that..."

"What else are you lying to me about?" This was it. She needed to come clean. Tell him everything. "You can trust me, Sarah."

Her eyes met his and he almost drowned in her green depths. "Nothing. I swear. I wanted to tell you. I almost told you that first night but...I was embarrassed."

"About what?" His hands caressed her shoulders.

She gulped down the rest of her drink. "I didn't want you to know that there'd been no one since you." She lifted her head, chin out. "I didn't want you to pity me or to gloat."

"Really?" He wanted to beat his chest like a caveman. He captured her face, staring into her eyes for the truth. "Don't lie to me about this. If you were with someone else before we got back together that's…fine." It wasn't but he'd deal with it.

"There's been no one but you." She smiled sadly. "As you now know, I don't get out much."

"Is that why you didn't move on…because you don't like to go out?" Once again, his heart waited for her answer. This was it, the perfect opening for her to tell him everything.

"No." Again it was a whisper of a word but this time it carried so much hope and promise.

"Then why?" His thumb caressed her chin. "Trust me." He was begging.

"I was busy and I…I couldn't stop thinking about you." She kissed his hand and then his lips, pressing her body into him.

"I'm glad, I am but…" She was rubbing his cock and he was losing focus and interest in this conversation. He grabbed her fingers, stopping her from moving but he didn't pull them away from his dick. "Is there anything else you want to tell me?" He kissed her. "I'll understand. I swear. Trust me." He kissed her again, this time deeper.

"No." Her eyes searched his. "There's been no one but you."

He stepped away from her, his temper starting to replace his lust. "I'm not talking about other men. I'm talking about you. Us."

"I don't know what you mean." Her eyes were wary now

389

like a cornered rabbit.

He could go in for the kill. Tell her he knew everything but that wouldn't make her trust him. "You need to stop lying to me."

"I'm not lying." She moved toward him and grabbed his hand. "I swear. I don't know what you want me to say. I haven't been with another man. I don't want another man."

"This isn't about other guys." He jerked his hand from her. "I believe you about that. This is about you not trusting me."

"I...I do."

"Now, you're lying. Again."

"I'm not...I'm trying." Her eyes were huge in her pale face.

"Are you? You had weeks to tell me about Peter and you didn't. If we were still going to my place to fuck, you'd still want to drive separately because you don't trust me to get you back here in time for Tank. You won't even let me help you with your business." He wanted to shake her, to hug her, to wrap her in his arms and protect her but she refused to let him.

"It's my business."

"And you don't have to take my fucking advice but you could talk to me about it. Jesus, it's what I do. I've made a god damn fortune helping small businesses but you won't even talk to me about yours."

"I...I didn't know it meant that much to you."

"You're my girlfriend. Of course what you do, your life, matters to me but you don't see that because you're so sure this is going to end."

"You can't tell me it won't." Now, she was getting mad. "You can't promise me that."

"No, but you can't promise me it will."

"I...I..."

"Except, you're doing everything you can to make sure that you're right. That this does end." He was tired of fighting with her, tired of her pushing him away. He needed to get out of there. "I know why you passed out at my sister's party—the real reason. I've been waiting weeks for you to tell me the truth, but you never did. You're killing this. Us." He felt like someone was tearing his insides out. "You know what? You win. I'm done. I can't do this anymore." He strode to the door and left.

CHAPTER 76: NICK

Nick had no idea how to fix his relationship and if he couldn't fix it who could? That's what he did. He was a fixer. He pulled into the parking lot of Patrick's office and walked into the building.

"He's expecting me," he lied to the receptionist.

She smiled and pressed the button that led to the upstairs suite of offices. He stopped at Patrick's door and knocked.

"One minute."

He shouldn't have come. It wasn't like he could tell Patrick everything. These were Sarah's secrets, not his. The door opened.

"Nick, is everything okay?" Patrick was rumpled—his hair, his shirt. Annie was behind him, also rumpled.

"Shit. I'm sorry." He turned to leave.

"Wait. Is everything okay?" repeated Patrick.

"Nick, you look terrible. Did something happen to Sarah? Your family?" Annie pushed in front of Patrick and grabbed Nick's arm, pulling him into the office and closing the door.

"No. Everyone's fine."

Patrick had moved to the bar and poured several drinks. He handed one to Nick. "Sit. Something's wrong."

He took the drink and dropped onto the couch. "Sarah and I...I think it's over."

"Oh, Nick." Annie sat next to him and gave him a quick hug. "I'm so sorry."

"Yeah. Me too." He was more than sorry; he was numb, empty.

She glanced at Patrick. "I'll leave you two."

"No." Nick grabbed her arm and then dropped his hand. He didn't need Patrick punching him again. Right now, he wouldn't fight back. "Stay. I could use a woman's opinion."

"Okay." She settled on the couch.

Patrick sat on his desk. "What happened?"

He sighed. "It wasn't only one thing. It's a lot of little things."

"Like what?" asked Patrick.

"She doesn't trust me."

"Of course, she does," said Annie.

"No. She doesn't. She never tells me anything. She won't let me in."

"You guys haven't been together that long. She may need more time," said Patrick.

"I get that, but I...I can't keep fighting with her about it. She's always pushing me away. Shit, I wouldn't even be living with her except I just kind of moved in."

"She didn't invite you?" Annie sounded a little appalled.

"No."

"So, how did it happen?" asked Annie. "Did you just bring your stuff over and never leave." She didn't sound like she was on his side.

"Yeah, kind of like that."

"You actually did that?" She looked at Patrick. "Who does that?"

Patrick shrugged. "Nick's a pushy guy."

"No kidding," said Annie.

"Hey. I know what I want and I go for it." There was nothing wrong with that.

"Everyone else be damned," said Patrick.

"It wasn't like that. She wanted me too."

Annie took his hand. "That's true, but was she ready for you to move in with her? That's a big step."

"I don't know." He pulled away. "That doesn't matter. Not now. She's fine with me living there. She's just not fine with telling me anything...like where she goes three times a week."

"You think she's having an affair?" asked Patrick.

"No. I mean, I did wonder about it at first but I don't anymore."

"That's good," said Annie, "But why don't you still think that?"

"Because I know where she's going and before you ask. I can't tell you." He tossed back his drink. "Sarah's had some...problems in the past and I can't talk about them. If she wants you to know, she'll tell you."

"I know." Patrick looked at Annie. "We know."

"She told you?" He pushed off the couch. "She'll tell you, a stranger, these things but she won't tell me she's going for counselling. This is exactly what I'm talking about."

"She didn't tell us, dumbass," said Patrick. "I have her file. My company does the background checks for the Club, remember?"

"You knew before the Viewing. That's cheating." He was going to kill Ethan. If he'd let Patrick have an interview with Sarah, she would've chosen him and Nick would've never touched her, kissed her...

"I hadn't seen the file then. Believe me, Ethan made sure of that. You know him and his rules."

"Then when?" He still wasn't sure he believed his friend.

Patrick's gaze fell on Annie. "When someone I know decided that you should have a chance to talk to Sarah and let her explain why she didn't agree to meet you after four months."

"Oh." That actually made sense. He dropped back onto the couch.

"I took the file home because I wanted to make sure there wasn't a good reason that she hadn't contacted you and"— Patrick sent Annie a disgusted look—"someone is kind of nosey."

"Hey! You left it on the table. Open. What was I supposed to do?" said Annie.

"Not look at it."

"Please." She made a face at him and then turned toward Nick. "Sarah is wonderful and she's crazy about you. You just need to have patience."

"Well, I don't. I did but I don't anymore."

"What are you saying?" asked Patrick.

"I'm saying that I've put up with enough of her crap. I dealt with her damn dog. I've even kept my mouth shut about her not letting me help her with practically anything. Even suggestions about her business and that's what I do, but this...this lack of trust....A relationship can't work without trust and she doesn't trust me." He stared over Patrick's head for a moment, trying to get himself under control. "I took her to a party."

"Oh, that probably wasn't a good idea," said Annie.

"No shit and I wouldn't have done it if I'd known, but she didn't tell me." He almost shouted the last part. "Instead, she had a panic attack. I thought she was fucking dying."

"Oh Nick, I'm so sorry," said Annie.

"And then what happened?" Patrick was watching him closely.

"This is when it gets really good. At the hospital, when she was having tests done, her shrink came by. Sarah's sister had called her and the good doctor lectured me because I haven't made time to come and see her." He snorted. "I would've made as much time as needed if Sarah would've told me."

"Did you explain that to the doctor?" asked Annie.

"Yeah. Of course."

"And then what happened," asked Patrick.

"You're repeating yourself," said Nick.

"Because you're not getting to the part where you fucked up," said Patrick.

"I didn't fuck up." But his conscience whispered that maybe he had.

"I know you. You're a good guy but once that temper goes, you're a jackass."

"Like you can talk."

Patrick shrugged. "Fair enough but I'm not at your office looking like my world has ended."

"She never told me. It's been almost two weeks and she still hasn't told me about the panic attack or the doctor. She said she passed out because of not eating."

"Give her time," said Patrick.

"I have."

"Give her more."

Annie took his hand. "It's good that she's getting help, but you're going to have to have patience. These kinds of things are hard. People don't get over them in a flash. My brother is going through something similar and he's getting better, but in baby steps not leaps."

"I don't need her to get better overnight but I do need her to trust me. Me. Not everyone in the world. Just me. Is that too much to ask?"

"Well, no." Annie spoke hesitantly as if suspecting a trap.

"What did you do, Nick? Why are you so sure it's over?" asked Patrick.

"I told you."

"No. You told me some problems the two of you are having, not why it's over."

"I left. Is that what you want me to say?" He stood. "I came home, found more things she was hiding from me. We fought and I left."

"You left?" asked Annie. "You know she has issues trusting men, trusting you to not leave her and you left? You did the exact thing she feared." Her voice had risen to a high pitch.

"I told you he did something stupid," said Patrick.

"It's not fucking stupid. Relationships need trust." It wasn't stupid. It wasn't.

"And, since she's not moving at your pace, trusting you when you say she should, you threw a fit and left." Patrick clapped his hands. "Bravo. You won. You walked out and ended the best thing in your life."

"Fuck you." He strode out of the office.

CHAPTER 77: NICK

Nick should've beaten the shit out of Patrick. Even if he'd lost, a good fight would've released some of his pent up frustration. He strode into the Club. Another great way to blow off steam was fucking. He should go inside and find someone—end this farce of a relationship once and for all—but instead he went upstairs to Ethan's office.

"Come in," said Ethan at his knock.

He walked inside. This office was familiar and comfortable but it made him remember the past—a past he no longer wanted.

"What happened to you?" Ethan was in the back room watching the Club through the cameras.

"Sarah and I....It's over."

"What happened?" Ethan turned off the monitors.

He grabbed a glass and a bottle and sat on the chair next to the couch. Ethan already had a drink. He filled his glass, took a large swallow and then told Ethan about Sarah's collapse at his sister's and their fight tonight.

"So, you're upset because she doesn't trust you?" asked Ethan.

"Yeah." He watched his friend over the glass as he took another gulp of his drink. Ethan had to be on his side about this. Of course, he'd thought the same about Patrick.

"You're also mad because her lover wasn't her lover at all."

"No. I'm happy about that." The fact that she'd been

celibate too made him want to strut around beating his chest. He finished his drink.

"But you fought with her about it."

"Because, she didn't tell me." He refilled his glass.

"She was probably embarrassed."

"About what? She knew I'd be thrilled to find out she hadn't been with anyone since me." He took a sip of his drink. "Any guy would be."

"I'm sure she understood that but think of it from her side. You're"—Ethan waved his hand—"you."

"What the hell does that mean?" He was starting to think he needed new friends.

"What that means is you're a guy who can and does fuck almost any woman he wants."

"So are you."

"Yes, but I can understand where a woman may not want a man...like either of us to know she sat around pining for him."

"That doesn't make sense. It'd make me happy. She should've wanted to tell me that right away."

"Right." Ethan leaned back against the couch. "Because she exists to make you happy."

Nick's mouth opened and shut. "I didn't say that."

"When did you confess your celibacy to her?" Ethan took a drink of his brandy, his blue eyes boring into Nick's.

"I've had enough." He tossed back his drink and stood.

"Never told her, did you?"

"No." He headed for the door.

"Why? Didn't you trust her?"

"Asshole."

He slammed the door behind him but not before he heard

Ethan holler, "Trust goes both ways, Nick. Stop being a jackass and apologize to her."

CHAPTER 78: SARAH

Sarah sat outside on the back porch. Tank and Sweetie were curled up next to her on the loveseat. Nick was gone. She'd known it would end. She'd predicted it but being right didn't make her feel any better, especially when deep down she knew this was her fault. She should've confided in him. He'd done nothing to make her think he didn't truly care for her. Their relationship may have ended eventually but ending right now was because of her.

She didn't want to live like this anymore—alone, isolated— with only Tank and Sweetie for company. She scratched Sweetie's head. "You're staying. I don't care that officially you're Nick's dog."

Sweetie licked her hand and she wrapped her arms around the warm, strong body and sobbed. Tank nudged her back, finally settling his head on her butt and she cried more.

She had no idea how long she'd stayed like that but by the time she sat up, she knew what she had to do. She called the dogs and went into her bedroom and started packing.

CHAPTER 79: NICK

Nick was done with all of them. His friends sucked. He drove, not going anywhere specific, but his subconscious had a different idea. He pulled into the parking lot of Dr. Smileworth's office. He stared at the building. He should leave, but he got out of the car and went inside. She was with a patient so he waited, and waited. Patrick, Ethan and Annie were wrong. He was the one in the right about this.

The doctor came out. "Is Sarah okay?"

"Yeah." He stood. "I know you're busy but I was wondering if you had a moment."

The doctor looked at her watch and then at him. "I suppose my husband won't mind waiting a few minutes for dinner."

"I'm sorry. Never mind." He hadn't realized it was so late.

"Nonsense. We've been married forty years. He's used to this." She waved him into her office. "Give me a moment to call him." She turned to her secretary. "You can go, dear."

"Are you sure?" The secretary eyed him suspiciously.

He must look like hell if the woman was scared to leave the doctor alone with him. Usually, women flirted with him, not stared at him like he had a disease.

"Yes, dear." The doctor put the phone to her ear and Nick went into the office and sat on the big comfy chair next to the couch.

The doctor came in a few minutes later. "Did Sarah finally ask you to come here?"

"No. We fought and...I left."

"Oh." Dr. Smileworth sat down on the chair by a small desk.

There was no visible change in her face but he knew she was disappointed. "I...I can't handle her not trusting me."

"That's understandable."

He blinked. He hadn't expected that. "It is? My friends think I'm being an ass. They said I should be patient."

"That doesn't come easily for you, does it?"

"No." How the fuck did she know?

"It wouldn't for a man like you."

"What the hell? I'm so tired of everyone judging me. You don't even know me."

"Everyone?"

"My friends."

"They know you."

"Yes and no. They know who I was at the Club...um...when we used to go out."

"I know all about La Petite Mort Club."

"You do?" An image of this elderly lady wearing black leather and carrying a whip flashed in his head.

"Sarah told me about how you met."

"Oh." He wanted to shake his head and erase the image like an Etch-A-Sketch.

"Is it only your friends who judge you?"

"No. Sarah does too." That bothered him the most. She should know him, see the real him, not the playboy but the man.

"I see."

"I don't think it's going to work out for us." He wanted it to but he couldn't keep doing this.

"I'm sorry to hear that."

He'd expected her to try and convince him to give it another chance.

"Sarah is an exceptional woman but she does have trust issues," said Dr. Smileworth.

"She has good reason."

"Yes, but that doesn't make them easier to deal with on a daily basis."

"No. It doesn't." This was exactly what he wanted to hear—confirmation, validation of how he'd acted and how he was feeling—but it wasn't making him happy, only more depressed.

"It's good you realized it isn't going to work."

"It is?" Now, he was confused.

"Of course."

"Look doctor, I kind of expected you to talk me into trying again."

"Why would I do that?"

"I don't know." Because he was good for Sarah. Because they belonged together.

"Sarah needs a man who has patience. One who understands that she isn't a toy or a car that can be magically fixed. It takes time. There will be good days and bad." The doctor took a deep breath. "Mostly, Sarah needs a person she can depend on to be there always and when that happens, she'll learn to trust again."

"No one can promise forever. No one can say that they'll always be there for someone else. Things change. People change."

"I think you have your answer."

"What do you mean? That didn't answer anything."

"Are your parents still alive?"

"Yes." He was wary. He didn't trust abrupt changes of topic.

"If you were to get a call that one of them was in the hospital, what would you do?"

"I'd go there."

"What if you were out of the country on business, a very important business trip? One that could make or break your company."

"I don't give a shit. I'd leave. I'd fly home on the first plane and be there for them."

"Even if it ruined your business?"

"I can start another one."

"That sounds like always to me."

It was like a slap in the face.

She stood. "I need to go home to my husband. Goodnight Nick."

CHAPTER 80: NICK

Nick barely remembered leaving the office and couldn't recall at all where he'd gone afterwards. He'd driven for hours, no destination, just the empty road and his thoughts. It was late when he turned the car down the street toward home—home to Sarah. The dogs barked as he pulled into the driveway. He walked to the house, praying she hadn't changed the locks already. If she had, he'd pound on the door, break it down. He'd make her listen to him. He breathed a sigh of relief when the key turned the lock. He stepped inside, shushing the dogs as he went into the bedroom.

Sarah sat up in bed, turning on the lamp on her nightstand. Her eyes were wide and her hair rumpled.

"I'm sorry." He wanted to fall into her and hold her, but he wasn't sure he still had that right.

Her eyes glimmered with tears. "No, Nick. It's my fault."

He didn't remember moving but he must've because he was on the bed holding her in his arms. She felt so good, warm and soft as she clung to him. He kissed her. It was supposed to be a soft kiss, a thank you for not kicking him out but as soon as his lips touched hers everything but his need for her disappeared. He had to know she was still his. That he hadn't fucked up the best thing that'd ever happened to him. "I need you." He whispered as his lips trailed down her cheek to her neck.

She pulled his shirt off as he removed hers. His hands

406

cupped her breasts as his tongue thrust into her mouth. He was desperate for her. He shoved her underwear down her legs and she kicked them off, her hands unzipping his pants and taking him out, stroking him.

"Stop, baby." He grabbed her hand. "I need to be inside you. Please." He snatched a condom from the nightstand and covered his cock.

She lay back on the bed, spreading her legs. He kissed her as he lowered his body to hers and pushed inside.

"Fuck. You feel so good." He loved the way she clung to him. She was perfect, perfect for him.

"You too." She wrapped her legs around him, tipping her hips and taking him farther inside.

"Wait." He stared into her eyes, so green and lush. "I'm sorry, Sarah. I shouldn't have left."

She cupped his cheek with one hand as the other tangled in his hair. "I should've told you."

"No. I understand." She was so hot and wet, so tight that his hips started moving on their own.

"Please." She kissed him. "We can talk later."

"Yeah." He pulled almost all the way out and pushed back in, the pleasure of her pussy clasping onto him shooting down his spine and into his balls. He wasn't going to last long. He hadn't thought he'd ever feel this again. He grabbed her leg, lifting it and adjusting his angle so he hit her g-spot. He thrust into her in hard fast jabs and she closed her eyes moaning.

"Oh, Nick. Right...there...please."

Her hands clawed at his back and her foot pushed on his ass as he thrust harder and faster. His balls tightened. He reached between them and skimmed his thumb over her clit, pushing her over the edge and making her body buck. She tightened around him almost to the point of pain and he came, collapsing onto her when he was done.

He rolled over, pulling her with him. He wrapped her in his arms, her ass to his front. "I have to tell you something."

"You don't need to ex—"

"I do. I-I haven't been with anyone since you."

"Really?" She wiggled until he let go so she could turn in his arms.

He stared into her eyes, no longer afraid she'd think he was whipped because he didn't care. "Yeah. I was celibate for four months, waiting for you."

She bit her lip and then laughed

"It's not exactly funny." It'd been excruciating.

"No. I know. I'm sorry." She continued to giggle. "It's just that...that explains why you were so pissed and...insatiable that first night."

"I was crazy for you. Still am." His hands skimmed down her back to her ass.

She sobered. "Why did you...Why were you celibate?"

He kissed her. "Because I wanted you to know that I was serious about this. About us."

"Oh Nick, you must've been so hurt when I didn't send the letter."

He shrugged and took a deep breath. Honesty. He needed to be honest with her. "Yeah. I was." He glanced away. "I was so sure you'd come to the Club."

"Oh no, you were actually there?"

"Yeah, I got there early. The guys were taking bets and teasing me. It was fine...until you didn't show."

"I'm so sorry." She pulled his head down and kissed him.

He wanted to sink into her but they were on the cusp of something beautiful, something more than sex and he needed her to go there with him. He broke the kiss. "Why didn't you contact Ethan?"

She rolled away from him. He almost grabbed her but he'd learned that sometimes she needed her space. She sat up, taking the sheet with her and covering her breasts. "I figured you'd forgotten about me the moment I was out of sight."

He sat up and leaned against the headboard—close to her but not touching. "Never. I waited for you. Everyone said I was crazy but...I didn't care." He shifted so he could watch her. "I was celibate for you. I haven't touched another woman since the day we signed the contract."

"Really?" Her eyes locked with his.

He shifted closer so there was only an inch or two separating him from her. "Really."

"Why?"

"I'd think it was obvious." His cock throbbed for her again. "I'm crazy about you. I can't get enough of you."

"Why? I-I'm not easy to be with."

"You're beautiful and smart and funny and I don't really know why I can't get enough of you but I can't. You're in my blood, Sarah." He should tell her she was in his heart but he faltered. He pulled her close, letting her feel his erection. "I need you."

She kissed him and rolled away, getting out of bed. "We need to talk." She grabbed her shirt and covered herself.

His stomach dropped to his toes. She couldn't be breaking up with him. They'd just fucked.

"I...as you know, I have some issues." She began to pace. "I'm sorry I didn't tell you. That wasn't fair to you."

"It's okay. We can work through this together. I'll go see Dr. Smileworth with you." He took her hand. If he kept touching her, she couldn't deny what they had. "I'm not going anywhere, Sarah. I swear."

"But I am."

"What?" He dropped her hand.

She sat on the bed next to him and kissed his cheek. "I need to go away. Get help."

"I thought you were doing that with Dr. Smileworth."

"I am but she thinks it'll go faster if I go away for a bit."

"You don't need to rush this. Not for me."

"I'm not doing this for you."

"Of course. God, I'm an arrogant ass. Even when I try not to be."

She touched his lips, silencing him. "I'm able to do this because of you."

"What do you mean?"

"I need you...I'm asking you to watch Tank and Sweetie while I'm gone. If you don't..."

He kissed her. "I'll do it. I'll do whatever you want."

"You will? It may be a month or two."

He'd die without her for that long. "Take however long you need." He kissed her again. "I'll take care of the dogs."

"Can you also help Peter with the business if he needs it? He can handle most things but....I know it's asking a lot, but..."

He took her head in his hands. "Baby, I'll take care of everything. I promise. You just take care of yourself." He kissed her. "Thank you for trusting me with this." He kissed her again.

It was slow and sweet. "When are you going?"

"Day after tomorrow."

"Oh." He wanted to beg her to stay with him, to get better slower but this was best for her and that was all that mattered.

"Dr. Smileworth wanted me to start tomorrow but...I wasn't sure I'd be able to get a hold of you."

He swallowed, hating the words that were going to come out of his mouth. "Talk to her. If you can still get in tomorrow you should go."

"No. I want to spend tomorrow with you."

"Are you sure?" He prayed she'd stay—give him one more day to worship her, to show her how he felt, to make memories that would have to last them both for months.

"Yes." She kissed him and pushed him back onto the bed, shoving the blankets aside and straddling him.

AFTER THE SEDUCTION

CHAPTER 81: NICK

Nick's stomach was in knots and his shirt was sticky with sweat as he got out of his car and walked to the facility. It'd been almost two months since he'd seen Sarah. They talked on the phone several times a week, but shortly after arriving she'd asked him not to visit.

It wasn't a good sign. She may not want him anymore. Maybe, she'd only wanted him because she'd been lonely...broken. Now that she was better, she might realize what an ass he'd been and kick him to the curb. He felt like he was going to puke, but he wiped his hand on his pants and grabbed the door handle. The cold blast of air from the air conditioner hit his face, helping to push back his nausea.

In a few minutes, he'd see her, take her home...and find out if he'd ruined everything by being a controlling ass. He took a deep breath and walked over to the reception area.

"Who are you here to see?" asked a pleasant, middle-aged woman.

"Sarah Daly." He was glad his voice didn't shake.

"Sign in. She'll be here shortly." The lady smiled at him as he signed his name on a list.

He moved over to some chairs by the wall but didn't sit. He was too nervous. His life was going to change today, either for better or worse, but he had to remember that no matter what, this was about her not him. He'd been seeing Dr. Smileworth since Sarah had been gone, getting ready for when she got out. He wanted to be the best boyfriend...No, he wanted more than that. He wanted to be the best husband she could have, but the doctor had warned him that things would be different when she came home. She'd be better but she may not want the same things that she'd wanted before—including him. Fuck. It'd kill him if she didn't want him anymore.

She stepped out of a room and walked down the hallway, carrying her suitcase and purse. His breath froze in his chest and his dick hardened. She looked good. She'd always looked good but now, she looked happy. Her eyes sparkled as she talked to a lady who was walking with her and her stride was confident and graceful. Her hair was pulled back in a ponytail and she wore jeans and a T-shirt. He wanted to tear them off with his teeth but he didn't move—content for the moment to just look at her.

The other lady said something and Sarah's gaze landed on him. Her smile faltered for a moment and his heart stalled.

"Nick..." It was a soft whisper but he felt it in his soul.

He moved toward her as if pulled by a string. He stopped in front of her, hands clasped at his sides so he didn't grab her and wrap her in his arms. "You look good."

"You too." Her eyes had softened and she stared at him as if seeing him for the first time.

"Ready?" He took her suitcase from her.

"Yeah. Let's go home."

His breath came easier now. She wouldn't have said it that way if she wanted him to leave, right?

CHAPTER 82: SARAH

Sarah kissed Maisie and hugged Peter and Kyle. Her mom had left a few hours earlier because she didn't like driving in the dark.

"I'll see you"—Maisie's eyes darted to Nick who was cleaning up the dishes in the kitchen—"next week."

"Next week? I thought we could go out for lunch tomorrow or the next day."

Maisie hugged her. "You two need time alone." She kissed her cheek. "Call me tomorrow."

"Okay." She closed the door behind them and the silence of the house bore down on her. The clinic had never been quiet. There'd always been machines and the soft sounds that people made just existing. She missed that. After years of only her and Tank, she realized that she needed more. Hopefully, she had more. She took a deep breath and walked into the kitchen.

"I've got this. You go rest." Nick glanced at her as he loaded the dishwasher.

"I'm fine." She started wiping the table. He'd been distant all day. Perhaps, he'd moved on. "Thank you for taking care of the dogs. Tank's doing well."

Nick's lips thinned but he nodded. "Yeah, he is. He and Sweetie are doing great. We go to the dog park at least once a week."

"And Tank is okay there?"

"He loves it."

She stared at her dog. She'd been holding him back all these years. Tank had been ready to move on, to live and she'd kept him prisoner.

"Why don't you get some rest? I've got this. Seriously."

"Maybe, I'll take a bath." She glanced at him. He was so handsome and kind and good and she had no idea if he was still hers. She wanted to ask him to join her, but his back was stiff and his face tight with tension. This hadn't been easy on him either. "Unless you want us to do something else?" There she'd hinted.

"No. You take your bath. I'll finish up in here and then...watch TV or something."

"Oh. Okay." The Nick she remembered would've been all over her subtle offer. *Maybe, he's nervous too.* If it weren't so sad, she'd laugh. Nick was never nervous about sex. He was controlling, commanding and often rough, but never nervous. She went into their room and shut the door, leaning against it. She'd find out soon enough if he still wanted her. "I think I'm going to go to bed after my bath," she hollered.

"Okay," he answered.

Had his voice gotten richer with desire or was that wishful thinking? Either way, maybe she could help persuade him into action. She had just the nightgown to do it too. It was green and black. His favorite colors on her. She opened the drawer and her breath caught in her throat. His clothes were gone. There was a large empty space next to her underwear where his used to be. She grabbed her phone and called Gina, her counselor.

"He's leaving." She inhaled deeply, trying to stay calm.

"Oh Sarah, I'm so sorry to hear that, but you can handle this," said Gina.

"I know but...I thought...hoped."

"People change. You'll get through this. Do you need me to come over?" Gina's no nonsense approach helped calm her nerves.

"No. I'm okay."

"Are you sure? You shouldn't be alone your first night."

"I'm not. Nick's here."

"He's there?"

"Yes."

"I thought you said he left," said Gina.

"Not yet, but he's going to. His clothes are gone." She'd fought so hard to believe she deserved and could have a relationship and now it was over before it began.

"Sarah, what are you talking about?"

"In our dresser. His clothes were there by mine, with mine, and now they're not."

"Did he tell you he wants out?"

"No, but he's been distant." And he doesn't want sex. For Nick, that meant it was over.

"Sarah, we talked about this."

She stared at the bathroom door. She should've never called Gina.

"You know what you have to do. You can't guess what others are going to do or think. If you want to know how someone else is feeling, what do you do?"

"Ask." She sounded like a pouty child. She didn't want to ask him because then her fears would be confirmed.

"It's always better to know, right?"

"I suppose," she lied. That was one of the mantras at the clinic that she hadn't quite embraced.

"Ask him."

"Okay."

"Swear?"

"I swear."

"When?" prodded Gina.

The woman knew her too well. "As soon as I get out of the shower." She was no longer in any mood to soak in the tub.

"Today. Out of the shower today."

"Yes, mother." Damn it, she'd hoped to slide that one by her friend. "Today. In fifteen minutes or so."

"Good."

"Goodbye...and thanks." Now, she wasn't only sad because Nick was leaving but dreading the conversation that was coming.

"You'll be fine. You're strong and capable but call me if you need to talk."

"I will." She hung up the phone and turned on the water, waiting for it to heat up before stepping inside the shower. The hot water soaked into her skin. She closed her eyes and breathed deeply. She'd be okay. Nick could go. She didn't want him to but she'd be okay if he did. She squirted soap onto the loofah and ran it over her body, wishing it were his hands touching her skin.

She wasn't ready to lose him. It wasn't fair. She'd been okay with not having him in her life before but...now she wanted him—a relationship with him. Of course, she could try and persuade him to stay. Unless he'd found someone else, maybe they could work through this. She'd talk to him like she'd promised Gina but she didn't have to wear her clothes. That nightgown would work nicely.

CHAPTER 83: NICK

Nick sat in the guest bedroom, listening to the shower running and imagining Sarah—her body wet and naked, warm and slippery. He could step inside, behind her. Her skin would be so soft and smooth. Damn, he needed to jerk off. Again.

The water stopped. She may need him for something. His dick rose even more. No. She didn't need that, not tonight. Maybe, never from him.

There was a tap on the door. "Nick? Are you in there?"

"Yeah." He grabbed a pillow and put it over his lap. Even wearing jeans she'd have to be blind to miss the bulge in his pants.

She opened the door and stepped inside. The breath left his body in a whoosh and his head spun. She was wearing a tiny, green nightgown with black lace over her chest. It only came to the top of her thighs and it was low cut. If she bent even a little he'd be able to see her breasts.

His eyes lingered on her chest. Her nipples were hard. She was probably wet and ready. She had to want him. There was no other reason for her to come to his room dressed like that. He sat on his hands so he didn't reach for her. That was old Nick's way of thinking. New Nick understood that there could be other reasons that would make her seek him out dressed like that. He couldn't come up with one but that was because all the blood had left his head and gone straight to his cock.

"I...I noticed that your clothes are gone and...Why are you

in here?"

He inhaled deeply and it was a mistake. He could smell her perfume or shampoo or just her and his body trembled. He needed sex. He needed a woman but more than that he needed her. "I thought...I...Fuck, this is hard."

Her eyes dropped to his lap as a blush crept up her cheeks. "I'm sorry. If you don't want..."

She started to turn. He couldn't let her leave, not like this.

"Wait. Let me try this again." He took a deep breath and tried to keep his eyes on her face. "It's been brought to my attention that I've been an overbearing ass."

"What?"

"I forced you to let me move in with you."

"I wouldn't say forced."

"You didn't invite me. I just came over and stayed."

"Well...yeah."

"I coerced you into being with me that first night." The entire time she'd been gone, he'd replayed that evening in his head. He hadn't forced her...not really, but he had pushed and persuaded.

"I wanted you too."

"You don't know how much I needed to hear that. Thank you." He held up his hand as she stepped closer. If she got within reach, he'd grab her. He wasn't strong enough not to. "Stay."

She frowned.

"I've been bullying you to do what I wanted and when I wanted it since the day we met."

"I've held my own."

"Yes, you did"—he smiled a little—"but that doesn't excuse

the way I acted." He took a shaky breath. "I thought that maybe...we can start over. You can decide what you want." He looked down at his hands that were grasping the pillow. "If you still want me,"—he glanced at her, praying she still did—"we can go as slow as you like. We can date." He almost cringed at the word. "I can stay here or move back to my place." His gaze fell on the two dogs who'd followed her down the hallway. "Whatever you decide, I think Sweetie should stay here. I'll pay for his care and visit him but I don't think it's fair to separate him and Tank." Just because he'd screwed up the best thing that'd ever happened to him, the dogs shouldn't suffer.

"You're right."

His shoulder's dropped. Being right had never felt so hollow.

"You have tried to push your agenda on me. No condoms. Anal. Meeting more than once a week." She stepped closer, her green eyes sparkling. "But I only agreed to the things that I wanted to do too."

"What about me living here?" His heart picked up its pace. There was hope.

"I may have been broken Nick but I still had a spine." She moved forward, stopping in front of him.

"You were never broken." The scent of her was making him dizzy with need. His hand shook as he captured hers. "You're the strongest person I know."

"The two aren't mutually exclusive."

"Are you still broken?" He ran his thumb over her skin. She was so soft and warm. He'd dreamt about this—touching her, being with her.

"A little but not as much."

420

"I fixed you then?" He pulled her closer, until she was between his legs. "It's what I do, you know. I fix things."

She smiled down at him. "I'm sorry, Nick but you didn't fix me. I fixed me." She grabbed the pillow and tossed it aside, her eyes widening at the bulge in his pants. "That looks like it hurts."

"Aches. For you." He grinned. "I bet you can fix that too."

"I can." She straddled his legs, brushing her hands over his face. "I want you to know that even though you didn't fix me, you did give me new pieces—ones that replaced the broken parts."

He almost moaned as she pressed against him, but the doctor had suggested they take it slow. "I can't believe I'm saying this, but are you sure about this...about us? If you need more time..." He'd died right here and now, his dick sticking up, but he'd wait if she wanted.

"I don't need more time. I'm crazy about you. I want you here in my...our home, in my life with me. If that's what you want." Now, her eyes were uncertain.

Her saying she was crazy about him didn't make him happy. She'd avoided the words just like he had but he was done being a coward. He took her face in his hands, wanting to bury himself in her softness, but needing to say this first. "I love you, Sarah. I want to spend the rest of my life with you."

She smiled sadly, pulling his hands away and kissing his knuckles. "You don't have to say that. I know we can't promise forever."

"But I can. I love my family. That isn't going to change. I love those damn dogs. That isn't going to change." He held her face again. "And I love you. That isn't going to change either. I love you with all my heart, Sarah. With everything I am." He rolled his hips upward, inhaling deeply as he rubbed against her. "Including my body."

"That's a very important part." She smiled as she pressed down on him. "Nick, I lo—"

He put a finger on her mouth. "I wasn't supposed to tell you how I felt, not yet. I was supposed to give you time. I don't want you to feel like I'm rushing you again because I'm not." He took a shaky breath. "Take all the time you need to decide exactly what you want. I'm not going anywhere." He kissed her forehead. "Think before you say anything. There's no changing your mind about this. Be super sure because for me, this is forever."

She nipped his finger, the slight pain going right to his cock. He couldn't stop from pressing his dick against her.

"My mind has been made up for a long time." She kissed him. "I love you too, Nick. I've loved you since our first night together. I was so scared and you were so kind and patient."

It was enough to send him over the edge. He grabbed her, pushing her down on the bed and taking her mouth. He'd never wanted anyone like he wanted her. She reached between them and caressed his cock.

He broke the kiss, moaning. "That feels so good."

She pushed against his chest. He wanted to hold her hands over her head and shove into her, but he rolled over instead. She straddled him, pulling off his shirt and tossing it aside. She bent, kissing her way down his body. Her mouth was hot and wet and he wanted it wrapped around his dick, but he couldn't do that, not this time.

He grabbed her hair. "Wait. Stop."

She was on her knees between his legs looking up at him with a mischievous glint in her beautiful, green eyes.

"Fuck baby, don't look at me like that." He scrambled off the bed and stood.

"What's the matter?" Her hand rubbed his dick through his pants.

"It's been too long." He should step away, but he was weak. He leaned into her touch. "I'll never last."

"That's okay." She undid his button. "I'll enjoy making you hard again."

"Sarah." His hand rested on her head. He wasn't pushing her toward his cock. He wasn't.

"Maybe, I'll tie you up and get the vibrator and make you watch as I pleasure myself."

"Fuck." His legs shook as she unzipped his pants. His hands tangled in her hair as her hot breath whispered over his dick. "Please, Sarah. I need to be inside you this time. You can suck me off later."

She leaned forward and kissed his dick through his underwear. His eyes almost rolled to the back of his head. He was a goner. He couldn't fight her.

She stood and put her hands on his chest, angling him toward the bed. "Okay Nick, but I've missed you so much you better make this fast." She shoved him, making him fall back onto the bed. She crawled up his body and straddled him, before kissing his chest. "I've missed you." She sat up and lifted the nightgown over her head, tossing it aside.

"God, you're beautiful." Her breasts were even more perfect than he'd remembered—soft and round, highlighting her slender body. He cupped them, squeezing and molding them to his touch. She was warm, silky perfection.

She bit her lip, her eyes half closing. "Oh Nick, I can't wait." She was rubbing against him, her rhythm getting faster and faster. "I need you inside me, now." She started shoving his pants down, trying to free his cock.

"Wait." He stopped her again.

"What?" she almost snapped.

"I have to get a condom. Let's go to your...our bedroom."

"Forget the condom." She pulled his dick from his pants, her hand tightening around him.

"Wait...Sarah..."

She kept stroking him as she lifted, pulling off her panties. She put his tip at her entrance. She was so fucking hot and wet. His hips rocked up and he slipped into her, just a little. She felt so good, so right but they couldn't do this. He almost ground his teeth to powder as he grabbed her hips and lifted her off him. A groan of pain escaped—his entire body revolting at his betrayal.

He dropped her on the bed and rolled on top of her, straddling her legs and keeping his cock away from her. "Are you sure about this? It's okay if you're not." He wanted, more than anything, to fuck her without a condom.

"I'm sure." She touched his cheek, her fingers a light caress. "I love you, Nick. I trust you. I want you. Just you and me. Nothing between us anymore."

"I love you too." He leaned down and kissed her, keeping his body away from hers because this one moment wasn't about sex. It was about so much more than that—love, their future, their forever.

Her leg came up, rubbing against his thigh. "Nick, please."

He lowered himself to her, bracing on his hands. "Put me

inside you."

She grabbed his cock, leading him to her. He kissed her quickly and then stared into her green eyes, so dark with passion, as he slid slowly into her. Her mouth opened in an "O" as she gasped.

"You feel so good. So tight." He slid out and back in a little farther, enjoying the feel, the heat.

She bent her knees making him slip in even more. He watched her face as he moved in and out, filling her more and more until he was inside her balls deep. He held still, relishing the feel of her tight body surrounding him, clinging to him but soon it wasn't enough. His body wanted...demanded more and his hips rocked back and forth, in and out. She wrapped her arms around him, her nails digging into his back and her legs tangling with his.

"That's it, baby." He moved faster and faster.

She was moaning now, soft little whimpers that drove him wild. His pace became faster, frenzied. She was clamping onto him tighter and tighter, squeezing him.

"Come for me, Sarah. Come for me." He reached between them and ran his fingers over her clit, stroking her until her body stiffened, her mouth opening in a silent scream. Her face was so beautiful in her orgasm that it pushed him over the edge. He came inside of her, filling her for the first time. Hopefully, one day, when they were both ready, she'd become pregnant.

He collapsed on top of her, unable to move for several moments. He breathed her in, her scent making him dizzy. He'd been too long without her, but never again. He kissed her neck and then rolled off her, pulling her into his arms. "I love you,

Sarah."

"I love you too, Nick."

"Marry me, Sarah." The words just slipped out. He'd been thinking them for months, but hadn't meant to say them.

"Nick, isn't this a little soon?"

He rolled over to look at her. "If it is for you, that's fine." It wasn't. It hurt. "But I've been thinking about this from that night of the banquet. Deep down, I knew I'd never let you go." He smiled at her. "I was lying to myself, hoping I'd tire of you."

"Oh." It was a soft whisper.

He kissed her. "I want you to know the truth. I didn't want a relationship. I was scared. Scared to love you. Scared you didn't feel the same."

"How could you not know how I felt?" She touched his face.

"You didn't contact Ethan. I thought you had a boyfriend."

"I'm sorry about that."

"Don't be. We're here now and if you aren't ready to be my wife, I'll wait." He touched her face, his fingers worshiping her. "Like I said, I'm not going anywhere."

"I...I'm not ready to be a wife."

"Okay." He kissed her to try and let her know it was okay. His heart was bruised but not defeated. "I'll ask again later."

"You don't need to."

Now, his heart was gone. Annihilated. She'd said she loved him. He stared down at her afraid to move because if he did, he'd leave and he'd promised he'd stay.

"Because I am ready to be your fiancé."

He was able to breathe again. "Really?"

"Yes, but I think we need a long engagement."

"Fine. Whatever you want." He kissed her, so grateful and happy and then he paused. "How long? Six months? A year?"

"How about a couple of years. Three sounds good."

"Three years? No. That's not going to work. I want everyone to know you belong to me." He ran his finger down her neck, over her collarbone and between her breasts. "Or would you rather I tattoo you again with my kisses?"

"You'd better never, ever do that again." She sounded mad but there was a smile in her eyes.

"Then a year." He kissed her neck, sucking gently before letting go. "Or else."

"I need more than a year. It takes a year to plan and...I can't focus on that right now."

"Oh, right. Shit, I'm sorry, babe. I'm such a selfish jerk." She'd just gotten out of the facility and he was pushing her, pressuring her to do what he wanted. He was doing the exact opposite of what the doctor had told him.

"Don't be. I love you, Nick." She kissed him. It was soft and sweet. "And I love it when you take charge, boss me around."

"You do?" That was good because no matter how hard he tried, he probably wouldn't stop doing that.

"Yes, because I only listen when I want to."

"You do argue with me a lot. You're going to have to learn to be a more obedient wife or I'll have to punish you." He swatted her ass.

"Oh, I see another fantasy coming. The naughty wife." She grabbed his head and kissed him, her tongue slipping into his mouth and her hand sliding down his body to fondle his hardening cock. "I'll need to be severely punished."

"I think you need that now."

"Do you?" She skimmed her nail gently over his balls.

"Yes." The word hissed from between his teeth. He rolled off her, hopped out of bed and grabbed her, tossing her over his shoulder.

"Nick," she laughed. "What are you doing?"

"Taking you to our room." Tank gave a warning rumble but he just patted the dog's head as he walked past.

"But this room—"

"Doesn't have the tools I need." He swatted her bottom and she squealed. "You, my love, need to be restrained."

"Oh please, Nick. Punish me. I've been a very naughty fiancé."

I hope you enjoyed Sarah and Nick's story.

Look below for a sneak peek at The Voyeur (Patrick and Annie's story). And it's free on all ebook retailers.

Sign up for my newsletter and you'll get special book offers, funny and educational emails about all things kinky, sneak peeks at book covers and a lot of other fun things.

Here's What You Get When You
Join My Readers' Group

Win Before You Can Buy
Exclusive Giveaways
Free Books
Sneak Peeks

Go to my website or email me for details:

http://www.EllisODay.com

authorellisoday@gmail.com

The Voyeur

CHAPTER 1: ANNIE

Annie finished making the bed and gathered the sheets from the floor, keeping them as far away from her body as possible. These sex rooms were disgusting and Ethan was a jerk making her work as a maid. She almost had her Bachelor's Degree in Culinary Arts, but he'd refused to hire her for the kitchen—too many men in the kitchen. The only job he'd give her at La Petite Mort Club was as a maid and unfortunately, she needed the money too badly to refuse.

She stuffed the dirty sheets into the cart and hurried out the door. She had almost thirty minutes before she had to be at the next "sex room." She hid the cart in a closet and darted down a back hallway, staying clear of the cameras. Julie, the woman who supervised the daytime maids, was a real bitch. If she were caught sneaking away from her duties, she'd be assigned to the orgy rooms every day. Right now, they all took turns cleaning that nightmare. She swore they should get hazard pay to even go in those rooms.

She slipped through a doorway and hurried to the one-way mirror. She stared at the couple in the next room. From her first day here, she'd been curious about the activities at the club. She was twenty-four and wasn't a virgin but she'd never, ever done some of these things.

The woman in the room below was tied to a table, legs spread and wearing some sort of leather outfit that left her large breasts free and her crotch exposed. She had shaved her pussy and her pink lower lips were swollen and glistening from her excitement. The man strolled around the table as if he had all night. He still had his pants on but had removed his shirt. His arms and chest were well defined but he had a slight paunch. His erection tented his pants and Annie felt wetness pool between her legs. She had no idea why watching this turned her on but it did. Ever since she'd accidentally barged in on that guy and girl in the Interview room, she couldn't stop watching.

The man below ran his hand up the woman's inner thigh, glancing over her pussy. The woman thrust her hips upward and Annie ran her own hand between her legs. The man's mouth moved but Annie couldn't hear anything and then he slapped the woman across the thigh hard enough to leave a red mark. Annie jumped. She wasn't into that, but she couldn't stop watching the woman's face. At first, it'd contorted in pain but then it'd morphed into pleasure. The man hit her again and then bent, kissing the red welts—

running his tongue across them as his fingers squeezed her nipple.

Annie clutched her thighs together, searching for some relief. Her panties were soaked. It wouldn't take but a few strokes to make her come. She started to slide her hand into her pants.

"Having fun?" asked a deep voice from behind her.

She spun around, her heart dropping into her stomach. "Ah…I was just finishing cleaning in here." Damn, she should've closed the door but she hadn't expected anyone in this area. The rooms were off limits on this floor until tonight and she was the only one assigned to clean here.

He shut the door and locked it before strolling toward her. She'd seen him around the Club, but more than that she remembered him from the military photos her brother, Vic, had sent to her. She carried one of the three of them—Vic, Ethan and this guy, Patrick—in her purse. He'd been attractive in the picture, but now that he was older and in person he was gorgeous. He had dark green eyes, brown hair and a perfect body. He stopped so close to her his chest almost brushed against her breasts. She was pretty sure it would if she inhaled deeply. She really wanted to take that deep breath and feel his hard chest against her breasts.

"Don't let me stop you from enjoying the show."

"I…I wasn't. I should go." She started to walk past him but he grabbed her hand.

His grip was warm and strong but loose enough that she could pull free if she wanted. She didn't. Even though she only knew him from her brother's pictures and letters, she'd had many fantasies about him when she'd been in high school. Her gaze dropped to the front of his pants and her mouth almost watered. He was definitely interested. She dragged her eyes up his body, stopping on his face. He smiled at her.

"There's nothing to be embarrassed about. Watching turns us all on." He kissed the back of her hand and she jumped as his tongue darted out, tasting her skin.

"I...I should go." She didn't move.

"No, you should watch." He dropped her hand and grabbed her shoulders, gently turning her toward the mirror. He trailed his hands up and down her arms. "Watch."

The man in the other room was now sucking on the woman's breast as his fingers caressed her pussy.

"Would you like to hear them? Or do you like it quiet?" His voice was a rough whisper against her ear.

"Sound, please." She wanted to hear their gasps and moans. She wanted to close her eyes and pretend it was her. She shifted, squeezing her thighs together.

He chuckled as he moved away. She felt his absence to her bones. He'd been strong and warm behind her and for a moment she'd felt safe, safer than she had since her brother had come back from the war, broken and sad, and her father had started drinking again.

The woman's moans filled the room and Patrick came back to stand behind her, this time placing his hands on her waist.

"I'm Patrick," he said against her ear.

She couldn't take her eyes from the scene in front of her. The woman was almost coming as the man thrust his fingers inside of her.

"What's your name?" He nipped her neck and she jumped.

"I...I..." If she told him her name, he might say something to Ethan. Ethan would kill her if he knew she was in here watching.

"Tell me your name." His lips trailed along her neck and she tipped her head giving him better access.

The guy was kissing his way down the woman's body. Annie wanted to touch herself, to make herself come but Patrick was here.

He nibbled her ear. "Why won't you tell me your name?"

"I...I'll get in trouble." She rubbed her ass against his erection, hopefully giving him a hint.

"Tease." His hand drifted down her stomach, stopping right above where she wanted him to touch. "Tell me your name or I'll make you suffer." He unbuttoned her pants and left his hand—warm, rough but immobile—resting on her abdomen.

"I can't." She stood on tip-toe, hoping his hand would lower a little but he was too tall or she was too short. He had to be almost six foot and she was barely five-foot four. "I could get fired and I need this job."

"Darling, Ethan won't fire you for fucking a customer."

"We can't." She spun around. She hadn't thought this through. He was her fantasy come to life and she wanted him to be hers just for a moment, but Ethan would find out and then she'd be in deep shit.

"Don't worry. I'm a member and you work here, so we're both clean." He hesitated, his hands tightening on her hips. "Are you protected?"

"What?" She had no idea what he was talking about.

"Ethan makes sure everyone at the Club is clean but only the…some of his employees are required to be on birth control." He ran his hands up her sides, getting closer and closer to her breasts. "Are you on birth control?" His eyes darkened as they dropped to her tits. "If not, it's okay. There are other things we can do."

Oh, she wanted to do everything his eyes promised, but she couldn't. "No, I'll get in trouble. I need this job. I have to go." She tried to move but her feet refused to obey, so she just stared at his handsome face.

"Are you sure?" He bent so he was almost eye level with her. "I promise. Ethan won't care. A lot of maids become…change jobs. The pay's a lot better." His eyes roamed over her frame. "Especially, for someone as cute as you."

Ethan would kill her before letting her become one of his pleasure associates.

"I could talk to Ethan for you." His hands moved up her body, stopping right below her breasts.

Her nipples hardened and she forgot everything but what he was making her feel. He ran his thumb over one of them and she leaned closer, wanting him to do it again.

He did. He continued rubbing her nipple as he spoke. "I could persuade him to let me…handle your initiation into club life."

Her heart raced in her chest. It could be just her and him doing all these things she'd seen. Her pussy throbbed but she couldn't do it. She wouldn't do it. She couldn't have sex for money. Her parents were both dead but they'd never understand and she couldn't disappoint them. "No. I can't do that…not for money." Her eyes darted to the door. She needed to get out of there before she did something she'd regret.

"That's even better." He smiled as he stepped closer. "We can keep this between us. No money. Only a man and a woman." He leaned down and whispered in her ear, "Giving each other pleasure. A lot of pleasure. In ways you haven't even imagined."

There were moans from the other room and she glanced over her shoulder. The man's face was buried between the woman's thighs.

Patrick turned her around, pulling her against him and wrapping his arms around her waist. "Are you wet?"

"What? No." She struggled in his arms, her ass brushing against his erection again.

"Oh fuck. Do that again." He kissed her neck, open mouthed and hot.

She stopped trying to get away. She wanted this...this moment. She shouldn't but she did, so she wiggled her butt against him again. He was hard and long and her body ached for him. It'd been too long since she'd had sex. She needed this.

"Would you like me to touch you?" His hands drifted over her hips and down her thighs.

She'd like him to do all sorts of things to her. She nodded.

"Say it." His words were a command she couldn't disobey.

"Yes."

"Yes, what?" He untucked her shirt from her pants.

"Touch me. Please." She was already pushing her hips toward his hand. She wanted his hand on her, his fingers inside of her.

"Are you wet?" he asked again.

She inhaled sharply as he unzipped her pants.

"Don't lie to me. I'll find out in a minute."

She'd never talked dirty during sex and she wasn't sure she was ready to do that with a stranger. Her heart skipped a beat. Maybe, she shouldn't be doing any of this with a stranger. She grabbed his hand. "Maybe, we shouldn't."

The woman below cried out and the man straightened, wiping his face and unbuttoning his pants.

"Watch. The main event is about to happen." Patrick's hot breath tickled her neck.

Her gaze locked on the man's penis. It was large and demanding. He straddled the woman, grabbing his cock.

"Don't you want to feel some of what they feel?" He nibbled on her ear and then neck. "I can help you."

She may not know him, but she trusted him. He was a former marine. He'd been a good friend of Vic's. He wouldn't hurt her and she needed to come. She loosened her grip, letting go of his hand. He slipped inside her pants, caressing her pussy through her underwear. His fingers were long and strong. She closed her eyes, leaning against him as he stroked her.

"You're already so wet and hot." His breath was a warm caress on her ear. "But, I'm going to make you wetter and then, I'm going to make you come." His other hand shoved her pants down, giving him more room to work. "Open your eyes and watch the show."

She did as he said. The man was inside the woman, thrusting hard and fast. The woman was moaning and trying to move but the restraints kept her mostly helpless.

"Fuck, you're soaked." Patrick's hand cupped her and she arched into his touch, rubbing her ass against his erection. He shoved his hand inside her underwear, his finger running along her folds until he slipped one inside.

"Oh." She grabbed his hand—not to push him away, but to make sure he didn't leave.

He smiled against her hair. "Don't worry, baby. I won't stop." He stroked his finger inside of her and his wrist brushed against her clit.

She needed more. She needed to touch him, feel him. She turned her head, wrapping her arms up and around his neck. He kissed her. It was desperate and wild, but he stopped too soon.

"They're almost done. You don't want to miss it."

She turned back to the mirror. The man below continued to fuck the woman as Patrick finger-fucked her. His other hand slipped under her shirt to her breast. His lips sucked her neck as he rocked his erection against her ass. He was everywhere, and she was so close. The muscles in her legs constricted. Her hips tipped upward.

"Wait, baby," he groaned in her ear, as he pushed a second finger inside of her. "Just a few more minutes."

His fingers were stretching her and it felt wonderful. She moaned, long and low as he thrust harder and faster, almost matching the pace of the man in the other room. She could almost imagine it was Patrick's cock and not his fingers inside of her.

"Oh...oh," she cried out. He was pushing her toward the edge. Her body was spiraling with each pump of his fingers. She was going to come—right here while watching that couple. It was so dirty and so wrong and it only made her hotter.

The woman below screamed and her body stiffened. The man thrust again and again and then grunted his release.

"Show's over." Patrick nipped her neck at the same time he pressed down on her clit with his thumb, sending her shooting into her orgasm.

She trembled and he pulled her close, his hand still cupping her pussy and his fingers still inside of her. When her heartbeat had settled, he removed his hand and bent, pulling off her shoes and removing her pants before lifting her and carrying her to the wall.

"My turn." He wrapped her legs around his waist.

Her phone rang. "My work phone. I…I have to answer it."

"When we're done." He unzipped his pants.

"Annie, answer the phone. I know you're around here. I can hear it ringing you stupid bitch," yelled Julie.

"Oh, shit." She shoved Patrick away, and ran across the room, grabbing her clothes off the floor. "It's my boss. She'll kill me if she finds me like this."

"I'll take care of Julie." He headed for the door, zipping up his fly. "Don't move." He grinned over his shoulder at her. "You can take off your pants again, but other than that, don't move."

"No. Please." She raced over to him, grabbing his arm. "I need this job." And Ethan could not find out about this.

"She won't fire you. She can't. Only Ethan can fire you." He bent and kissed her.

His lips were gentle and coaxing this time and her body swayed into him. He pulled her even closer and she could feel his cock, thick and heavy, pushing against her. Her pussy tightened again in anticipation.

"Damnit, Annie. This is going to be so much worse if I have to call your stupid phone again. Get out here!" Julie was only a few doors down.

She grabbed Patrick and tugged on his hand. "Please, hide." She glanced around, looking for somewhere that would conceal a six-foot muscular man.

"I'm not going to hide from Julie."

Coming soon:

TERRY'S STORY
ETHAN'S STORY
MATTIE'S STORY
JAKE'S STORY
HUNTER'S STORY
VIC'S STORY

Email me with questions, concerns or to let me know what you thought of the book. I love hearing from readers.
authorellisoday@gmail.com

Follow me.

Facebook
https://www.facebook.com/EllisODayRomanceAuthor/

Closed FB Group
https://www.facebook.com/groups/153238782143373

Twitter
https://twitter.com/ellis_o_day

Pinterest
http://www.pinterest.com/AuthorEllisODay

ABOUT THE AUTHOR

Ellis O. Day loves reading and writing about love and sex. She believes that although the two don't have to go together, it's best when they do (both in life and in fantasy).

www.ingramcontent.com/pod-product-compliance
Lightning Source LLC
Chambersburg PA
CBHW072252020726
47501CB00002B/238